A frightened hooker named Kim asked private investigator Matthew Scudder to help her get out of "the Life." Now she's dead, slashed to ribbons in a high-rise hotel. Finding her killer will be Scudder's penance. But there are lethal secrets hiding in Kim's past that are far dirtier than her trade—and many ways to die in this cruel and dangerous town.

EIGHT MILLION WAYS TO DIE

"First rate in all ways."
New York Times

"Lawrence Block is a master . . . The Matthew Scudder novels are among the finest detective books penned in this century."
Jonathan Kellerman

"Raymond Chandler and Dashiell Hammett still cast long shadows across the mystery genre. If there's one crime writer currently capable of matching their *noirish* legacies, it's Lawrence Block."
San Francisco Chronicle

"One of the best-written and most thought-provoking private eye series since the mid-'70s . . . [and] **EIGHT MILLION WAYS TO DIE** is the best book in the series."
Arizona Daily Star

Also by Lawrence Block

LAWRENCE BLOCK

EIGHT MILLION
WAYS TO DIE

A MATTHEW SCUDDER CRIME NOVEL

AVON BOOKS
An Imprint of HarperCollinsPublishers

AVON BOOKS
An Imprint of HarperCollins*Publishers*
10 East 53rd Street
New York, New York 10022-5299

Copyright © 1982 by Lawrence Block
Author photograph by Athena Gassoumis
ISBN: 0-380-71573-2
www.avonmystery.com

First Avon Books paperback printing: February 1993
First Avon Books special printing: December 1991

Avon Trademark Reg. U.S. Pat. Off. and in Other Countries, Marca Registrada, Hecho en U.S.A.
HarperCollins ® is a registered trademark of HarperCollins Publishers Inc.

Printed in the U.S.A.

10

In memory of
BILLY DUGAN
CLIFF
BOSTON JOHN
BAMBI
MARK THE DWARF
and
RED-HAIRED MAGGIE

The death of a beautiful woman is, unquestionably, the most poetical topic in the world.

—EDGAR ALLAN POE

EIGHT MILLION
WAYS TO DIE

Chapter 1

I saw her entrance. It would have been hard to miss. She had blonde hair that was close to white, the sort that's called towhead when it belongs to a child. Hers was plaited in heavy braids that she'd wrapped around her head and secured with pins. She had a high smooth forehead and prominent cheekbones and a mouth that was just a little too wide. In her western-style boots she must have run to six feet, most of her length in her legs. She was wearing designer jeans the color of burgundy and a short fur jacket the color of champagne. It had been raining on and off all day, and she wasn't carrying an umbrella or wearing anything on her head. Beads of water glinted like diamonds on her plaited hair.

She stood for a moment in the doorway getting her bearings. It was around three-thirty on a Wednesday afternoon, which is about as slow as it gets at Armstrong's. The lunch crowd was long gone and it was too early for the after-work people. In another fifteen minutes a couple of schoolteachers would stop in for a quick one, and then some nurses from Roosevelt Hospital whose shift ended at four, but for the moment there were three or four people at the bar and one couple finishing a carafe of wine at a front table and that was it. Except for me, of course, at my usual table in the rear.

She made me right away, and I caught the blue of her eyes all the way across the room. But she stopped at the bar to make sure before making her way between the tables to where I was sitting.

She said, "Mr. Scudder? I'm Kim Dakkinen. I'm a friend of Elaine Mardell's."

"She called me. Have a seat."

"Thank you."

She sat down opposite me, placed her handbag on the table between us, took out a pack of cigarettes and a disposable lighter, then paused with the cigarette unlit to ask if it was all right if she smoked. I assured her that it was.

Her voice wasn't what I'd expected. It was quite soft, and the only accent it held was Midwestern. After the boots and the fur and the severe facial planes and the exotic name, I'd been anticipating something more out of a masochist's fantasy: harsh and stern and European. She was younger, too, than I'd have guessed at first glance. No more than twenty-five.

She lit her cigarette and positioned the lighter on top of the cigarette pack. The waitress, Evelyn, had been working days for the past two weeks because she'd landed a small part in an off-Broadway showcase. She always looked on the verge of a yawn. She came to the table while Kim Dakkinen was playing with her lighter. Kim ordered a glass of white wine. Evelyn asked me if I wanted more coffee, and when I said yes Kim said, "Oh, are you having coffee? I think I'd like that instead of wine. Would that be all right?"

When the coffee arrived she added cream and sugar, stirred, sipped, and told me she wasn't much of a drinker, especially early in the day. But she couldn't drink it black the way I did, she'd never been able to drink black coffee, she had to have it sweet and rich, almost like dessert, and she supposed she was just lucky but she'd never had a weight problem, she could eat anything and never gain an ounce, and wasn't that lucky?

I agreed that it was.

Had I known Elaine long? For years, I said. Well, she hadn't really known her that long herself, in fact she hadn't even been in New York too terribly long, and she didn't know her that well either, but she thought Elaine was awfully nice. Didn't I agree? I agreed. Elaine was very level-headed, too, very sensible, and that was something, wasn't it? I agreed it was something.

I let her take her time. She had acres of small talk, she smiled and held your eyes with hers when she talked, and she could probably have walked off with the Miss Congeniality award in any beauty contest she didn't win outright, and if it took her awhile to get to the point that was fine with me. I had no place else to go and nothing better to do.

She said, "You used to be a policeman."

"A few years back."

"And now you're a private detective."

"Not exactly." The eyes widened. They were a very vivid blue, an unusual shade, and I wondered if she were wearing contact lenses. The soft lenses sometimes do curious things to eye color, altering some shades, intensifying others.

"I don't have a license," I explained. "When I decided I didn't want to carry a badge anymore I didn't figure I wanted to carry a license, either." Or fill out forms or keep records or check in with the tax collector. "Anything I do is very unofficial."

"But it's what you do? It's how you make your living?"

"That's right."

"What do you call it? What you do."

You could call it hustling a buck, except that I don't hustle a whole lot. The work finds me. I turn down more than I handle, and the jobs I accept are ones I can't think of a way to turn down. Right now I was wondering what this woman wanted from me, and what excuse I'd find to say no.

"I don't know what to call it," I told her. "You could say that I do favors for friends."

Her face lit up. She'd been doing a lot of smiling ever since she walked in the door but this was the first smile that got as far as her eyes. "Well, hell, that's perfect," she said. "I could use a favor. As far as that goes, I could use a friend."

"What's the problem?"

She bought some thinking time by lighting another cigarette, then lowered her eyes to watch her hands as she centered the lighter on top of the pack. Her nails were well manicured, long but not awkward, lacquered the color of tawny port. She wore a gold ring set with a large square-cut green stone on the third finger of her left hand. She said, "You know what I do. Same as Elaine."

"So I gathered."

"I'm a hooker."

I nodded. She straightened in her seat, squared her shoulders, adjusted the fur jacket, opened the clasp at her throat. I caught a trace of her perfume. I'd smelled that spicy scent before but couldn't recall the occasion. I picked up my cup, finished my coffee.

"I want out."

"Of the life?"

She nodded. "I've been doing this for four years. I came here four years ago in July. August, September, October, November. Four years and four months. I'm twenty-three years old. That's young, isn't it?"

"Yes."

"It doesn't feel so young." She adjusted the jacket again, refastened the clasp. Light glinted off her ring. "When I got off the bus four years ago I had a suitcase in one hand and a denim jacket over my arm. Now I've got this. It's ranch mink."

"It's very becoming."

"I'd trade it for the old denim jacket," she said, "if I could have the years back. No, I wouldn't. Because if I had them back I'd just do the same thing with them, wouldn't I? Oh to be nineteen again and know what I know now, but the only way that could be is if I started tricking at fifteen, and then I'd be dead by now. I'm just rambling. I'm sorry."

"No need."

"I want to get out of the life."

"And do what? Go back to Minnesota?"

"Wisconsin. No, I won't be going back. There's nothing there for me. Just because I want out doesn't mean I have to go back."

"Okay."

"I can make lots of trouble for myself that way. I reduce things to two alternatives, so if A is no good that means I'm stuck with B. But that's not right. There's the whole rest of the alphabet."

She could always teach philosophy. I said, "Where do I come in, Kim?"

"Oh. Right."

I waited.

"I have this pimp."

"And he won't let you leave?"

"I haven't said anything to him. I think maybe he knows, but I haven't said anything and *he* hasn't said anything and—" Her whole upper body trembled for a moment, and small beads of perspiration glistened on her upper lip.

"You're afraid of him."

"How'd you guess?"

"Has he threatened you?"

"Not really."

"What does that mean?"

"He never threatened me. But I *feel* threatened."

"Have other girls tried to leave?"

"I don't know. I don't know much about his other girls. He's very different from other pimps. At least from the ones I know about."

They're all different. Just ask their girls. "How?" I asked her.

"He's more refined. Subdued."

Sure. "What's his name?"

"Chance."

"First name or last name?"

"It's all anybody ever calls him. I don't know if it's a first name or a last name. Maybe it's neither, maybe it's a nickname. People in the life, they'll have different names for different occasions."

"Is Kim your real name?"

She nodded. "But I had a street name. I had a pimp before Chance, his name was Duffy. Duffy Green, he called himself, but he was also Eugene Duffy and he had another name he used sometimes that I forget." She smiled at a memory. "I was so green when he turned me out. He didn't pick me up right off the bus but he might as well."

"He a black man?"

"Duffy? Sure. So is Chance. Duffy put me on the street. The Lexington Avenue stroll, and sometimes when it was hot we'd go across the river to Long Island City." She closed her eyes for a moment. When she opened them she said, "I just got this rush of memory, what it was like on the street. My street name was Bambi. In Long Island City we did the johns in their cars. They would drive in from all over Long Island. On Lexington we had a hotel we could use. I can't believe I used to do that, I used to live like that. God, I was *green!* I wasn't innocent. I knew what I came to New York for, but I was green all right."

"How long were you on the street?"

"It must have been five, six months. I wasn't very good. I had the looks and I could, you know, perform, but I didn't have street smarts. And a couple of times I had anxiety attacks and I couldn't function. Duffy gave me stuff but all it ever did was make me sick."

"Stuff?"

"You know. Drugs."

"Right."

"Then he put me in this house, and that was better, but he didn't like it because he had less control that way. There was this big apartment near Columbus Circle and I went to work there like you would go to an office. I was in the house, I don't know, maybe another six months. Just about that. And then I went with Chance."

"How did that happen?"

"I was with Duffy. We were at this bar. Not a pimp bar, a jazz club, and Chance came and sat at our table. We all three sat and talked, and then they left me at the table and went off and talked some more, and Duffy came back alone and said I was to go with Chance. I thought he meant I should do him, you know, like a trick, and I was pissed because this was supposed to be our evening together and why should I be working. See, I didn't take Chance for a pimp. Then he explained that I was going to be Chance's girl from now on. I felt like a car he just sold."

"Is that what he did? Did he sell you to Chance?"

"I don't know what he did. But I went with Chance and it was all right. It was better than with Duffy. He took me out of that house and put me on a phone and it's been, oh, three years now."

"And you want me to get you off the hook."

"Can you do it?"

"I don't know. Maybe you can do it yourself. Haven't you said anything to him? Hinted at it, talked about it, something like that?"

"I'm afraid."

"Of what?"

"That he'd kill me or mark me or something. Or that he'd talk me out of it." She leaned forward, put her port-tipped fingers on my wrist. The gesture was clearly calculated but nonetheless effective for it. I breathed in her spicy scent and felt her sexual impact. I wasn't aroused and didn't want her but I could not be unaware of her sexual strength. She said, "Can't you help me, Matt?" And, immediately, "Do you mind if I call you Matt?"

I had to laugh. "No," I said. "I don't mind."

"I make money but I don't get to keep it. And I don't really make more money than I did on the street. But I have a little money."

"Oh?"

"I have a thousand dollars."

I didn't say anything. She opened her purse, found a plain white envelope, got a finger under the flap and tore it open. She took a sheaf of bills from it and placed them on the table between us.

"You could see him for me," she said.

I picked up the money, held it in my hand. I was being offered the opportunity to serve as intermediary between a blonde whore and a black pimp. It was not a role I'd ever hungered for.

I wanted to hand the money back. But I was nine or ten days out of Roosevelt Hospital and I owed money there, and on the first of the month my rent would be due, and I hadn't sent anything to Anita and the boys in longer than I cared to remember. I had money in my wallet and more money in the bank but it didn't add up to much, and Kim Dakkinen's money was as good as anybody else's and easier to come by, and what difference did it make what she'd done to earn it?

I counted the bills. They were used hundreds and there were ten of them. I left five on the table in front of me and handed the other five to her. Her eyes widened a little and I decided she had to be wearing contacts. Nobody had eyes that color.

I said, "Five now and five later. If I get you off the hook."

"Deal," she said, and grinned suddenly. "You could have had the whole thousand in front."

"Maybe I'll work better with an incentive. You want some more coffee?"

"If you're having some. And I think I'd like something sweet. Do they have desserts here?"

"The pecan pie's good. So's the cheesecake."

"I love pecan pie," she said. "I have a terrible sweet tooth but I never gain an ounce. Isn't that lucky?"

Chapter 2

There was a problem. In order for me to talk to Chance I had to find him, and she couldn't tell me how to do it.

"I don't know where he lives," she said. "Nobody does."

"Nobody?"

"None of his girls. That's the big guessing game if a couple of us should happen to be together and he's not in the room. Trying to guess where Chance lives. One night I remember this girl Sunny and I were together and we were just goofing, coming up with one outrageous idea after another. Like he lives in this tenement in Harlem with his crippled mother, or he has this mansion in Sugar Hill, or he has a ranch house in the suburbs and commutes. Or he keeps a couple of suitcases in his car and lives out of them, just sleeping a couple hours a night at one of our apartments." She thought a moment. "Except he never sleeps when he's with me. If we do go to bed he'll just lie there afterward for a little while and then he's up and dressed and out. He said once he can't sleep if there's another person in the room."

"Suppose you have to get in touch with him?"

"There's a number to call. But it's an answering service.

You can call the number any time, twenty-four hours a day, and there's always an operator that answers. He always checks in with his service. If we're out or something, he'll check in with them every thirty minutes, every hour."

She gave me the number and I wrote it in my notebook. I asked her where he garaged his car. She didn't know. Did she remember the car's license number?

She shook her head. "I never notice things like that. His car is a Cadillac."

"There's a surprise. Where does he hang out?"

"I don't know. If I want to reach him I leave a message. I don't go out looking for him. You mean is there a regular bar he drinks in? There's a lot of places he'll go sometimes, but nothing regular."

"What kind of things does he do?"

"What do you mean?"

"Does he go to ball games? Does he gamble? What does he do with himself?"

She considered the question. "He does different things," she said.

"What do you mean?"

"Depending who he's with. I like to go to jazz clubs so if he's with me that's where we'll go. I'm the one he calls if he's looking for that kind of an evening. There's another girl, I don't even know her, but they go to concerts. You know, classical music. Carnegie Hall and stuff. Another girl, Sunny, digs sports, and he'll take her to ball games."

"How many girls has he got?"

"I don't know. There's Sunny and Nan and the girl who likes classical music. Maybe there's one or two others. Maybe more. Chance is very private, you know? He keeps things to himself."

"The only name you've got for him is Chance?"

"That's right."

"You've been with him, what, three years? And you've got half a name and no address and the number of his answering service."

She looked down at her hands.

"How does he pick up the money?"

"From me, you mean? Sometimes he'll come by for it."

"Does he call first?"

"Not necessarily. Sometimes. Or he'll call and tell me to bring it to him. At a coffee shop or a bar or something, or to be on a certain corner and he'll pick me up."

"You give him everything you make?"

A nod. "He found me my apartment, he pays the rent, the phone, all the bills. We'll shop for my clothes and he'll pay. He likes picking out my clothes. I give him what I make and he gives me back some, you know, for walking-around money."

"You don't hold anything out?"

"Sure I do. How do you think I got the thousand dollars? But it's funny, I don't hold out much."

The place was filling up with office workers by the time she left. By then she'd had enough coffee and switched to white wine. She had one glass of the wine and left half of it. I stayed with black coffee. I had her address and phone in my notebook along with Chance's answering service, but I didn't have a whole lot more than that.

On the other hand, how much did I need? Sooner or later I would get hold of him, and when I did I would talk to him, and if it broke right I'd throw a bigger scare into him than he'd managed to throw into Kim. And if not, well, I still had five hundred dollars more than I had when I woke up that morning.

AFTER she left I finished my coffee and cracked one of her hundreds to pay my tab. Armstrong's is on Ninth Avenue between Fifty-seventh and Fifty-eighth, and my hotel is around the corner on Fifty-seventh Street. I went to it, checked the desk for mail and messages, then called Chance's service from the pay phone in the lobby. A woman answered on the third ring, repeating the four final digits of the number and asking if she could help me.

"I want to speak to Mr. Chance," I said.

"I expect to speak with him soon," she said. She sounded middle-aged, with a chain smoker's rasp to her voice. "May I take a message for him?"

I gave her my name and my phone number at the hotel. She asked what my call was in reference to. I told her it was personal.

When I hung up the phone I felt shaky, maybe from all the coffee I'd been sipping all day. I wanted a drink. I thought about going across the street to Polly's Cage for a quick one, or hitting the liquor store two doors down from Polly's and picking up a pint of bourbon. I could envision the booze, Jim Beam or J. W. Dant, some no-nonsense brown whiskey in a flat pint bottle.

I thought, C'mon, it's raining out there, you don't want to go out in the rain. I left the phone booth and turned toward the elevator instead of the front door and went up to my room. I locked myself in and pulled the chair over to the window and watched the rain. The urge to drink went away after a few minutes. Then it came back and then it went away again. It came and went for the next hour, winking on and off like a neon sign. I stayed where I was and watched the rain.

AROUND seven I picked up the phone in my room and called Elaine Mardell. Her machine answered, and when the beep sounded I said, "This is Matt. I saw your friend and I wanted to thank you for the referral. Maybe one of these days I can return the favor." I hung up and waited another half hour. Chance didn't return my call.

I wasn't especially hungry but I made myself go downstairs for something to eat. It had quit raining. I went over to the Blue Jay and ordered a hamburger and fries. A guy two tables over was having a beer with his sandwich and I decided to order one when the waiter brought my burger, but by the time that happened I'd changed my mind. I ate most of the hamburger and about half of the fries and drank two cups of coffee, then ordered cherry pie for dessert and ate most of it.

It was almost eight-thirty when I left there. I stopped at my hotel—no messages—and then walked the rest of the way to Ninth Avenue. There used to be a Greek bar on the corner, Antares and Spiro's, but it's a fruit and vegetable market now. I turned uptown and walked past Armstrong's and across Fifty-eighth Street, and when the light changed I crossed the avenue and walked on up past the hospital to St. Paul's. I walked around the side and down a narrow flight of stairs to the basement. A cardboard sign hung from the doorknob, but you'd have to be looking for it to see it.

A.A., it said.

They were just getting started when I walked in. There were three tables set up in a U, with people seated on either sides of the tables and perhaps a dozen other chairs arranged at the back. Another table off to the side held refreshments. I got a Styrofoam cup and drew coffee from the urn, then took a chair at the rear. A couple of people nodded to me and I nodded back.

The speaker was a fellow about my age. He was wearing a herringbone tweed jacket over a plaid flannel shirt. He told the story of his life from his first drink in his early teens until he came into the program and got sober four years ago. He was married and divorced a few times, cracked up several cars, lost jobs, hit a few hospitals. Then he stopped drinking and started going to meetings and things got better.

"*Things* didn't get better," he said, correcting himself. "*I* got better."

They say that a lot. They say a lot of things a lot and you get to hear the same phrases over and over. The stories are pretty interesting, though. People sit up there in front of God and everybody and tell you the goddamnedest things.

He spoke for half an hour. Then they took a ten-minute break and passed the basket for expenses. I put in a dollar, then helped myself to another cup of coffee and a couple of oatmeal cookies. A fellow in an old army jacket greeted me by name. I remembered his name was Jim and returned the greeting. He asked me how things were going and I told him they were going all right.

"You're here and you're sober," he said. "That's the important thing."

"I suppose."

"Any day I don't take a drink is a good day. You're staying sober a day at a time. The hardest thing in the world is for an alcoholic to not drink and you're doing it."

Except I wasn't. I'd been out of the hospital for nine or ten days. I would stay sober for two or three days and then I would pick up a drink. Mostly it was a drink or two drinks or three drinks and it stayed under control, but Sunday night I'd been bad drunk, drinking bourbon at a Blarney Stone on Sixth Avenue where I didn't figure to run into anybody I knew. I couldn't remember leaving the bar and didn't know how I got home, and Monday morning I had the shakes and a dry mouth and felt like walking death.

I didn't tell him any of this.

After ten minutes they started the meeting again and went around the room. People would say their names and say they were alcoholics and thank the speaker for his qualification, which is what they call the life story that he told. Then they would go on to talk about how they'd identified with the speaker, or recall some memory from their drinking days, or speak about some difficulty they were dealing with in the course of trying to lead a sober life. A girl not much older than Kim Dakkinen talked about problems with her lover, and a gay man in his thirties described a hassle he'd had that day with a customer at his travel agency. It made a funny story and got a lot of laughs.

One woman said, "Staying sober is the easiest thing in the world. All you have to do is don't drink, go to meetings, and be willing to change your whole fucking life."

When it got to me I said, "My name is Matt. I'll pass."

THE meeting ended at ten. I stopped at Armstrong's on my way home and took a seat at the bar. They tell you to stay out of bars if you're trying not to drink but I'm comfortable there and the coffee's good. If I'm going to drink I'll drink and it doesn't matter where I am.

By the time I left there the early edition of the *News* was on the street. I picked it up and went back to my room. There was still no message from Kim Dakkinen's pimp. I called his service again, which established that he had received my message. I left another message and said that it was important I hear from him as soon as possible.

I showered and put on a robe and read the paper. I read the national and international stories but I can never really focus on them. Things have to be on a smaller scale and happen closer to home before I can relate to them.

There was plenty to relate to. Two kids in the Bronx threw a young woman in front of the D train. She'd lain flat and, although six cars passed over her before the motorman got the train stopped, she'd escaped without injury.

Down on West Street, near the Hudson docks, a prostitute had been murdered. Stabbed, the story said.

A housing authority cop in Corona was still in critical condition. Two days ago I'd read how he'd been attacked by two men who hit him with lengths of pipe and stole his gun. He had a wife and four children under ten.

The telephone didn't ring. I didn't really expect it to. I couldn't think of any reason for Chance to return my call outside of curiosity, and perhaps he remembered what that had done to the cat. I could have identified myself as a cop—Mr. Scudder was easier to ignore than Police Officer Scudder, or Detective Scudder—but I didn't like to run that kind of game if I didn't have to. I was willing to let people jump to conclusions but reluctant to give them a push.

So I'd have to find him. That was just as well. It would give me something to do. In the meantime the messages I left with his service would fix my name in his head.

The elusive Mr. Chance. You'd think he'd have a mobile phone unit in his pimpmobile, along with the bar and the fur upholstery and the pink velvet sun visor. All those touches of class.

I read the sports pages and then went back to the hooker stabbing in the Village. The story was very sketchy. They didn't have a name or any description beyond identifying the victim as being about twenty-five years old.

I called the *News* to see if they had a name for the victim and was told they weren't giving out that information. Pending notification of kin, I suppose. I called the Sixth Precinct but Eddie Koehler wasn't on duty and I couldn't think of anyone else at the Sixth who might know me. I got out my notebook and decided it was too late to call her, that half the women in the city were hookers and there was no reason to suppose she'd been the one to get sliced up underneath the West Side Highway. I put the notebook away, and ten minutes later I dug it out again and dialed her number.

I said, "It's Matt Scudder, Kim. I just wondered if you happened to speak to your friend since I saw you."

"No, I haven't. Why?"

"I thought I might reach him through his service. I don't

think he's going to get back to me, so tomorrow I'll have to go out and look for him. You haven't said anything to him about wanting out?"

"Not a word."

"Good. If you see him before I do, just act as though nothing's changed. And if he calls and wants you to meet him somewhere, call me right away."

"At the number you gave me?"

"Right. If you reach me I'll be able to keep the appointment in your place. If not, just go ahead and play it straight."

I talked a little while longer, calming her down some after having alarmed her with the call in the first place. At least I knew she hadn't died on West Street. At least I could sleep easy.

Sure. I killed the light and got into bed and just lay there for a long time, and then I gave up and got up and read the paper again. The thought came to me that a couple of drinks would take the edge off and let me sleep. I couldn't banish the thought but I could make myself stay where I was, and when four o'clock came I told myself to forget it because the bars were closed now. There was an after-hours on Eleventh Avenue but I conveniently forgot about it.

I turned off the light and got in bed again and thought about the dead hooker and the housing cop and the woman who'd been run over by the subway train, and I wondered why anyone would think it a good idea to stay sober in this city, and I held onto that thought and fell asleep with it.

Chapter 3

I got up around ten-thirty, surprisingly well rested after six hours of skimming the surface of sleep. I showered and shaved, had coffee and a roll for breakfast, and went over to St. Paul's. Not to the basement this time but to the church proper, where I sat in a pew for ten minutes or so before lighting a couple of candles and slipping fifty dollars into the poor box. At the post office on Sixtieth Street I bought a two-hundred-dollar money order and an envelope with the stamp embossed. I mailed the money order to my ex-wife in Syosset. I tried to write a note to enclose but it came out apologetic. The money was too little and too late but she would know that without my having to tell her. I wrapped the money order in a blank sheet of paper and mailed it that way.

It was a gray day, on the cool side, with the threat of more rain. There was a raw wind blowing and it cut around corners like a scatback. In front of the Coliseum a man was chasing his hat and cursing, and I reached up reflexively and gave a tug to the brim of mine.

I walked most of the way to my bank before deciding I didn't have enough of Kim's advance left to necessitate for-

mal financial transactions. I went to my hotel instead and
paid half of the coming month's rent on account. By then I
had only one of the hundreds intact and I cracked that into
tens and twenties while I was at it.

Why hadn't I taken the full thousand in front? I remembered what I'd said about an incentive. Well, I had one.

My mail was routine—a couple of circulars, a letter from
my congressman. Nothing I had to read.

No message from Chance. Not that I'd expected one.

I called his service and left another message just for the
hell of it.

I got out of there and stayed out all afternoon. I took the
subway a couple of times but mostly walked. It kept threatening to rain but it kept not raining, and the wind got even
more of an edge to it but never did get my hat. I hit two police precinct houses and a few coffee shops and half a dozen
gin mills. I drank coffee in the coffee shops and Coca-Cola
in the bars, and I talked to a few people and made a couple
of notes. I called my hotel desk a few times. I wasn't expecting a call from Chance but I wanted to be in touch in case
Kim called. But no one had called me. I tried Kim's number
twice and both times her machine answered. Everybody's
got one of those machines and someday all the machines
will start dialing and talk to each other. I didn't leave any
messages.

Toward the end of the afternoon I ducked into a Times
Square theater. They had two Clint Eastwood movies paired,
ones where he's a rogue cop who settles things by shooting
the bad guys. The audience looked to be composed almost
entirely of the sort of people he was shooting. They cheered
wildly every time he blew somebody away.

I had pork fried rice and vegetables at a Cuban Chinese
place on Eighth Avenue, checked my hotel desk again,
stopped at Armstrong's and had a cup of coffee. I got into a
conversation at the bar and thought I'd stay there awhile, but

by eight-thirty I'd managed to get out the door and across the street and down the stairs to the meeting.

The speaker was a housewife who used to drink herself into a stupor while her husband was at his office and the kids were at school. She told how her kid would find her passed out on the kitchen floor and she convinced him it was a yoga exercise to help her back. Everybody laughed.

When it was my turn I said, "My name is Matt. I'll just listen tonight."

KELVIN Small's is on Lenox Avenue at 127th Street. It's a long narrow room with a bar running the length of it and a row of banquette tables opposite the bar. There's a small bandstand all the way at the back, and on it two dark-skinned blacks with close-cropped hair and horn-rimmed sunglasses and Brooks Brothers suits played quiet jazz, one on a small upright piano, the other using brushes on cymbals. They looked and sounded like half of the old Modern Jazz Quartet.

It was easy for me to hear them because the rest of the room went silent when I cleared the threshold. I was the only white man in the room and everybody stopped for a long look at me. There were a couple of white women, seated with black men at the banquette tables, and there were two black women sharing a table, and there must have been two dozen men in every shade but mine.

I walked the length of the room and went into the men's room. A man almost tall enough for pro basketball was combing his straightened hair. The scent of his pomade vied with the sharp reek of marijuana. I washed my hands and rubbed them together under one of those hot-air dryers. The tall man was still working on his hair when I left.

Conversation died again when I emerged from the men's room. I walked toward the front again, walked slowly and let my shoulders roll. I couldn't be sure about the musicians, but aside from them I figured there wasn't a man in the room who hadn't taken at least one felony bust. Pimps, drug dealers, gamblers, policy men. Nature's noblemen.

A man on the fifth stool from the front caught my eye. It took a second to place him because when I knew him years ago he had straight hair, but now he was wearing it in a modified Afro. His suit was lime green and his shoes were the skin of some reptile, probably an endangered species.

I moved my head toward the door and walked on past him and out. I walked two doors south on Lenox and stood next to a streetlamp. Two or three minutes went by and he came on out, walking loose-limbed and easy. "Hey, Matthew," he said, and extended his hand for a slap. "How's my man?"

I didn't slap his hand. He looked down at it, up at me, rolled his eyes, gave his head an exaggerated shake, clapped his hands together, dusted them against his trouser legs, then placed them on his slim hips. "Been some time," he said. "They run out of your brand downtown? Or do you just come to Harlem to use the little boy's room?"

"You're looking prosperous, Royal."

He preened a little. His name was Royal Waldron and I once knew a black cop with a bullet head who rang changes through Royal Flush to Flush Toilet and called him The Crapper. He said, "Well, I buy and sell. You know."

"I know."

"Give the folks an honest deal and you will never miss a meal. That's a rhyme my mama taught me. How come you uptown, Matthew?"

"I'm looking for a guy."

"Maybe you found him. You off the force these days?"

"For some years now."

"And you lookin' to buy something? What do you want and what can you spend?"

"What are you selling?"

"Most anything."

"Business still good with all these Colombians?"

"Shit," he said, and one hand brushed the front of his pants. I suppose he had a gun in the waistband of the lime green pants. There were probably as many handguns as people in Kelvin Small's. "Them Colombians be all right," he said. "You just don't ever want to cheat them is all. You didn't come up here to buy stuff."

"No."

"What you want, man?"

"I'm looking for a pimp."

"Shit, you just walked past twenty of 'em. And six, seven hoes."

"I'm looking for a pimp named Chance."

"Chance."

"You know him?"

"I might know who he is."

I waited. A man in a long coat was walking along the block, stopping at each storefront. He might have been looking in the windows except that you couldn't; every shop had steel shutters that descended like garage doors at the close of business. The man stopped in front of each closed store and studied the shutters as if they held meaning for him.

"Window shopping," Royal said.

A blue-and-white police car cruised by, slowed. The two uniformed officers within looked us over. Royal wished them a good evening. I didn't say anything and neither did they. When the car drove off he said, "Chance don't come here much."

"Where would I find him?"

"Hard to say. He'll turn up anyplace but it might be the last place you would look. He don't hang out."

"So they tell me."

"Where you been lookin'?"

I'd been to a coffee shop on Sixth Avenue and Forty-fifth Street, a piano bar in the Village, a pair of bars in the West Forties. Royal took all this in and nodded thoughtfully.

"He wouldn't be at Muffin-Burger," he said, "on account he don't run no girls on the street. That I *know* of. All the same, he might be there anyway, you dig? Just to *be* there. What I say, he'll turn up anywhere, but he don't hang out."

"Where should I look for him, Royal?"

He named a couple of places. I'd been to one of them already and had forgotten to mention it. I made a note of the others. I said, "What's he like, Royal?"

"Well, shit," he said, "He a pimp, man."

"You don't like him."

"He ain't to like or not like. My friends is business friends, Matthew, and Chance and I got no business with each other. We don't neither of us buy what the other be sellin'. He don't want to buy no stuff and I don't want to buy no pussy." His teeth showed in a nasty little smile. "When you the man with all the candy, you don't never have to pay for no pussy."

ONE of the places Royal mentioned was in Harlem, on St. Nicholas Avenue. I walked over to 125th Street. It was wide and busy and well lit, but I was starting to feel the not entirely irrational paranoia of a white man on a black street.

I turned north at St. Nicholas and walked a couple of blocks to the Club Cameroon. It was a low-rent version of Kelvin Small's with a jukebox instead of live music. The men's room was filthy, and in the stall toilet someone was inhaling briskly. Snorting cocaine, I suppose.

I didn't recognize anyone at the bar. I stood there and drank a glass of club soda and looked at fifteen or twenty black faces reflected in the mirrored back bar. It struck me, not for the first time that evening, that I could be looking at Chance and not knowing it. The description I had for him would fit a third of the men present and stretch to cover half of those remaining. I hadn't been able to see a picture of him. My cop contacts didn't recognize the name, and if it was his last name he didn't have a yellow sheet in the files.

The men on either side had turned away from me. I caught sight of myself in the mirror, a pale man in a colorless suit and a gray topcoat. My suit could have stood pressing and my hat would have looked no worse if the wind had taken it, and here I stood, isolated between these two fashion plates with their wide shoulders and exaggerated lapels and fabric-covered buttons. The pimps used to line up at Phil Kronfeld's Broadway store for suits like that, but Kronfeld's was closed and I had no idea where they went these days. Maybe I should find out, maybe Chance had a charge account and I could trace him that way.

Except people in the life didn't have charges because they did everything with cash. They'd even buy cars with cash, bop into Potamkin's and count out hundred dollar bills and take home a Cadillac.

The man on my right crooked a finger at the bartender. "Put it right in the same glass," he said. "Let it build up a taste." The bartender filled his glass with a jigger of Hennessy and four or five ounces of cold milk. They used to call that combination a White Cadillac. Maybe they still do.

Maybe I should have tried Potamkin's.

Or maybe I should have stayed home. My presence was creating tension and I could feel it thickening the air in the little room. Sooner or later someone would come over and ask me what the fuck I thought I was doing there and it was going to be hard to come up with an answer.

I left before it could happen. A gypsy cab was waiting for the light to change. The door on my side was dented and one fender was crumpled, and I wasn't sure what that said about the driver's ability. I got in anyway.

* * *

ROYAL had mentioned another place on West Ninety-sixth and I let the cab drop me there. It was after two by this time and I was starting to tire. I went into yet another bar where yet another black man was playing piano. This particular piano sounded out of tune, but it might have been me. The crowd was a fairly even mix of black and white. There were a lot of interracial couples, but the white women who were paired with black men looked more like girlfriends than hookers. A few of the men were dressed flashily, but nobody sported the full pimp regalia I'd seen a mile and a half to the north. If the room carried an air of fast living and cash trans-actions, it was nevertheless subtler and more muted than the Harlem clubs, or the ones around Times Square.

I put a dime in the phone and called my hotel. No mes-sages. The desk clerk that night was a mulatto with a cough-syrup habit that never seemed to keep him from functioning. He could still do the *Times* crossword puzzle with a fountain pen. I said, "Jacob, do me a favor. Call this number and ask to speak to Chance."

I gave him the number. He read it back and asked if that was Mr. Chance. I said just Chance.

"And if he comes to the phone?"

"Just hang up."

I went to the bar and almost ordered a beer but made it a Coke instead. A minute later the phone rang and a kid an-swered it. He looked like a college student. He called out, asking if there was anyone there named Chance. Nobody re-sponded. I kept an eye on the bartender. If he recognized the name he didn't show it. I'm not even certain he was paying attention.

I could have played that little game at every bar I'd been to, and maybe it would have been worth the effort. But it had taken me three hours to think of it.

I was some detective. I was drinking all the Coca-Cola in

Manhattan and I couldn't find a goddamned pimp. My teeth would rot before I got hold of the son of a bitch.

There was a jukebox, and one record ended and another began, something by Sinatra, and it triggered something, made some mental connection for me. I left my Coke on the bar and caught a cab going downtown on Columbus Avenue. I got off at the corner of Seventy-second Street and walked half a block west to Poogan's Pub. The clientele was a little less Superspade and a little more Young Godfather but I wasn't really looking for Chance anyway. I was looking for Danny Boy Bell.

He wasn't there. The bartender said, "Danny Boy? He was in earlier. Try the Top Knot, that's just across Columbus. He's there when he's not here."

And he was there, all right, on a bar stool all the way at the back. I hadn't seen him in years but he was no mean trick to recognize. He hadn't grown and he wasn't any darker.

Danny Boy's parents were both dark-skinned blacks. He had their features but not their color. He was an albino, as unpigmented as a white mouse. He was quite slender and very short. He claimed to be five two but I've always figured he was lying by an inch and a half or so.

He was wearing a three-piece banker's-stripe suit and the first white shirt I'd seen in a long time. His tie showed muted red and black stripes. His black shoes were highly polished. I don't think I've ever seen him without a suit and tie, or with scuffed shoes.

He said, "Matt Scudder. By God, if you wait long enough everybody turns up."

"How are you, Danny?"

"Older. It's been years. You're less than a mile away and when's the last time we saw each other? It has been, if you'll excuse the expression, a coon's age."

"You haven't changed much."

He studied me for a moment. "Neither have you," he said, but his voice lacked conviction. It was a surprisingly normal voice to issue from such an unusual person, of medium depth, unaccented. You expected him to sound like Johnny in the old Philip Morris commercials.

He said, "You were just in the neighborhood? Or you came looking for me?"

"I tried Poogan's first. They told me you might be here."

"I'm flattered. Purely a social visit, of course."

"Not exactly."

"Why don't we take a table? We can talk of old times and dead friends. And whatever mission brought you here."

THE bars Danny Boy favored kept a bottle of Russian vodka in the freezer. That was what he drank and he liked it ice-cold but without any ice cubes rattling around in his glass and diluting his drink. We settled in at a booth in the back and a speedy little waitress brought his drink of choice and Coke for me. Danny Boy lowered his eyes to my glass, then raised them to my face.

"I've been cutting back some," I said.

"Makes good sense."

"I guess."

"Moderation," he said. "I tell you, Matt, those old Greeks knew it all. Moderation."

He drank half his drink. He was good for perhaps eight like it in the course of a day. Call it a quart a day, all in a body that couldn't go more than a hundred pounds, and I'd never seen him show the effects. He never staggered, never slurred his words, just kept on keeping on.

So? What did that have to do with me?

I sipped my Coke.

We sat there and told each other stories. Danny Boy's business, if he had one, was information. Everything you told him got filed away in his mind, and by putting bits of data together and moving them around he brought in enough dollars to keep his shoes shined and his glass full. He would bring people together, taking a slice of their action for his troubles. His own hands stayed clean while he held a limited partnership in a lot of short-term enterprises, most of them faintly illicit. When I was on the force he'd been one of my best sources, an unpaid snitch who took his recompense in information.

He said, "You remember Lou Rudenko? Louie the Hat, they call him," I said I did. "You hear about his mother?"

"What about her?"

"Nice old Ukrainian lady, still lived in the old neighborhood on East Ninth or Tenth, wherever it was. Been a widow for years. Must have been seventy, maybe closer to eighty. Lou's got to be what, fifty?"

"Maybe."

"Doesn't matter. Point is this nice little old lady has a gentleman friend, a widower the same age as she is. He's over there a couple nights a week and she cooks Ukrainian food for him and maybe they go to a movie if they can find one that doesn't have people fucking all over the screen. Anyway, he comes over one afternoon, he's all excited, he found a television set on the street. Somebody put it out for the garbage. He says people are crazy, they throw perfectly good things away, and he's handy at fixing things and her own set's on the fritz and this one's a color set and twice the size of hers and maybe he can fix it for her."

"And?"

"And he plugs it in and turns it on to see what happens, and what happens is it blows up. He loses an arm and an eye and Mrs. Rudenko, she's right in front of it when it goes, she's killed instantly."

"What was it, a bomb?"

"You got it. You saw the story in the paper?"

"I must have missed it."

"Well, it was five, six months ago. What they worked out was somebody rigged the set with a bomb and had it delivered to somebody else. Maybe it was a mob thing and maybe it wasn't, because all the old man knew was what block he picked the set up on, and what does that tell you? Thing is, whoever received the set was suspicious enough to put it right out with the garbage, and it wound up killing Mrs. Rudenko. I saw Lou and it was a funny thing because he didn't know who to get mad at. 'It's this fucking city,' he told me. 'It's this goddamn fucking city.' But what sense does that make? You live in the middle of Kansas and a tornado comes and picks your house up and spreads it over Nebraska. That's an act of God, right?"

"That's what they say."

"In Kansas God uses tornadoes. In New York he uses gaffed television sets. Whoever you are, God or anybody else, you work with the materials at hand. You want another Coke?"

"Not right now."

"What can I do for you?"

"I'm looking for a pimp."

"Diogenes was looking for an honest man. You have more of a field to choose from."

"I'm looking for a particular pimp."

"They're all particular. Some of them are downright finicky. Has he got a name?"

"Chance."

"Oh, sure," Danny Boy said. "I know Chance."

"You know how I can get in touch with him?"

He frowned, picked up his empty glass, put it down. "He doesn't hang out anywhere," he said.

"That's what I keep hearing."

"It's the truth. I think a man should have a home base. I'm always here or at Poogan's. You're at Jimmy Armstrong's, or at least you were the last I heard."

"I still am."

"See? I keep tabs on you even when I don't see you. Chance. Let me think. What's today, Thursday?"

"Right. Well, Friday morning."

"Don't get technical. What do you want with him, if you don't mind the question?"

"I want to talk to him."

"I don't know where he is now but I might know where he'll be eighteen or twenty hours from now. Let me make a call. If that girl shows up, order me another drink, will you? And whatever you're having."

I managed to catch the waitress's eye and told her to bring Danny Boy another glass of vodka. She said, "Right. And another Coke for you?"

I'd been getting little drink urges off and on ever since I sat down and now I got a strong one. My gorge rose at the thought of another Coke. I told her to make it ginger ale this time. Danny Boy was still on the phone when she brought the drinks. She put the ginger ale in front of me and the vodka on his side of the table. I sat there and tried not to look at it and my eyes couldn't find anywhere else to go. I wished he would get back to the table and drink the damn thing.

I breathed in and breathed out and sipped my ginger ale and kept my hands off his vodka and eventually he came back to the table. "I was right," he said. "He'll be at the Garden tomorrow night."

"Are the Knicks back? I thought they were still on the road."

"Not the main arena. Matter of fact I think there's some rock concert. Chance'll be at the Felt Forum for the Friday night fights."

"He always goes?"

"Not always, but there's a welterweight named Kid Bascomb at the top of the prelim card and Chance has an interest in the young man."

"He owns a piece of him?"

"Could be, or maybe it's just an intellectual interest. What are you smiling at?"

"The idea of a pimp with an intellectual interest in a welter-weight."

"You never met Chance."

"No."

"He's not the usual run."

"That's the impression I'm getting."

"Point is, Kid Bascomb's definitely fighting, which doesn't mean Chance'll definitely be there, but I'd call it odds on. You want to talk to him, you can do it for the price of a ticket."

"How will I know him?"

"You never met him? No, you just said you didn't. You wouldn't recognize him if you saw him?"

"Not in a fight crowd. Not when half the house is pimps and players."

He thought about it. "This conversation you're going to have with Chance," he said. "Is it going to upset him a lot?"

"I hope not."

"What I'm getting at, is he likely to have a powerful resentment against whoever points him out?"

"I don't see why he should."

"Then what it's going to cost you, Matt, is the price of not one but two tickets. Be grateful it's an off-night at the Forum and not a title bout at the Main Garden. Ringside shouldn't be more than ten or twelve dollars, say fifteen at the outside. Thirty dollars at the most for our tickets."

"You're coming with me?"

"Why not? Thirty dollars for tickets and fifty for my time. I trust your budget can carry the weight?"

"It can if it has to."

"I'm sorry I have to ask you for money. If it were a track meet I wouldn't charge you a cent. But I've never cared for boxing. If it's any consolation, I'd want at least a hundred dollars to attend a hockey game."

"I guess that's something. You want to meet me there?"

"Out in front. At nine—that should give us plenty of lee-way. How does that sound?"

"Fine."

"I'll see if I can't wear something distinctive," he said, "so that you'll have no trouble recognizing me."

Chapter 4

He wasn't hard to recognize. His suit was a dove gray flannel and with it he wore a bright red vest over a black knit tie and another white dress shirt. He had sunglasses on, dark lenses in metal frames. Danny Boy contrived to sleep when the sun was out—neither his eyes nor his skin could take it—and wore dark glasses even at night unless he was in a dimly lit place like Poogan's or the Top Knot. Years ago he'd told me that he wished the world had a dimmer switch and you could just turn the whole thing down a notch or two. I remember thinking at the time that that was what whiskey did. It dimmed the lights and lowered the volume and rounded the corners.

I admired his outfit. He said, "You like the vest? I haven't worn it in ages. I wanted to be visible."

I already had our tickets. The ringside price was $15. I'd bought a pair of $4.50 seats that would have put us closer to God than to the ring. They got us through the gate, and I showed them to an usher down front and slipped a folded bill into his hand. He put us in a pair of seats in the third row.

"Now I might have to move you gentlemen," he said, "but probably not, and I guarantee you ringside."

After he'd moved off Danny Boy said, "There's always a way, isn't there? What did you give him?"

"Five dollars."

"So the seats set you back fourteen dollars instead of thirty. What do you figure he makes in a night?"

"Not much on a night like this. When the Knicks or Rangers play he might make five times his salary in tips. Of course he might have to pay somebody off."

"Everybody's got an angle," he said.

"It looks that way."

"I mean everybody. Even me."

That was my cue. I gave him two twenties and a ten. He put the money away, then took his first real look around the auditorium. "Well, I don't see him," he said, "but he'll probably just show for the Bascomb fight. Let me take a little walk."

"Sure."

He left his seat and moved around the room. I did some looking around myself, not trying to spot Chance but getting a sense of the crowd. There were a lot of men who might have been in the Harlem bars the previous night, pimps and dealers and gamblers and other uptown racket types, most of them accompanied by women. There were some white mob types; they were wearing leisure suits and gold jewelry and they hadn't brought dates. In the less expensive seats the crowd was the sort of mixed bag that turns up for any sporting event, black and white and Hispanic, singles and couples and groups, eating hot dogs and drinking beer from paper cups and talking and joking and, occasionally, having a look at the action in the ring. Here and there I saw a face straight out of any OTB horse room, one of those knobby on-the-come Broadway faces that only gamblers get. But there weren't too many of those. Who bets prizefights anymore?

I turned around and looked at the ring. Two Hispanic kids, one light and one dark, were being very careful not to risk serious injury. They looked like lightweights to me, and the fair-skinned kid was rangy with a lot of reach. I started getting interested, and in the final round the darker of the two figured out how to get in under the other kid's jab. He was working the body pretty good when they rang the bell. He got the decision, and most of the booing came from one spot in the audience. The other boy's friends and family, I suppose.

Danny Boy had returned to his seat during the final round. A couple minutes after the decision, Kid Bascomb climbed over the ropes and did a little shadowboxing. Moments later his opponent entered the ring. Bascomb was very dark, very muscular, with sloping shoulders and a powerful chest. His body might have been oiled the way the light glinted on it. The boy he was fighting was an Italian kid from South Brooklyn named Vito Canelli. He was carrying some fat around the waist and he looked soft as bread dough, but I had seen him before and knew him for a smart fighter.

Danny Boy said, "Here he comes. Center aisle."

I turned and looked. The same usher who'd taken my five bucks was leading a man and woman to their seats. She was about five five, with shoulder-length auburn hair and skin like fine porcelain. He was six one or two, maybe 190 pounds. Broad shoulders, narrow waist, trim hips. His hair was natural, short rather than long, and his skin was a rich brown. He was wearing a camel's-hair blazer and brown flannel slacks. He looked like a professional athlete or a hot lawyer or an up-and-coming black businessman.

I said, "You're sure?"

Danny Boy laughed. "Not your usual pimp, is he? I'm sure. That's Chance. I hope your friend didn't put us in his seats."

He hadn't. Chance and his girl were in the first row and a good deal closer to the center. They took their seats and he tipped the usher, acknowledged greetings from some of the other spectators, then approached Kid Bascomb's corner and said something to the fighter and his handlers. They huddled together for a moment. Then Chance returned to his seat.

"I think I'll leave now," Danny Boy said. "I don't really want to watch these two fools pummel each other. I hope you don't need me to introduce you?" I shook my head. "Then I'll slip out before the mayhem commences. In the ring, that is. Will he have to know I fingered him, Matt?"

"He won't hear it from me."

"Good. If I can be of further service—"

He made his way up the aisle. He probably wanted a drink and the bars in Madison Square Garden don't stock ice-cold Stolichnaya.

The announcer was introducing the fighters, calling out their ages and weights and hometowns. Bascomb was twenty-two and undefeated. Canelli didn't figure to change his status tonight.

There were two seats empty next to Chance. I thought about taking one but stayed where I was. The warning buzzer sounded, then the bell for round one. It was a slow, thoughtful round, with neither fighter anxious to commit himself. Bascomb jabbed nicely but Canelli managed to be out of range most of the time. Nobody landed anything solid.

The pair next to Chance were still empty at the round's end. I walked over there and sat next to him. He was looking very intently at the ring. He must have been aware of my presence but didn't indicate it if he was.

I said, "Chance? My name is Scudder."

He turned, looked at me. His eyes were brown flecked with gold. I thought of my client's eyes, that unreal blue. He'd been at her apartment last night while I was barhopping, dropped in unannounced to pick up some money. She'd told me about it earlier, called me at the hotel around noon. "I was afraid," she'd said. "I thought, suppose he asks about you, asks me some kind of questions. But it was cool."

Now he said, "Matthew Scudder. You left some messages with my service."

"You didn't return my calls."

"I don't know you. I don't call people I don't know. And you've been asking around town for me." His voice was deep and resonant. It sounded trained, as if he'd gone to broadcasting school. "I want to watch this fight," he said.

"All I want is a few minutes conversation."

"Not during the fight and not between rounds." A frown came and went. "I want to be able to concentrate. I bought that seat you're sitting in, you see, so I'd have some privacy."

The warning buzzer sounded. Chance turned, focused his eyes on the ring. Kid Bascomb was standing and his seconds were hauling the stool out of the ring. "Go back to your seat," Chance said, "and I'll talk to you after the fight ends."

"It's a ten-rounder?"

"It won't go ten."

IT didn't. In the third or fourth round Kid Bascomb started getting to Canelli, punishing him with the jab, putting a couple of combinations together. Canelli was smart but the Kid was young and fast and strong, with a way of moving that reminded me a little of Sugar Ray Robinson, not Leonard. In the fifth round he staggered Canelli with a short right hand to the heart and if I'd had a bet on the Italian I'd have written it off then and there.

Canelli looked strong by the end of the round but I'd seen the expression on his face when the blow landed, and I wasn't surprised a round later when Kid Bascomb dropped him with a looping left hook. He was up at three and took an eight-count, and then the Kid was all over him, hitting him with everything but the ring posts. Canelli went down again and got right up and the ref jumped between the two of them and looked in Canelli's eyes and stopped it.

There was some halfhearted booing from the diehards who never want a fight stopped, and one of Canelli's cornermen was insisting his fighter could have gone on, but Canelli himself seemed just as happy the show was over. Kid Bascomb did a little war dance and took his bows, then climbed nimbly over the ropes and left the ring.

On his way out he stopped to talk to Chance. The girl with the auburn hair sat forward and rested a hand on the fighter's glossy black arm. Chance and the Kid talked for a moment or two, and then the Kid headed for his dressing room.

I left my seat, walked over to Chance and the girl. They were standing by the time I got there. He said, "We're not staying for the main bout. If you'd planned on watching it—"

The top of the card matched two middleweights, a Panamanian contender and a black boy from South Philadelphia with a reputation as a spoiler. It would probably be a good bout, but that wasn't what I'd come for. I told him I was ready to leave.

"Then why don't you come with us," he suggested. "I have a car nearby." He headed up the aisle with the girl at his side. A few people said hello to him and some of them told him that the Kid had looked good in there. Chance didn't say much in reply. I tagged along, and when we got outside and hit the fresh air I realized for the first time how stale and smoky it had been inside the Garden.

On the street he said, "Sonya, this is Matthew Scudder. Mr. Scudder, Sonya Hendryx."

"It's nice to meet you," she said, but I didn't believe her. Her eyes told me she was withholding judgment until Chance cued her in one way or the other. I wondered if she was the Sunny that Kim had mentioned, the sports fan

Chance took to ball games. I wondered, too, if I would have pegged her for a hooker if I'd met her in other circumstances. I couldn't see anything unmistakably whorish about her, and yet she didn't look at all out of place hanging on a pimp's arm.

We walked a block south and half a block east to a parking lot where Chance collected his car and tipped the attendant enough to get thanked with more than the usual degree of enthusiasm. The car surprised me, just as the clothes and manner had surprised me earlier. I was expecting a pimpmobile, complete with custom paint and interior and the usual wretched excess, and what showed up was a Seville, the small Cadillac, silver on the outside with a black leather interior. The girl got in back, Chance sat behind the wheel, and I sat in front next to him.

The ride was smooth, silent. The car's interior smelled of wood polish and leather. Chance said, "There's a victory party for Kid Bascomb. I'll drop Sonya there now and join her after we've concluded our business. What did you think of the fight?"

"I thought it was hard to figure."

"Oh?"

"It looked fixed but the knockout looked real."

He glanced at me, and I saw interest in his gold-flecked eyes for the first time. "What makes you say that?"

"Canelli had an opening twice in the fourth round and he didn't follow it up either time. He's too smart a fighter for that. But he was trying to get through the sixth and he couldn't. At least that's how it looked from my seat."

"You ever box, Scudder?"

"Two fights at the Y when I was twelve or thirteen years old. Balloon gloves, protective headgear, two-minute rounds. I was too low and clumsy for it, I could never manage to land a punch."

"You have an eye for the sport."

"Well, I guess I've seen a lot of fights."

He was silent for a moment. A cab cut us off and he braked smoothly, avoiding a collision. He didn't swear or hit the horn. He said, "Canelli was set to go in the eighth. He was supposed to give the Kid his best fight until then, but not to get out in front or the knockout might not look right. That's why he held back in round four."

"But the Kid didn't know it was set up."

"Of course not. Most of his fights have been straight until tonight, but a fighter like Canelli could be dangerous to him, and why chance a bad mark on his record at this stage? He gains experience fighting Canelli and he gains confidence by beating him." We were on Central Park West now, heading uptown. "The knockout was real. Canelli would have gone in the tank in the eighth, but we hoped the Kid might get us home early, and you saw him do that. What do you think of him?"

"He's a comer."

"I agree."

"Sometimes he telegraphs the right. In the fourth round—"

"Yes," he said. "They've worked with him on that. The problem is that he generally manages to get away with it."

"Well, he wouldn't have gotten by with it tonight. Not if Canelli had been looking to win."

"Yes. Well, perhaps it's as well that he wasn't."

WE talked boxing until we got to 104th Street, where Chance turned the car around in a careful U-turn and pulled up next to a fire hydrant. He killed the motor but left the keys. "I'll be right down," he said, "after I've seen Sonya upstairs."

She hadn't said a word since she told me it was nice to meet me. He walked around the car and opened the door for her, and they strolled to the entrance of one of the two large apartment buildings that fronted on that block. I wrote the address in my notebook. In no more than five minutes he was back behind the wheel and we were heading downtown again.

Neither of us spoke for half a dozen blocks. Then he said, "You wanted to talk to me. It doesn't have anything to do with Kid Bascomb, does it?"

"No."

"I didn't really think so. What does it have to do with?"

"Kim Dakkinen."

His eyes were on the road and I couldn't see any change in his expression. He said, "Oh? What about her?"

"She wants out."

"Out? Out of what?"

"The life," I said. "The relationship she has with you. She wants you to agree to . . . break things off."

We stopped for a light. He didn't say anything. The light changed and we went another block or two and he said, "What's she to you?"

"A friend."

"What does that mean? You're sleeping with her? You want to marry her? Friend's a big word, it covers a lot of ground."

"This time it's a small word. She's a friend, she asked me to do her a favor."

"By talking to me."

"That's right."

"Why couldn't she talk to me herself? I see her frequently, you know. She wouldn't have had to run around the city asking after me. Why, I saw her just last night."

"I know."

"Do you? Why didn't she say anything when she saw me?"

"She's afraid."

"Afraid of me?"

"Afraid you might not want her to leave."

"And so I might beat her? Disfigure her? Stub out cigarettes on her breasts?"

"Something like that."

He fell silent again. The car's ride was hypnotically smooth. He said, "She can go."

"Just like that?"

"How else? I'm not a white slaver, you know." His tone put an ironic stress on the term. "My women stay with me out of their own will, such will as they possess. They're under no duress. You know Nietzsche? 'Women are like dogs, the more you beat them the more they love you.' But I don't beat them, Scudder. It never seems to be necessary. How does Kim come to have you for a friend?"

"We have an acquaintance in common."

He glanced at me. "You were a policeman. A detective, I believe. You left the force several years ago. You killed a child and resigned out of guilt."

That was close enough for me to let it pass. A stray bullet of mine had killed a young girl named Estrellita Rivera, but I don't know that it was guilt over the incident that propelled me out of the police department. What it had done, really, was change the way the world looked to me, so that being a cop was no longer something I wanted to do. Neither was being a husband and a father and living on Long Island, and in due course I was out of work and out of the marriage and living on Fifty-seventh Street and putting in the hours at Armstrong's. The shooting unquestionably set those currents in motion, but I think I was pointed in those directions anyway and would have gotten there sooner or later.

"Now you're a sort of half-assed detective," he went on "She hire you?"

"More or less."

"What's that mean?" He didn't wait for clarification. "Nothing against you, but she wasted her money. Or *my* money, according to how you look at it. If she wants to end our arrangement all she has to do is tell me so. She doesn't need anyone to do her talking for her. What's she plan to do? I hope she's not going back home."

I didn't say anything.

"I suspect she'll stay in New York. But will she stay in the life? I'm afraid it's the only trade she knows. What else will she do? And where will she live? I provide their apartments, you know, and pay their rent and pick out their clothes. Well, I don't suppose anyone asked Ibsen where Nora would find an apartment. I believe this is where you live, if I'm not mistaken."

I looked out the window. We were in front of my hotel. I hadn't been paying attention.

"I assume you'll be in touch with Kim," he said. "If you want, you can tell her you intimidated me and sent me slinking off into the night."

"Why would I do that?"

"So she'll think she got her money's worth from you."

"She got her money's worth," I said, "and I don't care whether she knows it or not. All I'll tell her is what you've told me."

"Really? While you're at it, you can let her know that I'll be coming to see her. Just to satisfy myself that all of this is really her idea."

"I'll mention it."

"And tell her she has no reason to fear me." He sighed. "They think they're irreplaceable. If she had any notion how easily she can be replaced she'd most likely hang herself. The buses bring them, Scudder. Every hour of every day they stream into Port Authority ready to sell themselves. And every day a whole slew of others decide there must be a better way than waiting tables or punching a cash register. I could open an office, Scudder, and take applications, and there'd be a line halfway around the block."

I opened the door. He said, "I enjoyed this. Especially earlier. You have a good eye for boxing. Please tell that silly
blonde whore that nobody's going to kill her."

"I'll do that."

"And if you need to talk to me, just call my service. I'll return your calls now that I know you."

I got out, closed the door. He waited for an opening, made
a U-turn, turned again at Eighth Avenue and headed uptown.
The U-turn was illegal and he ran the light making his left
turn on Eighth, but I don't suppose it worried him much. I
couldn't recall the last time I'd seen a cop ticket anyone for
a moving violation in the city of New York. Sometimes
you'll see five cars go on through after a light turns red.
Even the buses do it these days.

After he made his turn I took out my notebook, made an
entry. Across the street, near Polly's Cage, a man and
woman were having a loud argument. "You call yourself a
man?" she demanded. He slapped her. She cursed him and
he slapped her again.

Maybe he'd beat her senseless. Maybe this was a game
they played five nights out of seven. Try to break up that sort
of thing and as likely as not they'll both turn on you. When I
was a rookie cop, my first partner would do anything to
avoid interfering in a domestic argument. Once, facing down
a drunken husband, he'd been assaulted from behind by the
wife. The husband had knocked out four of her teeth but she
leaped to his defense, breaking a bottle over her savior's
head. He wound up with fifteen stitches and a concussion,
and he used to run his forefinger over the scar when he told
me the story. You couldn't see the scar, his hair covered it,
but his finger went right to the spot.

"I say let 'em kill each other," he used to say. "It don't
matter if she phoned in the complaint herself, she'll still turn
on you. Let 'em fucking kill each other."

Across the street, the woman said something I didn't

catch and the man hit her low with his closed fist. She cried out in what sounded like real pain. I put my notebook away and went into my hotel.

I called Kim from the lobby. Her machine answered and I had started to leave a message when she picked up the receiver and interrupted me. "I leave the machine on sometimes when I'm home," she explained, "so I can see who it is before I answer. I haven't heard from Chance since I spoke to you earlier."

"I just left him a few minutes ago."

"You saw him?"

"We rode around in his car."

"What did you think?"

"I think he's a good driver."

"I meant—"

"I know what you meant. He didn't seem terribly upset to hear that you want to leave him. He assured me that you've got nothing to fear from him. According to him, you didn't need me as your champion. All you had to do was tell him."

"Yes, well, he'd say that."

"You don't think it's true?"

"Maybe it is."

"He said he wants to hear it from you, and I gather he also wants to make some arrangements about your leaving the apartment. I don't know if you're afraid to be alone with him or not."

"I don't know either."

"You can keep the door locked and talk to him through it."

"He has keys."

"Don't you have a chain lock?"

"Yes."

"You can use that."

"I suppose."

"Shall I come over?"

"No, you don't have to do that. Oh, I suppose you want the rest of the money, don't you?"

"Not until you've talked to him and everything's settled. But I'll come over there if you want somebody on your side when he turns up."

"Is he coming tonight?"

"I don't know when he's coming. Maybe he'll handle the whole thing over the phone."

"He might not come until tomorrow."

"Well, I could hole up on the couch if you wanted."

"Do you think it's necessary?"

"Well, it is if you think it is, Kim. If you're uncomfortable—"

"Do you think I have anything to be afraid of?"

I thought for a moment, replayed the scene with Chance, assessed my own reactions after the fact. "No," I said. "I don't think so. But I don't really know the man."

"Neither do I."

"If you're nervous—"

"No, it's silly. Anyway it's late. I'm watching a movie on cable, but when it ends I'm going to sleep. I'll put the chain lock on. That's a good idea."

"You've got my number."

"Yes."

"Call me if anything happens, or if you just want to call me. All right?"

"Sure."

"Just to put your mind at rest, I think you spent some money you didn't have to spend, but it was money you held out so maybe it doesn't matter."

"Absolutely."

"The point is I think you're off the hook. He's not going to hurt you."

"I think you're right. I'll probably call you tomorrow. And Matt? Thanks."

"Get some sleep," I said.

I went upstairs and tried to take my own advice but I was wired. I gave up and got dressed and went around the corner to Armstrong's. I would have had something to eat but the kitchen was closed. Trina told me she could get me a piece of pie if I wanted. I didn't want a piece of pie.

I wanted two ounces of bourbon, neat, and another two ounces in my coffee, and I couldn't think of a single god-damned reason not to have it. It wouldn't get me drunk. It wouldn't put me back in the hospital. That had been the result of a bout of uncontrolled round-the-clock drinking, and I'd learned my lesson. I couldn't drink that way anymore, not safely, and I didn't intend to. But there was a fairly substantial difference between a nightcap and going out on a toot, wasn't there?

They tell you not to drink for ninety days. You're supposed to go to ninety meetings in ninety days and stay away from the first drink one day at a time, and after ninety days you can decide what you want to do next.

I'd had my last drink Sunday night. I'd been to four meetings since then, and if I went to bed without a drink I'd have five days.

So?

I had one cup of coffee, and on the way back to the hotel I stopped at the Greek deli and picked up a cheese danish and a half pint of milk. I ate the pastry and drank a little of the milk in my room.

I turned out the light, got into bed. Now I had five days. So?

Chapter 5

I read the paper while I ate breakfast. The housing cop in Corona was still in critical condition but his doctors now said they expected him to live. They said there might be some paralysis, which in turn might be permanent. It was too early to tell.

In Grand Central Station, someone had mugged a shopping-bag lady and had stolen two of her three bags. And, in the Gravesend section of Brooklyn, a father and son with arrest records for pornography and what the paper described as links to organized crime bolted from a car and sought sanctuary in the first house they could run to. Their pursuers opened up on them with pistols and a shotgun. The father was wounded, the son was shot dead, and the young wife and mother who'd just recently moved into the house was hanging something in a hall closet when enough of the shotgun blast came through the door to take most of her head off.

They have noon meetings six days a week at the YMCA on Sixty-third Street. The speaker said, "Just let me tell you how I got here. I woke up one morning and I said to myself, 'Hey, it's a beautiful day and I never felt better in my life. My health's tiptop, my marriage is in great shape, my career's going beautifully, and my state of mind has never been better. I think I'll go join AA.' "

The room rocked with laughter. After his talk they didn't go around the room. You raised your hand and the speaker called on you. One young fellow said shyly that he'd just reached ninety days. He got a lot of applause. I thought about raising my hand and tried to figure out what I might say. All I could think to talk about was the woman in Gravesend, or perhaps Lou Rudenko's mother, slain by a salvaged television set. But what did either of those deaths have to do with me? I was still looking for something to say when time ran out and we all stood up and said the Lord's Prayer. It was just as well. I probably wouldn't have gotten around to raising my hand anyway.

AFTER the meeting I walked for awhile in Central Park. The sun was out for a change and it was the first good day all week. I took a good long walk and watched the kids and the runners and the cyclists and the roller skaters and tried to reconcile all that wholesome innocent energy with the dark face of the city that showed itself every morning in the newspaper.

The two worlds overlap. Some of these riders would be robbed of their bicycles. Some of these strolling lovers would return home to burglarized apartments. Some of these laughing kids would pull holdups, and shoot or stab, and some would be held up or shot or stabbed, and a person could give himself a headache trying to make sense out of it.

On my way out of the park at Columbus Circle a bum with a baseball jacket and one milky eye hustled me for a dime toward a pint of wine. A few yards to the left of us, two colleagues of his shared a bottle of Night Train and watched our transaction with interest. I was going to tell him to piss off, then surprised myself by giving him a buck. Maybe I was reluctant to shame him in front of his friends. He started

to thank me more effusively than I could stomach, and then
I guess he saw something in my face that stopped him cold.
He backed off and I crossed the street and headed home.

THERE was no mail, just a message to call Kim. The clerk's
supposed to note the time of the call on the slip but this place
isn't the Waldorf. I asked if he remembered the time of the
call and he didn't.

I called her and she said, "Oh, I was hoping you'd call.
Why don't you come over and pick up the money I owe
you?"

"You heard from Chance?"

"He was here about an hour ago. Everything worked out
perfectly. Can you come over?"

I told her to give me an hour. I went upstairs and showered and shaved. I got dressed, then decided I didn't like
what I was wearing and changed. I was fussing with the knot
of my tie when I realized what I was doing. I was dressing
for a date.

I had to laugh at myself.

I put on my hat and coat and got out of there. She lived in
Murray Hill, Thirty-eighth between Third and Lex. I walked
over to Fifth, took a bus, then walked the rest of the way
east. Her building was a prewar apartment house, brick-
fronted, fourteen stories, with a tile floor and potted palms in
the lobby. I gave my name to the doorman and he called upstairs on the intercom and established that I was welcome
before pointing me to the elevator. There was something deliberately neutral about his manner, and I decided that he
knew Kim's profession and assumed I was a john and was
being very careful not to smirk.

I got off at the twelfth floor and walked to her door. It
opened as I approached it. She stood framed in the doorway,
all blonde braids and blue eyes and cheekbones, and for a
moment I could picture her carved on the prow of a Viking

ship. "Oh, Matt," she said, and reached to embrace me. She was just about my height and she gave me a good hard hug and I felt the pressure of firm breasts and thighs and recognized the sharp tang of her scent. "Matt," she said, drawing me inside, closing the door. "God, I'm so grateful to Elaine for suggesting I get in touch with you. You know what you are? You're my hero."

"All I did was talk to the man."

"Whatever you did, it worked. That's all I care about. Sit down, relax a moment. Can I get you anything to drink?"

"No thanks."

"Some coffee?"

"Well, if it's no trouble."

"Sit down. It's instant, if that's all right. I'm too lazy to make real coffee."

I told her instant was fine. I sat down on the couch and waited while she made the coffee. The room was a comfortable one, attractively if sparsely furnished. A recording of solo jazz piano played softly on the stereo. An all-black cat peered cautiously around the corner at me, then disappeared from view.

The coffee table held a few current magazines—*People, TV Guide, Cosmopolitan, Natural History*. A framed poster on the wall over the stereo advertised the Hopper show held a couple years back at the Whitney. A pair of African masks decorated another wall. A Scandinavian area rug, its abstract pattern a whirl of blue and green, covered the central portion of the limed oak floor.

When she returned with the coffee I admired the room. She said she wished she could keep the apartment. "But in a way," she said, "it's good I can't, you know? I mean, to go on living here, and then there'd be people showing up. You know. Men."

"Sure."

"Plus the fact that none of this is me. I mean, the only

thing in this room that I picked out is the poster. I went to that show and I wanted to take some of it home with me. The way that man painted loneliness. People together but not together, looking off in different directions. It got to me, it really did."

"Where will you live?"

"Someplace nice," she said confidently. She perched on the couch beside me, one long leg folded up beneath her, her coffee cup balanced on the other knee. She was wearing the same wine-colored jeans she'd worn at Armstrong's, along with a lemon yellow sweater. She didn't seem to be wearing anything under the sweater. Her feet were bare, the toenails the same tawny port as her fingernails. She'd been wearing bedroom slippers but kicked them off before sitting down.

I took in the blue of her eyes, the green of her square-cut ring, then found my eyes drawn to the rug. It looked as though someone had taken each of those colors and beaten them with a wire whisk.

She blew on her coffee, sipped it, leaned far forward and set the cup on the coffee table. Her cigarettes were on the table and she lit one. She said, "I don't know what you said to Chance but you really made an impression on him."

"I don't see how."

"He called this morning and said he would be coming over, and when he got here I had the door on the chain lock, and somehow I just knew I didn't have anything to fear from him. You know how sometimes you just know something?"

I knew, all right. The Boston Strangler never had to break a door down. All his victims opened the door and let him in.

She pursed her lips, blew out a column of smoke. "He was very nice. He said he hadn't realized I was unhappy and that he had no intention of trying to hold me against my will. He seemed hurt that I could have thought that of him. You know something? He had me just about feeling guilty. And he had me feeling I was making a big mistake, that I was throwing something away and I'd be sorry I couldn't ever get it back. He said, 'You know, I never take a girl back,' and I thought, God, I'm burning my bridges. Can you imagine?"

"I think so."

"Because he's such a con artist. Like I'm walking away from a great job and forfeiting my stake in the corporate pension plan. I mean, come *on!*"

"When do you have to be out of the apartment?"

"He said by the end of the month. I'll probably be gone before then. Packing's no big deal. None of the furniture's mine. Just clothes and records, and the Hopper poster, but do you want to know something? I think that can stay right here. I don't think I need the memories."

I drank some of my coffee. It was weaker than I preferred it. The record ended and was followed by a piano trio. She told me again how I had impressed Chance. "He wanted to know how I happened to call you," she said. "I was vague, I said you were a friend of a friend. He said I didn't need to hire you, that all I'd had to do was talk to him."

"That's probably true."

"Maybe. But I don't think so. I think I would have started talking to him, assuming I could work up the nerve, and we'd get into this conversation and gradually I would turn around and the whole subject would be shunted off to the side. And I'd leave it shunted off to the side, you know, because without ever coming out and saying it he'd manage to give me the impression that leaving him wasn't something I was going to be allowed to do. He might not say, 'Look, bitch, you stay where you're at or I'll ruin your face.' He might not say it, but that's what I'd hear."

"Did you hear it today?"

"No. That's the point. I didn't." Her hand fastened on my arm just above the wrist. "Oh, before I forget," she said, and my arm took some of her weight as she got up from the couch. Then she was across the room rummaging in her purse, and then she was back on the couch handing me five hundred-dollar bills, presumably the ones I'd returned to her three days earlier.

She said, "It seems like there ought to be a bonus."

"You paid me well enough."

"But you did such a good job."

She had one arm draped over the back of the sofa and she was leaning toward me. I looked at her blonde braids coiled around her head and thought of a woman I know, a sculptor with a loft in Tribeca. She did a head of Medusa with snakes for hair and Kim had the same broad brow and high cheekbones as Jan Keane's piece of sculpture.

The expression was different, though. Jan's Medusa had looked profoundly disappointed. Kim's face was harder to read.

I said, "Are those contacts?"

"What? Oh, my eyes? That's their natural color. It's kind of weird, isn't it?"

"It's unusual."

Now I could read her face. It was anticipation that I saw there.

"Beautiful eyes," I said.

The wide mouth softened into the beginning of a smile. I moved a little toward her and she came at once into my arms, fresh and warm and eager. I kissed her mouth, her throat, her lidded eyes.

Her bedroom was large and flooded with sunlight. The floor was thickly carpeted. The king-size platform bed was unmade, and the black kitten napped on a chintz-covered boudoir chair. Kim drew the curtains, glanced shyly at me, then began to undress.

Ours was a curious passage. Her body was splendid, the stuff of fantasy, and she gave herself with evident abandon. I was surprised by the intensity of my own desire, and yet it was almost wholly physical. My mind remained oddly detached from her body and from my own. I might have been viewing our performance from a distance.

The resolution provided relief and release and precious little pleasure. I drew away from her and felt as though I was in the midst of an infinite wasteland of sand and dry brush. There was a moment of astonishing sadness. Pain throbbed at the back of my throat and I felt myself close to tears.

Then the feeling passed. I don't know what brought it on or what took it away.

She said, "Well now," and smiled, and rolled on her side to face me and put a hand on my arm. "That was nice, Matt," she said.

I got dressed, turned down the offer of another cup of coffee. She took my hand at the doorway, thanked me again, and said she'd let me know her address and phone once she got relocated. I told her to feel free to call anytime for any reason. We didn't kiss.

In the elevator I remembered something she'd said. *"It seems like there ought to be a bonus."* Well, that was as good a word for it as any.

I walked all the way back to the hotel. I stopped a few times along the way, once for coffee and a sandwich, once in a church on Madison Avenue where I was going to put fifty dollars into the poor box until I realized I couldn't. Kim had paid me in hundreds and I didn't have enough in smaller bills.

I don't know why I tithe, or how I got in the habit in the first place. It was one of the things I began doing after I left Anita and the boys and moved into Manhattan. I don't know what the churches do with the money and I'm sure their need for it is no greater than my own, and of late I've tried to break myself of the habit. But whenever some money comes in I find there's a restlessness that comes with it that I cannot shed until I've handed over 10 percent of the sum to one church or another. I suppose it's superstition. I suppose I think that, having started this, I have to keep it up or something terrible will happen.

God knows it doesn't make any sense. Terrible things happen anyway, and will go on happening whether I give all or none of my income to churches.

This particular tithe would have to wait. I sat for a few minutes anyway, grateful for the peace the empty church provided. I let my mind wander for awhile. After I'd been there a few minutes an elderly man seated himself on the other side of the aisle. He closed his eyes and looked to be in deep concentration.

I wondered if he was praying. I wondered what prayer was like, and what people got out of it. Sometimes, in one church or another, it occurs to me to say a prayer, but I wouldn't know how to go about it.

If there'd been candles to light I would have lit one, but the church was Episcopalian and there weren't.

I went to the meeting that night at St. Paul's but couldn't keep my mind on the qualification. I kept drifting off. During the discussion the kid from the noon meeting told how he'd reached his ninety days, and once again he got a round of applause. The speaker said, "You know what comes after your ninetieth day? Your ninety-first day."

I said, "My name is Matt. I'll pass."

I made it an early night. I fell asleep easily but kept waking up out of dreams. They withdrew from the edge of thought as I tried to catch hold of them.

I got up finally, went out for breakfast, bought a paper and brought it back to the room. There's a Sunday noon meeting within walking distance. I'd never been to it but I had seen it listed in the meeting book. By the time I thought of going, it was already half over. I stayed in my room and finished the paper.

Drinking used to fill up the hours. I used to be able to sit in Armstrong's for hours, drinking coffee with bourbon in it, not getting loaded, just sipping one cup after another while the hours went by. You try and do the same thing without the booze and it doesn't work. It just doesn't work.

Around three I thought of Kim. I reached for the phone to call her and had to stop myself. We'd gone to bed because that was the sort of gift she knew how to bestow and one I didn't know how to reject, but that didn't make us lovers. It didn't make us anything to one another, and whatever business we'd had with each other was finished.

I remembered her hair and Jan Keane's Medusa and thought of calling Jan. And what would the conversation be like?

I could tell her I was halfway through my seventh sober day. I hadn't had any contact with her since she started going to meetings herself. They'd told her to stay away from people, places and things associated with drink, and I was in that category as far as she was concerned. I wasn't drinking today and I could tell her that, but so what? It didn't mean she would want to see me. For that matter, it didn't mean I would want to see her.

We'd had a couple evenings when we had a good time drinking together. Maybe we could have the same kind of enjoyment sober. But maybe it would be like sitting in Armstrong's for five hours with no bourbon in the coffee.

I got as far as looking up her number but never made the call.

The speaker at St. Paul's told a really low-bottom story. He'd been a heroin addict for several years, kicked that, then drank his way down to the Bowery. He looked as though he'd seen hell and remembered what it looked like.

During the break, Jim cornered me by the coffee urn and asked me how it was going. I told him it was going okay. He asked how long I'd been sober now.

"Today's my seventh day," I said.

"Jesus, that's great," he said. "That's really great, Matt."

During the discussion I thought maybe I'd speak up when it was my turn. I didn't know that I'd say I was an alcoholic because I didn't know that I was, but I could say something about it being my seventh day, or just that I was glad to be there, or something. But when it got to me I said what I always say.

After the meeting Jim came up to me while I was carrying my folded chair to where they stack them. He said, "You know, a bunch of us generally stop over to the Cobb's Corner for coffee after the meeting. Just to hang out and shoot the breeze. Why don't you come along?"

"Gee, I'd like to," I said, "but I can't tonight."

"Some other night, then."

"Sure," I said. "Sounds good, Jim."

I could have gone. I didn't have anything else to do. Instead I went to Armstrong's and ate a hamburger and a piece of cheesecake and drank a cup of coffee. I could have had the identical meal at Cobb's Corner.

Well, I always like Armstrong's on a Sunday night. You get a light crowd then, just the regulars. After I was done with my meal I carried my coffee cup over to the bar and chatted for awhile with a CBS technician named Manny and a musician named Gordon. I didn't even feel like drinking.

I went home and went to bed. I got up in the morning with a sense of dread and wrote it off as the residue of an unremembered dream. I showered and shaved and it was still there. I got dressed, went downstairs, dropped a bag of dirty clothes at the laundry and left a suit and a pair of pants at the dry cleaners. I ate breakfast and read the *Daily News*. One of their columnists had interviewed the husband of the woman who'd caught the shotgun blast in Gravesend. They'd just moved into that house, it was their dream house, their chance for a decent life in a decent neighborhood. And then these two gangsters, running for their lives, had picked that particular house to run to. "It was as if the finger of God had pointed to Clair Ryzcek," the columnist wrote.

In the "Metro Briefs" section, I learned that two Bowery derelicts had fought over a shirt one of them had found in a trash can in the Astor Place BMT subway station. One had stabbed the other dead with an eight-inch folding knife. The dead man was fifty-two, his killer thirty-three. I wondered if the item would have made the paper if it hadn't taken place belowground. When they kill each other in Bowery flophouses, it's not news.

I kept thumbing through the paper as if I expected to find something, and the vague feeling of foreboding persisted. I felt faintly hungover and I had to remind myself I'd had nothing to drink the night before. This was my eighth sober day.

I went to the bank, put some of my five-hundred-dollar fee in my account, changed the rest into tens and twenties. I went to St. Paul's to get rid of fifty bucks but there was a mass going on. I went to the Sixty-third Street Y instead and listened to the most boring qualification I'd heard yet. I think the speaker mentioned every drink he'd had from the age of eleven on. He droned on in a monotone for forty solid minutes.

I sat in the park afterward, bought a hot dog from a vendor, ate it. I got back to the hotel around three, took a nap, went out again around four-thirty. I picked up a *Post* and took it around the corner to Armstrong's. I must have looked at the headline when I bought the paper but somehow it didn't register. I sat down and ordered coffee and looked at the front page and there it was.

CALL GIRL SLASHED TO RIBBONS, it said.

I knew the odds and I also knew that the odds didn't matter. I sat for a moment with my eyes closed and the paper clenched in my fists, trying to alter the story by sheer force of will. Color, the very blue of her northern eyes, flashed behind my closed eyelids. My chest was tight and I could feel that pulse of pain again at the back of my throat.

I turned the goddamned page and there it was on page three just the way I knew it would be. She was dead. The bastard had killed her.

Chapter 6

Kim Dakkinen had died in a room on the seventeenth floor of the Galaxy Downtowner, one of the new high-rise hotels on Sixth Avenue in the Fifties. The room had been rented to a Mr. Charles Owen Jones of Fort Wayne, Indiana, who had paid cash in advance for a one-night stay upon checking in at 9:15 P.M. Sunday, after having phoned ahead for a room half an hour earlier. Since a preliminary check revealed no one of Mr. Jones's name in Fort Wayne, and since the street address he'd entered on the registration card did not seem to exist, he was presumed to have given a false name.

Mr. Jones had made no calls from his room, nor had he billed any charges to his hotel account. After an indeterminable number of hours he had left, and he'd done so without bothering to drop off his key at the desk. Indeed, he'd hung the DO NOT DISTURB sign on the door of his room, and the housekeeping staff had scrupulously honored it until shortly after the 11:00 A.M. checkout time Monday morning. At that time one of the maids put through a call to the room. When the phone went unanswered she knocked on the door; when that brought no response she opened it with her passkey.

She walked in on what the *Post* reporter called "a scene of indescribable horror." A nude woman lay on the carpet at the foot of the unmade bed. Bed and carpet were soaked with her blood. The woman had died of multiple wounds, having been stabbed and slashed innumerable times with what a deputy medical examiner guessed might have been a bayonet or machete. Her killer had hacked her face into "an unrecognizable mess," but a photograph retrieved by an enterprising reporter from Miss Dakkinen's "luxurious Murray Hill apartment" showed what he'd had to work with. Kim's blonde hair was quite different in the photograph, flowing down over her shoulders with one single braid wrapped around the crown like a tiara. She was clear-eyed and radiant in the photo, and looked like a grown-up Heidi.

Identification had been made on the basis of the woman's purse, found at the scene. A sum of cash in the purse had enabled police investigators to rule out money as a motive in the slaying.

No kidding.

I put down the paper. I noticed without much surprise that my hands were shaking. I was even shakier on the inside. I caught Evelyn's eye, and when she came over I asked her to bring me a double shot of bourbon.

She said, "Are you sure, Matt?"

"Why not?"

"Well, you haven't been drinking. Are you sure you want to start?"

I thought, What's it to you, kid? I took a breath and let it out and said, "Maybe you're right."

"How about some more coffee?"

"Sure."

I went back to the story. A preliminary examination fixed the time of death some time around midnight. I tried to think what I'd been doing when he killed her. I'd come to Armstrong's after the meeting, but what time had it been when I'd left? I made it a fairly early night, but even so it had probably been close to midnight by the time I packed it in. Of course the time of death was approximate, so I might have been already asleep when he started to chop her life away.

I sat there and I kept drinking coffee and I read the story over and over and over.

From Armstrong's I went to St. Paul's. I sat in a rear pew and tried to think. Images kept bouncing back and forth, flashes of my two meetings with Kim intercut with my conversation with Chance.

I put fifty futile dollars in the poor box. I lit a candle and stared at it as if I expected to see something dancing in its flame.

I went back and sat down again. I was still sitting there when a soft-spoken young priest came over and told me apologetically that they would be closing for the night. I nodded, got to my feet.

"You seem disturbed," he offered. "Could I help you in any way?"

"I don't think so."

"I've seen you come in here from time to time. Sometimes it helps to talk to someone."

Does it? I said, "I'm not even Catholic, Father."

"That's not a requirement. If there's something troubling you—"

"Just some hard news, Father. The unexpected death of a friend."

"That's always difficult."

I was afraid he'd hand me something about God's mysterious plan, but he seemed to be waiting for me to say more. I managed to get out of there and stood for a moment on the sidewalk, wondering where to go next.

It was around six-thirty. The meeting wasn't for another two hours. You could get there an hour early and sit around and have coffee and talk to people, but I never did. I had two hours to kill and I didn't know how.

They tell you not to let yourself get too hungry. I hadn't had anything to eat since that hot dog in the park. I thought of food and my stomach turned at the notion.

I walked back to my hotel. It seemed as though every place I passed was a bar or a liquor store. I went up to my room and stayed there.

I got to the meeting a couple of minutes early. Half a dozen people said hello to me by name. I got some coffee and sat down.

The speaker told an abbreviated drinking story and spent most of the time telling of all the things that had happened to him since he got sober four years ago. His marriage had broken up, his youngest son had been killed by a hit-and-run driver, he'd gone through a period of extended unemployment and several bad bouts of clinical depression.

"But I didn't drink," he said. "When I first came here you people told me there's nothing so bad that a drink won't make it worse. You told me the way to work this program is not drink even if my ass falls off. I'll tell you, sometimes I think I stay sober on sheer fucking stubbornness. That's okay. I figure whatever works is fine with me."

I wanted to leave at the break. Instead I got a cup of coffee and took a couple of Fig Newtons. I could hear Kim telling me that she had an awful sweet tooth. *"But I never gain an ounce. Aren't I lucky?"*

I ate the cookies. It was like chewing straw but I chewed them and washed them down.

During the discussion one woman got into a long riff about her relationship. She was a pain in the ass, she said the same thing every night. I tuned out.

I thought, My name is Matt and I'm an alcoholic. A woman I know got killed last night. She hired me to keep her from getting killed and I wound up assuring her that she was safe and she believed me. And her killer conned me and I believed him, and she's dead now, and there's nothing I can do about it. And it eats at me and I don't know what to do about that, and there's a bar on every corner and a liquor store on every block, and drinking won't bring her back to life but neither will staying sober, and why the hell do I have to go through this? Why?

I thought, My name is Matt and I'm an alcoholic and we sit around in these goddamned rooms and say the same damned things all the time and meanwhile out there all the animals are killing each other. We say Don't drink and go to meetings and we say The important thing is you're sober and we say Easy does it and we say One day at a time and while we natter on like brainwashed zombies the world is coming to an end.

I thought, My name is Matt and I'm an alcoholic and I need help.

When they got to me I said, "My name is Matt. Thanks for your qualification. I enjoyed it. I think I'll just listen tonight."

I left right after the prayer. I didn't go to Cobb's Corner and I didn't go to Armstrong's, either. Instead I walked to my hotel and past it and halfway around the block to Joey Farrell's on Fifty-eighth Street.

They didn't have much of a crowd. There was a Tony Bennett record on the jukebox. The bartender was nobody I knew.

I looked at the back bar. The first bourbon that caught my eye was Early Times. I ordered a straight shot with water back. The bartender poured it and set it on the bar in front of me.

I picked it up and looked at it. I wonder what I expected to see.

I drank it down.

Chapter 7

It was no big deal. I didn't even feel the drink at first, and then what I experienced was a vague headache and the suggestion of nausea.

Well, my system wasn't used to it. I'd been away from it for a week. When was the last time I'd gone a full week without a drink?

I couldn't remember. Maybe fifteen years, I thought. Maybe twenty, maybe more.

I stood there, a forearm on the bar, one foot on the bottom rung of the bar stool beside me, and I tried to determine just what it was that I felt. I decided that something didn't hurt quite so much as it had a few minutes ago. On the other hand, I felt a curious sense of loss. But of what?

"Another?"

I started to nod, then caught myself and shook my head. "Not right now," I said. "You want to let me have some dimes? I have to make a couple of calls."

He changed a dollar for me and pointed me toward the pay phone. I closed myself into the booth and took out my notebook and pen and started making calls. I spent a few dimes learning who was in charge of the Dakkinen case and a couple more reaching him, but finally I was plugged into the squad room at Midtown North. I asked to speak to Detective Durkin and a voice said, "Just a minute," and "Joe? For you," and after a pause another voice said, "This is Joe Durkin."

I said, "Durkin, my name is Scudder. I'd like to know if you've made an arrest in the Dakkinen murder."

"I didn't get that name," he said.

"It's Matthew Scudder, and I'm not trying to get information out of you, I'm trying to give it. If you haven't arrested the pimp yet I may be able to give you a lead."

After a pause he said, "We haven't made any arrests."

"She had a pimp."

"We know that."

"Do you have his name?"

"Look, Mr. Scudder—"

"Her pimp's name is Chance. That may be a first or last name or it may be an alias. There's no yellow sheet on him, not under that name."

"How would you know about a yellow sheet?"

"I'm an ex-cop. Look, Durkin, I've got a lot of information and all I want to do is give it to you. Suppose I just talk for a few minutes and then you can ask anything you want."

"All right."

I told him what I knew about Chance. I gave him a full physical description, added a description of his car and supplied the license number. I said he had a minimum of four girls on his string and that one of them was a Ms. Sonya Hendryx, possibly known as Sunny, and I described her. "Friday night he dropped Hendryx at 444 Central Park West. It's possible she lives there but more likely that she was going to attend a victory party for a prizefighter named Kid Bascomb. Chance has some sort of interest in Bascomb and it's probable that someone in that building was throwing a party for him."

He started to interrupt but I kept going. I said, "Friday night Chance learned that the Dakkinen girl wanted to end their relationship. Saturday afternoon he visited her on East Thirty-eighth Street and told her he had no objection. He told her to vacate the apartment by the end of the month. It was his apartment, he rented it and installed her in it."

"Just a minute," Durkin said, and I heard papers rustle. "The tenant of record is a Mr. David Goldman. That's also the name Dakkinen's phone's listed in."

"Have you been able to trace David Goldman?"

"Not yet."

"My guess is you won't, or else Goldman'll turn out to be a lawyer or accountant Chance uses to front for him. I'll tell you this much, Chance doesn't look like any David Goldman I ever met."

"You said he was black."

"That's right."

"You met him."

"That's right. Now he doesn't have a particular hangout, but there are several places he frequents." I ran down the list. "I wasn't able to learn where he lives. I gather he keeps that a secret."

"No problem," Durkin said. "We'll use the reverse directory. You gave us his phone number, remember? We'll look it up and get the address that way."

"I think the number's his answering service."

"Well, they'll have a number for him."

"Maybe."

"You sound doubtful."

"I think he likes to keep himself hard to find," I said.

"How'd you happen to find him? What's your connection to all of this, Scudder?"

I felt like hanging up. I'd given them what I had and I didn't feel like answering questions. But I was a lot easier to find than Chance, and if I hung up on Durkin he could have me picked up in no time.

I said, "I met him Friday night. Miss Dakkinen asked me to intercede for her."

"Intercede how?"

"By telling him she wanted to get off the hook. She was scared to tell him herself."

"So you told him for her."

"That's right."

"What, are you a pimp yourself, Scudder? She go from his stable to yours?"

My grip tightened on the receiver. I said, "No, that's not my line, Durkin. Why? Is your mother looking for a new connection?"

"What in—"

"Just watch your fucking mouth, that's all. I'm handing you things on a plate and I never had to call you at all."

He didn't say anything.

I said, "Kim Dakkinen was a friend of a friend. If you want to know about me there used to be a cop named Guzik who knew me. Is he still at Midtown North?"

"You're a friend of Guzik's?"

"We never liked each other much but he can tell you I'm straight. I told Chance she wanted out and he said it was fine with him. He saw her the next day and told her the same thing. Then last night somebody killed her. You still have the time of death figured as midnight?"

"Yeah, but that's approximate. It was twelve hours later that they found her. And the condition of the corpse, you know, the ME probably wanted to move on to something else."

"Bad."

"The one I feel sorry for is that poor little chambermaid. She's from Ecuador, I think she's an illegal, barely speaks a word of English, and she had to walk in on that." He snorted.

"You want to look at the body, give us a positive make? You'll see something'll stick in your memory."

"Don't you have an identification?"

"Oh, yeah," he said. "We got fingerprints. She was arrested once a few years back in Long Island City. Loitering with intent, fifteen days suspended. No arrests since then."

"She worked in a house after that," I said. "And then Chance put her in the apartment on Thirty-eighth Street."

"A real New York odyssey. What else have you got, Scudder? And how do I get hold of you if I need you?"

I didn't have anything else. I gave him my address and phone. We said a few more polite things to each other and I hung up and the phone rang. I owed forty-five cents for going over the three minutes my dime had bought me. I broke another dollar at the bar, put the money in the slot, and returned to the bar to order another drink. Early Times, straight up, water back.

This one tasted better. And after it hit bottom I felt something loosen up inside me.

At the meetings they tell you it's the first drink that gets you drunk. You have one and it triggers an irresistible compulsion and without meaning it you have another and another and you wind up drunk again. Well, maybe I wasn't an alcoholic because that wasn't what was happening. I'd had two drinks and I felt a whole lot better than I did before I'd had them and I certainly didn't feel any need to drink anymore.

I gave myself a chance, though. I stood there for a few minutes and thought about having a third drink.

No. No, I really didn't want it. I was fine the way I was.

I left a buck on the bar, scooped the rest of my change, and headed for home. I walked past Armstrong's and didn't feel like stopping in. I certainly didn't have the urge to stop for a drink.

The early *News* would be out by now. Did I want to walk down to the corner for it?

No, the hell with it.

I stopped at the desk. No messages. Jacob was on duty, riding a gentle codeine buzz, filling in the squares of a cross-word puzzle.

I said, "Say, Jacob, I want to thank you for what you did the other night. Making that phone call."

"Oh, well," he said.

"No, that was terrific," I said. "I really appreciate it."

I went upstairs and got ready for bed. I was tired and felt out of breath. For a moment, just before sleep came, I experienced again that odd sensation of having lost something. But what could I have lost?

I thought, Seven days. You had seven sober days and most of an eighth, and you lost them. They're gone.

Chapter 8

I bought the *News* the next morning. A new atrocity had already driven Kim Dakkinen off the front page. Up in Washington Heights a young surgeon, a resident at Columbia Presbyterian, had been shot dead in a robbery attempt on Riverside Drive. He hadn't resisted his assailant, who had shot him for no apparent reason. The victim's widow was expecting their first child in early February.

The call-girl slashing was on an inside page. I didn't learn anything I hadn't heard the previous night from Durkin.

I walked around a lot. At noon I dropped over to the Y but got restless and left during the qualification. I had a pastrami sandwich at a Broadway deli and drank a bottle of Prior Dark with it. I had another beer around dinnertime. At eight-thirty I went over to St. Paul's, walked once around the block and returned to my hotel without entering the basement meeting room. I made myself stay in my room. I felt like a drink, but I'd had two beers and I decided that two drinks a day would be my ration. As long as I didn't exceed that quota I didn't see how I could get in trouble. It didn't matter whether I had them first thing in the morning or last thing at night, in my room or at a bar, alone or in company.

The following day, Wednesday, I slept late and ate a late breakfast at Armstrong's. I walked to the main library and spent a couple hours there, then sat in Bryant Park until the drug dealers got on my nerves. They've so completely taken over the parks that they assume only a potential customer would bother coming there, so you can't read a paper without being constantly offered uppers and downers and pot and acid and God knows what else.

I went to the eight-thirty meeting that night. Mildred, one of the regulars, got a round of applause when she announced that it was her anniversary, eleven years since her last drink. She said she didn't have any secret, she just did it a day at a time.

I thought that if I went to bed sober I'd have one day. I decided, what the hell, I'd do that. After the meeting I went over to Polly's Cage instead and had my two drinks. I got into a discussion with a guy and he wanted to buy me a third drink, but I told the bartender to make it Coke instead. I was quietly pleased with myself, knowing my limit and sticking to it.

Thursday I had a beer with dinner, went to the meeting and left on the break. I stopped in at Armstrong's but something kept me from ordering a drink there and I didn't stay long. I was restless, I walked in and out of Farrell's and Polly's without ordering a drink in either place. The liquor store down the block from Polly's was still open. I bought a fifth of J. W. Dant and took it back to my room.

I took a shower first and got ready for bed. Then I broke the seal on the bottle, poured about two ounces of bourbon in a water glass, drank it down and went to sleep.

Friday I had another two ounces first thing when I got out of bed. I really felt the drink and it was a good feeling. I went all day without having another. Then around bedtime I had one more and fell asleep.

Saturday I awoke clearheaded with no desire for a morning drink. I couldn't get over how well I was controlling my drinking. I almost felt like going to a meeting and sharing my secret with them, but I could imagine the reaction I'd get. Knowing looks, knowing laughter. Holier-than-thou sobriety. Besides, just because I could control my drinking didn't mean I was justified in recommending it to other people.

I had two drinks before bed. I barely felt them, but Sunday morning I woke up a little rocky and poured myself a generous eye-opener to start the day. It did the job. I read the paper, then checked the meeting book and found an afternoon meeting in the Village. I went down there on the subway. The crowd was almost entirely gay. I left at the break.

I went back to the hotel and took a nap. After dinner I finished reading the paper and decided to have my second drink. I poured two or three ounces of bourbon into my glass and drank it off. I sat down and read some more but I couldn't concentrate very well on what I was reading. I thought of having another drink but I reminded myself I'd already had two that day.

Then I realized something. I'd had my morning drink more than twelve hours ago. More time had elapsed since then than had separated it from my last drink the night before. So that drink had long since left my system, and shouldn't properly be counted as part of *today's* drinks.

Which meant I was entitled to another drink before I went to bed.

I was pleased with having figured that out, and decided to reward myself for my insight by making the drink a respectable one. I filled the water glass to within a half inch of the top and took my time drinking it, sitting in my chair with it like a model in one of those Man of Distinction ads. I had the sense to realize that it was the number of drinks that was significant, not their size, and then it struck me that I'd cheated myself. My first drink, if you could call it that, had been a short measure. In a sense, I owed myself about four ounces of bourbon.

I poured what I judged to be four ounces and drained the glass.

I was pleased to note that the drinks hadn't had any discernible effect on me. I certainly wasn't drunk. As a matter of fact, I felt better than I'd felt in a long time. Too good, in fact, to sit around the room. I'd go out, find a congenial spot, have a Coke or a cup of coffee. Not a drink, because in the first place I didn't want any more and, just as important, I'd already had my two drinks for the day.

I had a Coke at Polly's. On Ninth Avenue I had a glass of ginger ale at a gay bar called Kid Gloves. Some of the other drinkers looked faintly familiar, and I wondered if any of them had been at the meeting that afternoon in the Village.

A block further downtown I realized something. I'd been controlling my drinking for days now, and before that I'd been off the sauce entirely for over a week, and that proved something. Hell, if I could limit myself to two drinks a day, that was fairly strong evidence that I didn't *need* to limit myself to two drinks a day. I'd had my problems with alcohol in the past, I couldn't very well deny it, but evidently I had outgrown that stage in my life.

So, although I certainly didn't *need* another drink, I could just as certainly have one if I wanted one. And I did want one, as a matter of fact, so why not have it?

I went into the saloon and ordered a double bourbon with water back. I remember the bartender had a shiny bald head, and I remember him pouring the drink, and I remember picking it up.

That's the last thing I remember.

Chapter 9

I woke up suddenly, consciousness coming on abruptly and at top volume. I was in a hospital bed.

That was the first shock. The second came a little later when I found out it was Wednesday. I couldn't remember anything after I picked up that third drink Sunday night.

I'd had occasional blackouts for years. Sometimes I'd lose the last half hour of the night. Sometimes I'd lose a few hours.

I'd never lost two whole days before.

THEY didn't want to let me go. I'd been admitted late the previous night and they wanted to keep me in detox for a full five days.

An intern said, "The booze isn't even out of your system yet. You'll walk around the corner and pick up a drink five minutes after you get out of here."

"No I won't."

"You just went through detox here a couple of weeks ago. It's on your chart. We cleaned you up and how long did you last?"

I didn't say anything.

"You know how you got here last night? You had a convulsion, a full-scale grand mal seizure. Ever have one of those before?"

"No."

"Well, you'll have them again. If you keep on drinking you can pretty much count on it. Not every time, but sooner or later. And sooner or later you'll die of it. If you don't die of something else first."

"Stop it."

He grabbed me by the shoulder. "No, I won't stop it," he said. "Why the hell should I stop it? I can't be polite and considerate of your feelings and expect to cut through all your bullshit at the same time. Look at me. *Listen* to me. You're an alcoholic. If you drink you'll die."

I didn't say anything.

He had it all figured out. I would spend ten days in detox. Then I'd go to Smithers for twenty-eight days of alcoholic rehabilitation. He let up on that part when he found out I didn't have medical insurance or the couple of thousand dollars rehab would cost, but he was still holding out for a five-day stay in the detox ward.

"I don't have to stay," I said. "I'm not going to drink."

"Everybody says that."

"In my case it's true. And you can't keep me here if I don't agree to stay. You have to let me sign out."

"If you do you'll be signing out AMA. Against Medical Advice."

"Than that's what I'll do."

He looked angry for a moment. Then he shrugged. "Suit yourself," he said cheerfully. "Next time maybe you'll listen to advice."

"There won't be a next time."

"Oh, there'll be a next time, all right," he said. "Unless you fall on your face closer to some other hospital. Or die before you get here."

* * *

THE clothes they brought me were a mess, dirty from rolling in the street, the shirt and jacket stained with blood. I'd been bleeding from a scalp wound when they brought me in and they'd stitched it up for me. I had evidently sustained the wound during the seizure, unless I'd acquired it earlier in my adventures.

I had enough cash on me for the hospital bill. A minor miracle, that.

It had rained during the morning and the streets were still wet. I stood on the sidewalk and felt the confidence drain out of me. There was a bar right across the street. I had money in my pocket for a drink and I knew it would make me feel better.

I went back to my hotel instead. I had to get up the nerve to approach the desk and collect my mail and messages, as if I'd done something shameful and owed some profound apology to the desk clerk. The worst of it was not knowing what I might have done during the time I was in blackout.

Nothing showed in the clerk's expression. Maybe I'd spent most of the lost time in my room, drinking in isolation. Maybe I'd never returned to the hotel since I left it Sunday night.

I went upstairs and ruled out the latter hypothesis. I'd evidently returned sometime either Monday or Tuesday, because I'd finished the bottle of J.W. Dant and there was a half-full quart of Jim Beam on the bureau beside the empty Dant bottle. The dealer's label indicated it was from a store on Eighth Avenue.

I thought, Well, here's the first test. Either you drink or you don't.

I poured the bourbon down the sink, rinsed out both bottles and put them in the trash.

The mail was all junk. I got rid of it and looked at my messages. Anita had called Monday morning. Someone named Jim Faber had called Tuesday night and left a number. And Chance had called once last night and once this morning.

I took a long hot shower and a careful shave and put on clean clothes. I threw out the shirt and socks and underwear I'd worn home from the hospital and put the suit aside. Maybe the dry cleaner would be able to do something with it. I picked up my messages and went through them again.

My ex-wife Anita. Chance, the pimp who'd killed Kim Dakkinen. And somebody named Faber. I didn't know anybody named Faber, unless he was some drunk who'd become a long-lost buddy during my drunken wanderings.

I discarded the slip with his number and weighed a trip downstairs against the hassle of placing a call through the hotel operator. If I hadn't poured out the bourbon I might have had a drink just about then. Instead I went downstairs and called Anita from the lobby booth.

It was a curious conversation. We were carefully polite, as we often are, and after we'd circled one another like first-round prizefighters she asked me why I'd called. "I'm just returning your call," I said. "I'm sorry it took me awhile."

"Returning my call?"

"There's a message that you called Monday."

There was a pause. Then she said, "Matt, we spoke Monday night. You called me back. Don't you remember?"

I felt a chill, as if someone had just scraped a piece of chalk on a blackboard. "Of course I remember," I said. "But how did this slip get back in my box? I thought you'd called a second time."

"No."

"I must have dropped the message slip and then some helpful idiot returned it to my box, and it got handed to me just now and I thought it was another call."

"That's what must have happened."

"Sure," I said. "Anita, I'd had a couple drinks when I

spoke to you the other night. My memory's a little vague. You want to remind me what we talked about in case there's anything I forgot?"

We had talked about orthodontia for Mickey. I'd told her to get another opinion. I remembered that part of the conversation, I assured her. Was there anything else? I had said I was hoping to send more money soon, a more substantial contribution than I'd made lately, and paying for the kid's braces shouldn't be any problem. I told her I remembered that part, too, and she said that was about all, except that of course I'd talked to the children. Oh, sure, I told her. I remembered my conversation with the boys. And that was all? Well, then, my memory wasn't so bad after all, was it?

I was shaking when I hung up the phone. I sat there and tried to summon up a memory of the conversation she had just described and it was hopeless. Everything was a blank from the moment just before the third drink Sunday night to the time I'd come out of it in the hospital. Everything, all of it, gone.

I tore up the message slip, tore it in half again, put the scraps in my pocket. I looked at the other message. The number Chance had left was his service number. I called Midtown North instead. Durkin wasn't in but they gave me his home number.

He sounded groggy when he answered. "Gimme a second, lemme light a cigarette," he said. When he came back on the line he sounded all right. "I was watching teevee," he said, "and I went and fell asleep in front of the set. What's on your mind, Scudder?"

"That pimp's been trying to reach me. Chance."

"Trying to reach you how?"

"By phone. He left a number for me to call. His answering service. So he's probably in town, and if you want me to set him up—"

"We're not looking for him."

For an awful moment I thought I must have spoken to
Durkin during my blackout, that one of us had called the
other and I didn't remember it. But he went on talking and I
realized that hadn't happened.

"We had him over at the station house and we sweated
him," he explained. "We put out a pickup order but he
wound up coming in on his own accord. He had a slick
lawyer with him and he was pretty slick himself."

"You let him go?"

"We didn't have one damn thing to hold him on. He had
an alibi for the whole stretch from several hours before the
estimated time of death to six or eight hours after. The alibi
looks solid and we haven't got anything to stack up against
it. The clerk who checked Charles Jones into the Galaxy
can't come up with a description. I mean he can't say for
sure if the man he signed in was black or white. He sort of
thinks he was white. How'd you like to hand that to the
D.A.?"

"He could have had someone else rent the room. Those
big hotels, they don't keep any track of who goes in and
out."

"You're right. He could have had someone rent the room.
He also could have had someone kill her."

"Is that what you figure he did?"

"I don't get paid to figure. I know we haven't got a case
against the son of a bitch."

I thought for a moment. "Why would he call me?"

"How would I know?"

"Does he know I steered you to him?"

"He didn't hear it from me."

"Then what does he want with me?"

"Why don't you ask him yourself?"

It was warm in the booth. I cracked the door, let a little air
in. "Maybe I'll do that."

"Sure. Scudder? Don't meet him in a dark alley, huh? Because if he's got some kind of a hard-on for you, you want to watch your back."

"Right."

"And if he does nail you, leave a dying message, will you? That's what they always do on television."

"I'll see what I can do."

"Make it clever," he said. "but not *too* clever, you know? Keep it simple enough so I can figure it out."

I dropped a dime and called his service. The woman with the smoker's rasp to her voice said, "Eight-oh-nine-two. May I help you?"

I said, "My name's Scudder. Chance called me and I'm returning his call."

She said she expected to be speaking to him soon and asked for my number. I gave it to her and went upstairs and stretched out on the bed.

A little less than an hour later the phone rang. "It's Chance," he said. "I want to thank you for returning my call."

"I just got the message an hour or so ago. Both of the messages."

"I'd like to speak with you," he said. "Face to face, that is."

"All right."

"I'm downstairs, I'm in your lobby. I thought we could get a drink or a cup of coffee in the neighborhood. Could you come down?"

"All right."

Chapter 10

He said, "You still think I killed her, don't you?"

"What does it matter what I think?"

"It matters to me."

I borrowed Durkin's line. "Nobody pays me to think."

We were in the back booth of a coffee shop a few doors from Eighth Avenue. My coffee was black. His was just a shade lighter than his skin tone. I'd ordered a toasted English muffin, figuring that I probably ought to eat something, but I hadn't been able to bring myself to touch it.

He said, "I didn't do it."

"All right."

"I have what you might call an alibi in depth. A whole roomful of people can account for my time that night. I wasn't anywhere near that hotel."

"That's handy."

"What's that supposed to mean?"

"Whatever you want it to mean."

"You're saying I could have hired it done."

I shrugged. I felt edgy, sitting across the table from him, but more than that I felt tired. I wasn't afraid of him.

"Maybe I could have. But I didn't."

"If you say so."

"God *damn*," he said, and drank some of his coffee. "She anything more to you than you let on that night?"

"No."

"Just a friend of a friend?"

"That's right."

He looked at me, and his gaze was like a too-bright light shining in my eyes. "You went to bed with her," he said. Before I could respond he said, "Sure, that's what you did. How else would she say thank you? The woman only spoke one language. I hope that wasn't the only compensation you got, Scudder. I hope she didn't pay the whole fee in whore's coin."

"My fees are my business," I said. "Anything that happened between us is my business."

He nodded. "I'm just getting a fix on where you're coming from, that's all."

"I'm not coming from anyplace and I'm not going anywhere. I did a piece of work and I was paid in full. The client's dead and I didn't have anything to do with that and it doesn't have anything to do with me. You say you had nothing to do with her death. Maybe that's true and maybe it isn't. I don't know and I don't have to know and I don't honestly give a damn. That's between you and the police. I'm not the police."

"You used to be."

"But I'm not anymore. I'm not the police and I'm not the dead girl's brother and I'm not some avenging angel with a flaming sword. You think it matters to me who killed Kim Dakkinen? You think I give a damn?"

"Yes."

I looked at him.

He said, "Yes, I think it matters to you. I think you care

who killed her. That's why I'm here." He smiled gently. "See," he said, "what I want is to hire you, Mr. Matthew Scudder. I want you to find out who killed her."

I took a while before I believed he was serious. Then I did what I could to talk him out of it. If there was any kind of trail leading to Kim's killer, I told him, the police had the best chance of finding and following it. They had the authority and the manpower and the talent and the connections and the skills. I had none of the above.

"You're forgetting something," he said.

"Oh?"

"They won't be looking. Far as they're concerned, they already *know* who killed her. They got no evidence so they can't do anything with it, but that's their excuse not to kill themselves trying. They'll say, 'Well, we know Chance killed her but we can't prove it so let's work on something else.' God knows they got plenty other things to work on. And if they did work on it, all they'd be looking for is some way to hang it onto me. They wouldn't even look to see if there's somebody else on earth with a reason for wanting her dead."

"Like who?"

"That's what you would be looking to find out."

"Why?"

"For money," he said, and smiled again. "I wasn't asking you to work for free. I have a lot of money coming in, all of it cash. I can pay a good fee."

"That's not what I meant. Why would you want me on the case? Why would you want the killer found, assuming I had any chance of finding him? It's not to get you off the hook because you're not on the hook. The cops haven't got a case against you and they're not likely to come up with one. What's it to you if the case stays on the books as unsolved?"

His gaze was calm, steady. "Maybe I'm concerned about my reputation," he suggested.

"How? It looks to me as though your reputation gets a boost. If the word on the street is that you killed her and got away with it, the next girl who wants to quit your string is going to have something else to think about. Even if you didn't have anything to do with her murder, I can see where you'd be just as happy to take the credit for it."

He flicked his index finger a couple times against his empty coffee cup. He said, "Somebody killed a woman of mine. Nobody should be able to do that and get away with it."

"She wasn't yours when she got killed."

"Who knew that? You knew it and she knew it and I knew it. My other girls, did they know? Did the people in the bars and on the street know? Do they know now? Far as the world knows, one of my girls got killed and the killer's getting away with it."

"And that hurts your reputation?"

"I don't see it helping it any. There's other things. My girls are afraid. Kim got killed and the guy who did it is still out there. Suppose he repeats?"

"Kills another prostitute?"

"Kills another of mine," he said levelly. "Scudder, that killer's a loaded gun and I don't know who he's pointed at. Maybe killing Kim's a way for somebody to get at me. Maybe another girl of mine is next on his list. I know one thing. My business is hurting already. I told my girls not to take any hotel tricks, that's for starters, and not to take any new johns if there's anything funny about them. That's like telling them to leave the phone off the hook."

The waiter drifted over with a pot of coffee and refilled our cups. I still hadn't touched my English muffin and the melted butter was starting to congeal. I got him to take it away. Chance added milk to his coffee. I remembered sitting with Kim while she drank hers heavily diluted with cream and sugar.

I said, "Why me, Chance?"

"I told you. The cops aren't going to kill themselves. The only way somebody's going to give this his best shot is if he's earning my money for it."

"There's other people who work private. You could hire a whole firm, get 'em working around the clock."

"I never did like team sports. Rather see somebody go one on one. 'Sides, you got an inside track. You knew the woman."

"I don't know how much of an edge that gives me."

"And I know you."

"Because you met me once?"

"And liked your style. That counts some."

"Does it? The only thing you know about me is I know how to look at a boxing match. That's not a whole lot."

"It's something. But I know more than that. I know how you handle yourself. And I've asked around, you know. A lot of folks know you and most of 'em said good things about you."

I was silent for a minute or two. Then I said, "It could have been a psycho that killed her. That's what he made it look like so maybe that's what it was."

"Friday I learn she wants out of my string of girls. Saturday I tell her it's cool. Sunday some crazy man flies in from Indiana and chops her up, just by coincidence. You figure?"

"Coincidences happen all the time," I said, "but no, I don't think it was coincidence." God, I felt tired. I said, "I don't much want the case."

"Why not?"

I thought, Because I don't want to have to do anything. I want to sit in a dark corner and turn the world off. I want a drink, damn it.

"You could use the money," he said.

That was true enough. I hadn't gotten all that much mileage out of my last fee. And my son Mickey needed braces on his teeth, and after that there'd be something else.

I said, "I've got to think it over."

"All right."

"I can't concentrate right now. I need a little time to sort out my thoughts."

"How much time?"

Months, I thought. "A couple of hours. I'll call you sometime tonight. Is there a number where I can reach you or do I just call the service?"

"Pick a time," he said. "I'll meet you in front of your hotel."

"You don't have to do that."

"It's too easy to say no over the phone. I figure the odds are better face to face. Besides, if the answer's yes we'll want to talk some. And you'll want some money from me."

I shrugged.

"Pick a time."

"Ten?"

"In front of your hotel."

"All right," I said. "If I had to answer now, it'd be no."

"Then it's good you got until ten."

He paid for the coffee. I didn't put up a fight.

I went back to the hotel and up to the room. I tried to think straight and couldn't. I couldn't seem to sit still, either. I kept moving from the bed to the chair and back again, wondering why I hadn't given him a final no right away. Now I had the aggravation of getting through the hours until ten o'clock and then finding the resolve to turn down what he was offering.

Without thinking too much about what I was doing I put on my hat and coat and went around the corner to Armstrong's. I walked in the door not knowing what I was going to order. I went up to the bar and Billie started shaking his head when he saw me coming. He said, "I can't serve you, Matt. I'm sorry as hell."

I felt the color mounting in my face. I was embarrassed and I was angry. I said, "What are you talking about? Do I look drunk to you?"

"No."

"Then how the hell did I get to be eighty-six around here?"

His eyes avoided mine. "I don't make the rules," he said. "I'm not saying you're not welcome here. Coffee or a Coke or a meal, hell, you're a valued longtime customer. But I'm not allowed to sell you booze."

"Who says?"

"The boss says. When you were in here the other night—"

Oh, God. I said, "I'm sorry about that, Billie. I'll tell you the truth, I had a couple of bad nights. I didn't even know I came in here."

"Don't worry about it."

Christ, I wanted to hide behind something. "Was I very bad, Billie? Did I make trouble?"

"Aw, shit," he said. "You were drunk, you know? It happens, right? I used to have this Irish landlady, I came in bagged one night and apologized the next day, and she would say, 'Jaysus, son, it could happen to a bishop.' You didn't make any trouble, Matt."

"Then—"

"Look," he said, and leaned forward. "I'll just repeat what I was told. He told me, he said, if the guy wants to drink himself to death I can't stop him, and if he wants to come in here he's welcome, but I'm not selling him the booze. This isn't me talking, Matt. I'm just saying what was said."

"I understand."

"If it was up to me—"

"I didn't come in for a drink anyway," I said. "I came in for coffee."

"In that case—"

"In that case the hell with it," I said. "In that case I think what I want is a drink and it shouldn't be all that hard to find somebody willing to sell it to me."

"Matt, don't take it that way."

"Don't tell me how to take it," I said. "Don't give me that shit."

There was something clean and satisfying about the rage I felt. I stalked out of there, my anger burning with a pure flame, and stood on the sidewalk trying to decide where to go for a drink.

Then someone was calling my name.

I turned. A fellow in an army jacket was smiling gently at me. I couldn't place him at first. He said it was good to see me and asked how I was doing, and then of course I knew who it was.

I said, "Oh, hi, Jim. I'm okay, I guess."

"Going to the meeting? I'll walk with you."

"Oh," I said. "Gee, I don't think I'm going to be able to make it tonight. I have to see a guy."

He just smiled. Something clicked, and I asked him if his last name was Faber.

"That's right," he said.

"You called me at the hotel."

"Just wanted to say hello. Nothing important."

"I didn't recognize the name. Otherwise I would have called you back."

"Sure. You sure you don't want to tag along to the meeting, Matt?"

"I wish I could. Oh, Jesus."

He waited.

"I've been having a little trouble, Jim."

"That's not so unusual, you know."

I couldn't look at him. I said, "I started drinking again. I went, I don't know, seven or eight days. Then I started again, and I was doing okay, you know, controlling it, and then one night I got into trouble."

"You got in trouble when you picked up the first one."

"I don't know. Maybe."

"That's why I called," he said gently. "I figured maybe you could use a little help."

"You knew?"

"Well, you were in pretty rocky shape at the meeting Monday night."

"I was at the meeting?"

"You don't remember, do you? I had a feeling you were in a blackout."

"Oh my God."

"What's the matter?"

"I went there drunk? I showed up drunk at an AA meeting?"

He laughed. "You make it sound like a mortal sin. You think you're the first person who ever did that?"

I wanted to die. "But it's terrible," I said.

"What's so terrible?"

"I can never go back. I can never walk into that room."

"You're ashamed of yourself, aren't you?"

"Of course."

He nodded. "I was always ashamed of my blackouts. I didn't want to know about them and I was always afraid of what I might have done. Just for the record, you weren't so bad. You didn't make trouble. You didn't talk out of turn. You spilled a cup of coffee—"

"Oh, God."

"It's not as if you spilled it *on* anybody. You were just drunk, that's all. In case you were wondering, you didn't look to be having a very good time. Matter of fact, you looked pretty miserable."

I found the courage to say, "I wound up in the hospital."

"And you're out already?"

"I signed myself out this afternoon. I had a convulsion, that's how I got there."

"That'll do it."

We walked a little ways in silence. I said, "I wouldn't be able to stay for the whole meeting. I have to meet a guy at ten o'clock."

"You could stay for most of the meeting."

"I guess so."

IT seemed to me as though everybody was staring at me. Some people said hello to me and I found myself reading implications into their greetings. Others didn't say anything and I decided they were avoiding me because my drunkenness had offended them. I was so maddeningly self-conscious I wanted to jump out of my own skin.

I couldn't stay in my seat during the qualification. I kept going back to the coffee urn. I was sure my constant visits to the urn were drawing disapproval but I seemed irresistibly drawn to it.

My mind kept going off on tangents of its own. The speaker was a Brooklyn fireman and he had a very lively story but I couldn't keep my mind on it. He told how everyone in his firehouse had been a heavy drinker and how anyone who didn't drink that way got transferred out. "The captain was an alcoholic and he wanted to surround himself with other alcoholics," he explained. "He used to say, 'Give me enough drunken firemen and I'll put out any fire there is.' And he was right. Man, we would do anything, we would go in anywhere, take any crazy goddamned chances. Because we were too drunk to know better."

It was such a goddamned puzzle. I'd been controlling my drinking and it had worked fine. Except when it didn't.

On the break I put a buck in the basket and went to the urn

for still another cup of coffee. This time I managed to make myself eat an oatmeal cookie. I was back in my seat when the discussion started.

I kept losing the thread but it didn't seem to matter. I listened as well as I could and I stayed there as long as I could. At a quarter of ten I got up and slipped out the door as unobtrusively as possible. I had the feeling every eye in the place was on me and I wanted to assure them all that I wasn't going for a drink, that I had to meet somebody, that it was a business matter.

It struck me later that I could have stayed for the end. St. Paul's was only five minutes from my hotel. Chance would have waited.

Maybe I wanted an excuse to leave before it was my turn to talk.

I was in the lobby at ten o'clock. I saw his car pull up and I went out the door and crossed the sidewalk to the curb. I opened the door, got in, swung it shut.

He looked at me.

"That job still open?"

He nodded. "If you want it."

"I want it."

He nodded again, put the car in gear, and pulled away from the curb.

Chapter 11

The circular drive in Central Park is almost exactly six miles around. We were on our fourth counterclockwise lap, the Cadillac cruising effortlessly. Chance did most of the talking. I had my notebook out, and now and then I wrote something in it.

At first he talked about Kim. Her parents were Finnish immigrants who had settled on a farm in western Wisconsin. The nearest city of any size was Eau Claire. Kim had been named Kiraa and grew up milking cows and weeding the vegetable garden. When she was nine years old her older brother began abusing her sexually, coming into her room every night, doing things to her, making her do things to him.

"Except one time she told the story and it was her uncle on her mother's side, and another time it was her father, so maybe it never happened at all outside of her mind. Or maybe it did and she changed it to keep it from being so real."

During her junior year in high school she had an affair with a middle-aged realtor. He told her he was going to leave his wife for her. She packed a suitcase and they drove to Chicago, where they stayed for three days at the Palmer House, ordering all their meals from room service. The realtor got maudlin drunk the second day and kept telling her he was ruining her life. He was in better spirits the third day, but the following morning she awoke to find him gone. A note explained that he had returned to his wife, that the room was paid for four more days, and that he would never forget Kim. Along with the note he left six hundred dollars in a hotel envelope.

She stayed out the week, had a look at Chicago, and slept with several men. Two of them gave her money without being asked. She'd intended to ask the others but couldn't bring herself to do so. She thought about going back to the farm. Then, on her final night at the Palmer House, she picked up a fellow hotel guest, a Nigerian delegate to some sort of trade conference.

"That burned her bridges," Chance said. "Sleeping with a black man meant she couldn't go back to the farm. First thing the next morning she went and caught a bus for New York."

She'd been all wrong for the life until he took her away from Duffy and put her in her own apartment. She had the looks and the bearing for the carriage trade, and that was good because she hadn't had the hustle to make it on the street.

"She was lazy," he said, and thought for a moment. "Whores are lazy."

He'd had six women working for him. Now, with Kim dead, he had five. He talked about them for a few moments in general terms, then got down to cases, supplying names and addresses and phone numbers and personal data. I made a lot of notes. We finished our fourth circuit of the park and he pulled off to the right, exited at West Seventy-second Street, drove two blocks and pulled over to the curb.

"Be a minute," he said.

I stayed where I was while he made a call from a booth on the corner. He'd left the motor idling. I looked at my notes and tried to see a pattern in the wisps and fragments I'd been given.

Chance returned to the car, checked the mirror, swung us around in a deft if illegal U-turn. "Just checking with my service," he said. "Just keeping in touch."

"You ought to have a phone in the car."

"Too complicated."

He drove downtown and east, pulling up next to a fire hydrant in front of a white brick apartment house on Seventeenth between Second and Third. "Collection time," he told me. Once again he left the motor idling, but this time fifteen minutes elapsed before he reappeared, striding jauntily past the liveried doorman, sliding nimbly behind the wheel.

"That's Donna's place," he said. "I told you about Donna."

"The poet."

"She's all excited. She got two poems accepted by this magazine in San Francisco. She'll get six free copies of the issue the poems appear in. That's as much pay as she'll get, just copies of the magazine."

A light turned red in front of us. He braked for it, looked left and right, then coasted through the light.

"Couple times," he said, "she's had poems in magazines that pay you for them. Once she got twenty-five dollars. That's the best she ever did."

"It sounds like a hard way to make a living."

"A poet can't make any money. Whores are lazy but this one's not lazy when it comes to her poems. She'll sit for six or eight hours to get the words right, and she's always got a dozen batches of poems in the mail. They come back from one place and she sends 'em out someplace else. She spends more on postage than they'll ever pay her for the poems." He fell silent for a moment, then laughed softly. "You know how much money I just took off of Donna? Eight hundred dollars, and that's just for the past two days. Of course there's days when her phone won't ring once."

"But it averages out pretty well."

"Pays better than poems." He looked at me. "Want to go for a ride?"

"Isn't that what we've been doing?"

"We been going around in circles," he said. "Now I'm gonna take you to a whole nother world."

WE drove down Second Avenue, through the Lower East Side, and over the Williamsburg Bridge into Brooklyn. Coming off the bridge we took enough turns to throw off my sense of direction, and the street signs didn't help much. I didn't recognize the names. But I watched the neighborhood change from Jewish to Italian to Polish and had a fair idea of where we were.

On a dark, silent street of two-family frame houses, Chance slowed in front of a three-story brick structure with a garage door in the middle. He used a remote-control unit to raise the door, then closed it after we had driven in. I followed him up a flight of stairs and into a spacious high-ceilinged room.

He asked if I knew where we were. I guessed Greenpoint. "Very good," he said. "I guess you know Brooklyn."

"I don't know this part of it very well. The meat market signs advertising kielbasa were a tip-off."

"I guess. Know whose house we're in? Ever hear of a Dr. Casimir Levandowski?"

"No."

"No reason why you should have. He's an old fellow. Retired, confined to a wheelchair. Eccentric, too. Keeps himself to himself. This place used to be a firehouse."

"I thought it must have been something like that."

"Two architects bought it some years ago and converted it.

They pretty much gutted the interior and started from scratch. They must have had a few dollars to play with because they didn't cut many corners. Look at the floors. Look at the window moldings." He pointed out details, commented on them. "Then they got tired of the place or each other, I don't know what, and they sold out to old Dr. Levandowski."

"And he lives here?"

"He don't exist," he said. His speech patterns kept shifting, from ghetto to university and back again. "The neighbors never see the old doc. They just see his faithful black servant and all they see him do is drive in and drive out. This is my house, Matthew. Can I give you the ten-cent tour?"

It was quite a place. There was a gym on the top floor, fully equipped with weights and exercise machines and furnished with sauna and Jacuzzi. His bedroom was on the same floor, and the bed, covered with a fur spread, was centered beneath a skylight. A library on the second floor contained one whole wall of books and an eight-foot pool table.

There were African masks all over the place, and occasional groups of free-standing African sculpture. Chance pointed out a piece from time to time, naming the tribe that had produced it. I mentioned having seen African masks at Kim's apartment.

"Poro Society masks," he said. "From the Dan tribe. I keep one or two African things in all my girls' apartments. Not the most valuable things, of course, but not junk, either. I don't own any junk."

He took a rather crudely fashioned mask from the wall and presented it for my inspection. The eye openings were square, the features all geometrically precise, the overall effect powerful in its primitiveness. "This is Dogon," he said. "Take hold of it. You can't appreciate sculpture with your eyes alone. The hands have to participate. Go ahead, handle it."

I took the mask from him. Its weight was greater than I

anticipated. The wood that composed it must have been very dense.

He lifted a telephone from a low teakwood table and dialed a number. He said, "Hey, darlin'. Any messages?" He listened for a moment, then put the phone down. "Peace and quiet," he said, "Shall I make some coffee?"

"Not if it's any trouble."

He assured me it wasn't. While the coffee brewed he told me about his African sculpture, how the craftsmen who produced it did not think of their work as art. "Everything they make has a specific function," he explained. "It's to guard your house or keep off spirits or to use in a particular tribal rite. If a mask doesn't have the power in it anymore they'll throw it away and somebody'll carve a new one. The old one's trash, you burn it up or toss it away cause it's no good."

He laughed. "Then the Europeans came and discovered African art. Some of those French painters got their inspiration from tribal masks. Now you've got a situation where there are carvers in Africa spending all their time making masks and statues for export to Europe and America. They follow the old forms because that's what their customers want, but it's a funny thing. Their work's no good. It doesn't have any feeling in it. It's not real. You look at it and you take it in your hand, and you do the same with the real thing, and you can tell the difference right away. If you have any feeling at all for the stuff. Funny, isn't it?"

"It's interesting."

"If I had any of the junk around I'd show you, but I don't own any. I bought some when I was starting out. You have to make mistakes to develop a feel for it. But I got rid of that stuff, burned it in the fireplace there." He smiled. "The very first piece I bought, I still have it. It's hanging in the bedroom. A Dan mask. Poro Society. I didn't know shit about African art but I saw it in an antique shop and I responded to the mask's artistic integrity." He stopped, shook his head. "Hell I did. What happened was I looked at that piece of smooth black wood and I was looking in a mirror. I saw myself, I saw my father, I was looking back through the damned ages. You know what I'm talking about?"

"I'm not sure."

"Hell. Maybe I don't know either." He gave his head a shake. "What do you figure one of those old carvers'd make of this? He'd say, 'Shit, what's this crazy nigger want with all these old masks? Why'd he go and hang 'em all over the damn wall?' That coffee's ready. You take yours black, right?"

HE said, "How's a detective go about detecting, anyway? Where do you start?"

"By going around and talking to people. Unless Kim got killed coincidentally by a maniac, her death grew out of her life." I tapped my notebook. "There's a lot you don't know about her life."

"I guess."

"I'll talk to people and see what they can tell me. Maybe it'll fit together and point somewhere. Maybe not."

"My girls'll know it's cool to talk to you."

"That'll help."

"Not that they necessarily know anything, but if they do."

"Sometimes people know things without knowing they know them."

"And sometimes they tell without knowing they told."

"That's true, too."

He stood up, put his hands on his hips. "You know," he said, "I didn't figure to bring you here. I didn't figure you needed to know about this house. And I brought you without you even asking."

"It's quite a house."

"Thank you."

"Was Kim impressed with it?"

"She never saw it. None of 'em ever did. There's an old German woman comes here once a week to clean. Makes the whole place shine. She's the only woman's ever been inside of this house. Since I owned it, anyway, and the architects who used to live here didn't have much use for women. Here's the last of the coffee."

It was awfully good coffee. I'd had too much of it already but it was too good to pass up. When I complimented it earlier he'd told me it was a mixture of Jamaica Blue Mountain and a dark roast Colombian bean. He'd offered me a pound of it, and I'd told him it wouldn't be much use to me in a hotel room.

I sipped the coffee while he made yet another call to his service. When he hung up I said, "You want to give me the number here? Or is that one secret you want to keep?"

He laughed. "I'm not here that much. It's easier if you just call the service."

"All right."

"And this number wouldn't do you much. I don't know it myself. I'd have to look at an old phone bill to make sure I got it right. And if you dialed it, nothing would happen."

"Why's that?"

"Because the bells won't ring. The phones are to make calls out. When I set this place up I got telephone service and I put in extensions so I'd never be far from a phone, but I never gave the number to anybody. Not even my service, not anybody."

"And?"

"And I was here one night, I think I was playing pool, and the damn phone rang. I like to jumped. It was somebody wanted to know did I want a subscription to the *New York Times*. Then two days later I got another call and it was a wrong number, and I realized the only calls I was ever going

to get were wrong numbers and somebody selling something, and I took a screwdriver and went around and opened
up each of the phones, and there's this little clapper that
rings the bell when a current passes through a particular
wire, and I just took the little clapper off each of the phones.
I dialed the number once from another phone, and you think
it rings because there's no telling the clapper's gone, but
there's no bell going off in this house."

"Clever."

"No doorbell, either. There's a thing you ring by the door
outside, but it's not connected to anything. That door's never
been opened since I moved in, and you can't see in the windows, and there's burglar alarms on everything. Not that you
get much burglary in Greenpoint, a nice settled Polish
neighborhood like this, but old Dr. Levandowski, he likes his
security and he likes his privacy."

"I guess he does."

"I'm not here much, Matthew, but when that garage door
closes behind me it keeps the whole world out. Nothing
touches me here. Nothing."

"I'm surprised you brought me here."

"So am I."

WE saved the money for last. He asked how much I wanted.
I told him I wanted twenty-five hundred dollars.

He asked what that bought.

"I don't know," I said. "I don't charge by the hour and I
don't keep track of my expenses. If I wind up laying out a lot
of money or if the thing goes on too long, I might wind up
asking you for more money. But I'm not going to send you a
bill and I'm not going to sue you if you don't pay."

"You keep it all very informal."

"That's right."

"I like that. Cash on the line and no receipts. I don't mind paying a price. The women bring in a lot of money, but there's a lot that has to go out, too. Rent. Operating costs. Payoffs. You got a whore installed in a building, you pay off the building. You can't give the doorman twenty dollars for Christmas and let it go at that, same as any other tenant. It's more like twenty a month and a hundred for Christmas, and it's the same for all the building employees. It adds up."

"It must."

"But there's a lot left. And I don't blow it on coke or waste it gambling. You said what? Twenty-five hundred? I paid more than twice that for the Dogon mask I gave you to hold. I paid $6,200, plus the auction galleries charge buyers a 10 percent commission these days. Comes to what? $6,820. And then there's sales tax."

I didn't say anything. He said, "Shit, I don't know what I'm proving. That I'm nigger-rich, I guess. Wait here a minute." He came back with a sheaf of hundreds and counted out twenty-five of them. Used bills, out of sequence. I wondered how much cash he kept around the house, how much he habitually carried on his person. Years ago I'd known a loan shark who made it a rule never to walk out his door with less than ten thousand dollars in his pocket. He didn't keep it a secret, and everybody who knew him knew about the roll he carried.

Nobody ever tried to take it off him, either.

HE drove me home. We took a different route back, over the Pulaski Bridge into Queens and through the tunnel to Manhattan. Neither of us talked much, and somewhere along the way I must have dozed off because he had to put a hand on my shoulder to waken me.

I blinked, straightened up in my seat. We were at the curb in front of my hotel.

"Door-to-door delivery service," he said.

I got out and stood on the curb. He waited for a couple of

cabs to pass, then made his U-turn. I watched until the Cadillac was out of sight.

Thoughts struggled in my brain like exhausted swimmers. I was far too tired to think. I went up to bed.

Chapter 12

"I didn't know her all that well. I met her a year or so ago at the beauty parlor and we had a cup of coffee together, and reading between the lines of her conversation I figured out she wasn't the Avon lady. We exchanged numbers and we would talk now and then over the phone, but we never got close. Then whenever it was, a couple weeks ago, she called and wanted to get together. I was surprised. We'd been out of touch for months."

We were in Elaine Mardell's apartment on Fifty-first between First and Second. White shag carpet on the floor, bold abstract oils on the walls, something inoffensive on the stereo. I had a cup of coffee. Elaine was drinking a diet soda.

"What did she want?"

"She told me she was leaving her pimp. She wanted to make the break without getting hurt. Which is where you came in, remember?"

I nodded. "Why'd she come to you?"

"I don't know. I had the feeling she didn't have too many friends. It wasn't the sort of thing she could talk over with one of Chance's other girls, and she probably wouldn't have wanted to discuss it with someone who was out of the life altogether. And she was young, you know, compared to me. She may have seen me as a sort of wise old aunt."

"That's you, all right."

"Isn't it just? What was she, about twenty-five?"

"She said twenty-three. I think it said twenty-four in the papers."

"Jesus, that's young."

"I know."

"More coffee, Matt?"

"I'm fine."

"You know why I think she picked me to have that little conversation with? I think it's because I don't have a pimp." She settled herself in her seat, uncrossed and recrossed her legs. I remembered other times in this apartment, one of us on the couch, the other on the Eames chair, the same sort of unobtrusive music softening the room's hard edges.

I said, "You never had one, did you?"

"No."

"Do most girls?"

"The ones she knew did. I think you pretty much have to on the street. Somebody's got to defend your right to a particular corner and bail you out when you get arrested. When you work out of an apartment like this, well, that's different. But even so, most of the hookers I know have boyfriends."

"Is that the same thing as a pimp?"

"Oh, no. A boyfriend isn't running a batch of girls. He just happens to be your boyfriend. And you don't turn your money over to him. But you buy him a lot of things, just because you want to, and you help out with cash when he hits a rough spot in life, or if there's some business opportunity he wants to take advantage of, or because he needs a little loan and, gee, it's not like you were *giving* him the money. That's what a boyfriend is."

"Sort of a one-woman pimp."

"Sort of, except every girl swears her boyfriend's different, her relationship's different, and what never changes is who earns the money and who spends it."

"And you never had a pimp, did you? Or a boyfriend?"

"Never. I had my palm read once and the woman who did it was impressed. 'You have a double head line, dear,' she told me. 'Your head rules your heart.' " She came over, showed me her hand. "It's this line right here. See?"

"Looks good to me."

"Damn straight." She went back for her glass of soda, then came and sat on the couch beside me. She said, "When I learned what happened to Kim, the first thing I did was call you. But you weren't in."

"I never got the message."

"I didn't leave one. I hung up and called a travel agent I know. A couple hours later I was on a plane for Barbados."

"Were you afraid you were on somebody's list?"

"Hardly that. I just figured Chance killed her. I didn't think he'd start knocking off all her friends and relations. No, I just knew it was time for a break. A week at a beach-front hotel. A little sun in the afternoon, a little roulette at night, and enough steel-drum music and limbo dancing to hold me for a long time."

"Sounds good."

"Second night out I met a fellow at the poolside cocktail party. He was staying at the next hotel over. Very nice fellow, tax lawyer, got divorced a year and a half ago and then went through a tough little affair with someone too young for him, and he's over that now, and who does he meet but me."

"And?"

"And we had a nice little romance for the rest of the week. Long walks on the beach. Snorkeling, tennis. Romantic dinners. Drinks on my terrace. I had a terrace looking out at the sea."

"Here you've got one looking at the East River."

"It's not the same. We had a great time, Matt. Good sex, too. I thought I'd have my work cut out for me, you know, acting shy. But I didn't have to act. I *was* shy, and then I got over my shyness."

"You didn't tell him—"

"Are you kidding? Of course not. I told him I work for art galleries. I restore paintings. I'm a freelance art restoration expert. He thought that was really fascinating and he had a lot of questions. It would have been easier if I'd had the sense to pick something a little more humdrum, but, see, I *wanted* to be fascinating."

"Sure."

She had her hands in her lap and she was looking at them. Her face was unlined but her years were beginning to show themselves on the back of her hands. I wondered how old she was. Thirty-six? Thirty-eight?

"Matt, he wanted to see me in the city. We weren't telling each other it was love, nothing like that, but there was this sense that we might have something that might go somewhere, and he wanted to follow it up and see where it led. He lives in Merrick. You know where that is?"

"Sure, out on the Island. It's not that far from where I used to live."

"Is it nice out there?"

"Parts of it are very nice."

"I gave him a phony number. He knows my name but the phone here is unlisted. I haven't heard from him and I don't expect to. I wanted a week in the sun and a nice little romance, and that's what I had, but once in a while I think I could call him and make up something about the wrong number. I could lie my way out of that one."

"Probably."

"But for what? I could even lie my way into being his wife or girlfriend or something. And I could give up this apartment and drop my john book in the incinerator. But for what?" She looked at me. "I've got a good life. I save my money. I always saved my money."

"And invested it," I remembered. "Real estate, isn't it? Apartment houses in Queens?"

"Not just Queens. I could retire now if I had to and I'd get by all right. But why would I want to retire and what do I need with a boyfriend?"

"Why did Kim Dakkinen want to retire?"

"Is that what she wanted?"

"I don't know. Why did she want to leave Chance?"

She thought it over, shook her head. "I never asked."

"Neither did I."

"I've never been able to understand why a girl would have a pimp in the first place, so I don't need an explanation when somebody tells me she wants to get rid of one."

"Was she in love with anybody?"

"Kim? Could be. She didn't mention it if she was."

"Was she planning to leave the city?"

"I didn't get that impression. But she wouldn't tell me if she was, would she?"

"Hell," I said. I put my empty cup on the end table. "She was involved someway with someone. I just wish I knew who."

"Why?"

"Because that's the only way I'm going to find out who killed her."

"You think that's how it works?"

"That's usually how it works."

"Suppose I got killed tomorrow. What would you do?"

"I guess I'd send flowers."

"Seriously."

"Seriously? I'd check tax lawyers from Merrick."

"There's probably a few of them, don't you think?"

"Could be. I don't suppose there's too many who spent a week in Barbados this month. You said he stayed at the next hotel down the beach from you? I don't think he'd be hard to find, or that I'd have much trouble tying him to you."

"Would you actually do all that?"

"Why not?"

"No one would be paying you."

I laughed. "Well, you and I, we go back a ways, Elaine."

And we did. When I was on the force we'd had an arrangement. I helped her out when she needed the kind of hand a cop could provide, whether with the law or with an unruly john. She, in turn, had been available to me when I wanted her. What, I wondered suddenly, had that made me? Neither pimp nor boyfriend, but what?

"Matt? Why did Chance hire you?"

"To find out who killed her."

"Why?"

I thought of the reasons he'd given. "I don't know," I said.

"Why'd you take the job?"

"I can use the money, Elaine."

"You don't care that much about money."

"Sure I do. It's time I started providing for my old age. I've got an eye on these apartment houses in Queens."

"Very funny."

"I'll bet you're some landlady. I'll bet they love it when you come around to collect the rent."

"There's a management firm that takes care of all that. I never see my tenants."

"I wish you hadn't told me that. You just ruined a great fantasy."

"I'll bet."

I said, "Kim took me to bed after I finished the job for her. I went over there and she paid me and then afterward we went to bed."

"And?"

"It was like a tip, almost. A friendly way of saying thank you."

"Beats ten dollars at Christmas time."

"But would she do that? If she was involved with somebody, I mean. Would she just go to bed with me for the hell of it?"

"Matt, you're forgetting something."

She looked, for just a moment, like somebody's wise old aunt. I asked what I was forgetting.

"Matt, she was a hooker."

"Were you a hooker in Barbados?"

"I don't know," she said. "Maybe I was and maybe I wasn't. But I can tell you this much. I was damn glad when the mating dance was over and we were in bed together because for a change I knew what I was doing. And going to bed with guys is what I do."

I thought a moment. Then I said, "When I called earlier you said to give you an hour. Not to come over right away."

"So?"

"Because you had a john booked?"

"Well, it wasn't the meter reader."

"Did you need the money?"

"Did I need the money? What kind of question is that? I *took* the money."

"But you would have made the rent without it."

"And I wouldn't have missed any meals, or had to wear the panty hose with the runs in it. What's this all about?"

"So you saw the guy today because that's what you do."

"I suppose."

"Well, you're the one who asked why I took the job."

"It's what you do," she said.

"Something like that."

She thought of something and laughed. She said, "When Heinrich Heine was dying—the German poet?"

"Yeah?"

"When he was dying he said, 'God will pardon me. It's His profession.' "

"That's not bad."

"It's probably even better in German. I shtup and you detect and God pardons." She lowered her eyes. "I just hope He does," she said. "When it's my turn in the barrel, I hope He's not down in Barbados for the weekend."

Chapter 13

When I left Elaine's the sky was growing dark and the streets were thick with rush-hour traffic. It was raining again, a nagging drizzle that slowed the commuters to a crawl. I looked at the swollen river of cars and wondered if one of them held Elaine's tax lawyer. I thought about him and tried to guess how he might have reacted when the number she gave him turned out to be a fake.

He could find her if he wanted to. He knew her name. The phone company wouldn't give out her unlisted number, but he wouldn't have to be too well connected to find somebody who could pry it out of them for him. Failing that, he could trace her without too much trouble through her hotel. They could tell him her travel agent and somewhere along the line he could pick up her address. I'd been a cop, I automatically thought of this sort of thing, but couldn't anybody make this sort of connection? It didn't seem terribly complicated to me.

Perhaps he'd been hurt when her number proved phony. Perhaps knowing she didn't want to see him would keep him from wanting to see her. But wouldn't his first thought be that the mistake might have been an accident? Then he'd try Information, and might guess that the unobtainable number differed from what she'd given him by no more than a transposed couple of digits. So why wouldn't he pursue it?

Maybe he never called her in the first place, never even learned that the number was phony. Maybe he'd discarded her number in the airplane washroom on the way home to his wife and kids.

Maybe he had a few guilt-ridden moments now and then, thinking of the art restorer waiting by her telephone for his call. Maybe he would find himself regretting his haste. No need, after all, to have thrown her number away. He might have been able to fit in a date with her from time to time. No reason she had to learn about the wife and kids. The hell, she'd probably be grateful for someone to take her away from her paint tubes and turpentine.

HALFWAY home I stopped at a deli and had soup and a sandwich and coffee. There was a bizarre story in the *Post*. Two neighbors in Queens had been arguing for months because of a dog that barked in its owner's absence. The previous night, the owner was walking the dog when the animal relieved itself on a tree in front of the neighbor's house. The neighbor happened to be watching and shot at the dog from an upstairs window with a bow and arrow. The dog's owner ran back into his house and came out with a Walther P-38, a World War II souvenir. The neighbor also ran outside with his bow and arrow, and the dog's owner shot him dead. The neighbor was eighty-one, the dog's owner was sixty-two, and the two men had lived side by side in Little Neck for over twenty years. The dog's age wasn't given, but there was a picture of him in the paper, straining against a leash in the hands of a uniformed police officer.

MIDTOWN North was a few blocks from my hotel. It was still raining in the same halfhearted fashion when I went over there a little after nine that night. I stopped at the front desk and a young fellow with a moustache and blow-dry hair pointed me to the staircase. I went up a flight and found the detective squad room. There were four plainclothes cops sitting at desks, a couple more down at the far end watching something on television. Three young black males in a holding pen paid some attention when I entered, then lost interest when they saw I wasn't their lawyer.

I approached the nearest desk. A balding cop looked up from the report he was typing. I told him I had an appointment with Detective Durkin.

A cop at another desk looked up and caught my eye. "You must be Scudder," he said. "I'm Joe Durkin."

His handshake was overly firm, almost a test of masculinity. He waved me into a chair and took his own seat, stubbed out a cigarette in an overflowing ashtray, lit a fresh one, leaned back and looked at me. His eyes were that pale shade of gray that doesn't show you a thing.

He said, "Still raining out there?"

"Off and on."

"Miserable weather. You want some coffee?"

"No thanks."

"What can I do for you?"

I told him I'd like to see whatever he could show me on the Kim Dakkinen killing.

"Why?"

"I told somebody I'd look into it."

"You told somebody you'd look into it? You mean you got a client?"

"You could say that."

"Who?"

"I can't tell you that."

A muscle worked along the side of his jaw. He was around thirty-five and a few pounds overweight, enough to make him look a little older than his years. He hadn't lost any hair yet and it was all dark brown, almost black. He wore it combed flat down on his head. He should have borrowed a blow dryer from the guy downstairs.

He said, "You can't hold that out. You don't have a license and it wouldn't be privileged information even if you did."

"I didn't know we were in court."

"We're not. But you come in here asking a favor—"

I shrugged. "I can't tell you my client's name. He has an interest in seeing her killer caught. That's all."

"And he thinks that'll happen faster if he hires you."

"Evidently."

"You think so too?"

"What I think is I got a living to make."

"Jesus," he said. "Who doesn't?"

I'd said the right thing. I wasn't a threat now. I was just a guy going through the motions and trying to turn a dollar. He sighed, slapped the top of his desk, got up and crossed the room to a bank of filing cabinets. He was a chunkily built, bandy-legged man with his sleeves rolled up and his collar open, and he walked with the rolling gait of a sailor. He brought back a manila accordion file, dropped into his chair, found a photograph in the files and pitched it onto the desk.

"Here," he said. "Feast your eyes."

It was a five-by-seven black and white glossy of Kim, but if I hadn't known that I don't see how I could have recognized her. I looked at the picture, fought off a wave of nausea, and made myself go on looking at it.

"Really did a job on her," I said.

"He got her sixty-six times with what the doc thinks was probably a machete or something like it. How'd you like the job of counting? I don't know how they do that work. I swear it's a worse job than the one I got."

"All that blood."

"Be grateful you're seeing it in black and white. It was worse in color."

"I can imagine."

"He hit arteries. You do that, you get spurting, you get blood all over the room. I never saw so much blood."

"He must have gotten blood all over himself."

"No way to avoid it."

"Then how did he get out of there without anybody noticing?"

"It was cold that night. Say he had a coat, he'd put that on over whatever else he was wearing." He drew on his cigarette. "Or maybe he wasn't wearing any clothes when he did the number on her. The hell, she was in her birthday suit, maybe he didn't want to feel overdressed. Then all he'd have to do afterward was take a shower. There was a nice beautiful bathroom there and he had all the time in the world so why not use it?"

"Were the towels used?"

He looked at me. The gray eyes were still unreadable, but I sensed a little more respect in his manner. "I don't remember any soiled towels," he said.

"I don't suppose they're something you'd notice, not with a scene like that in the same room."

"They ought to be inventoried, though." He thumbed through the file. "You know what they do, they take pictures of everything, and everything that might turn out to be evidence gets bagged and labeled and inventoried. Then it goes down to the warehouse, and when it's time to prepare a case nobody can find it." He closed the file for a moment, leaned forward. "You want to hear something? Two, three weeks ago I get a call from my sister. She and her husband live over in Brooklyn. The Midwood section. You familiar with the area?"

"I used to be."

"Well, it was probably nicer when you knew it. It's not so bad. I mean, the whole city's a cesspool, so it's not so bad in comparison. Why she called, they came home and found out there'd been a burglary. Somebody broke in, took a portable teevee, a typewriter, some jewelry. She called me to find out how to report it, who to call and everything. First thing I asked her is has she got insurance. No, she says, they didn't figure it was worth it. I told her to forget it. Don't report it, I told her. You'd just be wasting your time.

"So she says how are they gonna catch the guys if she doesn't report it? So I explain how nobody's got the time to investigate a burglary anymore. You fill out a report and it goes in a file, but you don't run around looking to see who did it. Catching a burglar in the act is one thing, but investigating, hell, it's low priority, nobody's got time for it. She says okay, she can understand that, but suppose they happen to recover the goods? If she never reported the theft in the first place, how will the stuff get returned to her? And then I had to tell her just how fucked up the whole system is. We got warehouses full of stolen goods we recovered, and we got files full of reports people filled out, stuff lost to burglars, and we can't get the shit back to the rightful owners. I went on and on, I won't bore you with it, but I don't think she really wound up believing me. Because you don't want to believe it's that bad."

He found a sheet in the file, frowned at it. He read, "One bath towel, white. One hand towel, white. Two wash cloths, white. Doesn't say used or unused." He drew out a sheaf of glossies and went rapidly through them. I looked over his shoulder at interior shots of the room where Kim Dakkinen had died. She was in some but not all of the pictures; the photographer had documented the murder scene by shooting virtually every inch of the hotel room.

A shot of the bathroom showed a towel rack with unused linen on it.

"No dirty towels," he said.

"He took them along."

"Huh?"

"He had to wash up. Even if he just threw a topcoat over his bloody clothes. And there aren't enough towels there.

There ought to be at least two of everything. A double room in a class hotel, they give you more than one bath towel and one hand towel."

"Why would he take 'em along?"

"Maybe to wrap the machete in."

"He had to have a case for it in the first place, some kind of a bag to get it into the hotel. Why couldn't he take it out the same way?"

I agreed that he could have.

"And why wrap it in the dirty towels? Say you took a shower and dried yourself off and you wanted to wrap a machete before you put it in your suitcase. There's clean towels there. Wouldn't you wrap it in a clean one instead of sticking a wet towel in your bag?"

"You're right."

"It's a waste of time worrying about it," he said, tapping the photo against the top of his desk. "But I shoulda noticed the missing towels. That's something I should have thought of."

We went through the file together. The medical report held few surprises. Death was attributed to massive hemorrhaging from multiple wounds resulting in excessive loss of blood. I guess you could call it that.

I read through witness interrogation reports, made my way through all the other forms and scraps of paper that wind up in a homicide victim's file. I had trouble paying attention. My head was developing a dull ache and my mind was spinning its wheels. Somewhere along the way Durkin let me go through the rest of the file on my own. He lit a fresh cigarette and went back to what he'd been typing earlier.

When I'd had as much as I could handle I closed the file and gave it back to him. He returned it to the cabinet, detouring on the way back to make a stop at the coffee machine.

"I got 'em both with cream and sugar," he said, setting mine before me. "Maybe that's not how you like it."

"It's fine," I said.

"Now you know what we know," he said. I told him I appreciated it. He said, "Listen, you saved us some time and aggravation with the tip about the pimp. We owed you one. If you can turn a buck for yourself, why not?"

"Where do you go from here?"

He shrugged. "We proceed in normal fashion with our investigation. We run down leads and assemble evidence until such time as we have something to present to the district attorney's office."

"That sounds like a recording."

"Does it?"

"What happens next, Joe?"

"Aw, Jesus," he said. "The coffee's terrible, isn't it?"

"It's okay."

"I used to think it was the cups. Then one day I brought my own cup, you know, so I was drinking it out of china instead of Styrofoam. Not fancy china, just, you know, an ordinary china cup like they give you in a coffee shop. You know what I mean."

"Sure."

"It tasted just as bad out of a real cup. And the second day after I brought the cup I was writing out an arrest report on some scumbag and I knocked the fucking cup off the desk and broke it. You got someplace you gotta be?"

"No."

"Then let's go downstairs," he said. "Let's go around the corner."

Chapter 14

He took me around the corner and a block and a half south on Tenth Avenue to a tavern that belonged at the end of somebody's qualification. I didn't catch the name and I'm not sure if it had one. They could have called it Last Stop Before Detox. Two old men in thrift-shop suits sat together at the bar, drinking in silence. A Hispanic in his forties stood at the far end of the bar, sipping an eight-ounce glass of red wine and reading the paper. The bartender, a rawboned man in a tee shirt and jeans, was watching something on a small black and white television set. He had the volume turned way down.

Durkin and I took a table and I went to the bar to get our drinks, a double vodka for him, ginger ale for myself. I carried them back to our table. His eyes registered my ginger ale without comment.

It could have been a medium-strength scotch and soda. The color was about right.

He drank some of his vodka and said, "Aw, Jesus, that helps. It really helps."

I didn't say anything.

"What you were asking before. Where do we go from here. Can't you answer that yourself?"

"Probably."

"I told my own sister to buy a new teevee and a new typewriter and hang some more locks on the door. But don't bother calling the cops. Where do we go with Dakkinen? We don't go anywhere."

"That's what I figured."

"We know who killed her."

"Chance?" He nodded. "I thought his alibi looked pretty good."

"Oh, it's gilt-edged. It's bottled in bond. So what? He still could have done it. The people he says he was with are people who would lie for him."

"You think they were lying?"

"No, but I wouldn't swear they weren't. Anyway, he could have hired it. We already talked about that."

"Right."

"If he did it he's clear. We're not going to be able to put a dent in that alibi. If he hired it we're not gonna find out who he hired. Unless we get lucky. That happens sometimes, you know. Things fall in your lap. One guy says something in a gin joint and somebody with a grudge passes it on, and all of a sudden we know something we didn't know before. But even if that happens, we'll be a long way from putting a case together. Meanwhile, we don't figure to kill ourselves over it."

What he was saying was no surprise but there was something deadening about the words. I picked up my ginger ale and looked at it.

He said, "Half the job is knowing the odds. Working the cases where you got a chance, letting the others flap in the breeze. You know the murder rate in this town?"

"I know it keeps going higher."

"Tell me about it. It's up every year. All crimes are up every year, except we're starting to get a statistical drop in some of the less serious ones because people aren't bothering to report them. Like my sister's burglary. You got mugged coming home and all that happened was he took your money? Well, shit, why make a federal case out of it, right? Be grateful you're alive. Go home and say a prayer of thanks."

"With Kim Dakkinen—"

"Screw Kim Dakkinen," he said. "Some dumb little bitch comes fifteen hundred miles to peddle her ass and give the money to a nigger pimp, who cares if somebody chopped her up? I mean why didn't she stay in fucking Minnesota?"

"Wisconsin."

"I meant Wisconsin. Most of 'em come from Minnesota."

"I know."

"The murder rate used to be around a thousand a year. Three a day in the five boroughs. That always seemed high."

"High enough."

"It's just about double that now." He leaned forward. "But that's *nothing*, Matt. Most homicides are husband-wife things, or two friends drinking together and one of 'em shoots the other and doesn't even remember it the next day. That rate never changes. It's the same as it always was. What's changed are stranger murders, where the killer and the victim don't know each other. That's the rate that shows you how dangerous it is to live somewhere. If you just take the stranger murders, if you throw out the other cases and put the stranger murders on a graph, the line goes up like a rocket."

"There was a guy in Queens yesterday with a bow and arrow," I said, "and the guy next door shot him with a .38."

"I read about that. Something about a dog shitting on the wrong lawn?"

"Something like that."

"Well, that wouldn't be on the chart. That's two guys who knew each other."

"Right."

"But it's all part of the same thing. People keep killing each other. They don't even stop and think, they just go ahead and do it. You been off the force what, a couple years now? I'll tell you this much. It's a lot worse than you remember."

"I believe you."

"I mean it. It's a jungle out there and all the animals are armed. Everybody's got a gun. You realize the number of people out there walking around with a piece? Your honest citizen, he's gotta have a gun now for his own protection, so he gets one and somewhere down the line he shoots himself or his wife or the guy next door."

"The guy with the bow and arrow."

"Whatever. But who's gonna tell him not to have a gun?" He slapped his abdomen, where his service revolver was tucked under his belt. "I gotta carry this," he said. "It's regulations. But I'll tell you, I wouldn't walk around out there without it. I'd feel naked."

"I used to think that. You get used to it."

"You don't carry anything?"

"Nothing."

"And it doesn't bother you?"

I went to the bar and got fresh drinks, more vodka for him, more ginger ale for me. When I brought them back to the table Durkin drank the whole thing in one long swallow and sighed like a tire going flat. He cupped his hands and lit a cigarette, inhaled deeply, blew out the smoke as if in a hurry to be rid of it.

"This fucking city," he said.

It was hopeless, he said, and he went on to tell me just how hopeless it was. He rang changes on the whole criminal justice system, from the cops to the courts to the jails, explaining how none of it worked and all of it was getting worse every day. You couldn't arrest a guy and then you couldn't convict him and finally you couldn't keep the son of a bitch in jail.

"The prisons are overcrowded," he said, "so the judges don't want to hand out long sentences and the parole boards release people early. And the D.A.s let the guys cop to a reduced charge, they plea bargain good cases down to nothing, because the court calendars are so jammed up and the courts are so careful to protect the rights of the accused that you just about need a photo of the guy committing the crime in order to get a conviction, and then you might get a reversal because you were violating his civil rights by taking his photograph without prior permission. And in the meantime there's no cops. The department's got ten thousand men below what it had twelve years ago. Ten thousand fewer cops on the street!"

"I know."

"Twice as many crooks and a third less cops and you wonder why it's not safe to walk down the street. You know what it is? The city's broke. There's no money for cops, no money to keep the subways running, no money for anything. The whole country's leaking money, it's all winding up in Saudi fucking Arabia. All those assholes are trading in their camels for Cadillacs while this country goes down the fucking tubes." He stood up. "My turn to buy."

"No, I'll get them. I'm on expenses."

"Right, you got a client." He sat down. I came back with another round and he said, "What are you drinking there?"

"Just ginger ale."

"Yeah, I thought that's what it looked like. Whyntcha have a real drink?"

"I'm sort of cutting back on it these days."

· "Oh yeah?" The gray eyes focused on me as he registered this information. He picked up his glass and drank about half of it, set it down on the worn wooden table with a thunk. "You got the right idea," he said, and I thought he meant the ginger ale, but he had shifted gears by then. "Quitting the job. Getting out. You know what I want? All I want is six more years."

"Then you got your twenty?"

"Then I got my twenty," he said, "and then I got my pension, and then I'm fucking well gone. Out of this job and out of this shithole of a city. Florida, Texas, New Mexico, someplace warm and dry and clean. Forget Florida, I heard things about Florida, all the fucking Cubans, they got crime like you get here. Plus they got all the dope coming in there. Those crazy Colombians. You know about the Colombians?"

I thought of Royal Waldron. "A fellow I know says they're all right," I said. "He said you just don't want to cheat 'em."

"You bet your ass you don't want to cheat 'em. You read about those two girls over in Long Island City? Must have been six, eight months ago. Sisters, one's twelve and one's fourteen, and they found 'em in the back room of this out-of-business gas station, hands tied behind their backs, each of 'em shot twice in the head with a small-caliber weapon, I think a .22, but who gives a shit?" He drank the rest of his drink. "Well, it didn't figure. No sex angle, nothing. It's an execution, but who executes a couple of teenage sisters?

"Well, it clears itself up, because a week later somebody breaks into the house where they lived and shoots their mother. We found her in the kitchen with dinner still cooking on the stove. See, the family's Colombian, and the father's in the cocaine business, which is the chief industry down there outside of smuggling emeralds—"

"I thought they grew a lot of coffee."

"That's probably a front. Where was I? The point is, the father turns up dead a month later in whatever's the capital of Colombia. He crossed somebody and he ran for it, and they wound up getting him in Colombia, but first they killed his kids and his wife. See, the Colombians, they play by a different set of rules. You fuck with them and they don't just kill you. They wipe out your whole family. Kids, any age, it don't matter. You got a dog and a cat and some tropical fish, they're dead too."

"Jesus."

"The Mafia was always considerate about family. They'd even make sure to arrange a hit so your family wouldn't be there to see it happen. Now we got criminals that kill the whole family. Nice?"

"Jesus."

He put his palms on the table for leverage, hoisted himself to his feet. "I'm getting this round," he announced. "I don't need some pimp payin' for my drinks."

BACK at the table he said, "He's your client, right? Chance?" When I failed to respond he said, "Well, shit, you met with him last night. He wanted to see you, and now you got a client that you won't say his name. Two and two's gotta be four, doesn't it?"

"I can't tell you how to add it."

"Let's just say I'm right and he's your client. For the sake of argument. You won't be givin' nothin' away."

"All right."

He leaned forward. "He killed her," he said. "So why would he hire you to investigate it?"

"Maybe he didn't kill her."

"Oh, sure he did." He dismissed the possibility of Chance's innocence with a wave of his hand. "She says she's quitting him and he says okay and the next day she's dead. Come on, Matt. What's that if it's not cut and dried?"

"Then we get back to your question. Why'd he hire me?"

"Maybe to take the heat off."

"How?"

"Maybe he'll figure we'll figure he must be innocent or he wouldn't have hired you."

"But that's not what you figured at all."

"No."

"You think he'd really think that?"

"How do I know what some coked-up spade pimp is gonna think?"

"You figure he's a cokehead?"

"He's got to spend it on something, doesn't he? It's not gonna go for country-club dues and a box at the charity ball. Lemme ask *you* something."

"Go ahead."

"You think there's a chance in the world he didn't kill her? Or set her up and hire it done?"

"I think there's a chance."

"Why?"

"For one thing, he hired me. And it wasn't to take the heat off because what heat are we talking about? You already said there wasn't going to be any heat. You're planning to clear the case and work on something else."

"He wouldn't necessarily know that."

I let that pass. "Take it from another angle," I suggested. "Let's say I never called you."

"Called me when?"

"The first call I made. Let's say you didn't know she was breaking with her pimp."

"If we didn't get it from you we'd of gotten it somewhere else."

"Where? Kim was dead and Chance wouldn't volunteer the information. I'm not sure anybody else in the world knew." Except for Elaine, but I wasn't going to bring her into it. "I don't think you'd have gotten it. Not right off the bat, anyway."

"So?"

"So how would you have figured the killing then?"

He didn't answer right away. He looked down at his near-empty glass, and a couple of vertical frown lines creased his forehead. He said, "I see what you mean."

"How would you have pegged it?"

"The way we did before you called. A psycho. You know we're not supposed to call 'em that anymore? There was a departmental directive went out about a year ago. From now on we don't call 'em psychos. From now on it's EDPs."

"What's an EDP?"

"Emotionally Disturbed Person. That's what some ass-hole on Centre Street's got nothing better to worry about. The whole city's up to its ass in more nuts than a fruitcake and our first priority is how we refer to them. We don't want to hurt their feelings. No, I'd figure a psycho, some new version of Jack the Ripper. Calls up a hooker, invites her over, chops her up."

"And if it was a psycho?"

"You know what happens then. You hope you get lucky with a piece of physical evidence. In this case fingerprints were hopeless, it's a transient hotel room, there's a million latents and no place to start with them. Be nice if there was a big bloody fingerprint and you knew it belonged to the killer, but we didn't have that kind of luck."

"Even if you did—"

"Even if we did, a single print wouldn't lead anywhere. Not until we had a suspect. You can't get a make from Washington on a single print. They keep saying you're gonna be able to eventually, but—"

"They've been saying that for years."

"It'll never happen. Or it will, but I'll have my six years by then and I'll be in Arizona. Barring physical evidence that leads somewhere, I guess we'd be waiting for the nut to do it again. You get another couple of cases with the same MO and sooner or later he fucks up and you got him, and then you match him to some latents in the room at the Galaxy and you wind up with a case." He drained his glass. "Then he plea bargains his way to manslaughter and he's out in three years tops and he does it again, but I don't want to get started on that again. I honest to Christ don't want to get started on that again."

I bought our next round. Any compunctions he had about having a pimp's money pay for his booze seemed to have been dissolved by the same alcohol that had given rise to them. He was visibly drunk now, but only if you knew where to look. The eyes had a glaze on them, and there was a matching glaze on his whole manner. He was holding up his end of a typical alcoholic conversation, wherein two drunks take polite turns talking aloud to their own selves.

I wouldn't have noticed this if I'd been matching him drink for drink. But I was sober, and as the booze got to him I felt the gulf widening between us.

I tried to keep the conversation on the subject of Kim Dakkinen but it wouldn't stay there. He wanted to talk about everything that was wrong with New York.

"You know what it is," he said, leaning forward, lowering his voice, as if we weren't the only two customers in the bar by now, just us and the bartender. "I'll tell you what it is. It's niggers."

I didn't say anything.

"And spics. The blacks and the Hispanics."

I said something about black and Puerto Rican cops. He rode right over it. "Listen, don't tell me," he said. "I got a guy I been partnered with a lot, Larry Haynes his name is, maybe you know him—" I didn't "—and he's as good as they come. I'd trust the man with my life. Shit, I *have* trusted him with my life. He's black as coal and I never met a better man in or out of the department. But that's got nothing to do with what I'm talking about." He wiped his mouth with the back of his hand. "Look," he said, "you ever ride the subway?"

"When I have to."

"Well, shit, nobody rides it by choice. It's the whole city in a nutshell, the equipment breaks down all the time, the cars are filthy with spray paint and they stink of piss and the transit cops can't make a dent in the crime down there, but what I'm talking about, shit, *I* get on a subway and I look around and you know where I am? I'm in a fucking foreign country."

"What do you mean?"

"I mean everybody's black or Spanish. Or oriental, we got all these new Chinese immigrants coming in, plus there's the Koreans. Now the Koreans are perfect citizens, they open up all these great vegetable markets all over the city, they work twenty hours a day and send their kids to college, but it's all part of something."

"Part of what?"

"Oh, shit, it sounds ignorant and bigoted but I can't help it. This used to be a white city and now there's days when I feel like I'm the only white man left in it."

The silence stretched. Then he said, "They smoke on the subway now. You ever notice?"

"I've noticed."

"Never used to happen. A guy might murder both his parents with a fire axe but he wouldn't dare light up a cigarette on the subway. Now you got middle-class people lighting their cigarettes, puffing away. Just in the last few months. You know how it started?"

"How?"

"Remember about a year ago? A guy was smoking on the PATH train and a PATH cop asked him to put it out, and the guy drew a gun and shot the cop dead? Remember?"

"I remember."

"That's what started it. You read about that and whoever you are, a cop or a private citizen, you're not in a rush to tell the guy across the aisle to put out his fucking cigarette. So a few people light up and nobody does anything about it, and more people do it, and who's gonna give a shit about smoking in the subway when it's a waste of time to report a major crime like burglary? Stop enforcing a law and people stop respecting it." He frowned. "But think about that PATH cop. You like that for a way to die? Ask a guy to put out a cigarette and bang, you're dead."

I found myself telling him about Rudenko's mother, dead of a bomb blast because her friend had brought home the wrong television set. And so we traded horror stories. He told of a social worker, lured onto a tenement roof, raped repeatedly and thrown off the building to her death. I recalled something I'd read about a fourteen-year-old shot by another boy the same age, both of them strangers to each other, the killer insisted that his victim had laughed at him. Durkin told me about some child-abuse cases that had ended in death, and about a man who had smothered his girlfriend's infant daughter because he was sick of paying for a baby-sitter everytime the two of them went to the movies. I mentioned the woman in Gravesend, dead of a shotgun blast while she hung clothes in her closet. There was an air of *Can You Top This?* to our dialogue.

He said, "The mayor thinks he's got the answer. The death penalty. Bring back the big black chair."

"Think it'll happen?"

"No question the public wants it. And there's one way it works and you can't tell me it doesn't. You fry one of these bastards and at least you know he's not gonna do it again. The hell, I'd vote for it. Bring back the chair and televise the fucking executions, run commercials, make a few dollars and hire a few more cops. You want to know something?"

"What?"

"We *got* the death penalty. Not for murderers. For ordinary citizens. Everybody out there runs a better chance of getting killed than a killer does of getting the chair. We get the death penalty five, six, seven times a day."

He had raised his voice and the bartender was auditing our conversation now. We'd lured him away from his program.

Durkin said, "I like the one about the exploding television set. I don't know how I missed that one. You think you heard 'em all but there's always something new, isn't there?"

"I guess."

"There are eight million stories in the naked city," he intoned. "You remember that program? Used to be on television some years back."

"I remember."

"They had that line at the end of every show. 'There are eight million stories in the naked city. This has been one of them.' "

"I remember it."

"Eight million stories," he said. "You know what you got in this city, this fucked-up toilet of a naked fucking city? You know what you got? You got eight million ways to die."

I got him out of there. Outside in the cool night air he fell silent. We circled a couple of blocks, wound up down the street from the station house. His car was a Mercury a few years old. It had been beaten up a little around the corners. The license plate had a prefix which would indicate to other cops that this was a vehicle used for police business and not to be ticketed. Some of the more knowledgeable crooks could also recognize it as a cop's car.

I asked if he was okay to drive. He didn't much care for the question. He said, "What are you, a cop?" and then the absurdity of the remark struck him and he started to laugh. He clung to the car's open door for support, helpless with laughter, and swung back and forth on the car door. "What are you, a cop?" he said, giggling. "What are you, a cop?"

That mood passed like a fast cut in a film. In an instant he was serious and apparently sober, eyes narrowed, jaw thrust forward like a bulldog's. "Listen," he said, voice low and hard. "Don't be so goddamn superior, you understand?"

I didn't know what he was talking about.

"You sanctimonious bastard. You're no better than I am, you son of a bitch."

He pulled out and drove off. He seemed to be driving all right for as far as I was able to track him. I hoped he didn't have too far to go.

Chapter 15

I walked straight back to my hotel. The liquor stores were closed but the bars were still open. I passed them without much effort, resisted too the call of street whores on Fifty-seventh Street on either side of the Holiday Inn. I gave Jacob a nod, confirmed that I'd had no calls, and went upstairs.

Sanctimonious bastard. No better than I am. He'd been ugly drunk, with that defensive belligerence of the drinker who had exposed too much of himself. His words didn't mean anything. He'd have addressed them to any companion, or to the night itself.

Still, they echoed in my head.

I got into bed but couldn't sleep, got up and put the light on and sat on the edge of the bed with my notebook. I looked over some of the notes I made, then jotted down a point or two from our conversation in the bar on Tenth Avenue. I made a few further notes to myself, playing with ideas like a kitten with a yarn ball. I put the notebook down when the process reached a point of diminishing returns, with the same thoughts turning over and over upon themselves. I picked up a paperback I'd bought earlier but couldn't get into it. I kept reading the same paragraph without getting the sense of it.

For the first time in hours I really wanted a drink. I was anxious and edgy and wanted to change it. There was a deli with a cooler full of beer just three doors from the hotel, and when had beer ever led me into a blackout?

I stayed where I was.

Chance hadn't asked my reason for working for him. Durkin had accepted money as a valid motive. Elaine was willing to believe I was doing it because it was what I did, even as she turned tricks and God pardoned sinners. And it was all true, I could indeed use the money and detecting was what I did insofar as I did anything, it was as much of a profession as I had.

But I had another motive, and perhaps it was a deeper one. Searching for Kim's killer was something I could do instead of drinking.

For awhile, anyway.

WHEN I woke up the sun was shining. By the time I showered and shaved and hit the street it was gone, tucked away behind a bank of clouds. It came and went all day, as if whoever was in charge didn't want to commit himself.

I ate a light breakfast, made some phone calls, then walked over to the Galaxy Downtowner. The clerk who'd checked in Charles Jones wasn't on duty. I'd read his interrogation report in the file and didn't really expect I could get more out of him than the cops could.

An assistant manager let me look at Jones's registration card. He'd printed "Charles Owen Jones" on the line marked "Name," and on the "Signature" line he'd printed "C. O. JONES" in block capitals. I pointed this out to the assistant manager, who told me the discrepancy was common. "People will put their full name on one line and a shorter version on the other," he said. "Either way is legal."

"But this isn't a signature."

"Why not?"

"He printed it."

He shrugged. "Some people print everything," he said. "The fellow made a telephone reservation and paid cash in advance. I wouldn't expect my people to question a signature under such circumstances."

That wasn't my point. What had struck me was that Jones had managed to avoid leaving a specimen of his handwriting, and I found that interesting. I looked at the name where he'd printed it in full. The first three letters of *Charles*, I found myself thinking, were also the first three letters of *Chance*. And what, pray tell, did that signify? And why look for ways to hang my own client?

I asked if there'd been any previous visits by our Mr. Jones in the past few months. "Nothing in the past *year*," he assured me. "We carry previous registrations alphabetically in our computer and one of the detectives had that information checked. If that's all—"

"How many other guests signed their names in block caps?"

"I've no idea."

"Suppose you let me look through the registration cards for the past two, three months."

"To look for what?"

"People who print like this guy."

"Oh, I really don't think so," he said. "Do you realize how many cards are involved? This is a 635-room hotel. Mr.—"

"Scudder."

"Mr. Scudder. That's over eighteen thousand cards a month."

"Only if all your guests leave after one night."

"The average stay is three nights. Even so, that's over six thousand registration cards a month, twelve thousand cards in two months. Do you realize how long it would take to look at twelve thousand cards?"

"A person could probably do a couple thousand an hour," I said, "since all he'd be doing is scanning the signature to see if it's in script or in block caps. We're just talking about a couple of hours. I could do it or you could have some of your people do it."

He shook his head. "I couldn't authorize that," he said. "I really couldn't. You're a private citizen, not a policeman, and while I did want to cooperate there's a limit to my authority here. If the police should make an official request—"

"I realize I'm asking a favor."

"If it were the sort of favor I could grant—"

"It's an imposition," I went on, "and I'd certainly expect to pay for the time involved, the time and inconvenience."

It would have worked at a smaller hotel, but here I was wasting my time. I don't think he even realized I was offering him a bribe. He said again that he'd be glad to go along if the police made the request for me, and this time I let it lie. I asked instead if I could borrow the Jones registration card long enough to have a photocopy made.

"Oh, we have a machine right here," he said, grateful to be able to help. "Just wait one moment."

He came back with a copy. I thanked him and he asked if there was anything else, his tone suggesting he was confident there wouldn't be. I said I'd like a look at the room she died in.

"But the police have quite finished there," he said. "The room's in a transitional state now. The carpet had to be replaced, you see, and the walls painted."

"I'd still like to see it."

"There's really nothing to see. I think there are workmen in there today. The painters are gone, I believe, but I think the carpet installers—"

"I won't get in their way."

He gave me a key and let me go up myself. I found the room and congratulated myself on my ability as a detective. The door was locked. The carpet installers looked to be on their lunch break. The old carpet had been removed, and new carpet covered about a third of the floor, with more of it rolled up awaiting installation.

I spent a few minutes there. As the man had assured me, there was really nothing to see. The room was as empty of traces of Kim as it was of furniture. The walls were bright with fresh paint and the bathroom fairly sparkled. I walked around like some psychic practitioner, trying to pick up vibrations through the tips of my fingers. If there were any vibrations present, they eluded me.

The window faced downtown, the view chopped up by the facades of other tall buildings. Through a gap between two of them I could catch a glimpse of the World Trade Center all the way downtown.

Had she had time to look out the window? Had Mr. Jones looked out the window, before or afterward?

I took the subway downtown. The train was one of the new ones, its interior a pleasing pattern of yellow and orange and tan. The inscribers of graffiti had already scarred it badly, scrawling their indecipherable messages over every available space.

I didn't notice anyone smoking.

I got off at West Fourth and walked south and west to Morton Street, where Fran Schecter had a small apartment on the top floor of a four-story brownstone. I rang her bell, announced myself over the intercom, and was buzzed through the vestibule door.

The stairwell was full of smells—baking smells on the first floor, cat odor halfway up, and the unmistakable scent of marijuana at the top. I thought that you could draw a building's profile from the aromas in its stairwell.

Fran was waiting for me in her doorway. Short curly hair, light brown in color, framed a round baby face. She had a button nose, a pouty mouth, and cheeks a chipmunk would have been proud of.

She said, "Hi, I'm Fran. And you're Matt. Can I call you Matt?" I assured her that she could, and her hand settled on my arm as she steered me inside.

The marijuana reek was much stronger inside. The apartment was a studio. One fairly large room with a pullman kitchen on one wall. The furniture consisted of a canvas sling chair, a pillow sofa, some plastic milk crates assembled as shelves for books and clothes, and a large waterbed covered with a fake-fur spread. A framed poster on one wall over the waterbed showed a room interior, with a railway locomotive emerging from the fireplace.

I turned down a drink, accepted a can of diet soda. I sat with it on the pillow sofa, which turned out to be more comfortable than it looked. She took the sling chair, which must have been more comfortable than it looked.

"Chance said you're investigating what happened to Kim," she said. "He said to tell you whatever you want to know."

There was a breathless little-girl quality to her voice and I couldn't tell how much of it was deliberate. I asked her what she knew about Kim.

"Not much. I met her a few times. Sometimes Chance'll take two girls at once out to dinner or a show. I guess I met everyone at one time or another. I just met Donna once, she's on her own trip, it's like she's lost in space. Have you met Donna?" I shook my head. "I like Sunny. I don't know if we're friends exactly, but she's the only one I'd call up to talk to. I'll call her once, twice a week, or she'll call me, you know, and we'll talk."

I just flashed that I'm the typical dumb hooker, thinks she's the only one the pimp loves. But you know what it is? I'm the only one he can relax with. He can come up here and take his shoes off and let his mind roll out. Do you know what a karmic tie is?"

"No."

"Well, it has something to do with reincarnation. I don't know if you believe in that."

"I never thought about it much."

"Well, I don't know if I believe in it either, but sometimes I think Chance and I knew each other in another life. Not necessarily as lovers or man and wife or anything like that. Like we could have been brother and sister, or maybe he was my father or I was his mother. Or we could even have both been the same sex because that can change from one lifetime to another. I mean we could have been sisters or something. Anything, really."

The telephone cut into her speculations. She crossed the room to answer it, standing with her back to me, one hand propped against her hip. I couldn't hear her conversation. She talked for a moment or two, then covered the mouthpiece and turned to me.

"Matt," she said, "I don't want to hassle you, but do you have any idea how long we're gonna be?"

"Not long."

"Like could I tell somebody it would be cool to come over in an hour?"

"No problem."

She turned again, finished the conversation quietly, hung up. "That was one of my regulars," she said. "He's a real nice guy. I told him an hour."

She sat down again. I asked her if she'd had the apartment before she hooked up with Chance. She said she'd been with Chance for two years and eight months and no, before that she shared a bigger place in Chelsea with three other girls.

Chance had had this apartment all ready for her. All she'd had to do was move into it.

"I just moved my furniture in," she said. "Except the waterbed. That was already here. I had a single bed that I got rid of. And I bought the Magritte poster, and the masks were here." I hadn't noticed the masks and had to turn in my seat to see them, a grouping of three solemn ebony carvings on the wall behind me. "He knows about them," she said. "What tribe made them and everything. He knows things like that."

I said that the apartment was an unlikely one for the use being made of it. She frowned, puzzled.

"Most girls in the game live in doorman buildings," I said. "With elevators and all."

"Oh, right. I didn't know what you meant. Yes, that's true." She grinned brightly. "This is something different," she said. "The johns who come here, they don't think they're johns."

"How do you mean?"

"They think they're friends of mine," she explained. "They think I'm this spacey Village chick, which I am, and that they're my friends, which they are. I mean, they come here to get laid, let's face it, but they could get laid quicker and easier in a massage parlor, no muss no fuss no bother, dig? But they can come up here and take off their shoes and smoke a joint, and it's a sort of a raunchy Village pad, I mean you have to climb three flights of stairs and then you roll around in a waterbed. I mean, I'm not a hooker. I'm a girlfriend. I don't get paid. They give me money because I got rent to pay and, you know, I'm a poor little Village chick who wants to make it as an actress and she's never going to. Which I'm not, and I don't care much, but I still take dancing lessons a couple mornings a week and I have an acting class with Ed Kovens every Thursday night, and I was in a showcase last May for three weekends in Tribeca. We did Ibsen, *When We*

Dead Awake, and do you believe that three of my johns came?"

She chatted about the play, then began telling me how her clients brought her presents in addition to the money they gave her. "I never have to buy any booze. In fact I have it to give away because I don't drink myself. And I haven't bought any grass in ages. You know who gets the best grass? Wall Street guys. They'll buy an ounce and we'll smoke a little and they'll leave me the ounce." She batted her long lashes at me. "I kind of like to smoke," she said.

"I guessed that."

"Why? Do I seem stoned?"

"The smell."

"Oh, right. I don't smell it because I'm here, but when I go out and then I come back in, whew! It's like a friend of mine has four cats and she swears they don't smell, but the smell could knock you down. It's just that she's used to it." She shifted in her seat. "Do you ever smoke, Matt?"

"No."

"You don't drink and you don't smoke, that's terrific. Can I get you another diet soda?"

"No thanks."

"Are you sure? Look, would it bother you if I smoked a quick joint? Just to unwind a little."

"Go ahead."

"Because I've got this fellow coming over and it'll help me be in the mood."

I told her it was fine with me. She fetched a plastic baggie of marijuana from a shelf over the stove and hand-rolled a cigarette with evident expertise. "He'll probably want to smoke," she said, and manufactured two more cigarettes. She lit one, put everything else away, and returned to the sling chair. She smoked the joint all the way down, chattering about her life between drags, finally stubbing the tiny roach and setting it aside for later. Her manner didn't change visibly for having smoked the thing. Perhaps she'd been smoking throughout the day and had been stoned when I arrived. Perhaps she just didn't show the effects of the drug, as some drinkers don't show their drinks.

I asked if Chance smoked when he came to see her and she laughed at the idea. "He never drinks, never smokes. Same as you. Hey, is that where you know him from? Do you both hang out in a nonbar together? Or maybe you both have the same undealer."

I managed to get the conversation back to Kim. If Chance didn't care for Kim, did Fran think she might have been seeing someone else?"

"He didn't care for her," she said. "You know something? I'm the only one he loves."

I could taste the grass in her speech now. Her voice was the same, but her mind made different connections, switching along paths of smoke.

"Do you think Kim had a boyfriend?"

"I have boyfriends. Kim had tricks. All of the others have tricks."

"If Kim had someone special—"

"Sure, I can dig it. Somebody who wasn't a john, and that's why she wanted to split with Chance. That what you mean?"

"It's possible."

"And then he killed her."

"Chance?"

"Are you crazy? Chance never cared enough about her to kill her. You know how long it'd take to replace her? Shit."

"You mean the boyfriend killed her."

"Sure."

"Why?"

"'Cause he's on the spot. She leaves Chance, there she is, all ready for happily ever after, and what does he want with that? I mean he's got a wife, he's got a job, he's got a family, he's got a house in Scarsdale—"

"How do you know all this?"

She sighed. "I'm just speedballing, baby. I'm just throwing chalk at the blackboard. Can you dig it? He's a married guy, he digs Kim, it's kicky being in love with a hooker and having her in love with you, and that way you get it for free, but you don't want anybody turning your life around. She says, Hey, I'm free now, time to ditch your wife and we'll run into the sunset, and the sunset's something he watches from the terrace at the country club and he wants to keep it that way. Next thing you know, zip, she's dead and he's back in Larchmont."

"It was Scarsdale a minute ago."

"Whatever."

"Who would he be, Fran?"

"The boyfriend? I don't know. Anybody."

"A john?"

"You don't fall in love with a john."

"Where would she meet a guy? And what kind of guy would she meet?"

She struggled with the notion, shrugged and gave up. The conversation never got any further than that. I used her phone, talked for a moment, then wrote my name and number on a pad next to the phone.

"In case you think of anything," I said.

"I'll call you if I do. You going? You sure you don't want another soda?"

"No thanks."

"Well," she said. She came over to me, stifled a lazy yawn with the back of her hand, looked up at me through the long lashes. "Hey, I'm really glad you could come over," she said. "Anytime you feel like company, you know, give me a call, okay? Just to hang out and talk."

"Sure."

"I'd like that," she said softly, coming up onto her toes, planting an astonishing kiss on my cheek. "I'd really like that, Matt," she said.

Halfway down the stairs I started laughing. How automatically she'd slipped into her whore's manner, warm and earnest at parting, and how good she was at it. No wonder those stockbrokers didn't mind climbing all those stairs. No wonder they turned out to watch her try to be an actress. The hell, she *was* an actress, and not a bad one, either.

Two blocks away I could still feel the imprint of her kiss on my cheek.

Chapter 16

Donna Campion's apartment was on the tenth floor of the white brick building on East Seventeenth Street. The living-room window faced west, and the sun was making one of its intermittent appearances when I got there. Sunlight flooded the room. There were plants everywhere, all of them vividly green and thriving, plants on the floor and the windowsills, plants hanging in the window, plants on ledges and tables throughout the room. The sunlight streamed through the curtain of plants and cast intricate patterns on the dark parquet flooring.

I sat in a wicker armchair and sipped a cup of black coffee. Donna was perched sideways on a backed oak bench about four feet wide. It had been a church pew, she'd told me, and it was English oak, Jacobite or possibly Elizabethan, dark with the passing years and worn smooth by three or four centuries of pious bottoms. Some vicar in rural Devon had decided to redecorate and in due course she'd bought the little pew at a University Place auction gallery.

She had the face to go with it, a long face that tapered from a high broad forehead to a pointed chin. Her skin was

very pale, as if the only sunlight she ever got was what
passed through the screen of plants. She was wearing a crisp
white blouse with a Peter Pan collar and a short pleated skirt
of gray flannel over a pair of black tights. Her slippers were
doeskin, with pointed toes.

A long narrow nose, a small thin-lipped mouth. Dark
brown hair, shoulder length, combed straight back from a
well-defined widow's peak. Circles under her eyes, tobacco
stains on two fingers of her right hand. No nail polish, no
jewelry, no visible makeup. No prettiness, certainly, but a
medieval quality that came quite close to beauty.

She didn't look like any whore I'd ever met. She did look
like a poet, though, or what I thought a poet ought to look
like.

She said, "Chance said to give you my complete cooperation. He said you're trying to find out who killed the Dairy
Queen."

"The Dairy Queen?"

"She looked like a beauty queen, and then I learned she
was from Wisconsin, and I thought of all that robust milk-
fed innocence. She was a sort of regal milkmaid." She
smiled softly. "That's my imagination talking. I didn't really
know her."

"Did you ever meet her boyfriend?"

"I didn't know she had one."

Nor had she known that Kim had been planning to leave
Chance, and she seemed to find the information interesting.
"I wonder," she said. "Was she an emigrant or an immi-
grant?"

"What do you mean?"

"Was she going from or to? It's a matter of emphasis.
When I first came to New York I was coming *to*. I'd also just
made a break with my family and the town I grew up in, but
that was secondary. Later on, when I split with my husband,

I was running from. The act of leaving was more important than the destination."

"You were married?"

"For three years. Well, together for three years. Lived together for one year, married for two."

"How long ago was that?"

"Four years?" She worked it out. "Five years this coming spring. Although I'm still married, technically. I never bothered to get a divorce. Do you think I should?"

"I don't know."

"I probably ought to. Just to tie off a loose end."

"How long have you been with Chance?"

"Going on three years. Why?"

"You don't seem the type."

"Is there a type? I don't suppose I'm much like Kim. Neither regal nor a milkmaid." She laughed. "I don't know which is which, but we're like the colonel's lady and Judy O'Grady."

"Sisters under the skin?"

She looked surprised that I'd recognized the quotation. She said, "After I left my husband I was living on the Lower East Side. Do you know Norfolk Street? Between Stanton and Rivington?"

"Not specifically."

"I knew it very specifically. I lived there and I had these little jobs in the neighborhood. I worked in a Laundromat, I waited tables. I clerked in shops. I would quit the jobs or the jobs would quit me and there was never enough money and I hated where I was living and I was starting to hate my life. I was going to call my husband and ask him to take me back just so he would take care of me. I kept thinking about it. One time I dialed his number but the line was busy."

And so she'd drifted almost accidentally into selling herself. There was a store owner down the block who kept coming on to her. One day without preplanning it she heard herself say, "Look, if you really want to ball me, would you give me twenty dollars?" He'd been flustered, blurting that he hadn't known she was a hooker. "I'm not," she told him, "but I need the money. And I'm supposed to be a pretty good fuck."   •

She started turning a few tricks a week. She moved from Norfolk Street to a better block in the same neighborhood, then moved again to Ninth Street just east of Tompkins Square. She didn't have to work now but there were other hassles to contend with. She was beaten up once, robbed several times. Again she found herself thinking of calling her ex-husband.

Then she met a girl in the neighborhood who worked in a midtown massage parlor. Donna tried out there and liked the security of it. There was a man in front to deal with anyone who tried to cause trouble, and the work itself was mechanical, almost clinical in its detachment. Virtually all her tricks were manual or oral. Her own flesh was uninvaded, and there was no illusion of intimacy beyond the pure fact of physical intimacy.

At first she welcomed this. She saw herself as a sexual technician, a kind of physiotherapist. Then it turned on her.

"The place had Mafia vibes," she said, "and you could smell death in the drapes and carpets. And it got like a job, I worked regular hours, I took the subway back and forth. It sucked—I love that word—it sucked the poetry right out of me."

And so she'd quit and resumed freelancing, and somewhere along the way Chance found her and everything fell into place. He'd installed her in this apartment, the first decent place she ever had in New York, and he got her phone number circulating and took all the hassles away. Her bills got paid, her apartment got cleaned, everything got done for her, and all she had to do was work on her poems and mail them off to magazines and be nice and charming whenever the telephone rang.

"Chance takes all the money you earn," I said. "Doesn't that bother you?"

"Should it?"

"I don't know."

"It's not real money anyway," she said. "Fast money doesn't last. If it did, all the drug dealers would own the stock exchange. But that kind of money goes out the way it comes in." She swung her legs around, sat facing forward on the church pew. "Anyway," she said, "I have everything I want. All I ever wanted was to be left alone. I wanted a decent place to live and time to do my work. I'm talking about my poetry."

"I realize that."

"You know what most poets go through? They teach, or they work a straight job, or they play the poetry game, giving readings and lectures and writing out proposals for foundation grants and getting to know the right people and kissing the right behinds. I never wanted to do all that shit. I just wanted to make poems."

"What did Kim want to do?"

"God knows."

"I think she was involved with somebody. I think that's what got her killed."

"Then I'm safe," she said. "I'm involved with no one. Of course you could argue that I'm involved with mankind. Would that put me in grave danger, do you suppose?"

I didn't know what she meant. With her eyes closed she said, " 'Any man's death diminishes me, because I am involved in Mankind,' John Donne. Do you know how she was involved, or with whom?"

"No."

"Does her death diminish me, do you suppose? I wonder if I was involved with her. I didn't know her, not really, and yet I wrote a poem about her."

"Could I see it?"

"I suppose so, but I don't see how it could tell you anything. I wrote a poem about the Big Dipper but if you want to know anything real about it you'd have to go to an astronomer, not to me. Poems are never about what they're about, you know. They're all about the poet."

"I'd still like to see it."

This seemed to please her. She went to her desk, a modern version of the old rolltop, and found what she was looking for almost immediately. The poem was hand-lettered on white bond paper with an italic-nibbed pen.

"I type them up for submission," she said, "but I like to see how they look on the page this way. I taught myself to do calligraphy. I learned from a book. It's easier than it looks."

I read:

> Bathe her in milk, let the white stream run
> Pure in its bovine baptism,
> Heal the least schism
> Under the soonest sun. Take her
> Hand, tell her it doesn't matter,
> Milk's not to cry over. Scatter
> Seed from a silver gun. Break her
> Bones in a mortar, shatter
> Wine bottles at her feet, let green glass
> Sparkle upon her hand. Let it be done.
> Let the milk run.
> Let it flow down, down to the ancient grass.

I asked if I could copy it into my notebook. Her laugh was light, merry. "Why? Does it tell who killed her?"

"I don't know what it tells me. Maybe if I keep it I'll figure out what it tells me."

"If you figure out what it means," she said, "I hope you'll tell *me*. That's an exaggeration. I sort of know what I'm getting at. But don't bother copying it. You can have that copy."

"Don't be silly. That's your copy."

She shook her head. "It's not finished. It needs more work. I want to get her eyes into it. If you met Kim you must have noticed her eyes."

"Yes."

"I originally wanted to contrast the blue eyes with the green glass, that's how that image got there in the first place, but the eyes disappeared when I wrote it. I think they were in an earlier draft but somewhere along the line they dropped out." She smiled. "They were gone in a wink. I've got the silver and the green and the white and I left the eyes out." She stood with her hand on my shoulder, looking down at the poem. "It's what, twelve lines? I think it should be fourteen anyway. Sonnet length, even if the lines are irregular. I don't know about *schism*, either. Maybe an off-rhyme would be better. Spasm, chasm, something."

She went on, talking more to herself than to me, discussing possible revisions in the poem. "By all means keep that," she concluded. "It's a long way from final form. It's funny. I haven't even looked at it since she was killed."

"You wrote it before she was killed?"

"Completely. And I don't think I ever thought of it as finished, even though I copied it in pen and ink. I'll do that with drafts. I can get a better idea of what does and doesn't work that way. I'd have kept on working on this one if she hadn't been killed."

"What stopped you? The shock?"

"Was I shocked? I suppose I must have been. 'This could happen to me,' Except of course I don't believe that. It's like

lung cancer, it happens to other people. 'Any man's death diminishes me.' Did Kim's death diminish me? I don't think
so. I don't think I'm as involved in mankind as John Donne
was. Or as he said he was."

"Then why did you put the poem aside?"

"I didn't put it aside. I left it aside. That's nitpicking, isn't
it?" She considered this. "Her death changed how I saw her.
I wanted to work on the poem, but I didn't want to get her
death into it. I had enough colors. I didn't need blood in
there, too."

Chapter 17

I had taken a cab from Morton Street to Donna's place on East Seventeenth. Now I took another to Kim's building on Thirty-seventh. As I paid the driver I realized I hadn't made it to the bank. Tomorrow was Saturday, so I'd have Chance's money on my hands all weekend. Unless some mugger got lucky.

I lightened the load some by slipping five bucks to the doorman for a key to Kim's apartment, along with some story about acting as the tenant's representative. For five dollars he was eager to believe me. I went up to the elevator and let myself in.

The police had been through the place earlier. I didn't know what they were looking for and couldn't say what they found. The sheet in the file Durkin showed me hadn't said much, but nobody writes down everything that comes to his attention.

I couldn't know what the officers on the scene might have noticed. For that matter, I couldn't be sure what might have stuck to their fingers. There are cops who'll rob the dead, doing so as a matter of course, and they are not necessarily men who are especially dishonest in other matters.

Cops see too much of death and squalor, and in order to go on dealing with it they often have the need to dehumanize the dead. I remember the first time I helped remove a corpse from a room in an SRO hotel. The deceased had died vomiting blood and had lain there for several days before his death was discovered. A veteran patrolman and I wrestled the corpse into a body bag and on the way downstairs my companion made sure the bag hit every single step. He'd have been more careful with a sack of potatoes.

I can still recall the way the hotel's other residents looked at us. And I can remember how my partner went through the dead man's belongings, scooping up the little cash he had to his name, counting it deliberately and dividing it with me.

I hadn't wanted to take it. "Put it in your pocket," he told me. "What do you think happens to it otherwise? Somebody else takes it. Or it goes to the state. What's the state of New York gonna do with forty-four dollars? Put it in your pocket, then buy yourself some perfumed soap and try to get this poor fucker's stink off your hands."

I put it in my pocket. Later on, I was the one who bounced bagged corpses down the stairs, the one who counted and divided their leavings.

Someday, I suppose, it'll come full circle, and I'll be the one in the bag.

I spent over an hour there. I went through drawers and closets without really knowing what I was looking for. I didn't find very much. If she'd had a little black book full of telephone numbers, the call girl's legendary stock in trade, someone else had found it before I did. Not that I had any reason to assume she'd had such a book. Elaine kept one, but Fran and Donna had both told me they didn't.

I didn't find any drugs or drug paraphernalia, which proved little in and of itself. A cop might appropriate drugs just as he'd take money from the dead. Or Chance might have picked up any contraband that he found lying around. He'd said that he visited the apartment once after her death. I noticed, though, that he'd left the African masks. They glared at me from their spot on the wall, guarding the premises on behalf of whatever eager young whore Chance would install in Kim's place.

The Hopper poster was still in place over the stereo. Would that stay behind for the next tenant, too?

Her spoor was all over the place. I breathed it when I went through the clothes in her dresser drawers and in her closet. Her bed was unmade. I lifted the mattress, looked under it. No doubt others had done so before me. I didn't find anything and I let the mattress fall back into place, and her spicy scent rose from the rumpled bedclothing and filled my nostrils.

In the living room, I opened a closet and found her fur jacket, other coats and jackets, and a shelf full of wine and liquor bottles. A fifth of Wild Turkey caught my eye, and I swear I could taste that rich overproof bourbon, could feel the bite of it in my throat, the hot rush flowing down to my stomach, the warmth spreading clear to my toes and fingers. I closed the door, crossed the room and sat down on the couch. I hadn't wanted a drink, hadn't so much as thought of a drink in hours, and the unexpected glimpse of a bottle of booze had caught me unawares.

I went back to the bedroom. She had a jewelry box on the top of her dressing table and I went through it. A lot of earrings, a couple of necklaces, a string of unconvincing pearls. Several bangle bracelets, including an attractive one made of ivory and trimmed in what looked to be gold. A gaudy class ring from LaFollette High in Eau Claire, Wisconsin. The ring was gold, stamped 14K on the inside, heavy enough by the feel of it to be worth something.

Who would get all of this? There had been some cash in her bag at the Galaxy Downtowner, four hundred bucks and

change according to the note in her file, and that would
probably wind up going to her parents in Wisconsin. But
would they fly in and claim her coats and sweaters? Would
they take possession of the fur jacket, the high school ring,
the ivory bracelet?

I stayed long enough to make a few notes and managed to
get out of there without again opening the front closet. I rode
the elevator to the lobby, waved at the doorman and nodded
at an entering tenant, an elderly woman with a small short-
haired dog on a rhinestone-studded leash. The dog yipped at
me, and I wondered for the first time what had become of
Kim's little black kitten. I'd seen no traces of the animal, no
litter pan in the bathroom. Someone must have taken it.

I caught a cab at the corner. I was paying it off in front of
my hotel when I found Kim's key with my pocket change. I
hadn't remembered to return it to the doorman, and he
hadn't thought to ask me for it.

THERE was a message for me. Joe Durkin had called and left
his number at the precinct. I called and was told he was out
but was expected back. I left my name and number.

I went up to my room, feeling winded and tired. I lay
down but I couldn't get any rest that way, couldn't turn off
the tapes in my head. I went downstairs again, had a cheese
sandwich and french fries and coffee. Over a second cup of
coffee I took Donna Campion's poem out of my pocket.
Something about it was trying to get through to me but I
couldn't figure out what. I read it again. I didn't know what
the poem meant; assuming that it was intended to have any
literal meaning. But it seemed to me that some element of it
was winking at me, trying to get my attention, and I was just
too brain damaged to catch on.

I went over to St. Paul's. The speaker told a horrible story
in a chatty matter-of-fact fashion. Both his parents had died

of alcoholism, his father of acute pancreatitis, his mother of suicide committed while drunk. Two brothers and a sister had died of the disease. A third brother was in a state hospital with a wet brain.

"After I was sober a few months," he said, "I started hearing how alcohol kills brain cells, and I got worried about how much brain damage I might have. So I went to my sponsor and told him what was on my mind. 'Well,' he said, 'maybe you've had some brain damage. It's possible. But let me ask you this. Are you able to remember where the meetings are from one day to the next? Can you find your way to them without any trouble?' 'Yeah,' I told him, 'I can manage that all right.' 'Well then,' he said, 'you got all the brain cells you need for the time being.'"

I left on the break.

THERE was another message from Durkin at the hotel desk. I called right back and he was out again. I left my name and number and went upstairs. I was having another look at Donna's poem when the phone rang.

It was Durkin. He said, "Hey, Matt. I just wanted to say I hope I didn't give you the wrong impression last night."

"About what?"

"Oh, things in general," he said. "Once in a while the whole business gets to me, you know what I mean? I have the need to break out, drink too much, run off at the mouth. I don't make a habit of it but once in awhile I have to do it."

"Sure."

"Most of the time I love the job, but there's things that get to you, things you try not to look at, and every now and then I have to get all that shit out of my system. I hope I didn't get out of line there toward the end."

I assured him that he'd done nothing wrong. I wondered how clearly he recalled the previous evening. He'd been drunk enough to be in a blackout, but not everybody has blackouts. Maybe he was just a little vague, and uncertain how I'd taken his outbursts.

I thought of what Billie's landlady had told him. "Forget it," I said. "It could happen to a bishop."

"Hey, I got to remember that one. It could happen to a bishop. And probably does."

"Probably."

"You getting anywhere with your investigation? Coming up with anything?"

"It's hard to tell."

"I know what you mean. If there's anything I can do for you—"

"Matter of fact, there is."

"Oh?"

"I went over to the Galaxy Downtowner," I said. "Talked to an assistant manager. He showed me the registration card Mr. Jones signed."

"The famous Mr. Jones."

"There was no signature on it. The name was hand-printed."

"Figures."

"I asked if I could go through the cards for the past few months and see if there were any other hand-printed signatures, and how they compared to Jones's printing. He couldn't authorize it."

"You should have slipped him a few bucks."

"I tried. He didn't even know what I was getting at. But you could have him pull the printed cards. He wouldn't do it for me because I've got no official standing, but he'd hop to it if a cop made the request."

He didn't say anything for a moment. Then he asked if I thought it was going to lead anywhere.

"It might," I said.

"You think whoever did it stayed at the hotel before? Under some other name?"

"It's possible."

"But not his own name, or he would have signed it in script instead of being cute. So what we'd wind up with, assuming we got very lucky and there was a card to be found and we actually came up with it, what we'd have is another alias for the same son of a bitch, and we wouldn't be any closer'n we are now to knowing who he is."

"There's another thing you could do, while you were at it."

"What's that?"

"Have other hotels in the area check their registrations for, oh, the past six months or a year."

"Check 'em for what? Printed registrations? Come on, Matt. You know the man-hours you're talking about?"

"Not printed registrations. Have them check for guests named Jones. I'm talking about hotels like the Galaxy Downtowner, modern hotels in that price range. Most of them'll be like the Galaxy and have their registrations on computer. They can pull their Jones registrations in five or ten minutes, but not unless someone with a tin shield asks 'em to."

"And then what have you got?"

"You pull the appropriate cards, look for a guest named Jones, probably with the first initial *C* or the initials *CO*, and you compare printing and see if you find him anywhere. If you come up with anything you see where it leads. I don't have to tell you what to do with a lead."

He was silent again. "I don't know," he said at length. "It sounds pretty thin."

"Maybe it is."

"I'll tell you what I think it is. I think it's a waste of time."

"It's not a waste of all that much time. And it's not that

thin. Joe, you'd do it if the case wasn't already closed in your mind."

"I don't know about that."

"Of course you would. You think it's a hired killer or a lunatic. If it's a hired killer you want to close it out and if it's a lunatic you want to wait until he does it again."

"I wouldn't go that far."

"You went that far last night."

"Last night was last night, for Christ's sake. I already explained about last night."

"It wasn't a hired killer," I said. "And it wasn't a lunatic just picking her out of the blue."

"You sound like you're sure of it."

"Reasonably sure."

"Why?"

"No hired hitman goes crazy that way. What did he hit her, sixty times with a machete?"

"I think it was sixty-six."

"Sixty-six, then."

"And it wasn't necessarily a machete. Something *like* a machete."

"He had her strip. Then he butchered her like that, he got so much blood on the walls that they had to paint the room. When did you ever hear of a professional hit like that?"

"Who knows what kind of animal a pimp hires? Maybe he tells the guy to make it ugly, do a real job on her, make an example out of her. Who knows what goes through his mind?"

"And then he hires me to look into it."

"I admit it sounds weird, Matt, but—"

"It can't be a crazy, either. It was somebody who *went* crazy, but it's not a psycho getting his kicks."

"How do you know that?"

"He's too careful. Printing his name when he signed in.

Carrying the dirty towels away with him. This is a guy who took the trouble to avoid leaving a shred of physical evidence."

"I thought he used the towels to wrap the machete."

"Why would he do that? After he washed the machete he'd put it back in the case the way he brought it. Or, if he wanted to wrap it in towels, he'd use clean towels. He wouldn't carry away the towels he washed up with unless he wanted to keep them from being found. But towels can hold things—a hair, a bloodstain—and he knew he might be a suspect because he knew something linked him to Kim."

"We don't know for sure the towels were dirty, Matt. We don't know he took a shower."

"He chopped her up and put blood all over the walls. You think he got out of there without washing up?"

"I guess not."

"Would you take wet towels home for a souvenir? He had a reason."

"Okay." A pause. "A psycho might not want to leave evidence. You're saying he's someone who knew her, who had a reason to kill her. You can't be sure of that."

"Why did he have her come to the hotel?"

"Because that's where he was waiting. Him and his little machete."

"Why didn't he take his little machete to her place on Thirty-seventh Street?"

"Instead of having her make house calls?"

"Right. I spent the day talking to hookers. They aren't nuts about outcalls because of the travel time. They'll do them, but they usually invite the caller to come to their place instead, tell him how much more comfortable it is. She probably would have done that but he wasn't having any."

"Well, he already paid for the room. Wanted to get his money's worth."

"Why wouldn't he just as soon go to her place?"

He thought about it. "She had a doorman," he said. "Maybe he didn't want to walk past the doorman."

"Instead he had to walk through a whole hotel lobby and sign a registration card and speak to a desk clerk. Maybe he didn't want to pass that doorman because the doorman had seen him before. Otherwise a doorman's a lot less of a challenge than an entire hotel."

"That's pretty iffy, Matt."

"I can't help it. Somebody did a whole batch of things that don't make sense unless he knew the girl and had a personal reason for wanting her dead. He may be emotionally disturbed. Perfectly levelheaded people don't generally go batshit with a machete. But he's more than a psycho picking women at random."

"How do you figure it? A boyfriend?"

"Something like that."

"She splits with the pimp, tells the boyfriend she's free, and he panics?"

"I was thinking along those lines, yes."

"And goes crazy with a machete? How does that mesh with your profile of a guy who decides he'd rather stay home with his wife?"

"I don't know."

"Do you know for sure she had a boyfriend?"

"No," I admitted.

"These registration cards. Charles O. Jones and all his aliases, if he ever had any. You think they're gonna lead anywhere?"

"They could."

"That's not what I asked you, Matt."

"Then the answer's no. I don't think they're going to lead to anything."

"But you still think it's worth doing."

"I'd have gone through the cards myself at the Galaxy Downtowner," I reminded him. "On my own time, if the guy would have let me."

"I suppose we could run the cards."

"Thanks, Joe."

"I suppose we can run the other check, too. First-class commercial hotels in the area, their Jones registrations for the past six months or whatever. That what you wanted?"

"That's right."

"The autopsy showed semen in her throat and esophagus. You happen to notice that?"

"I saw it in the file last night."

"First he had her blow him, then he chopped her up with his boy scout hatchet. And you figure it was a boyfriend."

"The semen could have been from an earlier contact. She was a hooker, she had a lot of contacts."

"I suppose," he said. "You know, they can type semen now. It's not like a fingerprint, more like a blood type. Makes useful circumstantial evidence. But you're right, with her lifestyle it doesn't rule a guy out if the semen type's not a match."

"And it doesn't rule him in if it is."

"No, but it'd fucking well give him a headache. I wish she'd scratched him, got some skin under her nails. That always helps."

"You can't have everything."

"For sure. If she blew him, you'd think she could have wound up with a hair or two between her teeth. Whole trouble is she's too ladylike."

"That's the trouble, all right."

"And my trouble is I'm starting to believe there's a case here, with a killer at the end of a rainbow. I got a desk full of shit I haven't got time for and you've got me pulling my chain with this one."

"Think how good you'll look if it breaks."

"I get the glory, huh?"

"Somebody might as well."

I had three more hookers to call, Sunny and Ruby and Mary Lou. Their numbers were in my notebook. But I'd talked to enough whores for one day. I called Chance's service, left word for him to call me. It was Friday night. Maybe he was at the Garden, watching a couple of boys hit each other. Or did he just go when Kid Bascomb was fighting?

I took out Donna Campion's poem and read it. In my mind's eye all the poem's colors were overlaid with blood, bright arterial blood that faded from scarlet to rust. I reminded myself that Kim had been alive when the poem was written. Why, then, did I sense a note of doom in Donna's lines? Had she picked up on something? Or was I seeing things that weren't really there?

She'd left out the gold of Kim's hair. Unless the sun was supposed to cover that base. I saw those gold braids wrapped around her head and thought of Jan Keane's Medusa. Without giving it too much thought I picked up the phone and placed a call. I hadn't dialed the number in a long time but memory supplied it, pushing it at me as a magician forces a card on one.

It rang four times. I was going to hang up when I heard her voice, low pitched, out of breath.

I said, "Jan, it's Matt Scuddder."

"Matt! I was just thinking of you not an hour ago. Give me a minute, I just walked in the door, let me get my coat off . . . There. How've you been? It's so good to hear from you."

"I've been all right. And you?"

"Oh, things are going well. A day at a time."

The little catchphrases. "Still going to those meetings?"

"Uh-huh. I just came from one, as a matter of fact. How are you doing?"

"Not so bad."

"That's good."

What was it, Friday? Wednesday, Thursday, Friday. "I've got three days," I said.

"Matt, that's wonderful!"

What was so wonderful about it? "I suppose," I said.

"Have you been going to meetings?"

"Sort of. I'm not sure I'm ready for all that."

We talked a little. She said maybe we'd run into each other at a meeting one of these days. I allowed that it was possible. She'd been sober almost six months, she'd qualified a couple of times already. I said it would be interesting sometime to hear her story. She said, "Hear it? God, you're *in* it."

She was just getting back to sculpture. She'd put it all on hold when she got sober, and it was hard to make the clay do what she wanted it to do. But she was working at it, trying to keep it all in perspective, putting her sobriety first and letting the rest of her life fall into shape at its own pace.

And what about me? Well, I said, I had a case, I was looking into a matter for an acquaintance. I didn't go into detail and she didn't press. The conversation slowed, and there were a few pauses in it, and I said, "Well, I just thought I'd call and say hello."

"I'm glad you did, Matthew."

"Maybe we'll run into each other one of these days."

"I'd like that."

I hung up and remembered drinking in her loft on Lispenard Street, warming and mellowing as the booze worked its magic in our veins. What a fine sweet evening that had been.

At meetings you'll hear people say, "My worst day sober is better than my best day drunk." And everybody nods like a plastic dog on a Puerto Rican's dashboard. I thought about that night with Jan and looked around my little cell of a room and tried to figure out why this night was better than the other had been.

I looked at my watch. The liquor stores were closed. The bars, though, would be open for hours yet.

I stayed where I was. Outside, a squad car went by with its siren open. The sound died down, the minutes slipped by, and my phone rang.

It was Chance. "You been working," he said with approval. "I've been getting reports. The girls cooperate okay?"

"They've been fine."

"You getting anywhere?"

"It's hard to tell. You pick up a piece here and a piece there and you never know if they're going to fit together. What did you take from Kim's apartment?"

"Just some money. Why?"

"How much?"

"Couple hundred. She kept cash in the top dresser drawer. It was no secret hiding place, just where she kept it. I looked around some to see if she had any holdout money stashed anywhere, but I couldn't find any. Didn't turn up any bankbooks, safe-deposit keys. Did you?"

"No."

"Or any money? S'pose it's finders keepers if you did, but I'm just asking."

"No money. That's all you took?"

"And a picture a nightclub photographer took of her and me. Couldn't see any rightful reason to leave that for the police. Why?"

"I just wondered. You went there before the police picked you up?"

"They didn't pick me up. I walked in voluntarily. And yes, I went there first, and it was before they got there, far as that goes. Or the couple hundred would have been gone."

Maybe, maybe not. I said, "Did you take the cat?"

"The cat?"

"She had a little black kitten."

"Right, she did. I never thought about the kitten. No, I didn't take it. I would have put out food for it if I thought. Why? Is it gone?"

I said it was, and its litter box too. I asked if the kitten had been around when he went to the apartment but he didn't know. He hadn't noticed a kitten, but then he hadn't been looking for one.

"And I was moving quickly, you know. I was in and out in five minutes. Kitten could have brushed against my ankles and I might not have paid it any mind. What's it matter? Kitten didn't kill her."

"No."

"You don't think she took the kitten to the hotel, do you?"

"Why would she do that?"

"*I* don't know, man. I don't know why we're *talking* about the kitten."

"Somebody must have taken it. Somebody besides you must have gone to her apartment after she died and took the kitten out of there."

"You sure the kitten wasn't there today? Animals get scared when a stranger comes around. They hide."

"The kitten wasn't there."

"Could have walked out when the cops came. Doors open, kitten runs out, goodbye kitty."

"I never heard of a cat taking its litter pan along."

"Maybe some neighbor took it. Heard it meowing, like they do, and didn't want it to go hungry."

"Some neighbor with a key?"

"Some people exchange keys with a neighbor. In case they get locked out. Or the neighbor could have got the key from the doorman."

"That's probably what happened."

"Must be."

"I'll check with the neighbors tomorrow."

He whistled softly. "You chase down everything, don't

you? Little thing like a kitten, you're at it like a dog at a bone."

"That's the way it's done. Goyakod."

"How's that?"

"Goyakod," I said, and spelled it out. "It stands for Get Off Your Ass and Knock On Doors."

"Oh, I like that. Say it again?"

I said it again.

" 'Get off your ass and knock on doors.' I like that."

Chapter 18

Saturday was a good day for knocking on doors. It usually is because more people are at home than during the week. This Saturday the weather didn't invite them out. A fine rain was falling out of a dark sky and there was a stiff wind blowing, whipping the rain around.

Wind sometimes behaves curiously in New York. The tall buildings seem to break it up and put a spin on it, like English on a billiard ball, so that it takes odd bounces and blows in different directions on different blocks. That morning and afternoon it seemed to be always in my face. I would turn a corner and it would turn with me, always coming at me, always driving the spray of rain at me. There were moments when I found it invigorating, others when I hunched my shoulders and lowered my head and cursed the wind and the rain and myself for being out in them.

My first stop was Kim's building, where I nodded and walked past the doorman, key in hand. I hadn't seen him before and I doubt that I was any more familiar to him than he was to me, but he didn't challenge my right to be there. I rode upstairs and let myself into Kim's apartment.

Maybe I was making sure the cat was still missing. I had

no other reason to go in. The apartment was as I had left it, as far as I could tell, and I couldn't find a kitten or a litter pan anywhere. While I thought of it I checked the kitchen. There were no cans or boxes of cat food in the cupboards, no bag of kitty litter, no nonspill bowl for a cat to eat out of. I couldn't detect any cat odor in the apartment, and I was beginning to wonder if my memory of the animal might have been a false one. Then, in the refrigerator, I found a half-full can of Puss 'n Boots topped with a plastic lid.

How about that, I thought. The great detective found a clue.

Not long after that the great detective found a cat. I walked up and down the hallway and knocked on doors. Not everyone was home, rainy Saturday or no, and the first three people who were had no idea that Kim had ever owned a cat, let alone any information on its present whereabouts.

The fourth door that opened to my knock belonged to an Alice Simkins, a small woman in her fifties whose conversation was guarded until I mentioned Kim's cat.

"Oh, Panther," she said. "You've come for Panther. You know, I was afraid someone would. Come in, won't you?"

She led me to an upholstered chair, brought me a cup of coffee, and apologized for the excess of furniture in the room. She was a widow, she told me, and had moved to this small apartment from a suburban house, and while she'd rid herself of a great many things she'd made the mistake of keeping too much furniture.

"It's like an obstacle course in here," she said, "and it's not as if I just moved in yesterday. I've been here almost two years. But because there's no real urgency I seem to find it all too easy to put it off and put it off."

She had heard about Kim's death from someone in the building. The following morning she was at her desk at the office when she thought of Kim's cat. Who would feed it? Who would take care of it?

"I made myself wait until lunch hour," she said, "because I decided I just wasn't crazy enough to run out of the office lest a kitten go an extra hour without food. I fed the kitten and cleaned out the litter pan and freshened its water, and I checked on it that evening when I came home from the office, and it was evident that no one had been in to care for it. I thought about the poor little thing that night, and the next morning when I went to feed it I decided it might as well live with me for the time being." She smiled. "It seems to have adjusted. Do you suppose it misses her?"

"I don't know."

"I don't suppose it'll miss me, either, but I'll miss it. I never kept a cat before. We had dogs years ago. I don't think I'd want to keep a dog, not in the city, but a cat doesn't seem to be any trouble. Panther was declawed so there's no problem of furniture scratching, although I almost wish he'd scratched some of this furniture, it might move me to get rid of it." She laughed softly. "I'm afraid I took all his food from her apartment. I can get all of that together for you. And Panther's hiding somewhere, but I'm sure I can find him."

I assured her I hadn't come for the cat, that she could keep the animal if she wanted. She was surprised, and obviously relieved. But if I hadn't come for the cat, what was I there for? I gave her an abbreviated explanation of my role. While she was digesting that I asked her how she'd gained access to Kim's apartment.

"Oh, I had a key. I'd given her a key to my apartment some months ago. I was going out of town and wanted her to water my plants, and shortly after I came back she gave me her key. I can't remember why. Did she want me to feed Panther? I really can't remember. Do you suppose I can change his name?"

"I beg your pardon?"

"It's just that I don't much care for the cat's name, but I don't know if it's proper to change it. I don't believe he recognizes it. What he recognizes is the whirr of the electric can opener, announcing that dinner is served." She smiled. "T. S. Eliot wrote that every cat has a secret name, known only to the cat himself. So I don't suppose it really matters what name *I* call him."

I turned the conversation to Kim, asked how close a friend she'd been.

"I don't know if we were friends," she said. "We were neighbors. We were good neighbors, I kept a key to her apartment, but I'm not sure we were friends."

"You knew she was a prostitute?"

"I suppose I knew. At first I thought she was a model. She had the looks for it."

"Yes."

"But somewhere in the course of things I gathered what her actual profession was. She never mentioned it. I think it may have been her failure to discuss her work that made me guess what it was. And then there was that black man who visited her frequently. Somehow I found myself assuming he was her pimp."

"Did she have a boyfriend, Mrs. Simkins?"

"Besides the black man?" She thought about it, and while she did so a black streak darted across the rug, leaped onto a couch, leaped again and was gone. "You see?" the woman said. "He's not at all like a panther. I don't know what he is like, but he's nothing like a panther. You asked if she had a boyfriend."

"Yes."

"I just wonder. She must have had some sort of secret plan because she hinted at it the last time we talked—that she'd be moving away, that her life was going to take a turn for the better. I'm afraid I wrote it off as a pipe dream."

"Why?"

"Because I assumed she meant she and her pimp were go-ing to run off into the sunset and live happily ever after, only she wouldn't say as much to me because she'd never come out and told me that she *had* a pimp, that she was a prostitute. I understand pimps will assure a girl that their other girls are unimportant, that as soon as enough money's saved they'll go off and buy a sheep station in Australia or something equally realistic."

I thought of Fran Schecter on Morton Street, convinced she and Chance were bound by karmic ties, with innumerable lifetimes ahead of them.

"She was planning on leaving her pimp," I said.

"For another man?"

"That's what I'm trying to find out."

She'd never seen Kim with anyone in particular, never paid much attention to the men who visited Kim's apartment. Such visitors were few at night, anyway, she explained, and she herself was at work during the day.

"I thought she'd bought the fur herself," she said. "She was so proud of it, as if someone had bought it for her, but I thought she wanted to conceal her shame at having had to buy it for herself. I'll bet she did have a boyfriend. She showed it off with that air, as if it had been a gift from a man, but she didn't come out and say so."

"Because the relationship was a secret."

"Yes. She was proud of the fur, proud of the jewelry. You said she was leaving her pimp. Is that why she was killed?"

"I don't know."

"I try not to think about her having been killed, or how or why it happened. Did you ever read a book called *Watership Down?*" I hadn't. "There's one colony of rabbits in the book, a sort of semidomesticated colony. The food's in good supply there because human beings leave food for the rabbits. It's sort of rabbit heaven, except that the men who do this do so in order to set snares and provide themselves with a rabbit dinner from time to time. And the surviving rabbits, they never refer to the snare, they never mention any of their fellows who've been killed that way. They have an unspoken agreement to pretend that the snare does not exist, and that their dead companions never existed." She'd been looking to one side as she spoke. Now her eyes found mine. "Do you know, I think New Yorkers are like those rabbits. We live here for whatever it is that the city provides—the culture, the job opportunities, whatever it is. And we look the other way when the city kills off our friends and neighbors. Oh, we read about it and we talk about it for a day or two days but then we blink it all away. Because otherwise we'd have to do something about it, and we can't. Or we'd have to move, and we don't want to move. We're like those rabbits, aren't we?"

I left my number, told her to call if she thought of anything. She said she would. I took the elevator to the lobby, but when it got there I stayed in the car and rode it back to twelve again. Just because I'd located the black kitten didn't mean I'd be wasting my time knocking on a few more doors.

Except that's what I did. I talked to half a dozen people and didn't learn a thing, other than that they and Kim did a good job of keeping to themselves. One man had even managed to miss out on the knowledge that a neighbor of his had been murdered. The others knew that much, but not a great deal more.

When I'd run out of doors to knock on I found myself approaching Kim's door, key in hand. Why? Because of the fifth of Wild Turkey in the front closet?

I put her key in my pocket and got out of there.

THE meeting book led me to a noon meeting just a few blocks from Kim's. The speaker was just finishing her qualification when I walked in. At first glance I thought she was Jan, but when I took another look I saw there was no real resemblance. I got a cup of coffee and took a seat at the back.

The room was crowded, thick with smoke. The discussion

seemed to center itself on the spiritual side of the program, and I wasn't too clear on what that was, nor did anything I hear clarify it for me.

One guy said something good, though, a big fellow with a voice like a load of gravel. "I came in here to save my ass," he said, "and then I found out it was attached to my soul."

IF Saturday was a good day for knocking on doors, it was equally good for visiting hookers. While a Saturday-afternoon trick may not be unheard of, it's the exception.

I ate some lunch, then rode uptown on the Lexington IRT. The car was uncrowded, and directly opposite me a black kid in a pea jacket and heavy-soled boots was smoking a cigarette. I remembered my conversation with Durkin and wanted to tell the kid to put out the cigarette.

Jesus, I thought, mind your own business. Leave it alone.

I got off at Sixty-eighth Street and walked a block north and two blocks east. Ruby Lee and Mary Lou Barcker lived in apartment buildings diagonally opposite one another. Ruby's was on the southwest corner and I went there first because I came to it first. The doorman announced me over the intercom and I shared the elevator with a florist's delivery boy. He had his arms full of roses and the car was heavy with their scent.

Ruby opened the door to my knock, smiled coolly, led me inside. The apartment was sparsely if tastefully furnished. The furniture was contemporary and neutral, but there were other items to give the place an oriental cast—a Chinese rug, a group of Japanese prints in black lacquered frames, a bamboo screen. They weren't enough to render the apartment exotic, but Ruby managed that all by herself.

She was tall, though not so tall as Kim, and her figure was lithe and willowy. She showed it off in a black sheath dress with a skirt slit to show a flash of thigh when she walked. She put me in a chair and offered me a drink, and I heard myself ask for tea. She smiled and came back with tea for both of us. It was Lipton's, I noted. God knows what I expected.

Her father was half French and half Senegalese, her mother Chinese. She'd been born in Hong Kong, lived for a time in Macao, then came to America via Paris and London. She didn't tell me her age and I didn't ask, nor could I have possibly guessed it. She might have been twenty or forty-five or almost anything in between.

She had met Kim once. She didn't really know anything about her, didn't know much about any of the girls. She herself had been with Chance for a time and found their arrangement comfortable.

She didn't know if Kim had had a boyfriend. Why, she wondered, would a woman want two men in her life? Then she would have to give money to both of them.

I suggested that Kim might have had a different sort of relationship with her boyfriend, that he might have given her gifts. She seemed to find the idea baffling. Did I mean a customer? I said that was possible. But a customer was not a boyfriend, she said. A customer was just another man in a long line of men. How could one feel anything for a customer?

ACROSS the street, Mary Lou Barcker poured me a Coke and set out a plate of cheese and crackers. "So you met the Dragon Lady," she said. "Striking, isn't she?"

"That's putting it mildly."

"Three races blended into one absolutely stunning woman. Then the shock comes. You open the door and nobody's home. Come here a minute."

I joined her at the window, looked where she was pointing.

"That's her window," she said. "You can see her apartment from mine. You'd think we'd be great friends, wouldn't you? Dropping in at odd hours to borrow a cup of sugar or complain about premenstrual tension. Figures, doesn't it?"

"And it hasn't worked out that way?"

"She's always polite. But she's just not there. The woman doesn't relate. I've known a lot of johns who've gone over there. I've steered some business her way, as far as that goes. A guy'll say he's had fantasies about oriental girls, for example. Or I might just tell a guy that I know a girl he might like. You know something? It's the safest thing in the world. They're grateful because she *is* beautiful, she *is* exotic, and I gather she knows her way around a mattress, but they almost never go back. They go once and they're glad they went, but they don't go back. They'll pass her number on to their buddies instead of ringing it again themselves. I'm sure she keeps busy but I'll bet she doesn't know what a steady trick is, I'll bet she's never had one."

She was a slender woman, dark haired, a little taller than average, with precise features and small even teeth. She had her hair pulled back and done in a chignon, I think they call it, and she was wearing aviator glasses, the lenses tinted a pale amber. The hair and the glasses combined to give her a rather severe look, an effect of which she was by no means unaware. "When I take off the glasses and let my hair down," she said at one point, "I look a whole lot softer, a good deal less threatening. Of course some johns want a woman to look threatening."

Of Kim she said, "I didn't know her well. I don't know any of them really well. What a crew they are! Sunny's the good-time party girl, she thinks she's made a huge leap in status by becoming a prostitute. Ruby's a sort of autistic adult, untouched by human minds. I'm sure she's socking away the dollars, and one of these days she'll go back to Macao or Port Said and open up an opium den. Chance probably knows she's holding out and has the good sense to let her."

She put a slice of cheese on a biscuit, handed it to me, took some for herself, sipped her red wine. "Fran's a charming kook out of *Wonderful Town*. I call her the Village Idiot. She's raised self-deception to the level of an art form. She must have to smoke a ton of grass to support the structure of illusion she's created. More Coke?"

"No thanks."

"You sure you wouldn't rather have a glass of wine? Or something stronger?"

I shook my head. A radio played unobstrusively in the background, tuned to one of the classical music stations. Mary Lou took off her glasses, breathed on them, wiped them with a napkin.

"And Donna," she said. "Whoredom's answer to Edna St. Vincent Millay. I think the poetry does for her what the grass does for Fran. She's a good poet, you know."

I had Donna's poem with me and showed it to Mary Lou. Vertical frown lines appeared in her forehead as she scanned the lines.

"It's not finished," I said. "She still has work to do on it."

"I don't know how poets know when they're finished. Or painters. How do they know when to stop? It baffles me. This is supposed to be about Kim?"

"Yes."

"I don't know what it means, but there's something, she's onto something here." She thought for a moment, her head cocked like a bird's. She said, "I guess I thought of Kim as the archetypical whore. A spectacular ice blonde from the northern Midwest, the kind that was just plain born to walk through life on a black pimp's arm. I'll tell you something. I wasn't surprised when she was murdered."

"Why not?"

"I'm not entirely sure. I was shocked but not surprised. I guess I expected her to come to a bad end. An abrupt end. Not necessarily as a murder victim, but as some sort of victim of the life. Suicide, for instance. Or one of those unholy combinations of pills and liquor. Not that she drank much, or took drugs as far as I know. I suppose I expected suicide, but murder would do as well, wouldn't it? To get her out of the life. Because I couldn't see her going on with it forever. Once that corn-fed innocence left her she wouldn't be able to handle it. And I couldn't see her finding her way out, either."

"She *was* getting out. She told Chance she wanted out."

"Do you know that for a fact?"

"Yes."

"And what did he do?"

"He told her it was her decision to make."

"Just like that?"

"Evidently."

"And then she got killed. Is there a connection?"

"I think there has to be. I think she had a boyfriend and I think the boyfriend's the connection. I think he's why she wanted to get away from Chance and I think he's also the reason she was killed."

"But you don't know who he was."

"No."

"Does anybody have a clue?"

"Not so far."

"Well, I'm not going to be able to change that. I can't remember the last time I saw her, but I don't remember her eyes being agleam with true love. It would fit, though. A man got her into this. She'd probably need another man to get her out."

And then she was telling me how she'd gotten into it. I hadn't thought to ask but I got to hear it anyway.

Someone had pointed Chance out to her at an opening in SoHo, one of the West Broadway galleries. He was with Donna, and whoever pointed him out told Mary Lou he was a pimp. Fortified by an extra glass or two of the cheap wine they were pouring, she approached him, introduced herself, told him she'd like to write a story about him.

She wasn't exactly a writer. At the time she'd been living in the West Nineties with a man who did something incomprehensible on Wall Street. The man was divorced and still half in love with his ex-wife, and his bratty kids came over every weekend, and it wasn't working out. Mary Lou did free-lance copyediting and had a part-time proofreading job, and she'd published a couple of articles in a feminist monthly newspaper.

Chance met with her, took her out to dinner, and turned the interview inside out. She realized over cocktails that she wanted to go to bed with him, and that the urge stemmed more from curiosity than sexual desire. Before dinner was over he was suggesting that she forget about some surface article and write something real, a genuine inside view of a prostitute's life. She was obviously fascinated, he told her. Why not use that fascination, why not go with it, why not buy the whole package for a couple of months and see where she went with it?

She made a joke out of the suggestion. He took her home after dinner, didn't make a pass, and managed to remain oblivious to her sexual invitation. For the next week she couldn't get his proposal out of her mind. Everything about her own life seemed unsatisfactory. Her relationship was exhausted, and she sometimes felt she only stayed with her lover out of reluctance to hunt an apartment of her own. Her career was dead-ended and unsatisfying, and the money she earned wasn't enough to live on.

"And the book," she said, "the book was suddenly everything. De Maupassant obtained human flesh from a morgue and ate it so that he could describe its taste accurately. Couldn't I spend a month as a call girl in order to write the best book ever written on the subject?"

Once she accepted Chance's offer, everything was taken

care of. Chance moved her out of her place on West Ninety-fourth and installed her where she was now. He took her out, showed her off, took her to bed. In bed he told her precisely what to do, and she found this curiously exhilarating. Other men in her experience had always been reticent that way, expecting you to read their minds. Even johns, she said, had trouble telling you what they wanted.

For the first few months she still thought she was doing research for a book. She took notes every time a john left, writing down her impressions. She kept a diary. She detached herself from what she was doing and from who she was, using her journalistic objectivity as Donna used poetry and as Fran used marijuana.

When it dawned on her that whoring was an end in itself she went through an emotional crisis. She had never considered suicide before, but for a week she hovered on its brink. Then she worked it out. The fact that she was whoring didn't mean she had to label herself a whore. This was something she was doing for a while. The book, just an excuse to get into the life, might someday turn out to be something she really wanted to do. It didn't really matter. Her individual days were pleasant enough, and the only thing that was unsettling was when she pictured herself living this way forever. But that wouldn't happen. When the time was right, she would drift out of the life as effortlessly as she had drifted in.

"So that's how I keep my particular cool, Matt. I'm not a hooker. I'm just 'into hooking.' You know, there are worse ways to spend a couple of years."

"I'm sure there are."

"Plenty of time, plenty of creature comforts. I read a lot, I get to movies and museums and Chance likes to take me to concerts. You know the bit about the blind men and the elephant? One grabs the tail and thinks the elephant is like a snake, another touches the side of the elephant and thinks it's like a wall?"

"So?"

"I think Chance is the elephant and his girls are the blind men. We each see a different person."

"And you all have some African sculpture on the premises."

Hers was a statue about thirty inches high, a little man holding a bundle of sticks in one hand. His face and hands were rendered in blue and red beadwork, while all the rest of him was covered with small seashells.

"My household god," she said. "That's a Batum ancestor figure from Cameroun. Those are cowry shells. Primitive societies all over the world use the cowry shell as a medium of exchange, it's the Swiss franc of the tribal world. You see how it's shaped?"

I went and had a look.

"Like the female genitalia," she said. "So men automatically use it to buy and sell. Can I get you some more of that cheese?"

"No thanks."

"Another Coke?"

"No."

"Well," she said, "if there's anything you'd like, just let me know what it is."

Chapter 19

Just as I was leaving her building, a cab pulled up in front to discharge a passenger. I got in and gave the address of my hotel.

The windshield wiper on the driver's side didn't work. The driver was white; the picture on the posted license showed a black man. A sign cautioned, NO SMOKING/DRIVER ALLERGIC. The cab's interior reeked of marijuana.

"Can't see a fucking thing," the driver said.

I sat back and enjoyed the ride.

I called Chance from the lobby, went up to my room. About fifteen minutes later he got back to me. "Goyakod," he said. "I'll tell you, I like that word. Knock on many doors today?"

"A few."

"And?"

"She had a boyfriend. He bought her presents and she showed them off."

"To who? To my girls?"

"No, and that's what makes me sure it was something she wanted to keep secret. It was one of her neighbors who mentioned the gifts."

"Neighbor turn out to have the kitten?"

"That's right."

"Goyakod. Damn if it don't work. You start with a missing cat and you wind up with a clue. What presents?"

"A fur and some jewelry."

"Fur," he said. "You mean that rabbit coat?"

"She said it was ranch mink."

"Dyed rabbit," he said. "I bought her that coat, took her shopping and paid cash for it. Last winter, that was. The neighbor said it was mink, shit, I'd like to sell the neighbor a couple of minks just like it. Give her a good price on 'em."

"Kim said it was mink."

"Said it to the neighbor?"

"Said it to me." I closed my eyes, pictured her at my table in Armstrong's. "Said she came to town in a denim jacket and now she was wearing ranch mink and she'd trade it for the denim jacket if she could have the years back."

His laughter rang through the phone wire. "Dyed rabbit," he said with certainty. "Worth more than the rag she got off the bus with, maybe, but no king's ransom. And no boyfriend bought it for her 'cause *I* bought it for her."

"Well—"

"Unless I was the boyfriend she was talking about."

"I suppose that's possible."

"You said jewelry. All she had was costume, man. You see the jewelry in her jewelry box? Wasn't nothing valuable there."

"I know."

"Fake pearls, a school ring. The one nice thing she had was somethin' else I got her. Maybe you saw it. The bracelet?"

"Was it ivory, something like that?"

"Elephant tusk ivory, *old* ivory, and the fittings are gold. The hinge and the clasp. Not a lot of gold, but gold's gold, you know?"

"You bought it for her?"

"Got it for a hundred dollar bill. Cost you three hundred in a shop, maybe a little more, if you were to find one that nice."

"It was stolen?"

"Let's just say I didn't get no bill of sale. Fellow who sold it to me, he never said it was stolen. All he said was he'd take a hundred dollars for it. I should have picked that up when I got the photograph. See, I bought it 'cause I liked it, and then I gave it to her because I wasn't about to wear it, see, and I thought it'd look good on her wrist. Which it did. You still think she had a boyfriend?"

"I think so."

"You don't sound so sure no more. Or maybe you just sound tired. You tired?"

"Yes."

"Knockin' on too many doors. Wha'd this boyfriend of hers do besides buy her all these presents that don't exist?"

"He was going to take care of her."

"Well, shit," he said. "That's what *I* did, man. What else did I do for that girl but take care of her?"

I stretched out on the bed and fell asleep with my clothes on. I'd knocked on too many doors and talked to too many people. I was supposed to see Sunny Hendryx, I'd called and told her I would be coming over, but I took a nap instead. I dreamed of blood and a woman screaming, and I woke up bathed in sweat and with a metallic taste in the back of my mouth.

I showered and changed my clothes. I checked Sunny's number in my notebook, dialed it from the lobby. No answer.

I was relieved. I looked at my watch, headed over to St. Paul's.

* * *

THE speaker was a soft-spoken fellow with receding light brown hair and a boyish face. At first I thought he might be a clergyman.

He turned out to be a murderer. He was homosexual, and one night in a blackout he had stabbed his lover thirty or forty times with a kitchen knife. He had, he said quietly, faint memories of the incident, because he'd kept going in and out of blackout, coming to with the knife in his hand, being struck by the horror of it, and then slipping back into the darkness. He'd served seven years at Attica and had been sober three years now on the outside.

It was disturbing, listening to him. I couldn't decide how I felt about him. I didn't know whether to be glad or sorry that he was alive, that he was out of prison.

On the break I got to talking with Jim. Maybe I was reacting to the qualification, maybe I was carrying Kim's death around with me, but I started talking about all the violence, all the crime, all the killings. "It gets to me," I said. "I pick up the paper and I read some damn thing or other and it gets to me."

"You know that vaudeville routine? 'Doctor, it hurts when I do this.' 'So don't do this!' "

"So?"

"So maybe you should stop picking up the paper." I gave him a look. "I'm serious," he said. "Those stories bother me, too. So do the stories about the world situation. If the news was good they wouldn't put it in the paper. But one day it struck me, or maybe I got the idea from somebody else, but it came to me that there was no law saying I had to read that crap."

"Just ignore it."

"Why not?"

"That's the ostrich approach, isn't it? What I don't look at can't hurt me?"

"Maybe, but I see it a little differently. I figure I don't

have to make myself crazy with things I can't do anything about anyway."

"I can't see myself overlooking that sort of thing."

"Why not?"

I thought of Donna. "Maybe I'm involved with mankind."

"Me too," he said. "I come here, I listen, I talk. I stay sober. That's how I'm involved in mankind."

I got some more coffee and a couple of cookies. During the discussion people kept telling the speaker how much they appreciated his honesty.

I thought, Jesus, I never did anything like that. And my eyes went to the wall. They hang these slogans on the wall, gems of wisdom like Keep It Simple and Easy Does It, and the sign my eyes went to as if magnetized read There But For The Grace Of God.

I thought, no, screw that. I don't turn murderous in blackouts. Don't tell me about the grace of God.

When it was my turn I passed.

"But you never called Kim?"

"Oh, no. I never had her number, even." She thought for a moment. "She had beautiful eyes. I can close my eyes and picture the color of them."

Her own eyes were large, somewhere between brown and green. Her eyelashes were unusually long, and it struck me that they were probably false. She was a short girl of the body type they call a pony in Las Vegas chorus lines. She was wearing faded Levi's with the cuffs turned up and a hot pink sweater that was stretched tight over her full breasts.

She hadn't known that Kim had planned to leave Chance, and she found the information interesting. "Well, I can understand that," she said after some thought. "He didn't really care for her, you know, and you don't want to stay forever with a man who doesn't care for you."

"What makes you say he didn't care for her?"

"You pick these things up. I suppose he was glad to have her around, like she didn't make trouble and she brought in the bread, but he didn't have a feeling for her."

"Does he have a feeling for the others?"

"He has a feeling for me," she said.

"And anybody else?"

"He likes Sunny. Everybody likes Sunny, she's fun to be with. I don't know if he *cares* for her. Or Donna, I'm sure he doesn't care for Donna, but I don't think she cares for him either. I think that's strictly business on both sides. Donna, I don't think Donna cares for anybody. I don't think she knows there are people in the world."

"How about Ruby?"

"Have you met her?" I hadn't. "Well, she's like, you know, exotic. So he'd like that. And Mary Lou's very intelligent and they go to concerts and shit, like Lincoln Center, classical music, but that doesn't mean he has a feeling for her."

She started to giggle. I asked her what was so funny. "Oh,

Chapter 20

Danny Boy held his glass of Russian vodka aloft so that he could look at the light shine through it. "Purity. Clarity. Precision," he said, rolling the words, pronouncing them with elaborate care, "The best vodka is a razor, Matthew. A sharp scalpel in the hand of a skilled surgeon. It leaves no ragged edges."

He tipped back the glass and swallowed an ounce or so of purity and clarity. We were at Poogan's and he was wearing a navy suit with a red stripe that barely showed in the bar's halflight. I was drinking club soda with lime. At another stop along the way a freckled-faced waitress had informed me that my drink was called a Lime Rickey. I had a feeling I'd never ask for it by that name.

Danny Boy said, "Just to recapitulate. Her name was Kim Dakkinen. She was a big blonde, early twenties, lived in Murray Hill, got killed two weeks ago in the Galaxy Downtowner."

"Not quite two weeks ago."

"Right. She was one of Chance's girls. And she had a boyfriend, and that's what you want. The boyfriend."

"That's right."

"And you're paying for whoever can give you the skinny on this. How much?"

I shrugged. "A couple of dollars."

"Like a bill? Like a half a K? How many dollars?"

I shrugged again. "I don't know, Danny. It depends on the information and where it comes from and where it goes. I haven't got a million dollars to play with but I'm not strapped either."

"You said she was one of Chance's girls."

"Right."

"You were looking for Chance a little over two weeks ago, Matthew. And then you took me to the boxing matches just so I could point him out to you."

"That's right."

"And a couple of days after that, your big blonde had her picture in the papers. You were looking for her pimp, and now she's dead, and here you are looking for her boyfriend."

"So?"

He drank the rest of his vodka. "Chance know what you're doing?"

"He knows."

"You talk to him about it?"

"I've talked to him."

"Interesting." He raised his empty glass to the light, squinted through it. Checking it, no doubt, for purity and clarity and precision. He said, "Who's your client?"

"That's confidential."

"Funny how people looking for information are never looking to furnish it. No problem. I can ask around, put the word out in certain quarters. That's what you want?"

"That's what I want."

"Do you know anything about this boyfriend?"

"Like what?"

"Like is he old or young, wise or straight, married or single? Does he walk to school or take his lunch?"

"He may have given her presents."

"That narrows the field."

"I know."

"Well," he said, "all we can do is try."

It was certainly all *I* could do. I'd gone back to the hotel after the meeting and found a message waiting for me. *Call Sunny*, it said, and included the number which I'd called earlier. I rang her from the booth in the lobby and got no answer. Didn't she have a machine? Didn't they all have machines nowadays?

I went to my room but I couldn't stay in it. I wasn't tired, the nap had taken the edge off my tiredness, and all the coffee I'd drunk at the meeting had me restless and edgy. I went through my notebook and reread Donna's poem and it struck me that I was very likely looking for an answer someone else already knew.

That's very often the case in police work. The easiest way to find out something is to ask someone who knows. The hard part is figuring out who that person is, the one with the answer.

Who might Kim have confided in? Not the girls I'd talked to so far. Not her neighbor on Thirty-seventh Street. Who, then?

Sunny? Maybe. But Sunny wasn't answering her phone. I tried her again, placing the call through the hotel switchboard.

No answer. Just as well. I didn't much feel like spending the next hour drinking ginger ale with yet another hooker.

What had they done, Kim and her faceless friend? If they'd spent all their time behind closed doors, rolling together on a mattress and swearing eternal love, never saying a word to anyone else, then I might be up against it. But maybe they'd gone out, maybe he'd shown her off in some circle or other. Maybe he talked to somebody who talked to somebody else, maybe—

I wouldn't learn the answers in my hotel room. The hell, it wasn't such a bad night. The rain had quit sometime during the meeting and the wind had died down some. Time to get off my ass, time to take a few taxis and spend a little money. I didn't seem to be putting it in the bank or stuffing it into poor boxes or shipping it home to Syosset. Might as well spread it around.

AND so I'd been doing that. Poogan's Pub was perhaps the ninth place I'd hit and Danny Boy Bell perhaps the fifteenth person I'd talked to. Some of the places were ones I'd visited while looking for Chance, but others were not. I tried saloons in the Village, gin joints in Murray Hill and Turtle Bay, singles bars on First Avenue. I kept doing this after I left Poogan's, spending frequent small sums on cabs and drink orders, having the same conversation over and over again.

No one knew anything. You live in hope when you run that sort of fool's errand. There's always the chance that you'll deliver your spiel and the person you're talking to will turn and point and say, "That's him, that's her boyfriend, that big guy in the corner over there."

It almost never happens that way. What does happen, if you're lucky, is that the word gets around. There may be eight million people in the goddamned city but it's amazing how they all talk to each other. If I did this right, it wouldn't be long before a fair share of those eight million knew that a dead whore had a boyfriend and a guy named Scudder was looking for him.

Two cabbies in a row refused to go to Harlem. There's a law that says they have to. If an orderly fare requests a destination anywhere in the five boroughs of New York City, the driver has to take him there. I didn't bother citing the relevant statute. It was easier to walk a block and catch a subway.

The station was a local stop, the platform deserted. The attendant sat in the bulletproof token booth, locked in. I wondered if she felt secure in there. New York taxis have thick Plexiglas partitions to protect the drivers, but the cabbies I'd hailed weren't willing to go uptown, partition or no.

Not long ago an attendant had had a heart attack in one of those token booths. The CPR team couldn't get into the locked booth to revive him and so the poor bastard had died in there. Still, I suppose they protect more people than they kill.

Of course they hadn't protected the two women at the Broad Channel stop on the A train. A couple of kids had a grudge against an attendant who'd reported them for turnstile jumping, so they'd filled a fire extinguisher with gasoline, pumped it into the booth, and lit a match. The whole booth exploded, incinerated both women. One more way to die.

That had been in the paper a year ago. Of course there was no law saying I had to read the papers.

I bought tokens. When my train came I rode it uptown. I worked Kelvin Small's and a few other places on Lenox Avenue. I ran into Royal Waldron at a rib joint, had the same conversation with him I'd been having with everybody else. I drank a cop of coffee on 125th Street, walked the rest of the way to St. Nicholas, had a glass of ginger ale at the bar of Club Cameroon.

The statue in Mary Lou's apartment was from Cameroun. An ancestor statue, encrusted with cowry shells.

I found no one at the bar I knew well enough to talk to. I looked at my watch. It was getting late. On Saturday night the bars in New York close an hour early, at three instead of four. I've never understood why. Perhaps so that the heavy hitters can sober up in time for church.

I motioned to the bartender, asked about after-hours joints. He just looked at me, his face impassive. I found myself laying my rap on him, telling him I was looking for information about Kim's boyfriend. I knew I wasn't going to get an answer from him, knew I wouldn't get the time of day from him, but I was getting the message across all the same. He'd hear me and so would the men on either side of me, and they'd all talk to people, and that was how it worked.

"'Fraid I can't help you," he said. "Whatever you lookin' for, you lookin' awful far uptown for it."

I suppose the boy followed me out of the bar. I didn't notice, and I should have. You have to pay attention to that sort of thing.

I was walking along the street, my mind jumping all over the place, from Kim's mysterious boyfriend to the speaker who'd stabbed his lover. By the time I sensed movement alongside of me there was no time left to react. I was just starting to turn when his hand fastened on my shoulder and propelled me into the mouth of the alley.

He came right in after me. He was an inch or so shorter than me but his bushy Afro made up those two inches and more. He was eighteen or twenty or twenty-two, with a drooping moustache and a burn scar on one cheek. He was wearing a flight jacket with zippered pockets and a pair of tight black jeans, and he had a little gun in his hand and it was pointed right at me.

He said, "Motherfucker, fucking motherfucker. Gimme your money, you motherfucker. Gimme it, gimme all of it, gimme it or you dead, you motherfucker."

I thought, Why didn't I get to the bank? Why didn't I leave some of it at my hotel? I thought, Jesus, Mickey could forget getting his teeth straightened, St. Paul's could forget about their ten percent.

And I could forget about tomorrow.

"Motherfucking honky bastard, dirty motherfucker—"

Because he was going to kill me. I reached in my pocket for my wallet and I looked at his eyes and at his finger on the trigger and I knew it. He was working himself up, he was primed, and whatever money I had wasn't going to be enough for him. He'd be scoring big, better than two grand, but I'd be dead whatever money I had.

We were in an alley about five feet wide, just a gap between two brick tenements. Light from a streetlamp spilled into the alley, illuminating the passage for another ten or fifteen yards beyond where we stood. There was rain-soaked litter on the ground, scraps of paper, beer cans, broken bottles.

Fine place to die. Fine *way* to die, not even a very original one. Shot dead by a mugger, crime in the streets, a terse paragraph on a back page.

I drew the wallet out of my pocket. I said, "You can have it, everything I've got, you're welcome to it," knowing it wasn't enough, knowing he'd resolved to shoot me for five dollars or five thousand. I extended the wallet, hand shaking, and I dropped it.

"I'm sorry," I said, "very sorry, I'll get it," and bent to retrieve it, hoping he'd bend forward also, figuring he had to. I bent at the knees and I gathered my feet under me and I thought *Now!* and I straightened up hard and fast, slapping at the gun as I drove my head full force into his chin.

The gun went off, deafening in that enclosed space. I thought I must have been hit but I didn't feel anything. I grabbed and butted him again, then shoved hard and he stumbled back against the wall behind him, eyes glazed, the gun held loose in his hand. I kicked his wrist and the gun went flying.

He came off the wall, his eyes full of murder. I feinted with a left and hit him with my right in the pit of the stomach. He made a retching sound and doubled up, and I grabbed that son of a bitch, one hand gripping the nylon flight jacket, the other tangled up in his mop of hair, and I ran him right into the wall, three quick steps that ended with his face smacking into the bricks. Three, four times I drew him back by the hair and smashed his face into the wall. When I let go of him he dropped like a marionette with the strings cut, sprawling on the floor of the alley.

My heart was pounding as if I'd run at top speed up ten flights of stairs. I couldn't catch my breath. I leaned against the brick wall, panting for breath, waiting for the cops to come.

Nobody came. There had been a noisy scuffle, hell, there had been a gunshot, but nobody came and nobody was going to come. I looked down at the young man who would have killed me if he could. He lay with his mouth open, showing teeth broken off at the gumline. His nose was smashed flat against his face and blood flowed from it in a stream.

I checked, made sure I wasn't shot. Sometimes, I understand, you can take a bullet and not feel it at the time. Shock and adrenaline anesthetize the pain. But he'd missed me. I examined the wall behind where I was standing, found a fresh indentation in the brick where the bullet had dug out a chip before ricocheting. I figured out where I'd been standing and calculated that he hadn't missed me by much.

Now what?

I found my wallet, put it back in my pocket. I rooted around until I located the gun, a .32-caliber revolver with a spent cartridge in one of its chambers and live rounds in the other five. Had he killed anyone else with it? He'd seemed nervous, so maybe I'd been scheduled to be his first. Then again, maybe some people always get nervous before they pull the trigger, just as some actors always feel anxious before they step onstage.

I knelt down and frisked him. He had a switch knife in one pocket, another knife tucked into his sock. No wallet, no ID, but he had a thick roll of bills on his hip. I slipped off the rubber band and gave the roll a fast count. He had over three hundred dollars, the bastard. He hadn't been looking to make the rent money or score a bag of dope.

And what the hell was I going to do with him?

Call the cops? And hand them what? No evidence, no witnesses, and the guy on the ground was the one who'd sustained the damages. There was nothing good enough for a courtroom, not even anything to hold him on. They'd rush him to the hospital, fix him up, even give him his money back. No way to prove it was stolen. No way to prove it wasn't rightfully his.

They wouldn't give him the gun back. But they couldn't hang a weapons charge on him, either, because I couldn't prove he'd been carrying it.

I put his roll of bills in my own pocket, took out the gun that I'd placed there earlier. I turned the gun over and over in my hand, trying to recall the last time I'd handled one. It had been a while.

He lay there, his breath bubbling through the blood in his nose and throat, and I crouched at his side. After a moment or two I stuck the gun into his ruined mouth and let my finger curl around the trigger.

Why not?

Something stopped me, and it wasn't fear of punishment, not in this world or the next. I'm not sure what it was, but after what seemed like a long time I sighed and withdrew the gun from his mouth. There were traces of blood on the barrel, glowing like brass in the soft light of the alley. I wiped the gun on his jacket front, put it back in my pocket.

I thought, Damn you, goddamn you, what am I going to do with you?

I couldn't kill him and I couldn't hand him to the cops. What could I do? Leave him there?

What else?

I stood up. A wave of dizziness came over me and I stumbled, reached out, caught onto the wall for support. After a moment the dizziness passed and I was all right.

I took a deep breath, let it out. I bent down again and grabbed him by the feet, dragged him some yards back into the alley to a ledge about a foot high, the top frame of a barred basement window. I stretched him out across the alley on his back with his feet up on the ledge and his head wedged against the opposite wall.

I stamped full force on one of his knees, but that didn't do it. I had to jump into the air and come down with both feet. His left leg snapped like a matchstick on my first attempt, but it took me four times to break the right one. He remained unconscious throughout, moaning a bit, then crying out when the right leg broke.

I stumbled, fell, landed on one knee, got up again. Another wave of dizziness hit me, this one accompanied by nausea, and I clung to the wall and gave myself up to dry heaves. The dizziness passed, and the nausea, but I still couldn't catch my breath and I was shaking like a leaf. I held my hand out in front of me and watched my fingers tremble. I'd never seen anything like that before. I'd faked the shaking when I took out my wallet and dropped it, but this shaking was perfectly real, and I couldn't control it by force of will. My hands had a will of their own and they wanted to shake.

The shakes were even worse on the inside.

I turned, took a last look at him. I turned again and made my way over the littered pavement to the street. I was still shaking and it wasn't getting any better.

Well, there was a way to stop the shakes, the ones on the outside and the inner ones as well. There was a specific remedy for that specific disease.

Red neon winked at me from the other side of the street. BAR, it said.

Chapter 21

I didn't cross the street. The kid with the smashed face and broken legs was not the only mugger in the neighborhood, and it struck me that I wouldn't want to meet another one with drink in me.

No, I had to get to my home ground. I was only going to have one drink, maybe two, but I couldn't guarantee that was all I would have, nor could I say with assurance what one or two drinks would do to me.

The safe thing would be to get back to my neighborhood, have one or at the most two shots in a bar, then take a couple of beers back to my room.

Except that there was no safe way to drink. Not for me, not anymore. Hadn't I proved that? How many times did I have to go on proving it?

So what was I supposed to do? Shake until I fell apart? I wasn't going to be able to sleep without a drink. I wasn't going to be able to sit still without a drink, for Christ's sake.

Well, fuck it. I had to have one. It was medicinal. Any doctor who looked at me would prescribe it.

Any doctor? How about that intern at Roosevelt? I could feel his hand on my shoulder, right where the mugger had grabbed me to shove me into the alley. *"Look at me. Listen to me. You're an alcoholic. If you drink you'll die."*

I'd die anyway, in one of eight million ways. But if I had the choice, at least I could die closer to home.

I walked over to the curb. A gypsy cab, the only kind that cruises Harlem, slowed as it approached. The driver, a middle-aged Hispanic woman wearing a brimmed cap over kinky red hair, decided I looked all right. I got in the back seat, closed the door, told her to take me to Fifty-eighth and Ninth.

On the way there my mind was all over the place. My hands were still trembling, though not so violently as before, but the internal shakes were as bad as ever. The ride seemed to take forever, and then before I knew it the woman was asking me which corner I wanted. I told her to pull up in front of Armstrong's. When the light changed she nosed the cab across the intersection and stopped where I'd told her. When I made no move she turned around to see what was wrong.

I'd just remembered that I couldn't get a drink at Armstrong's. Of course they might have forgotten by now that Jimmy had eighty-sixed me, but maybe they hadn't, and I felt myself burning with resentment already at the thought of walking in there and being refused service. No, fuck them, I wouldn't walk through their goddamned door.

Where, then? Polly's would be closed, they never ran all the way to closing hour. Farrell's?

That was where I'd had the first drink after Kim's death. I'd had eight sober days before I picked up that drink. I remembered that drink. Early Times, it was.

Funny how I always remember what brand I was drinking. It's all the same crap, but that's the sort of detail that sticks in your mind.

I'd heard someone make that very observation at a meeting a while back.

What did I have now? Four days? I could go up to my room and just make myself stay there and when I woke up I'd be starting my fifth day.

Except that I'd never fall asleep. I wouldn't even stay in the room. I'd try, but I couldn't stay anywhere, not the way I felt right now, not with only my own whirling mind to keep me company. If I didn't drink now I'd drink an hour from now.

"Mister? You okay?"

I blinked at the woman, then dug my wallet out of my pocket and found a twenty. "I want to make a phone call," I said. "From the booth right there on the corner. You take this and wait for me. All right?"

Maybe she'd drive off with the twenty. I didn't really care. I walked to the corner, dropped a dime, stood there listening to the dial tone.

It was too late to call. What time was it? After two, much too late for a social call.

Hell, I could go to my room. All I had to do was stay put for an hour and I'd be in the clear. At three the bars would close.

So? There was a deli that would sell me beer, legally or not. There was an after-hours on Fifty-first, way west between Eleventh and Twelfth. Unless it had closed by now; I hadn't been there in a long time.

There was a bottle of Wild Turkey in Kim Dakkinen's front closet. And I had her key in my pocket.

That scared me. The booze was right there, accessible to me at any hour, and if I went there I'd never stop after one or two drinks. I'd finish the bottle, and when I did there were a lot of other bottles to keep it company.

I made my call.

SHE'D been sleeping. I heard that in her voice when she answered the phone.

I said, "It's Matt. I'm sorry to call you so late."

"That's all right. What time is it? God, it's after two."

"I'm sorry.

"It's all right. Are you okay, Matthew?

"No."

"Have you been drinking?"

"No."

"Then you're okay."

"I'm falling apart," I said. "I called you because it was the only way I could think of to keep from drinking."

"You did the right thing."

"Can I come over?"

There was a pause. Never mind, I thought. Forget it. One quick drink at Farrell's before they closed, then back to the hotel. Never should have called her in the first place.

"Matthew, I don't know if it's a good idea. Just take it an hour at a time, a minute at a time if you have to, and call me as much as you want. I don't mind if you wake me, but—"

I said, "I almost got killed half an hour ago. I beat a kid up and broke his legs for him. I'm shaking like I never shook before in my life. The only thing that's going to make me feel right is a drink and I'm afraid to take one and scared I'll do it anyway. I thought being with someone and talking with someone might get me through it but it probably wouldn't anyway, and I'm sorry, I shouldn't have called. I'm not your responsibility. I'm sorry."

"Wait!"

"I'm here."

"There's a clubhouse on St. Marks Place where they have meetings all night long on the weekends. It's in the book, I can look it up for you."

"Sure."

"You won't go, will you?"

"I can't talk up at meetings. Forget it, Jan. I'll be all right."

"Where are you?"

"Fifty-eighth and Ninth."

"How long will it take you to get here?"

I glanced over at Armstrong's. My gypsy cab was still parked there. "I've got a cab waiting," I said.

"You remember how to get here?"

"I remember."

THE cab dropped me in front of Jan's six-story loft building on Lispenard. The meter had eaten up most of the original twenty dollars. I gave her another twenty to go with it. It was too much but I was feeling grateful, and could afford to be generous.

I rang Jan's bell, two long and three short, and went out in front so that she could toss the key down to me. I rode the industrial elevator to the fifth floor and stepped out into her loft.

"That was quick," she said. "You really did have a cab waiting."

She'd had time to dress. She was wearing old Lee jeans and a flannel shirt with a red-and-black checkerboard pattern. She's an attractive woman, medium height, well fleshed, built more for comfort than for speed. A heart-shaped face, her hair dark brown salted with gray and hanging to her shoulders. Large well-spaced gray eyes. No makeup.

She said, "I made coffee. You don't take anything in it, do you?"

"Just bourbon."

"We're fresh out. Go sit down, I'll get the coffee."

When she came back with it I was standing by her Medusa, tracing a hair-snake with my fingertip. "Her hair reminded me of your girl here," I said. "She had blonde braids but she wrapped them around her head in a way that made me think of your Medusa."

"Who?"

"A woman who got killed. I don't know where to start."

"Anywhere," she said.

I talked for a long time and I skipped all over the place, from the beginning to that night's events and back and forth again. She got up now and then to get us more coffee, and when she came back I'd start in where I left off. Or I'd start somewhere else. It didn't seem to matter.

I said, "I didn't know what the hell to do with him. After I'd knocked him out, after I'd searched him. I couldn't have him arrested and I couldn't stand the thought of letting him go. I was going to shoot him but I couldn't do it. I don't know why. If I'd just smacked his head against the wall a couple more times it might have killed him, and I'll tell you, I'd have been glad of it. But I couldn't shoot him while he was lying there unconscious."

"Of course not."

"But I couldn't leave him there, I didn't want him walking the streets. He'd just get another gun and do it again. So I broke his legs. Eventually the bones'll knit and he'll be able to resume his career, but in the meantime he's off the streets." I shrugged. "It doesn't make any sense. But I couldn't think of anything else to do."

"The important thing is you didn't drink."

"Is that the important thing?"

"I think so."

"I almost drank. If I'd been in my own neighborhood, or if I hadn't reached you. God knows I wanted to drink. I *still* want to drink."

"But you're not going to."

"No."

"Do you have a sponsor, Matthew?"

"No."

"You should. It's a big help."

"How?"

"Well, a sponsor's someone you can call anytime, someone you can tell anything to."

"You have one?"

She nodded. "I called her after I spoke to you."

"Why?"

"Because I was nervous. Because it calms me down to talk to her. Because I wanted to see what she would say."

"What did she say?"

"That I shouldn't have told you to come over." She laughed. "Fortunately, you were already on your way."

"What else did she say?"

The big gray eyes avoided mine. "That I shouldn't sleep with you."

"Why'd she say that?"

"Because it's not a good idea to have relationships during the first year. And because it's a terrible idea to get involved with anybody who's newly sober."

"Christ," I said. "I came over because I was jumping out of my skin, not because I was horny."

"I know that."

"Do you do everything your sponsor says?"

"I try to."

"Who is this woman that she's the voice of God on earth?"

"Just a woman. She's my age, actually she's a year and a half younger. But she's been sober almost six years."

"Long time."

"It seems like a long time to me." She picked up her cup, saw it was empty, put it down again. "Isn't there someone you could ask to be your sponsor?"

"Is that how it works? You have to ask somebody?"

"That's right."

"Suppose I asked you?"

She shook her head. "In the first place, you should get a male sponsor. In the second place, I haven't been sober long enough. In the third place we're friends."

"A sponsor shouldn't be a friend?"

"Not that kind of friend. An AA friend. In the fourth place, it ought to be somebody in your home group so you have frequent contact."

I thought unwillingly of Jim. "There's a guy I talk to sometimes."

"It's important to pick someone you can talk to."

"I don't know if I can talk to him. I suppose I could."

"Do you respect his sobriety?"

"I don't know what that means."

"Well, do you—"

"This evening I told him I got upset by the stories in the newspapers. All the crime in the streets, the things people keep doing to each other. It gets to me, Jan."

"I know it does."

"He told me to quit reading the papers. Why are you laughing?"

"It's just such a program thing to say."

"People talk the damnedest crap. 'I lost my job and my mother's dying of cancer and I'm going to have to have my nose amputated but I didn't drink today so that makes me a winner.' "

"They really sound like that, don't they?"

"Sometimes. What's so funny?"

" 'I'm going to have my nose amputated.' A *nose* amputated?"

"Don't laugh," I said. "It's a serious problem."

A little later she was telling me about a member of her home group whose son had been killed by a hit-and-run driver. The man had gone to a meeting and talked about it, drawing strength from the group, and evidently it had been an inspirational experience all around. He'd stayed sober, and his sobriety had enabled him to deal with the situation and bolster the other members of his family while fully experiencing his own grief.

I wondered what was so wonderful about being able to experience your grief. Then I found myself speculating what would have happened some years ago if I'd stayed sober after an errant bullet of mine ricocheted and fatally wounded a six-year-old girl named Estrellita Rivera. I'd dealt with the resultant feelings by pouring bourbon on them. It had certainly seemed like a good idea at the time.

Maybe it hadn't been. Maybe there were no shortcuts, no detours. Maybe you had to go through things.

I said, "You don't worry about getting hit by a car in New York. But it happens here, the same as anywhere else. Did they ever catch the driver?"

"No."

"He was probably drunk. They usually are."

"Maybe he was in a blackout. Maybe he came to the next day and never knew what he'd done."

"Jesus," I said, and thought of that night's speaker, the man who stabbed his lover. "Eight million stories in the Emerald City. And eight million ways to die."

"The naked city."

"Isn't that what I said?"

"You said the Emerald City."

"I did? Where did I get that from?"

"*The Wizard of Oz.* Remember? Dorothy and Toto in Kansas? Judy Garland going over the rainbow?"

"Of course I remember."

" 'Follow the Yellow Brick Road.' It led to the Emerald City, where the wonderful wizard lived."

"I remember. The Scarecrow, the Tin Man, the Cowardly Lion, I remember the whole thing. But where'd I get emeralds from?"

"You're an alcoholic," she suggested. "You're missing a couple of brain cells, that's all."

I nodded. "Must be it," I said.

THE sky was turning light when we went to sleep. I slept on the couch wrapped up in a couple of spare blankets. At first I thought I wouldn't be able to sleep, but the tiredness came over me like a towering wave. I gave up and let it take me wherever it wanted.

I can't say where it took me because I slept like a dead man. If I dreamed at all I never knew about it. I awoke to the smells of coffee perking and bacon frying, showered, shaved with a disposable razor she'd laid out for me, then got dressed and joined her at a pine plank table in the kitchen. I drank orange juice and coffee and ate scrambled eggs and bacon and whole wheat muffins with peach preserves, and I couldn't remember when my appetite had been so keen.

There was a group that met Sunday afternoons a few blocks to the east of us, she informed me. She made it one of her regular meetings. Did I feel like joining her?

"I ought to do some work," I said.

"On a Sunday?"

"What's the difference?"

"Are you really going to be able to accomplish anything on a Sunday afternoon?"

I hadn't really accomplished anything since I'd started. Was there anything I could do today?

I got out my notebook, dialed Sunny's number. No answer. I called my hotel. Nothing from Sunny. Nothing from Danny Boy Bell or anyone else I'd seen last night. Well, Danny Boy would still be sleeping at this hour, and so might most of the others.

There was a message to call Chance. I started dialing his number, then stopped myself. If Jan was going to a meeting,

I didn't want to sit around her loft waiting for him to call back. Her sponsor might not approve.

The meeting was on the second floor of a synagogue on Forsythe Street. You couldn't smoke there. It was an unusual experience being in an AA meeting that wasn't thick with cigarette smoke.

There were about fifty people there and she seemed to know most of them. She introduced me to several people, all of whose names I promptly forgot. I felt self-conscious, uncomfortable with the attention I was getting. My appearance didn't help, either. While I hadn't slept in my clothes, they looked as though I had, showing the effects of last night's fight in the alley.

And I was feeling the fight's effects, too. It wasn't until we left her loft that I realized how much I ached. My head was sore where I'd butted him and I had a bruise on one forearm and one shoulder was black and blue and ached. Other muscles hurt when I moved. I hadn't felt anything after the incident but all those aches and pains turn up the next day.

I got some coffee and cookies and sat through the meeting. It was all right. The speaker qualified very briefly, leaving the rest of the meeting for discussion. You had to raise your hand to get called on.

Fifteen minutes from the end, Jan raised her hand and said how grateful she was to be sober and how much of a role her sponsor played in her sobriety, how helpful the woman was when she had something bothering her or didn't know what to do. She didn't get more specific than that. I had a feeling she was sending me a message and I wasn't too crazy about that.

I didn't raise my hand.

Afterward she was going out with some people for coffee and asked me if I'd like to come along. I didn't want any more coffee and I didn't want company, either. I made an excuse.

Outside, before we went separate ways, she asked me how I felt. I said I felt all right.

"Do you still feel like drinking?"

"No," I said.

"I'm glad you called last night."

"So am I."

"Call anytime, Matthew. Even in the middle of the night if you have to."

"Let's hope I don't have to."

"But if you do, call. All right?"

"Sure."

"Matthew? Promise me one thing?"

"What?"

"Don't have a drink without calling me first."

"I'm not going to drink today."

"I know. But if you ever decide to, if you're going to, call me first. Promise?"

"Okay."

On the subway heading uptown I thought about the conversation and felt foolish for having made the promise. Well, it had made her happy. What was the harm in it if it made her happy?

THERE was another message from Chance. I called from the lobby, told his service I was back at my hotel. I bought a paper and took it upstairs with me to kill the time it took him to call back.

The lead story was a honey. A family in Queens—father, mother, two kids under five—had gone for a ride in their shiny new Mercedes. Someone pulled up next to them and emptied both barrels of a shotgun into the car, killing all four of them. A police search of their apartment in Jamaica Estates had revealed a large amount of cash and a quantity of uncut cocaine. Police theorized the massacre was drug related.

No kidding.

There was nothing about the kid I'd left in the alley. Well, there wouldn't be. The Sunday papers were already on the street when he and I encountered one another. Not that he'd be much likelier to make tomorrow's paper, or the next day's. If I'd killed him he might have earned a paragraph somewhere, but what was the news of a black youth with a pair of broken legs?

I was pondering that point when someone knocked on my door.

Funny. The maids have Sunday off, and the few visitors I get call from downstairs. I got my coat off the chair, took the .32 from the pocket. I hadn't gotten rid of it yet, or of the two knives I'd taken from my broken-legged friend. I carried the gun over to the door and asked who it was.

"Chance."

I dropped the gun in a pocket, opened the door. "Most people call," I said.

"The fellow down there was reading. I didn't want to disturb him."

"That was considerate."

"That's my trademark." His eyes were taking me in, appraising me. They left me to scan my room. "Nice place," he said.

The words were ironic but the tone of voice was not. I closed the door, pointed to a chair. He remained standing. "It seems to suit me," I said.

"I can see that. Spartan, uncluttered."

He was wearing a navy blazer and gray flannel slacks. No topcoat. Well, it was a little warmer today and he had a car to get around in.

He walked over to my window, looked out of it. "Tried you last night," he said.

"I know."

"You didn't call back."

"I didn't get the message until a little while ago and I wasn't where I could be reached."

"Didn't sleep here last night?"

"No."

He nodded. He had turned to face me and his expression was guarded and hard to read. I hadn't seen that look on his face before.

He said, "You speak to all my girls?"

"All but Sunny."

"Yeah. You didn't see her yet, huh?"

"No. I tried her a few times last night and again around noon today. I didn't get any answer."

"You didn't."

"No. I had a message from her last night, but when I called back she wasn't there."

"She called you last night."

"That's right."

"What time?"

I tried to remember. "I left the hotel around eight and got back a little after ten. The message was waiting for me. I don't know what time it came in. They're supposed to put the time on the message slip but they don't always bother. Anyway, I probably threw away the slip."

"No reason to hang onto it."

"No. What difference does it make when she called?"

He looked at me for a long moment. I saw the gold flecks in the deep brown eyes. He said, "Shit, I don't know what to do. I'm not used to that. Most of the time I at least *think* I know what to do."

I didn't say anything.

"You're my man, like you're working for me. But I don't know as I'm sure what that means."

"I don't know what you're getting at, Chance."

"Shit," he said. "Question is, how much can I trust you? What I keep coming back to is whether I can or not. I *do* trust you. I mean, I took you to my *house*, man. I never took anybody else to my house. Why'd I do that?"

"I don't know."

"I mean, was I showing off? Was I saying something along the lines of, Look at the class this here nigger has got? Or was I inviting you inside for a look at my soul? Either way, shit, I got to believe I trust you. But am I right to do it?"

"I can't decide that for you."

"No," he said, "you can't." He pinched his chin between thumb and forefinger. "I called her last night. Sunny. Couple of times, same as you, didn't get no answer. Well, okay, that's cool. No machine, but that's cool, too, 'cause sometimes she'll forget to put it on. Then I called again, one-thirty, two o'clock maybe, and again no answer, so what I did, I drove over there. Naturally I got a key. It's my apartment. Why shouldn't I have a key?"

By now I knew where this was going. But I let him tell it himself.

"Well, she was there," he said. "She's still there. See, what she is, she's dead."

Chapter 22

She was dead, all right. She lay on her back, nude, one arm flung back over her head and her face turned to that side, the other arm bent at the elbow with the hand resting on her rib cage just below her breast. She was on the floor a few feet from her unmade bed, her auburn hair spread out above and behind her head, and alongside her lipsticked mouth an ellipse of vomit floated on the ivory carpet like scum on a pond. Between her well-muscled white thighs, the carpet was dark with urine.

There were bruises on her face and forehead, another on her shoulder. I touched her wrist automatically, groping for a pulse, but her flesh was far too cold to have any life left in it.

Her eye was open, rolled up into her head. I wanted to coax the eyelid shut with a fingertip. I left it alone.

I said, "You move her?"

"No way. I didn't touch a thing."

"Don't lie to me. You tossed Kim's apartment after she was dead. You must have looked around."

"I opened a couple of drawers. I didn't take anything."

"What were you looking for?"

"I don't know, man. Just anything I ought to know about.

I found some money, couple hundred dollars. I left it there. I found a bankbook. I left it, too."

"What did she have in the bank?"

"Under a thousand. No big deal. What I found, she had a ton of pills. That's how she did this here."

He pointed to a mirrored vanity across the room from the corpse. There, among innumerable jars and bottles of makeup and scent, were two empty plastic vials containing prescription labels. The patient's name on both was S. Hendryx, although the prescriptions had been written by different physicians and filled at different pharmacies, both nearby. One prescription had been for Valium, the other for Seconal.

"I always looked in her medicine chest," he was saying. "Just automatically, you know? And all she ever had was this antihistamine stuff for her hay fever. Then I open this drawer last night and it's a regular drugstore in there. All prescription stuff."

"What kind of stuff?"

"I didn't read every label. Didn't want to leave any prints where they shouldn't be. From what I saw, it's mostly downs. A lot of tranks. Valium, Librium, Elavil. Sleeping pills like the Seconal here. A couple things of ups, like whatchacallit, Ritalin. But mostly downs." He shook his head. "There's things I never heard of. You'd need a doctor to tell you what everything was."

"You didn't know she took pills?"

"Had no idea. Come here, look at this." He opened a dresser drawer carefully so as not to leave prints. "Look," he said, pointing. At one side of the drawer, beside a stack of folded sweaters, stood perhaps two dozen pill bottles.

"That's somebody who's into this shit pretty heavy," he said. "Somebody who's scared to run out. And I didn't know about it. That gets to me, Matt. You read that note?"

The note was on the vanity, anchored with a bottle of Norell cologne. I nudged the bottle aside with the back of my hand and carried the note over to the window. She'd written it in brown ink on beige notepaper and I wanted to read it in decent light.

I read:

> *Kim, you were lucky. You found someone to do it for you, I have to do it myself.*
>
> *If I had the guts I would use the window. I could change my mind halfway down and laugh the rest of the way. But I haven't got the guts and the razor blade didn't work.*
>
> *I hope I took enough this time.*
>
> *It's no use. The good times are all used up. Chance, I'm sorry. You showed me good times but they're gone. The crowds went home in the eighth inning. All the cheering stopped. Nobody's even keeping score anymore.*
>
> *There's no way off the merry-go-round. She grabbed the brass ring and it turned her finger green.*
>
> *Nobody's going to buy me emeralds. Nobody's going to give me babies. Nobody's going to save my life.*
>
> *I'm sick of smiling. I'm tired of trying to catch up and catch on. All the good times are gone.*

I looked out the window across the Hudson at the Jersey skyline. Sunny had lived and died on the thirty-second floor of a high-rise apartment complex called Lincoln View Gardens, though I hadn't seen any trace of garden beyond the potted palms in the lobby.

"That's Lincoln Center down there," Chance said.

I nodded.

"I should have put Mary Lou here. She likes concerts, she could just walk over. Thing is, she used to live on the West Side. So I wanted to move her to the East Side. You want to do that, you know. Make a big change in their lives right away."

I didn't much care about the philosophy of pimping. I said, "She do this before?"

"Kill herself?"

"Try to. She wrote 'I hope I took enough this time.' Was there a time she didn't take enough?"

"Not since I've known her. And that's a couple years."

"What does she mean when she says the razor blade didn't work?"

"I don't know."

I went to her, examined the wrist of the arm stretched out above her head. There was a clearly perceptible horizontal scar. I found an identical scar on her other wrist. I stood up, read the note again.

"What happens now, man?"

I got out my notebook and copied what she'd written word for word. I used a Kleenex to remove what prints I'd left on it, then put it back where I'd found it and anchored it again with the cologne bottle.

I said, "Tell me again what you did last night."

"Just what I already told you. I called her and I got a feeling, I don't know why, and I came here."

"What time?"

"After two. I didn't notice the exact time."

"You came right upstairs?"

"That's right."

"The doorman see you?"

"We sort of nodded at each other. He knows me, thinks I live here."

"Will he remember you?"

"Man, I don't know what he remembers and what he forgets."

"He just work weekends or was he on Friday as well?"

"I don't know. What's the difference?"

"If he's been on every night he might remember he saw you but not remember when. If he just works Saturdays—"

"I get you."

In the small kitchen a bottle of Georgi vodka stood on the sink board with an inch's depth of liquor left in it. Beside it was an empty cardboard quart of orange juice. A glass in the sink held a residue of what looked like a mixture of the two, and there'd been a faint trace of orange in the reek of her vomit. You didn't need to be much of a detective to put those pieces together. Pills, washed down with a batch of strong screwdrivers, their sedative effect boosted by the alcohol.

I hope I took enough this time.

I had to fight the impulse to pour the last of the vodka down the drain.

"How long were you here, Chance?"

"I don't know. Didn't pay attention to the time."

"Talk to the doorman on the way out?"

He shook his head. "I went down to the basement and out through the garage."

"So he wouldn't have seen you."

"Nobody saw me."

"And while you were here—"

"Like I said. I looked in the drawers and closets. I didn't touch many things and I didn't move anything."

"You read the note?"

"Yeah. But I didn't pick it up to do it."

"Make any phone calls?"

"My service, to check in. And I called you. But you weren't there."

No, I hadn't been there. I'd been breaking a boy's legs in an alley three miles to the north.

I said, "No long-distance calls."

"Just those two calls, man. That ain't a long distance. You can just about throw a rock from here to your hotel."

And I could have walked over last night, after my meeting, when her number failed to answer. Would she still have been alive by then? I imagined her, lying on the bed, waiting for the pills and vodka to do their work, letting the phone ring and ring and ring. Would she have ignored the doorbell the same way?

Maybe. Or maybe she'd have been unconscious by then. But I might have sensed that something was wrong, might have summoned the super or kicked the door in, might have gotten to her in time—

Oh, sure. And I could have saved Cleopatra from the fucking asp, too, if I hadn't been born too late.

I said, "You had a key to this place?"

"I have keys to all their places."

"So you just let yourself in."

He shook his head. "She had the chain lock on. That's when I knew something was wrong. I used the key and the door opened two, three inches and stopped on account of the chain, and I knew there was trouble. I busted the chain and came on in and just knew I was gonna find something I didn't want to see."

"You could have gone right out. Left the chain on, gone home."

"I thought of that." He looked full at me and I was seeing his face less armored than I'd seen it before. "You know something? When that chain was on, the thought came to me right away that she killed herself. First thing I thought of, *only* thing I thought of. Reason I broke that chain, I figured maybe she was still alive, maybe I could save her. But it was too late."

I went to the door, examined the chain lock. The chain itself had not broken; rather, the assembly had ripped loose from its moorings on the doorjamb and hung from the door itself. I hadn't noticed it when we let ourselves into the apartment.

"You broke this when you came in?"

"Like I said."

"The chain could have been unfastened when you let yourself in. Then you could have locked it and broken it from inside."

"Why would I do that?"

"To make it look as though the apartment was locked from the inside when you got here."

"Well, it was. I didn't have to. I don't get where you're comin' from, man."

"I'm just making sure she was locked in when you got here."

"Didn't I say she was?"

"And you checked the apartment? There wasn't anybody else here?"

"Not unless they was hiding in the toaster."

It was a pretty clear suicide. The only thing problematic was his earlier visit. He'd sat on the knowledge of her death for over twelve hours without reporting it.

I thought for a moment. We were north of Sixtieth Street, so that put us in the Twentieth Precinct and out of Durkin's bailiwick. They'd close it as a suicide unless the medical evidence didn't match, in which case his earlier visit would come to light later on.

I said, "There's a few ways we could do it. We could say that you couldn't reach her all night and you got worried.

You talked to me this afternoon and we came over here to-gether. You had a key. You opened the door and we found her and called it in."

"All right."

"But the chain lock gets in the way. If you weren't here before, how did it get broken? If somebody else broke it, who was he and what was he doing here?"

"What if we say we broke it getting in?"

I shook my head. "That doesn't work. Suppose they come up with solid evidence that you were here last night. Then I'm caught swearing to a lie. I could lie for you to the extent of treating something you told me as confidential, but I'm not going to get nailed to a lie that cuts across the grain of the facts. No, I have to say the chain lock was broken when we got here."

"So it's been broken for weeks."

"Except the break's fresh. You can see where the screws came out of the wood. The one thing you don't want to do is get caught in that kind of a lie, where your story and the evidence wind up pointing in different directions. I'll tell you what I think you have to do."

"What's that?"

"Tell the truth. You came here, you kicked the door in, she was dead and you split. You drove around, tried to sort things out in your mind. And you wanted to reach me before you did anything, and I was hard to reach. Then you called me and we came here and called it in."

"That's the best way?"

"It looks like it to me."

"All because of that chain thing?"

"That's the most obvious loose end. But even without the chain lock you're better off telling the truth. Look, Chance, you didn't kill her. She killed herself."

"So?"

"If you didn't kill her, the best thing you can do is tell the truth. If you're guilty, the best thing to do is say nothing, not a word. Call a lawyer and keep your mouth shut. But anytime you're innocent, just tell the truth. It's easier, it's simpler, and it saves trying to remember what you said before. Because I'll tell you one thing. Crooks lie all the time and cops know it and they hate it. And once they get hold of a lie they pull on it until something comes loose. You're looking to lie to save yourself a hassle, and it might work, it's an obvious suicide, you might get by with it, but if it doesn't work you're going to get ten times the hassle you're trying to avoid."

He thought about it, then sighed. "They're gonna ask why I didn't call right away."

"Why didn't you?"

" 'Cause I didn't know what to do, man. I didn't know whether to shit or go blind."

"Tell them that."

"Yeah, I guess."

"What did you do after you got out of here?"

"Last night? Like you said, I drove around some. Drove around the park a few times. Drove over the George Washington Bridge, up the Palisades Parkway. Like a Sunday drive, only a little early." He shook his head at the memory. "Came back, drove over to see Mary Lou. Let myself in, didn't have to bust no chain lock. She was sleepin'. I got in bed with her, woke her up, stayed with her a little. Then I went on home."

"To your house?"

"To my house. I'm not gonna tell 'em about my house."

"No need to. You got a little sleep at Mary Lou's."

"I never sleep when someone else is around. I can't. But they don't have to know that."

"No."

"I was at my house for awhile. Then I came on into town, lookin' for you."

"What did you do at your house?"

"Slept some. A couple hours. I don't need a whole lot of sleep, but I got what I needed."

"Uh-huh."

"And I was just there, you know?" He walked over to the wall, took a staring mask from the nail where it hung. He started telling me about it, the tribe, their geographical location, the purpose of the mask. I didn't pay much attention. "Now I got fingerprints on it," he said. "Well, that's okay. You can tell 'em while we were waiting for them I took the mask off the wall and told you its history. I might as well tell the truth. Wouldn't want to get caught in some nasty old little white lie." He smiled at the last phrase. "Little black lie," he said. "Whyn't you make that call?"

Chapter 23

It wasn't half the hassle it might have been. I didn't know either of the cops who came out from the Twentieth, but it couldn't have gone much smoother if I had. We answered questions on the scene and went back to the station house on West Eighty-second to give our statements. The on-scene medical evidence all seemed to be consistent with what we'd reported. The cops were quick to point out that Chance should have called in as soon as he found the dead girl, but they didn't really jump on him for taking his time. Walking in on an unexpected corpse is a shock, even if you're a pimp and she's a whore, and this, after all, was New York, the city of the uninvolved, and what was remarkable was not that he'd called it in late but that he'd called it in at all.

I was at ease by the time we got to the station house. I'd only been anxious early on when it occurred to me that it might occur to them to frisk us. My coat was a small-time arsenal, still holding the gun and the two knives I'd taken from the kid in the alley. The knives were both illegal weapons. The gun was that and possibly more; God only knew what kind of a provenance it had. But we'd done nothing to rate a frisk, and, happily, we didn't get one.

*   *   *

"Whores'll kill themselves," Joe Durkin said. "It's something they do, and this one had a history. You saw the wrist scars? Those were a few years old, according to the report. What you might not know is she tried the pill route a little less than a year ago. A girlfriend took her over to St. Clare's to get her stomach pumped."

"There was something in the note. She hoped she had enough this time, something like that."

"Well, she got her wish."

We were at the Slate, a Tenth Avenue steak house that draws a lot of cops from John Jay College and Midtown North. I'd been back at my hotel, changing my clothes, finding places to stow the weapons and some of the money I'd been carrying, when he called to suggest I buy him a dinner. "I thought I'd hit you up for a meal now," he said, "before all your client's girls are dead and your expense account gets trimmed."

He had the mixed grill and drank a couple of Carlsbergs with it. I ordered the chopped sirloin and drank black coffee with my meal. We talked a little about Sunny's suicide but it didn't carry us very far. He said, "If it wasn't for the other one, the blonde, you wouldn't even think to look at it twice. All the medical evidence fits in with suicide. The bruises, that's easy. She was groggy, she didn't know what she was doing, she fell and bumped into things. Same reason she was on the floor instead of the bed. There was nothing special about the bruises. Her prints were where they belonged—the bottle, the glass, the pill bottles. The note matches other samples of her handwriting. If we buy your guy's story, she was even in a locked room when he found her. Locked from inside, the chain on. You figure that for the truth?"

"His whole story sounded true to me."

"So she killed herself. It even fits with the Dakkinen death two weeks ago. They were friends and she was depressed by what happened to her friend. You see any way it was anything but suicide?"

I shook my head. "It's the hardest kind of suicide to stage. What do you do, stuff the pills down her throat with a funnel? Make her take them at gunpoint?"

"You can dissolve the contents, let her take them without knowing it. But they found traces of the Seconal capsules in the stomach contents. So forget that. It's suicide."

I tried to remember the annual suicide rate in the city. I couldn't even come up with an educated guess, and Durkin was no help. I wondered what the rate was, and if it was on the rise like everything else.

Over coffee he said, "I had a couple of clerks go through the registration cards at the Galaxy Downtowner since the first of the year. Pulling the block-printed ones. Nothing ties into the Jones registration."

"And the other hotels?"

"Nothing that fits. A batch of people called Jones, it's a common enough name, but they're all signatures and credit cards and they look bona fide. Waste of time."

"Sorry."

"Why? Ninety percent of what I do is a waste of time. You were right, it was worth checking. If this had been a big case, front-page stuff, top brass putting pressure on, you can believe I'd have thought of it myself and we'd be checking every hotel in the five boroughs. How about you?"

"What about me?"

"You getting anywhere with Dakkinen?"

I had to think. "No," I said, finally.

"It's aggravating. I went over the file again and you know what got stuck in my throat? That desk clerk."

"The one I talked to?"

"That was a manager, assistant manager, something like that. No, the one who checked the killer in. Now here's a guy comes in, prints his name instead of writing it, and pays

cash. Those are two unusual things for a person to do, right?
I mean, who pays cash in front for a hotel nowadays? I don't
mean in a hot-pillow joint, I mean a decent hotel where
you're going to spend sixty or eighty dollars for a room.
Everything's plastic nowadays, credit cards, that's the whole
business. But this guy paid cash and the desk clerk doesn't
remember shit about him."

"Did you check him out?"

He nodded. "I went and talked to him last night. Well,
he's this South American kid, up from one of those countries. He was in a fog when I talked to him. He was probably
in a fog when the killer checked in. He probably lives his life
in a fog. I don't know where his fog comes from, whether he
smokes it or snorts it or what he does, but I think he probably comes by it honestly. You know the percentage of this
city that's stoned all the time?"

"I know what you mean."

"You see 'em at lunch hour. Office workers, midtown,
Wall Street, I don't care what neighborhood you're talking
about. They buy the fucking joints in the street and spend
their lunch hour smoking 'em in the park. How does anybody get any work done?"

"I don't know."

"And there's all these pillheads. Like this woman who
killed herself. Taking all those pills all the time, and she
wasn't even breaking the law. Drugs." He sighed, shook his
head, smoothed his dark hair. "Well, what I'm gonna have is
a brandy," he said, "if you think your client can afford it."

I got over to St. Paul's in time for the last ten minutes of the
meeting. I had coffee and a cookie and barely listened to
what was being said. I didn't even have to say my name, and
I ducked out during the prayer.

I went back to the hotel. There were no messages. I'd had
a couple of calls, the desk man told me, but nobody'd left a

name. I went upstairs and tried to sort out how I felt about Sunny's suicide, but all I seemed to feel so far was numb. It was tempting to beat myself up with the thought that I might have learned something if I hadn't saved her interrogation for last, might even have said or done something to forestall her suicide, but I couldn't get much mileage out of that one. I'd talked to her on the phone. She could have said something and she hadn't. And suicide, after all, was something she'd tried at least twice in the past, and very likely a time or two of which there'd been no record.

TRY something long enough, sooner or later you get it right.

In the morning I had a light breakfast and went over to the bank, where I deposited some cash and bought a money order. I went to the post office and mailed it to Anita. I hadn't given a whole lot of thought to my son's orthodontia and now I could forget it altogether.

I walked on to St. Paul's and lit a candle for Sonya Hendryx. I sat in a pew, giving myself a few minutes to remember Sunny. There wasn't much to remember. We'd barely met. I couldn't even recall very clearly what she looked like because her image in death pushed my dim memory of the living Sunny to the side.

It occurred to me that I owed the church money. Ten percent of Chance's fee came to $250, and they were further entitled to a tithe of the three hundred bucks and change I'd taken off the kid who'd tried mugging me. I didn't have an exact count but $350 struck me as a fair estimate, so I could give them $285 and call it even.

But I'd put most of my money in the bank. I had a few hundred dollars in my wallet but if I gave the church $285 I'd be strapped for walk-around money. I weighed the nuisance of another trip to the bank, and then the fundamental insanity of my little game struck me like a kidney punch.

What was I doing anyway? Why did I figure I owed any-body money? And who did I owe it to? Not the church, I didn't belong to any church. I gave my tithes to whatever house of worship came along at the right time.

To whom, then, was I in debt? To God?

Where was the sense in that? And what was the nature of this debt? How did I owe it? Was I repaying borrowed funds? Or had I invented some sort of bribe scheme, some celestial protection racket?

I'd never had trouble rationalizing it before. It was just a custom, a minor eccentricity. I didn't file a tax return so I paid a tithe instead.

I'd never really let myself ask myself why.

I wasn't sure I liked the answer. I remembered, too, a thought that had crossed my mind momentarily in that alley off St. Nicholas Avenue—that I was going to get killed by this boy because I hadn't paid my tithe. Not that I'd really believed it, not that I thought the world worked that way, but how remarkable that I'd had such a thought at all.

After awhile I took out my wallet, counted out the $285. I sat there with the money in my hand. Then I put it all back in my wallet, all but a dollar.

At least I could pay for the candle.

THAT afternoon I walked all the way to Kim's building. The weather wasn't bad and I didn't have anything better to do. I walked past the doorman and let myself into her apartment.

The first thing I did was pour the bottle of Wild Turkey down the sink.

I don't know how much sense that made. There was plenty of other booze there and I didn't feel like doing my Carrie Nation imitation. But the Wild Turkey had taken on the status of a symbol. I pictured the bottle every time I thought of going to that apartment, and the picture was ac-companied more often than not by a vivid memory of the taste and smell. When the last of it went down the sink I was able to relax.

Then I went back to the front closet and checked out the fur coat hanging there. A label sewn to the lining identified the garment as consisting of dyed lapin. I used the Yellow Pages, called a furrier at random and learned that *lapin* was the French word for "rabbit." "You could find it in a dictionary," I was told. "A regular American dictionary. It's an English word now, it came into the language from the fur business. Plain old rabbit."

Just as Chance had said.

ON the way home something triggered the thought of having a beer. I don't even recall what the stimulus was, but the response was a picture of myself with a shoulder pressed against a bar and one foot up on the brass rail, bell-shaped glass in hand, sawdust on the floor, my nostrils full of the smell of a musty old tavern.

It wasn't a strong drink urge and I never considered acting on it, but it put me in mind of what I'd promised Jan. Since I wasn't going to have a drink I felt no compulsion to call her but decided to anyway. I spent a dime and dialed her number from a booth around the corner from the main public library.

Our conversation had traffic noises for competition, and so we kept it brief and light. I didn't get around to telling her about Sunny's suicide. I didn't mention the bottle of Wild Turkey, either.

I read the *Post* while I ate dinner. Sunny's suicide had had a couple of paragraphs in the *News* that morning, which is as much as it merited, but the *Post* would hype anything that might sell papers, and their hook was that Sunny had the same pimp as Kim, who'd been chopped to pieces in a hotel just two weeks ago. Nobody had been able to turn up a picture of Sunny so they ran the shot of Kim again.

The story, though, couldn't fulfill the promise of the head-lines. All they had was a suicide and some airy speculation that Sunny had killed herself because of what she knew about Kim's murder.

I couldn't find anything about the boy whose legs I'd bro-ken. But there was the usual complement of crime and deaths scattered throughout the paper. I thought about what Jim Faber had said about giving up newspapers. It didn't seem like I'd be giving up all that much.

After dinner I picked up my mail at the desk. The mail was the usual junk, along with a phone message to call Chance. I called his service and he rang back to ask how things were going. I said that they weren't, really. He asked if I was going to keep at it.

"For a while," I said. "Just to see if it goes anywhere."

The cops, he said, had not been hassling him. He'd spent his day arranging funeral services for Sunny. Unlike Kim, whose body had been shipped back to Wisconsin, Sunny didn't have parents or kin to claim her. There was a question about when Sunny's body would be released from the morgue, so he'd made arrangements to have a memorial service at Walter B. Cooke's on West Seventy-second Street. That would take place Thursday, he told me, at two in the af-ternoon.

"I should have done the same for Kim," he said, "but I never thought of it. It's mostly for the girls. They're in a state, you know."

"I can imagine."

"They're all thinking the same thing. That business about death comes in threes. They're all worrying about who's next."

I went to my meeting that night. It struck me during the qualification that a week ago I'd been in a blackout, wander-ing around doing God knows what.

"My name's Matt," I said when my turn came. "I'll just listen tonight. Thanks."

WHEN the meeting broke up a guy followed me up the stairs to street level, then fell into step with me. He was about thirty, wearing a plaid lumber jacket and a peaked cap. I couldn't recall seeing him before.

He said, "Your name is Matt, right?" I allowed that it was. "You like that story tonight?"

"It was interesting," I said.

"You wanna hear an interesting story? I heard a story about a man uptown with a broken face and two broken legs. That's some story, man."

I felt a chill. The gun was in my dresser drawer, all rolled up in a pair of socks. The knives were in the same drawer.

He said, "You got some pair of balls, man. You got *cojones*, you know what I mean?" He cupped his groin with one hand like a baseball player adjusting his jock. "All the same," he said, "You don' wanna look for trouble."

"What are you talking about?"

He spread his hands. "What do I know? I'm Western Union, man. I bring the message, tha's all I do. Some chick gets herself iced in a hotel, man, is one thing, but who her friends are is another. Is not important, you know?"

"Who's the message from?"

He just looked at me.

"How'd you know to find me at the meeting?"

"Followed you in, followed you out." He chuckled. "That *maricón* with the broken legs, that was too much, man. That was too much."

Chapter 24

Tuesday was largely devoted to a game of Follow the Fur.

It started in that state that lies somewhere between dreaming and full consciousness. I'd awakened from a dream and dozed off again, and I found myself running a mental videotape of my meeting with Kim at Armstrong's. I began with a false memory, seeing her as she must have been when she arrived on the bus from Chicago, a cheap suitcase in one hand, a denim jacket tight on her shoulders. Then she was sitting at my table, her hand at her throat, light glinting off her ring while she toyed with the clasp at the throat of her fur jacket. She was telling me that it was ranch mink but she'd trade it for the denim jacket she'd come to town in.

The whole sequence played itself off and my mind moved on to something else. I was back in that alley in Harlem, except now my assailant had help. Royal Waldron and the messenger from the night before were flanking him on either side. The conscious part of my mind tried to get them the hell out of there, perhaps to even the odds a little, and then a realization screamed at me and I tossed my legs over the side of my bed and sat up, the dream images all scurrying off into the corners of the mind where they live.

It was a different jacket.

I showered and shaved and got out of there. I cabbed first to Kim's building to check her closet yet again. The lapin coat, the dyed rabbit Chance had bought her, was not the garment I had seen in Armstrong's. It was longer, it was fuller, it didn't fasten with a clasp at the throat. It was not what she'd been wearing, not what she'd described as ranch mink and offered to trade for her old denim jacket.

Nor was the jacket I remembered to be found anywhere else in the apartment.

I took another cab to Midtown North. Durkin wasn't on duty. I got another cop to call him at home and finally got unofficial access to the file, and yes, the inventory of impounded articles found in the room at the Galaxy Downtowner included a fur jacket. I checked the photos in the file and couldn't find the jacket in any of them.

A subway took me downtown to One Police Plaza, where I talked to some more people and waited while my request went through some channels and around others. I got to one office just after the guy I was supposed to see left for lunch. I had my meeting book with me, and it turned out there was a meeting less than a block away at St. Andrew's Church, so I killed an hour there. Afterward I got a sandwich at a deli and ate it standing up.

I went back to One Police Plaza and finally got to examine the fur jacket Kim had had with her when she died. I couldn't have sworn it was the one I'd seen in Armstrong's but it seemed to match my memory. I ran my hand over the rich fur and tried to replay the tape that had run in my mind that morning. It all seemed to go together. This fur was the right length, the right color, and there was a clasp at the throat that her port-tipped fingers might have toyed with.

The label sewn to the lining told me it was genuine ranch mink and that a furrier named Arvin Tannenbaum had made it.

The Tannenbaum firm was on the third floor of a loft building on West Twenty-ninth, right in the heart of the fur district. It would have simplified things if I could have taken Kim's fur along, but NYPD cooperation, official or otherwise, only went so far. I described the jacket, which didn't help much, and I described Kim. A check of their sales records revealed the purchase of a mink jacket six weeks previously by Kim Dakkinen, and the sales slip led us to the right salesman and he remembered the sale.

The salesman was round faced and balding, with watery blue eyes behind thick lenses. He said, "Tall girl, very pretty girl. You know, I read that name in the newspaper and it rang a bell but I couldn't think why. Terrible thing, such a pretty girl."

She'd been with a gentleman, he recalled, and it was the gentleman who had paid for the coat. Paid cash for it, he remembered. And no, that wasn't so unusual, not in the fur business. They only did a small volume of retail sales and a lot of it was people in the garment trade or people who knew somebody in the trade, although of course anyone could walk in off the street and buy any garment in the place. But mostly it was cash because the customer didn't usually want to wait for his check to clear, and besides a fur was often a luxury gift for a luxury friend, so to speak, and the customer was happier if no record of the transaction existed. Thus payment in cash, thus the sales slip not in the buyer's name but in Miss Dakkinen's.

The sale had come to just under twenty-five hundred dollars with the tax. A lot of cash to carry, but not unheard of. I'd been carrying almost that myself not too long ago.

Could he describe the gentleman? The salesman sighed. It was much easier, he explained, to describe the lady. He could picture her now, those gold braids wrapped around her head, the piercing blue of her eyes. She'd tried on several jackets, she looked quite elegant in fur, but the man—

Thirty-eight, forty years old, he supposed. Tall rather than short, as he remembered, but not tall as the girl had been tall.

"I'm sorry," he said. "I have a sense of him but I can't picture him. If he'd been wearing a fur I could tell you more than you'd want to know about it, but as it was—"

"What was he wearing?"

"A suit, I think, but I don't remember it. He was the type of man who'd wear a suit. I can't recall what he was wearing, though."

"Would you recognize him if you saw him again?"

"I might pass him on the street and not think twice."

"Suppose he was pointed out to you."

"Then I would probably recognize him, yes. You mean like a lineup? Yes, I suppose so."

I told him he probably remembered more than he thought he did. I asked him the man's profession.

"I don't even know his name. How would I know what he did for a living?"

"Your impression," I said. "Was he an auto mechanic? A stockbroker? A rodeo performer?"

"Oh," he said, and thought it over. "Maybe an accountant," he said.

"An accountant?"

"Something like that. A tax lawyer, an accountant. This is a game, I'm just guessing, you understand that—"

"I understand. What nationality?"

"American. What do you mean?"

"English, Irish, Italian—"

"Oh," he said. "I see, more of the game. I would say Jewish, I would say Italian, I would say dark, Mediterranean. Because she was so blonde, you know? A contrast. I don't know that he was dark, but there was a contrast. Could be Greek, could be Spanish."

"Did he go to college?"

"He didn't show me a diploma."

"No, but he must have talked, to you or to her. Did he sound like college or did he sound like the streets?"

"He didn't sound like the streets. He was a gentleman, an educated man."

"Married?"

"Not to her."

"To anybody?"

"Aren't they always? You're not married, you don't have to buy mink for your girlfriend. He probably bought another one for his wife, to keep her happy."

"Was he wearing a wedding ring?"

"I don't remember a ring." He touched his own gold band. "Maybe yes, maybe no. I don't recall a ring."

He didn't recall much, and the impressions I'd pried out of him were suspect. They might have been valid, might as easily have grown out of an unconscious desire to supply me with the answers he thought I wanted. I could have kept going—*"All right, you don't remember his shoes, but what kind of shoes would a guy like him wear? Chukka boots? Penny loafers? Cordovans? Adidas? What?"* But I'd reached and passed a point of diminishing returns. I thanked him and got out of there.

THERE was a coffee shop on the building's first floor, just a long counter with stools and a takeout window. I sat over coffee and tried to assess what I had.

She had a boyfriend. No question. Somebody bought her that jacket, counted out hundred dollar bills, kept his own name out of the transaction.

Did the boyfriend have a machete? There was a question I hadn't asked the fur salesman. *"All right, use your imagination. Picture this guy in a hotel room with the blonde. Let's say he wants to chop her. What does he use? An axe? A cavalry saber? A machete? Just give me your impression."*

Sure. He was an accountant, right? He'd probably use a

pen. A Pilot Razor Point, deadly as a sword in the hands of a samurai. Zip zip, take that, you bitch.

The coffee wasn't very good. I ordered a second cup anyway. I interlaced my fingers and looked down at my hands. That was the trouble, my fingers meshed well enough but nothing else did. What kind of accountant type went batshit with a machete? Granted, anyone could explode that way, but this had been a curiously planned explosion, the hotel room rented under a false name, the murder performed with no traces left of the murderer's identity.

Did that sound like the same man who bought the fur?

I sipped my coffee and decided it didn't. Nor did the picture I got of the boyfriend jibe with the message I'd been given after last night's meeting. The fellow in the lumber jacket had been muscle, pure and simple, even if he hadn't been called upon to do anything more with that muscle than flex it. Would a mild-mannered accountant command that sort of muscle?

Not likely.

Were the boyfriend and Charles Owen Jones one and the same? And why such an elaborate alias, middle name and all? People who used a surname like Smith or Jones for an alias usually picked Joe or John to go with it. Charles Owen Jones?

Maybe his name was Charles Owens. Maybe he'd started to write that, then changed his mind in the nick of time and dropped the last letter of Owens, converting it to a middle name. Did that make sense?

I decided that it didn't.

The goddamned room clerk. It struck me that he hadn't been interrogated properly. Durkin had said he was in a fog, and evidently he was South American, possibly somewhat at a loss in English. But he'd have had to be reasonably fluent to get hired by a decent hotel for a position that put him in contact with the public. No, the problem was that nobody

pushed him. If he'd been questioned the way I questioned
the fur salesman, say, he'd have let go of something. Witnesses always remember more than they think they remember.

THE room clerk who checked in Charles Owen Jones was
named Octavio Calderón, and he'd worked last on Saturday
when he was on the desk from four to midnight. Sunday afternoon he'd called in sick. There had been another call yesterday and a third call an hour or so before I got to the hotel
and braced the assistant manager. Calderón was still sick.
He'd be out another day, maybe longer.

I asked what was the matter with him. The assistant manager sighed and shook his head. "*I* don't know," he said. "It's
hard to get a straight answer out of these people. When they
want to turn evasive their grasp of the English language
weakens considerably. They slip off into the convenient little
world of *No comprendo*."

"You mean you hire room clerks who can't speak English?"

"No, no. Calderón's fluent. Someone else called in for
him." He shook his head again. "He's a very diffident young
man, 'Tavio is. I suspect he reasoned that if he had a friend
make the call, I couldn't intimidate him over the phone. The
implication, of course, is that he's not hale and hearty
enough to get from his bed to the phone. I gather he lives in
some sort of rooming house with the telephone in the hallway. Someone with a much heavier Latin accent than 'Tavio
made the call."

"Did he call yesterday?"

"Someone called for him."

"The same person who called today?"

"I'm sure I don't know. One Hispanic voice over the
phone is rather like another. It was a male voice both times.

I think it was the same voice, but I couldn't swear to it. What difference does it make?"

None that I could think of. How about Sunday? Had Calderón done his own telephoning then?

"I wasn't here Sunday."

"You have a phone number for him?"

"It rings in the hall. I doubt that he'll come to the phone."

"I'd like the number anyway."

He gave it to me, along with an address on Barnett Avenue in Queens. I'd never heard of Barnett Avenue and I asked the assistant manager if he knew what part of Queens Calderón lived in.

"I don't know anything about Queens," he said. "You're not going out there, are you?" He made it sound as though I'd need a passport, and supplies of food and water. "Because I'm sure 'Tavio will be back on the job in a day or two."

"What makes you so sure?"

"It's a good job," he said. "He'll lose it if he's not back soon. And he must know that."

"How's his absenteeism record?"

"Excellent. And I'm sure his sickness is legitimate enough. Probably one of those viruses that runs its course in three days. There's a lot of that going around."

I called Octavio Calderón's number from a pay phone right there in the Galaxy lobby. It rang for a long time, nine or ten rings, before a woman answered it in Spanish. I asked for Octavio Calderón.

"No está aquí," she told me.

I tried to form questions in Spanish. *Es enfermo?* Is he sick? I couldn't tell if I was making myself understood. Her replies were delivered in a Spanish that was very different in inflection from the Puerto Rican idiom I was used to hearing around New York, and when she tried to accommodate me in English her accent was heavy and her vocabulary inadequate. *No está aquí*, she kept saying, and it was the one thing she said that I understood with no difficulty. *No está aquí*. He is not here.

I went back to my hotel. I had a pocket atlas for the five boroughs in my room and I looked up Barnett Avenue in the Queens index, turned to the appropriate page and hunted until I found it. It was in Woodside. I studied the map and wondered what a Hispanic rooming house was doing in an Irish neighborhood.

Barnett Avenue extended only ten or twelve blocks, running east from Forty-third Street and ending at Woodside Avenue. I had my choice of trains. I could take either the E or F on the Independent line or the IRT Flushing Line.

Assuming I wanted to go there at all.

I called again from my room. Once again the phone rang for a long time. This time a man answered it. I said, "Octavio Calderón, *por favor*."

"*Momento*," he said. Then there was a thumping sound, as if he let the receiver hang from its cord and it was knocking against the wall. Then there was no sound at all except that of a radio in the background tuned to a Latin broadcast. I was thinking about hanging up by the time he came back on the line.

"*No está aquí*," he said, and rang off before I could say anything in any language.

I looked in the pocket atlas again and tried to think of a way to avoid a trip to Woodside. It was rush hour already. If I went now I'd have to stand up all the way out there. And what was I going to accomplish? I'd have a long ride jammed into a subway car like a sardine in a can so that someone could tell me *No está aquí* face to face. What was the point? Either he was taking a drug-assisted vacation or he was really sick, and either way I didn't stand much chance of getting anything out of him. If I actually managed to run him down, I'd be rewarded with *No lo se* instead of *No está aquí*. I don't know, he's not here, I don't know, he's not here—

Shit.

Joe Durkin had done a follow-up interrogation of Calderón on Saturday night, around the time that I was passing the word to every snitch and hanger-on I could find. That same night I took a gun away from a mugger and Sunny Hendryx washed down a load of pills with vodka and orange juice.

The very next day, Calderón called in sick. And the day after that a man in a lumber jacket followed me in and out of an AA meeting and warned me off Kim Dakkinen's trail.

The phone rang. It was Chance. There'd been a message that he'd called, but evidently he'd decided not to wait for me to get back to him.

"Just checking," he said. "You getting anywhere?"

"I must be. Last night I got a warning."

"What kind of a warning?"

"A guy told me not to go looking for trouble."

"You sure it was about Kim?"

"I'm sure."

"You know the guy?"

"No."

"What are you fixing to do?"

I laughed. "I'm going to go looking for trouble," I said. "In Woodside."

"Woodside?"

"That's in Queens."

"I know where Woodside is, man. What's happening in Woodside?"

I decided I didn't want to get into it. "Probably nothing," I said, "and I wish I could save myself the trip, but I can't. Kim had a boyfriend."

"In Woodside?"

"No, Woodside's something else. But it's definite she had a boyfriend. He bought her a mink jacket."

He sighed. "I *told* you about that. Dyed rabbit."

"I know about the dyed rabbit. It's in her closet."

"So?"

"She also had a short jacket, ranch mink. She was wearing it the first time I met her. She was also wearing it when she went to the Galaxy Downtowner and got killed. It's in a lockbox at One Police Plaza."

"What's it doin' there?"

"It's evidence."

"Of what?"

"Nobody knows. I got to it and I traced it and I talked to the man who sold it to her. She's the buyer of record, her name's on the sales slip, but there was a man with her and he counted out the money and paid for it."

"How much?"

"Twenty-five hundred."

He thought it over. "Maybe she held out," he said. "Be easy to do, couple hundred a week, you know they hold out from time to time. I wouldn'ta missed it."

"The man paid out the money, Chance."

"Maybe she gave it to him to pay with. Like a woman'll slip a man money for a restaurant check, so it don't look bad."

"How come you don't want it to be that she had a boyfriend?"

"Shit," he said. "I don't care about that. I want it to be whatever way it was. I just can't believe it, that's all."

I let it go.

"Could be a trick instead of a boyfriend. Sometimes a john wants to pretend like he's a special friend, he don't have to pay, so he wants to give presents instead of cash. Maybe he was just a john and she was like hustling him for the fur."

"Maybe."

"You think he was a boyfriend?"

"That's what I think, yes."

"And he killed her?"

"I don't know who killed her."

"And whoever killed her wants you to drop the whole thing."

"I don't know," I said. "Maybe the killing had nothing to do with the boyfriend. Maybe it was a psycho, the way the cops want to figure it, and maybe the boyfriend just doesn't want to get roped into any investigation."

"He wasn't in it and he wants to stay out of it. That what you mean?"

"Something like that."

"I don't know, man. Maybe you should let it go."

"Drop the investigation?"

"Maybe you should. A warning, shit, you don't want to get killed over it."

"No," I said. "I don't."

"What are you gonna do, then?"

"Right now I'm going to catch a train to Queens."

"To Woodside."

"Right."

"I could bring the car around. Drive you out there."

"I don't mind the subway."

"Be faster in the car. I could wear my little chauffeur's cap. You could sit in the back."

"Some other time."

"Suit yourself," he said. "Call me after, huh?"

"Sure."

I wound up taking the Flushing line to a stop at Roosevelt Avenue and Fifty-second Street. The train came up out of the ground after it left Manhattan. I almost missed my stop because it was hard to tell where I was. The station signs on

the elevated platforms were so disfigured with graffiti that
their messages were indecipherable.

A flight of steel steps led me back down to street level. I
checked my pocket atlas, got my bearings, and set out for
Barnett Avenue. I hadn't walked far before I managed to figure out what a Hispanic rooming house was doing in Woodside. The neighborhood wasn't Irish anymore. There were
still a few places with names like the Emerald Tavern and
the Shamrock scattered in the shadow of the El, but most of
the signs were Spanish and most of the markets were *bode-
gas* now. Posters in the window of the Tara Travel Agency
offered charter flights to Bogotá and Caracas.

Octavio Calderón's rooming house was a dark two-story
frame house with a front porch. There were five or six plastic lawn chairs lined up on the porch, and an upended orange
crate holding magazines and newspapers. The chairs were
unoccupied, which wasn't surprising. It was a little chilly for
porch sitting.

I rang the doorbell. Nothing happened. I heard conversation within, and several radios playing. I rang the bell again,
and a middle-aged woman, short and very stout, came to the
door and opened it. *"Sí?"* she said, expectant.

"Octavio Calderón," I said.

"No está aquí."

She may have been the woman I spoke to the first time I
called. It was hard to tell and I didn't care a whole lot. I
stood there talking through the screen door, trying to make
myself understood in a mixture of Spanish and English. After awhile she went away and came back with a tall hollow-
cheeked man with a severely trimmed moustache. He spoke
English, and I told him that I wanted to see Calderón's room.

But Calderón wasn't there, he told me.

"No me importa," I said. I wanted to see his room anyway. But there was nothing to see, he replied, mystified.

Calderón was not there. What was I to gain by seeing a room?

They weren't refusing to cooperate. They weren't even particularly reluctant to cooperate. They just couldn't see the point. When it became clear that the only way to get rid of me, or at least the easiest way, was to show me to Calderón's room, that was what they did. I followed the woman down a hallway and past a kitchen to a staircase. We climbed the stairs, walked the length of another hallway. She opened a door without knocking on it, stood aside and gestured for me to enter.

There was a piece of linoleum on the floor, an old iron bedstead with the mattress stripped of linen, a chest of drawers in blonde maple, and a little writing table with a folding chair in front of it. A wing chair slipcovered in a floral print stood on the opposite side of the room near the window. There was a table lamp with a patterned paper shade on the chest of drawers, an overhead light fixture with two bare bulbs in the center of the ceiling.

And that's all there was.

"Entiende usted ahora? No está aquí."

I went through the room mechanically, automatically. It could hardly have been emptier. The small closet held nothing but a couple of wire hangers. The drawers in the blonde chest and the single drawer in the writing table were utterly empty. Their corners had been wiped clean.

With the hollow-cheeked man as interpreter, I managed to question the woman. She wasn't a mine of information in any language. She didn't know when Calderón had left. Sunday or Monday, she believed. Monday she had come into his room to clean it and discovered he had removed all his possessions, leaving nothing behind. Understandably enough, she took this to mean that he was relinquishing the room. Like all of her tenants, he had paid by the week. He'd had a couple of days left before his rent was due, but evidently he had had someplace else to go, and no, it was not remarkable that he had left without telling her. Tenants did that with some frequency, even when they were not behind in their rent. She and her daughter had given the room a good cleaning, and now it was ready to be rented to someone else. It would not be vacant long. Her rooms never stood vacant long.

Had Calderón been a good tenant? *Sí*, an excellent tenant, but she had never had trouble with her tenants. She rented only to Colombians and Panamanians and Ecuadorians and never had trouble with any of them. Sometimes they had to move suddenly because of the Immigration Service. Perhaps that was why Calderón had left so abruptly. But that was not her business. Her business was cleaning his room and renting it to someone else.

Calderón wouldn't have had trouble with Immigration, I knew. He wasn't an illegal or he wouldn't have been working at the Galaxy Downtowner. A big hotel wouldn't employ an alien without a green card.

He'd had some other reason for leaving in a hurry.

I spent about an hour interviewing other tenants. The picture of Calderón that emerged didn't help a bit. He was a quiet young man who kept to himself. His hours at work were such that he was likely to be out when the other tenants were at home. He did not, to anyone's knowledge, have a girlfriend. In the eight months that he'd lived on Barnett Avenue, he had not had a visitor of either sex, nor had he had frequent phone calls. He'd lived elsewhere in New York before moving to Barnett Avenue, but no one knew his previous address or even if it had been in Queens.

Had he used drugs? Everyone I spoke to seemed quite shocked by the suggestion. I gathered that the fat little landlady ran a tight ship. Her tenants were all regularly employed and they led respectable lives. If Calderón smoked marijuana, one of them assured me, he certainly hadn't done so in his room. Or the landlady would have detected the smell and he would have been asked to leave.

"Maybe he is homesick," a dark-eyed young man suggested. "Maybe he is fly back to Cartagena."

"Is that where he came from?"

"He is Colombian. I think he say Cartagena."

So that was what I learned in an hour, that Octavio Calderón had come from Cartagena. And nobody was too certain of that, either.

Chapter 25

I called Durkin from a Dunkin' Donuts on Woodside Avenue. There was no booth, just a pay phone mounted on the wall. A few feet from me a couple of kids were playing one of those electronic games. Somebody else was listening to disco music on a satchel-sized portable radio. I cupped the telephone mouthpiece with my hand and told Durkin what I'd found out.

"I can put out a pickup order on him. Octavio Calderón, male Hispanic, early twenties. What is he, about five seven?"

"I never met him."

"That's right, you didn't. I can check the hotel for a description. You sure he's gone, Scudder? I talked to him just a couple of days ago."

"Saturday night."

"I think that's right. Yeah, before the Hendryx suicide. Right."

"That's still a suicide?"

"Any reason why it shouldn't be?"

"None that I know of. You talked to Calderón Saturday night and that's the last anybody's seen of him."

"I have that effect on a lot of people."

"Something spooked him. You think it was you?"

He said something but I couldn't hear it over the din. I asked him to repeat it.

"I said he didn't seem to be paying that much attention. I thought he was stoned."

"The neighbors describe him as a pretty straight young man."

"Yeah, a nice quiet boy. The kind that goes batshit and wipes out his family. Where are you calling from, it's noisy as hell there?"

"A donut shop on Woodside Avenue."

"Couldn't you find a nice quiet bowling alley? What's your guess on Calderón? You figure he's dead?"

"He packed everything before he left his room. And somebody's been calling in sick for him. That sounds like a lot of trouble to go through if you're going to kill somebody."

"The calling in sounds like a way to give him a head start. Let him get a few extra miles before they start the bloodhounds."

"That's what I was thinking."

"Maybe he went home," Durkin said. "They go home all the time, you know. It's a new world these days. My grandparents came over here, they never saw Ireland again outside of the annual calendar from Treaty Stone Wines & Liquors. These fucking people are on a plane to the islands once a month and they come back carrying two chickens and another fucking relative. Of course, my grandparents worked, maybe that's the difference. They didn't have welfare giving 'em a trip around the world."

"Calderón worked."

"Well, good for him, the little prick. Maybe what I'll check is the flights out of Kennedy the past three days. Where's he from?"

"Somebody said Cartagena."

"What's that, a city? Or is it one of those islands?"

"I think it's a city. And it's in either Panama or Colombia or Ecuador or she wouldn't have rented him a room. I think it's Colombia."

"The gem of the ocean. The calling in fits if he went home. He had somebody phone for him so the job'd be there when he gets back. He can't call up every afternoon from Cartagena."

"Why'd he clear out of the room?"

"Maybe he didn't like it there. Maybe the exterminator came and knocked off all his pet cockroaches. Maybe he owed rent and he was skipping."

"She said no. He was paid up through the week."

He was silent a moment. Then, reluctantly, he said, "Somebody spooked him and he ran."

"It looks that way, doesn't it?"

"I'm afraid it does. I don't think he left the city, either. I think he moved a subway stop away, picked himself a new name, and checked into another furnished room. There's something like half a million illegals in the five boroughs. He doesn't have to be Houdini to hide where we're not gonna find him."

"You could get lucky."

"Always a chance. I'll check the morgue first, and then the airlines. We'll stand the best chance if he's dead or out of the country." He laughed, and I asked what was so funny. "If he's dead or out of the country," he said, "he's not gonna be a whole lot of good to us, is he?"

THE train back to Manhattan was one of the worst, its interior vandalized beyond recognition. I sat in a corner and tried to fight off a wave of despair. My life was an ice floe that had broken up at sea, with the different chunks floating off in different directions. Nothing was ever going to come together, in this case or out of it. Everything was senseless, pointless, and hopeless.

Nobody's going to buy me emeralds. Nobody's going to give me babies. Nobody's going to save my life.

All the good times are gone.

Eight million ways to die, and among them there's a wide variety suitable for the do-it-yourselfer. For all that was wrong with the subways, they still did the job when you threw yourself in front of them. And the city has no end of bridges and high windows, and stores stay open twenty-four hours a day selling razor blades and clothesline and pills.

I had a .32 in my dresser drawer, and my hotel room window was far enough from the pavement to make death a certainty. But I've never tried that sort of thing, and I've somehow always known I never will. I'm either too scared or too stubborn, or perhaps my particular despair is never as unequivocal as I think it is. Something seems to keep me going.

Of course all bets were off if I drank. I'd heard a man at a meeting who told of coming out of a blackout on the Brooklyn Bridge. He was over the railing and he had one foot in space when he came to. He retrieved the foot, climbed back over the railing, and got the hell out of there.

Suppose he'd come to a second later, with both feet in the air.

IF I drank I'd feel better.

I couldn't get the thought out of my head. The worst of it was that I knew it was true. I felt horrible, and if I had a drink the feeling would go away. I'd regret it in the long run, I'd feel as bad and worse again in the long run, but so what? In the long run we're all dead.

I remembered something I'd heard at a meeting. Mary,

one of the regulars at St. Paul's, had said it. She was a bird-like woman with a tiny voice, always well dressed and well groomed and soft-spoken. I'd heard her qualify once, and evidently she'd been the next thing to a shopping-bag lady before she hit bottom.

One night, speaking from the floor, she'd said, "You know, it was a revelation to me to learn that I don't have to be comfortable. Nowhere is it written that I *must* be comfortable. I always thought if I felt nervous or anxious or unhappy I had to do something about it. But I learned that's not true. Bad feelings won't kill me. Alcohol will kill me, but my feelings won't."

The train plunged into the tunnel. As it dropped below ground level all the lights went out for a moment. Then they came back on again. I could hear Mary, pronouncing each word very precisely. I could see her, her fine-boned hands resting one on top of the other in her lap as she spoke.

Funny what comes to mind.

When I emerged from the subway station at Columbus Circle I still wanted a drink. I walked past a couple of bars and went to my meeting.

THE speaker was a big beefy Irishman from Bay Ridge. He looked like a cop, and it turned out he'd been one, retiring after twenty years and currently supplementing his city pension as a security guard. Alcohol never interfered with his job or his marriage, but after a certain number of years it began to get to him physically. His capacity decreased, his hangovers worsened, and a doctor told him his liver was enlarged.

"He told me the booze was threatening my life," he said. "Well, I wasn't some derelict, I wasn't some degenerate drunk, I wasn't some guy who had to drink to get rid of the blues. I was just your normal happy-go-lucky guy who liked a shot an' a beer after work and a six-pack in front of the television set. So if it's gonna kill me, the hell with it, right? I walked out of that doctor's office and resolved to stop drinking. And eight years later that's just what I did."

A drunk kept interrupting the qualification. He was a well-dressed man and he didn't seem to want to make trouble. He just seemed incapable of listening quietly, and after his fifth or sixth outburst a couple of members escorted him out and the meeting went on.

I thought how I'd come to the meeting myself in blackout. God, had I been like that?

I couldn't keep my mind on what I was hearing. I thought about Octavio Calderón and I thought about Sunny Hendryx and I thought how little I'd accomplished. I'd been just a little bit out of synch from the very beginning. I could have seen Sunny before she killed herself. She might have done it anyway, I wasn't going to carry the weight for her self-destruction, but I could have learned something from her first.

And I could have talked to Calderón before he did his disappearing act. I'd asked for him on my first visit to the hotel, then forgot about him when he proved temporarily unavailable. Maybe I couldn't have gotten anything out of him, but at least I might have sensed that he was holding something back. But it didn't occur to me to pursue him until he'd already checked out and headed for the woods.

My timing was terrible. I was always a day late and a dollar short, and it struck me that it wasn't just this one case. It was the story of my life.

Poor me, poor me, pour me a drink.

During the discussion, a woman named Grace got a round of applause when she said it was her second anniversary. I clapped for her, and when the applause died down I counted up and realized today was my seventh day. If I went to bed sober, I'd have seven days.

How far did I get before my last drink? Eight days?

Maybe I could break that record. Or maybe I couldn't, maybe I'd drink tomorrow.

Not tonight, though. I was all right for tonight. I didn't feel any better than I'd felt before the meeting. My opinion of myself was certainly no higher. All the numbers on the scorecard were the same, but earlier they'd added up to a drink and now they didn't.

I didn't know why that was. But I knew I was safe.

Chapter 26

There was a message at the desk to call Danny Boy Bell. I dialed the number on the slip and the man who answered said, "Poogan's Pub." I asked for Danny Boy and waited until he came on the line.

He said, "Matt, I think you should come up and let me buy you a ginger ale. That's what I think you should do."

"Now?"

"What better time?"

I was almost out of the door when I turned, went upstairs, and got the .32 out of my dresser. I didn't really think Danny Boy would set me up but I didn't want to bet my life that he wouldn't. Either way, you never knew who might be drinking in Poogan's.

I'd received a warning last night and I'd spent the intervening hours disregarding it. And the clerk who gave me Danny Boy's message had volunteered that I'd had a couple of other calls from people who'd declined to leave their names. They might have been friends of the chap in the lumber jacket, calling to offer a word to the wise.

I dropped the gun into a pocket, went out and hailed a cab.

* * *

DANNY BOY insisted on buying the drinks, vodka for himself, ginger ale for me. He looked as natty as ever, and he'd been to the barber since I last saw him. His cap of tight white curls was closer to his scalp, and his manicured nails showed a coating of clear polish.

He said, "I've got two things for you. A message and an opinion."

"Oh?"

"The message first. It's a warning."

"I thought it might be."

"You should forget about the Dakkinen girl."

"Or what?"

"Or what? Or else, I suppose. Or you get what she got, something like that. You want a specific warning so you can decide whether it's worth it or not?"

"Who's the warning come from, Danny?"

"I don't know."

"What spoke to you? A burning bush?"

He drank off some of his vodka. "Somebody talked to somebody who talked to somebody who talked to me."

"That's pretty roundabout."

"Isn't it? I could give you the person who talked to me, but I won't, because I don't do that. And even if I did it wouldn't do you any good, because you probably couldn't find him, and if you did he still wouldn't talk to you, and meanwhile somebody's probably going to whack you out. You want another ginger ale?"

"I've still got most of this one."

"So you do. I *don't* know who the warning's from, Matt, but from the messenger they used I'd guess it's some very heavy types. And what's interesting is I get absolutely nowhere trying to find anybody who saw Dakkinen on the town with anybody but our friend Chance. Now if she's going with somebody with all this firepower, you'd think he'd show her around, wouldn't you? Why not?"

I nodded. For that matter, why would she need me to ease her out of Chance's string?

"Anyway," he was saying, "that's the message. You want the opinion?"

"Sure."

"The opinion is I think you should heed the message. Either I'm getting old in a hurry or this town's gotten nastier in the past couple of years. People seem to pull the trigger a lot quicker than they used to. They used to need more of a reason to kill. You know what I mean?"

"Yes."

"Now they'll do it unless they've got a reason not to. They'll sooner kill than not. It's an automatic response. I'll tell you, it scares me."

"It scares everybody."

"You had a little scene uptown a few nights back, didn't you? Or was somebody making up stories?"

"What did you hear?"

"Just that a brother jumped you in the alley and wound up with multiple fractures."

"News travels."

"It does for a fact. Of course there's more dangerous things in this city than a young punk on angel dust."

"Is that what he was on?"

"Aren't they all? I don't know. I stick to basics, myself." He underscored the line with a sip of his vodka. "About Dakkinen," he said. "I could pass a message back up the line."

"What kind of message?"

"That you're letting it lay."

"That might not be true, Danny Boy."

"Matt—"

"You remember Jack Benny?"

"Do I remember Jack Benny? Of course I remember Jack Benny."

"Remember that bit with the stickup man? The guy says, 'Your money or your life,' and there's a long pause, a really long pause, and Benny says, 'I'm thinking it over.' "

"That's the answer? You're thinking it over?"

"That's the answer."

OUTSIDE on Seventy-second Street I stood in the shadows in the doorway of a stationery store, waiting to see if anyone would follow me out of Poogan's. I stood there for a full five minutes and thought about what Danny Boy had said. A couple of people left Poogan's while I was standing there but they didn't look like anything I had to worry about.

I went to the curb to hail a cab, then decided I might as well walk half a block to Columbus and get one going in the right direction. By the time I got to the corner I decided it was a nice night and I was in no hurry, and an easy stroll fifteen blocks down Columbus Avenue would probably do me good, make sleep come that much easier. I crossed the street and headed downtown and before I'd covered a block I noticed that my hand was in my coat pocket and I was holding onto the little gun.

Funny. No one had followed me. What the hell was I afraid of?

Just something in the air.

I kept walking, displaying all the street smarts I hadn't shown Saturday night. I stayed at the edge of the sidewalk near the curb, keeping my distance from buildings and doorways. I looked left and right, and now and then I turned to see if anyone was moving up behind me. And I went on clutching the gun, my finger resting lightly alongside the trigger.

I crossed Broadway, walked on past Lincoln Center and O'Neal's. I was on the dark block between Sixtieth and Sixty-first, across the street from Fordham, when I heard the car behind me and spun around. It was slanting across the wide avenue toward me and had cut off a cab. Maybe it was his brakes I heard, maybe that's what made me turn.

I threw myself down on the pavement, rolled away from the street toward the buildings, came up with the .32 in my hand. The car was even with me now, its wheels straightened out. I'd thought it was going to vault the curb but it wasn't. And the windows were open and someone was leaning out the rear window, looking my way, and he had something in his hand—

I had the gun pointed at him. I was prone, elbows braced in front of me, holding the gun in both hands. I had my finger on the trigger.

The man leaning out the window threw something, tossed it underhand. I thought, *Jesus, a bomb*, and I aimed at him and felt the trigger beneath my finger, felt it tremble like some little live thing, and I froze, I froze, I couldn't pull the fucking trigger.

Time froze, too, like a stop-frame sequence in a film. Eight or ten yards from me a bottle struck the brick wall of a building and smashed. There was no explosion beyond the shattering of the glass. It was just an empty bottle.

And the car was just a car. I watched now as it went on careening south on Ninth Avenue, six kids in it, six drunken kids, and they might well kill somebody, they were drunk enough to do it, but when they did it would be an accident. They weren't professional killers, hitmen dispatched to murder me. They were just a bunch of kids who'd had more to drink than they could handle. Maybe they'd cripple someone, maybe they'd total their car, maybe they'd make it home without bending a fender.

I got up slowly, looked at the gun in my hand. Thank God I hadn't fired it. I could have shot them, I could have killed them.

God knows I'd wanted to. I'd *tried* to, thinking logically enough that they were trying to kill me.

But I'd been unable to do it. And if it *had* been pros, if the object I'd seen had been not a whiskey bottle but the gun or bomb I'd thought it was, I'd have been no more able to pull the trigger. They'd have killed me and I'd have died with an unfired revolver in my hands.

Jesus.

I dropped the useless gun in my pocket. I held out my hand, surprised that it wasn't shaking. I didn't even feel particularly shaky inside, and I was damned if I could figure out why not.

I went over to examine the broken bottle, if only to make sure it was just that and not a Molotov cocktail that had providentially failed to ignite. But there was no puddle, no reek of gasoline. There was a slight whiskey smell, unless I imagined it, and a label attached to one chunk of glass indicated that the bottle had contained J & B Scotch. Other fragments of green glass sparkled like jewels in the light of the streetlamp.

I bent over and picked up a little cube of glass. I placed it in the palm of my hand and stared at it like a gypsy at a crystal. I thought of Donna's poem and Sunny's note and my own slip of the tongue.

I started walking. It was all I could do to keep from running.

Chapter 27

"Jesus, I need a shave," Durkin said. He'd just dropped what was left of his cigarette into what was left of his coffee, and he was running one hand over his cheek, feeling the stubble. "I need a shave, I need a shower, I need a drink. Not necessarily in that order. I put out an APB on your little Colombian friend. Octavio Ignacio Calderón y La Barra. Name's longer'n he is. I checked the morgue. They haven't got him down there in a drawer. Not yet, anyway."

He opened his top desk drawer, withdrew a metal shaving mirror and a cordless electric shaver. He leaned the mirror against his empty coffee cup, positioned his face in front of it and began shaving. Over the whirr of the shaver he said, "I don't see anything in her file about a ring."

"Mind if I look?"

"Be my guest."

I studied the inventory sheet, knowing the ring wouldn't be on it. Then I went over the photographs of the death scene. I tried to look only at her hands. I looked at every picture, and in none of them could I spot anything that suggested she was wearing a ring.

I said as much to Durkin. He switched off the shaver,

reached for the photographs, went through them carefully and deliberately. "It's hard to see her hands in some of these," he complained. "All right, there's definitely no ring on that hand. What's that, the left hand? No ring on the left hand. Now in this shot, okay, definitely no ring on that hand. Wait a minute. Shit, that's the left hand again. It's not clear in this one. Okay, here we go. That's definitely her right hand and there's no ring on it." He gathered the photos together like cards to be shuffled and dealt. "No ring," he said. "What's that prove?"

"She had a ring when I saw her. Both times I saw her."

"And?"

"And it disappeared. It's not at her apartment. There's a ring in her jewelry box, a high school class ring, but that's not what I remember seeing on her hand."

"Maybe your memory's false."

I shook my head. "The class ring doesn't even have a stone. I went over there before I came here, just to check my memory. It's one of those klutzy school rings with too much lettering on it. It's not what she was wearing. She wouldn't have worn it, not with this mink and the wine-colored nails."

I wasn't the only one who'd said so. After my little epiphany with the bit of broken glass, I'd gone straight to Kim's apartment, then used her phone to call Donna Campion. "It's Matt Scudder," I said. "I know it's late, but I wanted to ask you about a line in your poem."

She'd said, "What line? What poem?"

"Your poem about Kim. You gave me a copy."

"Oh, yes. Just give me a moment, will you? I'm not completely awake."

"I'm sorry to call so late, but—"

"That's all right. What was the line?"

"Shatter / Wine bottles at her feet, let green glass / Sparkle upon her hand."

"*Sparkle*'s wrong."

"I've got the poem right here, it says—"

"Oh, I know that's what I wrote," she said, "but it's wrong. I'll have to change it. I *think*. What about the line?"

"Where did you get the green glass from?"

"From the shattered wine bottles."

"Why green glass on her hand? What's it a reference to?"

"Oh," she said. "Oh, I see what you mean. Her ring."

"She had a ring with a green stone, didn't she?"

"That's right."

"How long did she have it?"

"I don't know." She thought it over. "The first time I saw it was just before I wrote the poem."

"You're sure of that?"

"At least that's the first time I noticed it. It gave me a handle on the poem, as a matter of fact. The contrast of the blue of her eyes and the green of the ring, but then I lost the blue when I got working on the poem."

She'd told me something along those lines when she first showed me the poem. I hadn't known then what she was talking about.

She wasn't sure when that might have been. How long had she been working on one or another version of the poem? Since a month before Kim's murder? Two months?

"I don't know," she said. "I have trouble placing events in time. I don't tend to keep track."

"But it was a ring with a green stone."

"Oh, yes. I can picture it now."

"Do you know where she got it? Who gave it to her?"

"I don't know anything about it," she said. "Maybe—"

"Yes?"

"Maybe she shattered a wine bottle."

To Durkin I said, "A friend of Kim's wrote a poem and mentioned the ring. And there's Sunny Hendryx's suicide note." I got out my notebook, flipped it open. I read, " 'There's no way off the merry-go-round. She grabbed the brass ring and it turned her finger green. Nobody's going to buy me emeralds.' "

He took the book from me. "*She* meaning Dakkinen, I suppose," he said. "There's more here. 'Nobody's going to give me babies. Nobody's going to save my life.' Dakkinen wasn't pregnant and neither was Hendryx, so what's this shit about babies? And neither one of them had her life saved." He closed the book with a snap, handed it across the desk to me. "I don't know where you can go with this," he said. "It doesn't look to me like something you can take to the bank. Who knows when Hendryx wrote this? Maybe after the booze and the pills started working, and who can say where she was coming from?"

Behind us, two men in plainclothes were putting a young white kid in the holding cage. A desk away, a sullen black woman was answering questions. I picked up the top photo on the stack and looked at Kim Dakkinen's butchered body. Durkin switched on the razor and finished shaving.

"What I don't understand," he said, "is what you think you got. You think she had a boyfriend and the boyfriend gave her the ring. Okay. You also figured she had a boyfriend and he gave her the fur jacket, and you traced that and it looks as though you were right, but the jacket won't lead to the boyfriend because he kept his name out of it. If you can't trace him with a jacket that we've got, how can you trace him with a ring that all we know about it is it's missing? You see what I mean?"

"I see what you mean."

"That Sherlock Holmes thing, the dog that didn't bark, well what you got is a ring that isn't there, and what does it prove?"

"It's gone."

"Right."

"Where'd it go?"

"Same place a bathtub ring goes. Down the fucking drain. How do I know where it went?"

"It disappeared."

"So? Either it walked away or someone took it."

"Who?"

"How do I know who?"

"Let's say she wore it to the hotel where she was killed."

"You can't know that."

"Let's just say so, all right?"

"Okay, run with it."

"Who took it? Some cop yank it off her finger?"

"No," he said. "Nobody'd do that. There's people who'll take cash if it's loose, we both know that, but a ring off a murder victim's finger?" He shook his head. "Besides, nobody was alone with her. It's something nobody'd do with somebody else watching."

"How about the maid? The one who discovered the body?"

"Jesus, no way. I questioned the poor woman. She took one look at the body and started screaming and she'd still be screaming now if she had the breath left. You couldn'ta got her close enough to Dakkinen to touch her with a mop handle."

"Who took the ring?"

"Assuming she wore it there—"

"Right."

"So the killer took it."

"Why?"

"Maybe he's queer for jewelry. Maybe green's his favorite color."

"Keep going."

"Maybe it's valuable. You got a guy who goes around killing people, his morals aren't the best. He might not draw the line at stealing."

"He left a few hundred dollars in her purse, Joe."

"Maybe he didn't have time to go through her bag."

"He had time to take a shower, for Christ's sake. He had time to go through her bag. In fact, we don't know that he didn't go through her bag. We just know he didn't take the money."

"So?"

"But he took the ring. He had time to take hold of her bloody hand and tug it off her finger."

"Maybe it came off easy. Maybe it wasn't a snug fit."

"Why'd he take it?"

"He wanted it for his sister."

"Got any better reasons?"

"No," he said. "No, goddamn it, I don't have any better reasons. What are you getting at? He took it because it could be traced to him?"

"Why not?"

"Then why didn't he take the fur? We fucking *know* a boyfriend bought her the fur. Maybe he didn't use his name, but how can he be sure of what he let slip and what the salesman remembers? He took towels, for Christ's sake, so he wouldn't leave a fucking pubic hair behind, but he left the fur. And now you say he took the ring. Where did this ring come from besides left field? Why have I got to hear about this ring tonight when I never heard of it once in the past two and a half weeks?"

I didn't say anything. He picked up his cigarettes, offered me one. I shook my head. He took one for himself and lit it. He took a drag, blew out a column of smoke, then ran a hand over his head, smoothing down the dark hair that already lay flat upon his scalp.

He said, "Could be there was some engraving. People do that with rings, engraving on the inside. To Kim from Freddie, some shit like that. You think that's it?"

"I don't know."

"You got a theory?"

I remembered what Danny Boy Bell had said. If the boyfriend commanded such muscle, was so well connected, how come he hadn't shown her off? And if it was someone else with the muscle and the connections and the insufficient words to the wise, how did that someone else fit in with the boyfriend? Who was this accountant type who paid for her mink, and why wasn't I getting a smell of him from anywhere else?

And why did the killer take the ring?

I reached into my pocket. My fingers touched the gun, felt its cool metal, slipped beneath it to find the little cube of broken green glass that had started all of this. I took it from my pocket and looked at it, and Durkin asked me what it was.

"Green glass," I said.

"Like the ring."

I nodded. He took the piece of glass from me, held it to the light, dropped it back in my palm. "We don't know she wore the ring to the hotel," he reminded me. "We just said so for the sake of argument."

"I know."

"Maybe she left it at the apartment. Maybe someone took it from there."

"Who?"

"The boyfriend. Let's say he didn't kill her, let's say it was an EDP like I said from the beginning—"

"You really use that expression?"

"You get so you use the expressions they want you to use, you know how it works. Let's say the psycho killed her and the boyfriend's worried he'll be tied into it. So he goes to the apartment, he's got a key, and he takes the ring. Maybe he bought her other presents and he took them, too. He would've taken the fur, too, but it was in the hotel. Why isn't that theory just as good as the killer yanking the ring off her finger?"

Because it wasn't a psycho, I thought. Because a psycho killer wouldn't be sending men in lumber jackets to warn me off, wouldn't be passing messages to me through Danny Boy Bell. Because a psycho wouldn't have worried about handwriting or fingerprints or towels.

Unless he was some sort of Jack the Ripper type, a psycho who planned and took precautions. But that wasn't it, that couldn't be it, and the ring had to be significant. I dropped the piece of glass back into my pocket. It meant something, it had to mean something.

Durkin's phone rang. He picked it up, said "Joe Durkin" and "Yeah, right, right." He listened, grunting acknowledgment from time to time, darting a pointed look in my direction, making notes on a memo pad.

I went over to the coffee machine and got us both coffee. I couldn't remember what he took in his coffee, then remembered how bad the coffee was out of that machine and added cream and sugar to both cups.

He was still on the phone when I got back to the desk. He took the coffee, nodded his thanks, sipped it, lit a fresh cigarette to go with it. I drank some of my own coffee and made my way through Kim's file, hoping something I saw might bridge a gap for me. I thought of my conversation with Donna. What was wrong with the word *sparkle?* Hadn't the ring sparkled on Kim's finger? I remembered how it had looked with the light striking it. Or was I just fabricating the memory to reinforce my own theory? And did I even have a theory? I had a missing ring and no hard evidence that the ring had even existed. A poem, a suicide note, and my own remark about eight million stories in the Emerald City. Had the ring triggered that subconsciously? Or was I just identifying with the crew on the Yellow Brick Road, wishing I had a brain and a heart and a dose of courage?

Durkin said, "Yeah, it's a pisser, all right. Don't go 'way, okay? I'll be right out."

He hung up, looked at me. His expression was a curious one, self-satisfaction mixed with something that might have been pity.

He said, "The Powhattan Motel, you know where Queens Boulevard cuts the Long Island Expressway? It's just past the intersection. I don't know just where, Elmhurst or Rego Park. Right about where they run into each other."

"So?"

"One of those adult motels, waterbeds in some of the rooms, X-rated movies on the teevee. They get cheaters, the hot-sheet trade, take a room for two hours. They'll turn a room five, six times a night if they get the volume, and a lot of it's cash, they can skim it. Very profitable, motels like that."

"What's the point?"

"Guy drove up, rented a room a couple of hours ago. Well, that business, you make up the room soon as the customer leaves it. Manager noticed the car was gone, went to the room. Do Not Disturb sign hanging on the door. He knocks, no answer, he knocks again, still no answer. He opens the door and guess what he finds?"

I waited.

"Cop named Lennie Garfein responded to the call, first thing that struck him was the similarity to what we had at the Galaxy Downtowner. That was him on the phone. We won't know until we get the medical evidence, direction of thrust, nature of wounds, all that, but it sure as hell sounds identical. Killer even took a shower, took the towels with him when he left."

"Was it—"

"Was it what?"

It wasn't Donna. I'd just spoken to her. Fran, Ruby, Mary Lou—

"Was it one of Chance's women?"

"Hell," he said, "how do I know who Chance's women are? You think all I do is keep tabs on pimps?"

"Who was it?"

"Not one of anybody's women," he said. He crushed out his cigarette, started to help himself to a fresh one, changed his mind and pushed it back into the pack. "Not a woman," he said.

"Not—"

"Not who?"

"Not Calderón. Octavio Calderón, the room clerk."

He let out a bark of laughter. "Jesus, what a mind you got," he said. "You really want things to make sense. No, not a woman, and not your boy Calderón either. This was a transsexual hooker off the Long Island City stroll. Preoperative, from what Garfein said. Means the tits are there, the silicone implants, but she's still got her male genitals. You hear me? *Her* male genitals. Jesus, what a world. Of course maybe she got the operation tonight. Maybe that was surgery there, with a machete."

I couldn't react. I sat there, numb. Durkin got to his feet, put a hand on my shoulder. "I got a car downstairs. I'm gonna run out there, take a look at what they got. You want to tag along?"

Chapter 28

The body was still there, sprawled full-length on the king-size bed. It had bled white, leaving the skin with the translucence of old china. Only the genitalia, hacked almost beyond recognition, identified the victim as male. The face was that of a woman. So was the smooth and hairless skin, the slender but full-breasted body.

"She'd fool you," Garfein said. "See, she had the preliminary surgery. The breast implants, the Adam's apple, the cheekbones. And of course the hormone shots all along. That keeps down the beard and the body hair, makes the skin nice and feminine. Look at the wound in the left breast there. You can see the silicone sac. See?"

Blood all over, and the smell of fresh death in the air. Not the stale reek of a late-found corpse, not the stench of decomposition, but the horrible odor of a slaughterhouse, the raw throat-catching smell of fresh blood. I felt not so much nauseated as overpowered, oppressed by the warmth and density of the air.

"What was lucky is I recognized her," Garfein was saying. "That way I knew right off she was a pross and that made the connection in my mind with that case of yours, Joe. Was the one you caught as bloody as this?"

"Same thing," Durkin said.

I said, "You recognized her?"

"Oh, right away. I did a hitch not that long ago with the Pussy Posse over in Long Island City. They still got a stroll there, they've had street prostitution in that same location for forty or fifty years, but now you're getting a lot of middle-class people moving in there, converting lofts for residential use, buying up the old brownstones and converting them back from rooming houses to nice homes. They sign the lease in the daytime and then they move in and they look at what's around them and they aren't happy, and the pressure comes down to clean up the street." He pointed at the figure on the bed. "I must have arrested her, oh, say three times."

"You know her name?"

"Which name do you want? They've all got more than one. Her street name was Cookie. That was the name that came to me when I saw her. Then I called in to the station house at Fiftieth and Vernon and had somebody pull her file. She was calling herself Sara but back when she made her bar mitzvah the name they wrote down was Mark Blaustein."

"She had a bar mitzvah?"

"Who knows? I wasn't invited. But she's a nice Jewish girl from Floral Park is the point I'm making. A nice Jewish girl who used to be a nice Jewish boy."

"Sara Blaustein?"

"Sara Bluestone a/k/a Sara Blue. A/k/a Cookie. Notice the hands and feet? They're on the large side for a girl. That's one way you can tell a transsexual. Of course it's not foolproof, you get girls with big hands and boys with small ones. She'd fool you, wouldn't she?"

I nodded.

"She would have had the rest of the surgery soon. Probably already had herself scheduled for the operation. Law says they have to live as a woman for a year before Medicaid'll pick up the tab. Of course they all got Medicaid, they all got welfare. They'll turn ten or twenty tricks a night, all quickie blow jobs in the johns' cars for ten or twenty bucks a pop, they'll bring in a couple of hundred dollars a night seven nights a week, all of it tax free, and they got Medicaid and welfare and the ones with kids get ADC and half the pimps are on SSI."

He and Durkin batted that ball around a little. Meanwhile the technical people were busy around us, measuring things, taking photographs, dusting for prints. We got out of their way and stood together in the motel parking lot.

Durkin said, "You know what we got, don't you? We got us Jack the fucking Ripper."

"I know it," Garfein said.

"You get anything with the other guests? She musta made some noise."

"You kidding? Cheaters? 'I didn't see nothin', I didn't hear nothin', I gotta go now.' Even if she did some screaming, in a job like this everybody'd figure it was a new way to have fun. Assuming they weren't too busy having their own fun to notice."

"First he checks into a decent midtown hotel and phones up a fancy call girl. Then he picks up a TV streetwalker and drags her to a cheater's motel. You figure the cock and balls came as a shock to him?"

Garfein shrugged. "Maybe. You know, half your street prostitutes are guys in drag. Some sections it's more than half."

"The West Side docks it's a lot more than half."

"I've heard that," Garfein said. "You talk to the johns, some of 'em'll admit they prefer if it's a guy. They say a guy gives better head. Of course there's nothing queer about them, see, because they're just receiving it."

"Well, go figure a john," Durkin said.

"Whether he knew or not, I don't think it put him off much. He went and did his number all the same."

"Figure he had sex with her?"

"Hard to tell unless there's traces on the sheets. He doesn't figure as her first trick of the evening."

"He took a shower?"

Garfein shrugged, showed his hands palms up. "Go know," he said. "The manager says there's towels missing. When they make up the room they put out two bath towels and two hand towels, and both of the bath towels are missing."

"He took towels from the Galaxy."

"Then he probably took 'em here, but who knows in a dump like this? I mean who knows if they always remember to make up the room right. Same with the shower. I don't figure they gave it a scrub after the last party left."

"Maybe you'll find something."

"Maybe."

"Fingerprints, something. You see any skin under her nails?"

"No. But that's not to say the lab boys won't." A muscle worked in his jaw. "I'll say one thing. Thank God I'm not a medical examiner or a technician. It's bad enough being a cop."

"Amen to that," Durkin said.

I said, "If he picked her up on the street, somebody might have seen her get into the car."

"A couple of guys are out there now trying to take statements. We might get something. If anybody saw anything, and if they remember, and if they feel like talking."

"Lots of ifs," Durkin said.

"The manager here must have seen him," I said. "What does he remember?"

"Not a whole lot. Let's go talk to him some more."

* * *

THE manager had a night worker's sallow complexion and a pair of red-rimmed eyes. There was alcohol on his breath but he didn't have a drinker's way about him, and I guessed he'd tried to fortify himself with liquor after discovering the body. It only made him vague and ineffectual. "This is a decent place," he insisted, and the statement was so palpably absurd no one responded to it. I suppose he meant murder wasn't a daily occurrence.

He never saw Cookie. The man who had presumably killed her had come in alone, filled out the card, paid cash. This was not unusual. It was common practice for the woman to wait in the car while the man checked in. The car had not stopped directly in front of the office, so he hadn't seen it while the man was checking in. In fact he hadn't really seen the car at all.

"You saw it was missing," Garfein reminded him. "That's how you knew the room was empty."

"Except it wasn't. I opened the door and—"

"You thought it was empty because the car was gone. How'd you know it was gone if you never saw it?"

"The parking space was empty. There's a space in front of each unit, the spaces are numbered same as the units. I looked out, that space was empty, that meant his car was gone."

"They always park in the proper spaces?"

"They're supposed to."

"Lots of things people are supposed to do. Pay their taxes, don't spit on the sidewalk, cross only at corners. A guy's in a hurry to dip his wick, what does he care about a number on a parking space? You got a look at the car."

"I—"

"You looked once, maybe twice, and the car was parked in the space. Then you looked later and it wasn't and that's when you decided they were gone. Isn't that what happened?"

"I guess so."

"Describe the car."

"I didn't really look at it. I looked to see that it was there, that's all."

"What color was it?"

"Dark."

"Terrific. Two door? Four door?"

"I didn't notice."

"New? Old? What make?"

"It was a late-model car," he said. "American. Not a foreign car. As far as the make, when I was a kid they all looked different. Now every car's the same."

"He's right," Durkin said.

"Except American Motors," he said. "A Gremlin, a Pacer, those you can tell. The rest all look the same."

"And this wasn't a Gremlin or a Pacer."

"No."

"Was it a sedan? A hatchback?"

"I'll tell you the truth," the man said. "All I noticed is it was a car. It says on the card, the make and model, the plate number."

"You're talking about the registration card?"

"Yeah. They have to fill all that in."

The card was on the desk, a sheet of clear acetate over it to preserve prints until the lab boys had their shot at it. *Name: Martin Albert Ricone. Address: 211 Gilford Way. City: Fort Smith, Arkansas. Make of Auto: Chevrolet. Year: 1980. Model: Sedan. Color: Black. License No.: LJK-914. Signature: M.A. RICONE.*

"Looks like the same hand," I told Durkin. "But who can tell with printing?"

"The experts can say. Same as they can tell you if he had

the same light touch with the machete. Guy likes forts, you notice? Fort Wayne, Indiana and Fort Smith, Arkansas."

"A subtle pattern begins to emerge," Garfein said.

"Ricone," Durkin said. "Must be Italian."

"M. A. Ricone sounds like the guy who invented the radio."

"That's Marconi," Durkin said.

"Well, that's close. This guy's Macaroni. Stuck a feather in his hat and called it Macaroni."

"Stuck a feather up his ass," Durkin said.

"Maybe he stuck it up Cookie's ass and maybe it wasn't a feather. Martin Albert Ricone, that's a fancy alias. What did he use last time?"

"Charles Owen Jones," I said.

"Oh, he likes middle names. He's a cute fucker, isn't he?"

"Very cute," Durkin said.

"The cute ones, the really cute ones, usually everything means something. Like *Jones* is slang, it means a habit. You know, like a heroin jones. Like a junkie says he's got a hundred-dollar jones, that's what his habit costs him per day."

"I'm really glad you explained that for me," Durkin said.

"Just trying to be helpful."

" 'Cause I only got fourteen years in, I never had any contact yet with smack addicts."

"So be a smart fuck," Garfein said.

"The license plate go anywhere?"

"It's gonna go the same place as the name and address. I got a call in to Arkansas Motor Vehicles but it's a waste of time. A place like this, even the legitimate guests make up the plate number. They don't park in front of the window when they sign in so our guy here can't check. Not that he would anyway, would you?"

"There's no law says I have to check," the man said.

"They use false names, too. Funny our boy used Jones at

the Galaxy and Ricone here. They must get a lot of Joneses here, along with the usual run of Smiths and Browns. You get a lot of Smiths?"

"There's no law says I'm supposed to check ID," the man said.

"Or wedding rings, huh?"

"Or wedding rings or marriage licenses or anything. Consenting adults, the hell, it's none of my business."

"Maybe Ricone means something in Italian," Garfein suggested.

"Now you're thinking," Durkin said. He asked the manager if he had an Italian dictionary. The man stared at him, baffled. "And they call this place a motel," he said, shaking his head. "There's probably no Gideon Bibles, either."

"Most of the rooms have them."

"Jesus, really? Right next to the television with the X-rated movies, right? Conveniently located near the waterbed."

"Only two of the units have waterbeds," the poor bastard said. "There's an extra charge for a waterbed."

"Good thing our Mr. Ricone's a cheap prick," Garfein said. "Cookie'da wound up underwater."

"Tell me about this guy," Durkin said. "Describe him again."

"I told you—"

"You're gonna get to tell this again and again. How tall was he?"

"Tall."

"My height? Shorter? Taller?"

"I—"

"What was he wearing? He have a hat on? He wearing a tie?"

"It's hard to remember."

"He walks in the door, asks you for a room. Now he's filling out the card. Pays you in cash. What do you get for a room like that, incidentally?"

"Twenty-eight dollars."

"That's not such a bad deal. I suppose the porn movies are extra."

"It's coin-operated."

"Handy. Twenty-eight's fair, and it's a good deal for you if you can flip the room a few times a night. How'd he pay you?"

"I told you. Cash."

"I mean what kind of bills? What'd he give you, a pair of fifteens?"

"A pair of—"

"He give you a twenty and a ten?"

"I think it was two twenties."

"And you gave him twelve bucks back? Wait, there must have been tax, right?"

"It's twenty-nine forty with the tax."

"And he gave you forty bucks and you gave him the change."

Something registered. "He gave me two twenties and forty cents in change," the man said. "And I gave him a ten and a one."

"See? You remember the transaction."

"Yeah, I do. Sort of."

"Now tell me what he looked like. He white?"

"Yeah, sure. White."

"Heavy? Thin?"

"Thin but not too thin. On the thin side."

"Beard?"

"No."

"Moustache?"

"Maybe. I don't know."

"There was something about him, though, something that stuck in your memory."

"What?"

"That's what we're trying to get, John. That what they call you? John?"

"Mostly it's Jack."

"Okay, Jack. You're doin' fine now. What about his hair?"

"I didn't pay attention to his hair."

"Sure you did. He bent over to sign in and you saw the top of his head, remember?"

"I don't—"

"Full head of hair?"

"I don't—"

"THEY'LL sit him down with one of our artists," Durkin said, "and he'll come up with something. And when this fucking psycho ripper steps on his cock one of these days, when we catch him in the act or on his way out the door, he'll look as much like the police artist's sketch as I look like Sara fucking Blaustein. She looked like a woman, didn't she?"

"Mostly she looked dead."

"I know. Meat in a butcher's window." We were in his car, driving over the bumpy surface of the Queensboro Bridge. The sky was starting to lighten up already. I was beyond tiredness by now, with the ragged edges of my emotions perilously close to the surface. I could feel my own vulnerability; the smallest thing could nudge me to tears or laughter.

"You gotta wonder what it would be like," he said.

"What?"

"Picking up somebody who looked like that. On the street or in a bar, whatever. Then you get her someplace and she takes her clothes off and surprise. I mean, how do you react?"

"I don't know."

"'Course if she already had the operation, you could go with her and never know. Her hands didn't look so big to me. There's women with big hands and men with little hands, far as that goes."

"Uh-huh."

"She had a couple rings on, speaking of her hands. You happen to notice?"

"I noticed."

"One on each hand, she had."

"So?"

"So he didn't take 'em."

"Why would he take her rings?"

"You were saying he took Dakkinen's."

I didn't say anything.

Gently he said, "Matt, you don't still think Dakkinen got killed for a reason?"

I felt rage swelling up within me, bulging like an aneurysm in a blood vessel. I sat there trying to will it away.

"And don't tell me about the towels. He's a ripper, he's a cute fucking psycho who makes plans and plays by his own private rules. He's not the first case like that to come along."

"I got warned off the case, Joe. I got very professionally warned off the case."

"So? She got killed by a psycho and there could still be something about her life that some friends of hers don't want to come out in the open. Maybe she had a boyfriend and he's a married guy, just like you figured, and even if what she died of was scarlet fucking fever he wouldn't want you poking around in the ashes."

I gave myself the Miranda warning. *You have the right to remain silent*, I told myself, and exercised the right.

"Unless you figure Dakkinen and Blaustein are tied together. Long-lost sisters, say. Excuse me, brother and sister. Or maybe they were brothers, maybe Dakkinen had her operation a few years ago. Tall for a girl, wasn't she?"

"Maybe Cookie was a smokescreen," I said.

"How's that?"

I went on talking in spite of myself. "Maybe he killed her to take the heat off," I said. "Make it look like a train of random murders. To hide his motive for killing Dakkinen."

"To take the heat off. What heat, for Christ's sake?"

"I don't know."

"There's been no fucking heat. There will be now. Nothing turns the fucking press on like a series of random killings. The readers eat it up, they pour it on their corn flakes. Anything gives 'em a chance to run a sidebar on the original Jack the Ripper, those editors go crazy for it. You talk about heat, there'll be enough heat now to scorch his ass for him."

"I suppose."

"You know what you are, Scudder? You're stubborn."

"Maybe."

"Your problem is you work private and you only carry one case at a time. I got so much shit on my desk it's a pleasure when I get to let go of something, but with you it's just the opposite. You want to hang onto it as long as you can."

"Is that what it is?"

"I don't know. It sounds like it." He took one hand off the wheel, tapped me on the forearm. "I don't mean to bust balls," he said. "I see something like that, somebody chopped up like that, I try to clamp a lid on it and it comes out in other directions. You did a lot of good work."

"Did I?"

"No question. There were things we missed. It might give us a little jump on the psycho, some of the stuff you came up with. Who knows?"

Not I. All I knew was how tired I was.

He fell silent as we drove across town. In front of my hotel he braked to a stop and said, "What Garfein said there. Maybe Ricone means something in Italian."

"It won't be hard to check."

"Oh, of course not. Everything should be that easy to run

down. No, we'll check, and you know what we'll find? It'll turn out it means Jones."

I went upstairs and got out of my clothes and into bed. Ten minutes later I got up again. I felt unclean and my scalp itched. I stood under a too-hot shower and scrubbed myself raw. I got out of the shower, told myself it didn't make any sense to shave before going to bed, then lathered up and shaved anyway. When I was done I put a robe on and sat down on the edge of my bed, then moved to the chair.

They tell you not to let yourself get too hungry, too angry, too lonely or too tired. Any of the four can put you off balance and turn you in the direction of a drink. It seemed to me that I'd touched all four bases, I'd boxed that particular compass in the course of the day and night. Oddly enough, I didn't feel the urge for a drink.

I got the gun from my coat pocket, I started to return it to the dresser drawer, then changed my mind and sat in the chair again, turning the gun in my hands.

When was the last time I'd fired a gun?

I didn't really have to think very hard. It had been that night in Washington Heights when I chased two holdup men into the street, shot them down and killed that little girl in the process. In the time I remained on the force after that incident, I never had occasion to draw my service revolver, let alone discharge it. And I certainly hadn't fired a gun since I left the force.

And tonight I'd been unable to do it. Because something clued me that the car I was aiming at held drunken kids instead of assassins? Because some subtle intuitive perception made me wait until I was certain what I was shooting at?

No. I couldn't make myself believe that.

I had frozen. If instead of a kid with a whiskey bottle I'd seen a thug with a tommy gun, I wouldn't have been any more capable of squeezing the trigger. My finger'd been paralyzed.

I broke the gun, shook the bullets out of the cylinder, closed it up again. I pointed the empty weapon at the wastebasket across the room and squeezed the trigger a couple of times. The *click* the hammer made as it fell upon an empty chamber was surprisingly loud and sharp in my little room.

I aimed at the mirror over the dresser. *Click!*

Proved nothing. It was empty, I knew it was empty. I could take the thing to a pistol range, load it and fire at targets, and that wouldn't prove anything either.

It bothered me that I'd been unable to fire the gun. And yet I was grateful it had happened that way, because otherwise I'd have emptied the gun into that car of kids, probably killed a few of them, and what would that have done to my peace of mind? Tired as I was, I went a few hard rounds with that particular conundrum. I was glad I hadn't shot anyone and frightened of the implications of not shooting, and my mind went around and around, chasing its tail.

I took off the robe, got into bed, and couldn't even begin to loosen up. I got dressed again in street clothes, used the back end of a nail file as a screwdriver, and took the revolver apart for cleaning. I put its parts in one pocket, and in another I stowed the four live cartridges along with the two knives I'd taken from the mugger.

It was morning and the sky was bright. I walked over to Ninth Avenue and up to Fifty-eighth Street, where I dropped both knives into a sewer grating. I crossed the street and walked to another grating and stood near it with my hands in my pockets, one holding the four cartridges, the other touching the pieces of the disassembled revolver.

Why carry a gun you're not going to shoot? Why own a gun you can't carry?

I stopped in a deli on the way back to the hotel. The customer ahead of me bought two six-packs of Old English 800 Malt Liquor. I picked out four candy bars and paid for them, ate one as I walked and the other three in my room. Then I took the revolver's parts from my pocket and put them back together again. I loaded four of the six chambers and put the gun in the dresser drawer.

I got into bed, told myself I'd stay there whether I could sleep or not, and smiled at the thought as I felt myself drifting off.

Chapter 29

The telephone woke me. I fought my way out of sleep like an underwater swimmer coming up for air. I sat up, blinking and trying to catch my breath. The phone was still ringing and I couldn't figure out what was making that damned sound. Then I caught on and answered it.

It was Chance. "Just saw the paper," he said. "What do you figure? That the same guy as got Kim?"

"Give me a minute," I said.

"You asleep?"

"I'm awake now."

"Then you don't know what I'm talkin' about. There was another killing, this time in Queens, some sex-change street-walker cut to ribbons."

"I know."

"How do you know if you been sleeping?"

"I was out there last night."

"Out there in Queens?"

He sounded impressed. "Out there on Queens Boulevard," I told him. "With a couple of cops. It was the same killer."

"You sure of that?"

"They didn't have the scientific evidence sorted out when I was there. But yes, I'm sure of it."

He thought about it. "Then Kim was just unlucky," he said. "Just in the wrong place at the wrong time."

"Maybe."

"Just maybe?"

I got my watch from the nightstand. It was almost noon.

"There are elements that don't fit," I said. "At least it seems that way to me. A cop last night told me my problem is I'm too stubborn. I've only got the one case and I don't want to let go of it."

"So?"

"He could be right, but there are still some things that don't fit. What happened to Kim's ring?"

"What ring?"

"She had a ring with a green stone."

"Ring," he said, and thought about it. "Was it Kim had that ring? I guess it was."

"What happened to it?"

"Wasn't it in her jewelry box?"

"That was her class ring. From high school back home."

"Yeah, right. I recall the ring you mean. Big green stone. Was a birthstone ring, something like that."

"Where'd she get it?"

"Out of a Crackerjack box, most likely. Think she said she bought it for herself. It was just a piece of junk, man. Chunk of green glass is all."

Shatter wine bottles at her feet.

"It wasn't an emerald?"

"You shuckin', man? You know what emeralds cost?"

"No."

"More'n diamonds. Why's the ring important?"

"Maybe it's not."

"What do you do next?"

"I don't know," I said. "If Kim got killed by a psycho

striking at random, I don't know what I can do that the cops can't do better. But there's somebody who wants me off the case, and there's a hotel clerk who got scared into leaving town, and there's a missing ring."

"That maybe doesn't mean anything."

"Maybe."

"Wasn't there something in Sunny's note about a ring turning somebody's finger green? Maybe it was a cheap ring, turned Kim's finger green, and she got rid of it."

"I don't think that's what Sunny meant."

"What did she mean, then?"

"I don't know that either." I took a breath. "I'd like to connect Cookie Blue and Kim Dakkinen," I said. "That's what I'd like to do. If I can manage that I can probably find the man who killed them both."

"Maybe. You be at Sunny's service tomorrow?"

"I'll be there."

"Then I'll see you. Maybe we can talk a little afterward."

"Fine."

"Yeah," he said. "Kim and Cookie. What could they have in common?"

"Didn't Kim work the streets for a while? Didn't she take a bust on that Long Island City stroll?"

"Years ago."

"She had a pimp named Duffy, didn't she? Did Cookie have a pimp?"

"Could be. Some of the TVs do. Most of 'em don't, from what I know. Maybe I could ask around."

"Maybe you could."

"I haven't seen Duffy in months. I think I heard he was dead. But I'll ask around. Hard to figure, though, that a girl like Kim had anything in common with a little Jewish queen from the Island."

A Jewish queen and a Dairy Queen, I thought, and thought of Donna.

"Maybe they were sisters," I suggested.

"Sisters?"

"Under the skin."

I wanted breakfast, but when I hit the street I bought a paper before I did anything else, and I could see right away that it wasn't going to make a good accompaniment for my bacon and eggs. *Hotel Ripper Claims Second Victim*, the top teaser headline announced. And then, in big block caps, SEX-CHANGE HOOKER BUTCHERED IN QUEENS.

I folded it, tucked it under my arm. I don't know what I thought I was going to do first, read the paper or eat, but my feet decided for me and picked neither of those choices. I walked two blocks before I realized I was heading for the Y on West Sixty-third, and that I was going to get there just in time for the twelve-thirty meeting.

What the hell, I thought. Their coffee was as good as anybody else's.

I got out of there an hour later and had breakfast in a Greek joint around the corner on Broadway. I read the paper while I ate. It didn't seem to bother me now.

There wasn't much in the story I didn't already know. The victim was described as having lived in the East Village; I'd somehow assumed she lived across the river in Queens. Garfein had mentioned Floral Park, just across the line in Nassau County, and evidently that was where she'd grown up. Her parents, according to the *Post*, had both died several years earlier in an air crash. Mark/Sara/Cookie's sole surviving relative was a brother, Adrian Blaustein, a wholesale jeweler residing in Forest Hills with offices on West Forty-seventh Street. He was out of the country and had not yet been notified of his brother's death.

His brother's death? Or his sister's? How did a relative relate to someone who'd changed sex? How did a respectable

businessman regard a brother-turned-sister who turned
quick tricks in strangers' parked cars? What would Cookie
Blue's death mean to Adrian Blaustein?

What did it mean to me?

*Any man's death diminishes me, because I am involved in
mankind.* Any man's death, any woman's death, any death in
between. But did it diminish me? And was I truly involved?

I could still feel the trigger of the .32 trembling beneath
my finger.

I ordered another cup of coffee and turned to a story about
a young soldier home on furlough, playing pickup basketball at a sandlot game in the Bronx. A gun had apparently
fallen out of some bystander's pocket, discharging on impact, and the bullet had struck this young serviceman and
killed him instantly. I read the story through a second time
and sat there shaking my head at it.

One more way to die. Jesus, there really were eight million of them, weren't there?

At twenty to nine that evening I slipped into the basement of
a church on Prince Street in SoHo. I got myself a cup of coffee, and while I looked for a seat I scanned the room for Jan.
She was near the front on the right-hand side. I sat further
back near the coffee.

The speaker was a woman in her thirties who drank for
ten years and spent the last three of them on the Bowery,
panhandling and wiping windshields to get money for wine.
"Even on the Bowery," she said, "there are some people who
know how to take care of themselves. Some of the men
down there always carry a razor and a bar of soap. I gravi-
tated straight to the other kind, the ones who don't shave and
don't wash and don't change their clothes. A little voice in
my head said, 'Rita, you're right where you belong.' "

During the break I ran into Jan on her way to the coffee
urn. She seemed pleased to see me. "I was in the neighbor-

hood," I explained, "and it got to be meeting time. It occurred to me I might see you here."

"Oh, this is one of my regular meetings," she said. "We'll go for coffee after, okay?"

"Sure."

A dozen of us wound up around a couple of tables in a coffee shop on West Broadway. I didn't take a very active part in the conversation, or pay too much attention to it. Eventually the waiter distributed separate checks. Jan paid hers and I paid mine and the two of us headed downtown toward her place.

I said, "I didn't just happen to be in the neighborhood."

"There's a big surprise."

"I wanted to talk to you. I don't know if you read today's paper—"

"About the killing in Queens? Yes, I did."

"I was out there. I'm all wound up and I feel the need to talk about it."

We went up to her loft and she made a pot of coffee. I sat with a cup of coffee in front of me and by the time I stopped talking and took a sip it was cold. I brought her up to date, told her about Kim's fur jacket, about the drunken kids and the broken wine bottle, about the trip to Queens and what we'd found there. And I told her, too, how I'd spent this afternoon, riding the subway across the river and walking around Long Island City, returning to knock on doors in Cookie Blue's East Village tenement, then crossed the island to work the gay bars on Christopher Street and up and down West Street.

By then it had been late enough to get in touch with Joe Durkin and learn what the lab had come up with.

"It was the same killer," I told Jan. "And he used the same weapon. He's tall, right handed, and pretty powerful, and he keeps a sharp edge on his machete, or whatever the hell he uses."

Phone checks with Arkansas yielded nothing. The Fort Smith street address was a phony, predictably enough, and the auto license plate belonged to an orange Volkswagen owned by a nursery school teacher in Fayetteville.

"And she only drove it on Sundays," Jan said.

"Something like that. He made up the whole Arkansas business the same as he made up Fort Wayne, Indiana. But the license plate was real, or almost real. Somebody thought to check the hot-car sheet, and there was a navy blue Impala stolen off the street in Jackson Heights just a couple hours before Cookie was killed. The plate number's the same as he used checking in except for a pair of digits reversed, and of course it's a New York plate instead of Arkansas.

"The car fits the motel clerk's description, such as it was. It also fits what they got from some other hookers who were on the stroll when Cookie was picked up. They say there was a car like that cruising around for a while before the dude in it made up his mind and picked up Cookie.

"The car hasn't turned up yet, but that doesn't mean he's still driving it. It can take a long time before an abandoned stolen car turns up. Sometimes the thieves leave 'em in a No Parking zone and the police tow truck hauls them to the pound. That's not supposed to happen, somebody's supposed to check towed cars against the hot sheet, but it doesn't always go the way it's supposed to. It doesn't matter. It'll turn out the killer dumped the car twenty minutes after he finished with Cookie, and that he wiped it clean of prints."

"Matt, can't you let go of it?"

"Of the whole business?"

She nodded. "It's police procedure from here on in, isn't it? Sifting evidence, running down all the details."

"I suppose so."

"And it's not as though they're likely to put this on the shelf and forget about it, the way you thought they might when it was just Kim who was dead. The papers wouldn't let them shelve it even if they wanted to."

"That's true."

"So is there a reason why you have to push yourself on this? You already gave your client his money's worth."

"Did I?"

"Didn't you? I think you worked harder for the money than he did."

"I guess you're right."

"So why stay with it? What can you do that the whole police force can't?"

I wrestled with that one. After a moment I said, "There's got to be a connection."

"What kind of connection?"

"Between Kim and Cookie. Because, damnit, otherwise they don't make sense. A psycho killer always has a pattern for what he's doing, even if it only exists in his own mind. Kim and Cookie didn't look alike and didn't have similar lives. For Christ's sake, they weren't even the same sex to start with. Kim worked off a phone in her own apartment and had a pimp. Cookie was a transsexual streetwalker doing the johns in their cars. She was an outlaw. Chance is doing some double-checking to see if she had a pimp nobody knew about, but it doesn't look likely."

I drank some cold coffee. "And he *picked* Cookie," I went on. "He took his time, he drove up and down those streets, he made sure he got her and not somebody else. Where's the connection? It's not a matter of type. She was a completely different physical type from Kim."

"Something in her personal life?"

"Maybe. Her personal life's hard to trace. She lived in the East Village and tricked in Long Island City. I couldn't find anybody in the West Side gay bars who knew her. She didn't have a pimp and she didn't have a lover. Her neighbors on East Fifth Street never knew she was a prostitute, and only a few of them suspected she wasn't a woman. Her only family's her brother and he doesn't even know she's dead."

I talked some more. *Ricone* wasn't an Italian word, and if it was a name it was an uncommon one. I'd checked telephone directories for Manhattan and Queens without finding a single Ricone listed.

When I ran dry she got more coffee for both of us and we sat for a few minutes without speaking. Then I said, "Thanks."

"For the coffee?"

"For listening. I feel better now. I had to talk my way through it."

"Talking always helps."

"I suppose so."

"You don't talk at meetings, do you?"

"Jesus, I couldn't talk about this stuff."

"Not specifically, maybe, but you could talk about what you're going through and the way it makes you feel. That might help more than you think, Matt."

"I don't think I could do it. Hell, I can't even say I'm an alcoholic. 'My name is Matt and I pass.' I could phone it in."

"Maybe that'll change."

"Maybe."

"How long have you been sober, Matt?"

I had to think. "Eight days."

"Gee, that's terrific. What's so funny?"

"Something I've noticed. One person asks another how long he's been sober, and whatever the answer is, the reply is, 'Gee, that's terrific, that's wonderful.' If I said eight days or eight years the reaction'd be the same. 'Gee, isn't that great, isn't that terrific.' "

"Well, it is."

"I guess."

"What's terrific is that you're sober. Eight years is terrific and so is eight days."

"Uh-huh."

"What's the matter?"

"Nothing. Sunny's funeral is tomorrow afternoon."

"Are you going?"

"I said I would."

"Are you worried about that?"

"Worried?"

"Nervous, anxious."

"I don't know about that. I'm not looking forward to it." I looked into her large gray eyes, then looked away. "Eight days is as long as I've gone," I said casually. "I had eight days last time, and then I drank."

"That doesn't mean you have to drink tomorrow."

"Oh, shit, I know that. I'm not going to drink tomorrow."

"Take someone with you."

"What do you mean?"

"To the funeral. Ask someone from the program to go along with you."

"I couldn't ask anyone to do that."

"Of course you could."

"Who? There's nobody I know well enough to ask."

"How well do you have to know somebody to sit next to them at a funeral?"

"Well?"

"Well what?"

"Would you go with me? Never mind, I don't want to put you on the spot."

"I'll go."

"Really?"

"Why not? Of course I might look pretty dowdy. Next to all those flashy hookers."

"Oh, I don't think so."

"No?"

"No, I don't think so at all."

I tipped up her chin and tasted her mouth with mine. I touched her hair. Dark hair, lightly salted with gray. Gray to match her eyes.

She said, "I was afraid this would happen. And then I was afraid it wouldn't."

"And now?"

"Now I'm just afraid."

"Do you want me to leave?"

"Do I want you to leave? No, I don't want you to leave. I want you to kiss me again."

I kissed her. She put her arms around me and drew me close and I felt the warmth of her body through our clothing.

"Ah, darling," she said.

AFTERWARD, lying in her bed and listening to my own heartbeat, I had a moment of utter loneliness and desolation. I felt as though I had taken the cover off a bottomless well. I reached over and laid a hand on her flank, and the physical contact cut the thread of my mood.

"Hello," I said.

"Hello."

"What are you thinking?"

She laughed. "Nothing very romantic. I was trying to guess what my sponsor's going to say."

"Do you have to tell her?"

"I don't have to do anything, but I will tell her. 'Oh, by the way, I hopped into bed with a guy who's eight days sober.'"

"That's a mortal sin, huh?"

"Let's just say it's a no-no."

"What'll she give you? Six Our Fathers?"

She laughed again. She had a good laugh, full and hearty. I'd always liked it.

"She'll say, 'Well, at least you didn't drink. That's the important thing.' And she'll say, 'I hope you enjoyed it.'"

"Did you?"

"Enjoy it?"

"Yeah."

"Hell, no. I was faking orgasm."

"Both times, huh?"

"You betcha." She drew close to me, put her hand on my chest. "You'll stay over, won't you?"

"What would your sponsor say?"

"Probably that I might as well hang for a sheep as a lamb. Oh, shit, I almost forgot."

"Where are you going?"

"Gotta make a phone call."

"You're actually calling your sponsor?"

She shook her head. She'd put a robe on and now she was paging through a small address book. She dialed a number and said, "Hi, this is Jan. You weren't sleeping, were you? Look, this is out of left field, but does the word *Ricone* mean anything to you?" She spelled it. "I thought it might be a dirty word or something. Uh-huh." Then she listened for a moment and said, "No, nothing like that. I'm doing crossword puzzles in Sicilian, that's all. On nights when I can't sleep. Listen, you can only spend so much time reading the Big Book."

She finished the conversation, hung up and said, "Well, it was a thought. I figured if it was a dialect or an obscenity it might not be in the dictionary."

"What obscenity did you think it might be? And when did the thought happen to cross your mind?"

"None of your business, wiseass."

"You're blushing."

"I know, I can feel it. That'll teach me to try to help a friend solve a murder."

"No good deed goes unpunished."

"That's what they say. Martin Albert Ricone and Charles Otis Jones? Are those the names he used?"

"Owen. Charles Owen Jones."

"And you think it means something."

"It has to mean something. Even if he's a lunatic, anything that elaborate would have to mean something."

"Like Fort Wayne and Fort Smith?"

"Like that, maybe, but I think the names he used are more significant than that. Ricone's such an unusual name."

"Maybe he started by writing *Rico*."

"I thought of that. There are plenty of Ricos in the phone book. Or maybe he's from Puerto Rico."

"Why not? Everybody else is. Maybe he's a Cagney fan."

"Cagney?"

"In the death scene. 'Mother of mercy, is this the end of Rico?' Remember?"

"I thought that was Edward G. Robinson."

"Maybe it was. I was always drunk when I watched the 'Late Show' and all those Warner Brothers gangsters tend to merge in my mind. It was one of those ballsy guys. 'Mother of mercy, is this the—' "

"Some pair of balls," I said.

"Huh?"

"Jesus Christ."

"What's the matter?"

"He's a comedian. A fucking comedian."

"What are you talking about?"

"The killer. C. O. Jones and M. A. Ricone. I thought they were names."

"They're not?"

"Cojones. Maricón."

"That's Spanish."

"Right."

"Cojones means 'balls,' doesn't it?"

"And *maricón* means 'faggot.' I don't think there's an E on the end of it, though."

"Maybe it's especially nasty with an E on the end."

"Or maybe he's just a lousy speller."

"Well, hell," she said. "Nobody's perfect."

Chapter 30

Around mid-morning I went home to shower and shave and put on my best suit. I caught a noon meeting, ate a Sabrett hot dog on the street, and met Jan as arranged at the papaya stand at Seventy-second and Broadway. She was wearing a knit dress, dove gray with touches of black. I'd never seen her in anything that dressy.

We went around the corner to Cooke's, where a professionally sympathetic young man in black determined which set of bereaved we belonged to and ushered us through a hallway to Suite Three, where a card in a slot on the open door said HENDRYX. Inside, there were perhaps six rows of four chairs each on either side of a center aisle. In the front, to the left of the lectern on a raised platform, an open casket stood amid a glut of floral sprays. I'd sent flowers that morning but I needn't have bothered. Sunny had enough of them to see a Prohibition-era mobster on his way to the Promised Land.

Chance had the aisle seat in the front row on the right. Donna Campion was seated beside him, with Fran Schecter and Mary Lou Barcker filling out the row. Chance was wearing a black suit, a white shirt, and a narrow black silk tie.

The women were all wearing black, and I wondered if he'd taken them shopping the previous afternoon.

He turned at our entrance, got to his feet. Jan and I walked over there and I managed the introductions. We stood awkwardly for a moment, and then Chance said, "You'll want to view the body," and gave a nod toward the casket.

Did anyone ever want to view a body? I walked over there and Jan walked beside me. Sunny was laid out in a brightly colored dress on a casket lining of cream-colored satin. Her hands, clasped upon her breast, held a single red rose. Her face might have been carved from a block of wax, and yet she certainly looked no worse than when I'd seen her last.

Chance was standing beside me. He said, "Talk to you a moment?"

"Sure."

Jan gave my hand a quick squeeze and slipped away. Chance and I stood side by side, looking down at Sunny.

I said, "I thought the body was still at the morgue."

"They called yesterday, said they were ready to release it. The people here worked late getting her ready. Did a pretty good job."

"Uh-huh."

"Doesn't look much like her. Didn't look like her when we found her, either, did it?"

"No."

"They'll cremate the body after. Simpler that way. The girls look right, don't they? The way they're dressed and all?"

"They look fine."

"Dignified," he said. After a pause he said, "Ruby didn't come."

"I noticed."

"She doesn't believe in funerals. Different cultures, different customs, you know? And she always kept to herself, hardly knew Sunny."

I didn't say anything.

"After this is over," he said, "I be taking the girls to their homes, you know. Then we ought to talk."

"All right."

"You know Parke Bernet? The auction gallery, the main place on Madison Avenue. There's a sale tomorrow and I wanted to look at a couple of lots I might bid on. You want to meet me there?"

"What time?"

"I don't know. This here won't be long. Be out of here by three. Say four-fifteen, four-thirty?"

"Fine."

"Say, Matt?" I turned. " 'Preciate your coming."

There were perhaps ten more mourners in attendance by the time the service got underway. A party of four blacks sat in the middle on the left-hand side, and among them I thought I recognized Kid Bascomb, the fighter I'd watched the one time I met Sunny. Two elderly women sat together in the rear, and another elderly man sat by himself near the front. There are lonely people who drop in on the funerals of strangers as a way of passing the time, and I suspected these three were of their number.

Just as the service started, Joe Durkin and another plain-clothes detective slipped into a pair of seats in the last row.

The minister looked like a kid. I don't know how thoroughly he'd been briefed, but he talked about the special tragedy of a life cut short in its prime, and about God's mysterious ways, and about the survivors being the true victims of such apparently senseless tragedy. He read passages from Emerson, Teilhard de Chardin, Martin Buber, and the Book of Ecclesiastes. Then he suggested that any of Sunny's friends who wished to might come forward and say a few words.

Donna Campion read two short poems which I assumed she'd written herself. I learned later that they were by Sylvia

Plath and Anne Sexton, two poets who had themselves committed suicide. Fran Schecter followed her and said, "Sunny, I don't know if you can hear me but I want to tell you this anyway," and went on to say how she'd valued the dead girl's friendship and cheerfulness and zest for living. She started off light and bubbly herself and wound up breaking down in tears, and the minister had to help her off stage. Mary Lou Barcker spoke just two or three sentences, and those in a low monotone, saying that she wished she'd known Sunny better and hoped she was at peace now.

Nobody else came forward. I had a brief fantasy of Joe Durkin mounting the platform and telling the crowd how the NYPD was going to get it together and win this one for the Gipper, but he stayed right where he was. The minister said a few more words—I wasn't paying attention—and then one of the attendants played a recording, Judy Collins singing "Amazing Grace."

OUTSIDE, Jan and I walked for a couple of blocks without saying anything. Then I said, "Thanks for coming."

"Thanks for asking me. God, that sounds foolish. Like a conversation after the Junior Prom. 'Thanks for asking me. I had a lovely time.' " She took a handkerchief from her purse, dabbed at her eyes, blew her nose. "I'm glad you didn't go to that alone," she said.

"So am I."

"And I'm glad I went. It was so sad and so beautiful. Who was that man who spoke to you on the way out?"

"That was Durkin."

"Oh, was it? What was he doing there?"

"Hoping to get lucky, I suppose. You never know who'll show up at a funeral."

"Not many people showed up at this one."

"Just a handful."

"I'm glad we were there."

"Uh-huh."

I bought her a cup of coffee, then put her in a cab. She insisted she could take the subway but I got her into a cab and made her take ten bucks for the fare.

A lobby attendant at Parke Bernet directed me to the second-floor gallery where Friday's African and Oceanic art was on display. I found Chance in front of a set of glassed-in shelves housing a collection of eighteen or twenty small gold figurines. Some represented animals while others depicted human beings and various household articles. One I recall showed a man sitting on his haunches and milking a goat. The largest would fit easily in a child's hand, and many of them had a droll quality about them.

"Ashanti gold weights," Chance explained. "From the land the British called the Gold Coast. It's Ghana now. You see plated reproductions in the shops. Fakes. These are the real thing."

"Are you planning to buy them?"

He shook his head. "They don't speak to me. I try to buy things that do. I'll show you something."

We crossed the room. A bronze head of a woman stood mounted on a four-foot pedestal. Her nose was broad and flattened, her cheekbones pronounced. Her throat was so thickly ringed by bronze necklaces that the overall appearance of the head was conical.

"A bronze sculpture of the lost Kingdom of Benin," he announced. "The head of a queen. You can tell her rank by the number of necklaces she's wearing. Does she speak to you, Matt? She does to me."

I read strength in the bronze features, cold strength and a merciless will.

"Know what she says? She says, 'Nigger, why you be

lookin' at me dat way? You know you ain't got de money to take me home.'" He laughed. "The presale estimate is forty to sixty thousand dollars."

"You won't be bidding?"

"I don't know what I'll be doing. There are a few pieces I wouldn't mind owning. But sometimes I come to auctions the way some people go to the track even when they don't feel like betting. Just to sit in the sun and watch the horses run. I like the way an auction room feels. I like to hear the hammer drop. You seen enough? Let's go."

His car was parked at a garage on Seventy-eighth Street. We rode over the Fifty-ninth Street Bridge and through Long Island City. Here and there street prostitutes stood along the curb singly or in pairs.

"Not many out last night," he said. "I guess they feel safer in daylight."

"You were here last night?"

"Just driving around. He picked up Cookie around here, then drove out Queens Boulevard. Or did he take the expressway? I don't guess it matters."

"No."

We took Queens Boulevard. "Want to thank you for coming to the funeral," he said.

"I wanted to come."

"Fine-looking woman with you."

"Thank you."

"Jan, you say her name was?"

"That's right."

"You go with her or—"

"We're friends."

"Uh-huh." He braked for a light. "Ruby didn't come."

"I know."

"What I told you was a bunch of shit. I didn't want to contradict what I told the others. Ruby split, she packed up and went."

"When did this happen?"

"Sometime yesterday, I guess. Last night I had a message on my service. I was running around all yesterday, trying to get this funeral organized. I thought it went okay, didn't you?"

"It was a nice service."

"That's what I thought. Anyway, there's a message to call Ruby and a 415 area code. That's San Francisco. I thought, huh? And I called, and she said she had decided to move on. I thought it was some kind of a joke, you know? Then I went over there and checked her apartment, and all her things were gone. Her clothes. She left the furniture. That makes three empty apartments I got, man. Big housing shortage, nobody can find a place to live, and I'm sitting on three empty apartments. Something, huh?"

"You sure it was her you spoke to?"

"Positive."

"And she was in San Francisco?"

"Had to be. Or Berkeley or Oakland or some such place. I dialed the number, area code and all. She had to be out there to have that kind of number, didn't she?"

"Did she say why she left?"

"Said it was time to move on. Doing her inscrutable oriental number."

"You think she was afraid of getting killed?"

"Powhattan Motel," he said, pointing. "That's the place, isn't it?"

"That's the place."

"And you were out here to find the body."

"It had already been found. But I was out here before they moved it."

"Must have been some sight."

"It wasn't pretty."

"That Cookie worked alone. No pimp."

"That's what the police said."

"Well, she coulda had a pimp that they didn't know about. But I talked to some people. She worked alone, and if she ever knew Duffy Green, nobody ever heard tell of it." He turned right at the corner. "We'll head back to my house, okay?"

"All right."

"I'll make us some coffee. You liked that coffee I fixed last time, didn't you?"

"It was good."

"Well, I'll fix us some more."

His block in Greenpoint was almost as quiet by day as it had been by night. The garage door ascended at the touch of a button. He lowered it with a second touch of the button and we got out of the car and walked on into the house. "I want to work out some," he said. "Do a little lifting. You like to work out with weights?"

"I haven't in years."

"Want to go through the motions?"

"I think I'll pass."

My name is Matt and I pass.

"Be a minute," he said.

He went into a room, came out wearing a pair of scarlet gym shorts and carrying a hooded terry-cloth robe. We went to the room he'd fitted out as a gym, and for fifteen or twenty minutes he worked out with loose weights and on the Universal machine. His skin became glossy with perspiration as he worked and his heavy muscles rippled beneath it.

"Now I want ten minutes in the sauna," he said. "You didn't earn the sauna by pumping the iron, but we could grant a special dispensation in your case."

"No thanks."

"Want to wait downstairs then? Be more comfortable."

I waited while he took a sauna and shower. I studied some of his African sculpture, thumbed through a couple of magazines. He emerged in due course wearing light blue jeans and a navy pullover and rope sandals. He asked if I was ready for coffee. I told him I'd been ready for half an hour.

"Won't be long," he said. He started it brewing, then came back and perched on a leather hassock. He said, "You want to know something? I make a lousy pimp."

"I thought you were a class act. Restraint, dignity, all of that."

"I had six girls and I got three. And Mary Lou'll be leaving soon."

"You think so?"

"I know it. She's a tourist, man. You ever hear how I turned her out?"

"She told me."

"First tricks she did, she got to tell herself she was a reporter, a journalist, this was all research. Then she decided she was really into it. Now she's finding out a couple of things."

"Like what?"

"Like you can get killed, or kill yourself. Like when you die there's twelve people at your funeral. Not much of a turnout for Sunny, was there?"

"It was on the small side."

"You could say that. You know something? I could have filled that fucking room three times over."

"Probably."

"Not just probably. Definitely." He stood up, clasped his hands behind his back, paced the floor. "I thought about that. I could have taken their biggest suite and filled it. Uptown people, pimps and whores, and the ringside crowd. Could have mentioned it to people in her building. Might be she had some neighbors who would have wanted to come. But see, I didn't want too many people."

"I see."

"It was really for the girls. The four of them. I didn't

know they'd be down to three when I organized the thing. Then I thought, shit, it might be pretty grim, just me and the four girls. So I told a couple of other people. It was nice of Kid Bascomb to come, wasn't it?"

"Yes."

"I'll get that coffee."

He came back with two cups. I took a sip, nodded my approval.

"You'll take a couple pounds home with you."

"I told you last time. It's no good to me in a hotel room."

"So you give it to your lady friend. Let her make you a cup of the best."

"Thanks."

"You just drink coffee, right? You don't drink booze?"

"Not these days."

"But you used to."

And probably will again, I thought. But not today.

"Same as me," he said. "I don't drink, don't smoke dope, don't do any of that shit. Used to."

"Why'd you stop?"

"Didn't go with the image."

"Which image? The pimp image?"

"The connoisseur," he said. "The art collector."

"How'd you learn so much about African art?"

"Self-taught," he said. "I read everything I could find, went around to the dealers and talked to them. And I had a feel for it." He smiled at something. "Long time ago I went to college."

"Where was that?"

"Hofstra. I grew up in Hempstead. Born in Bedford-Stuyvesant, but my folks bought a house when I was two, three years old. I don't even remember Bed-Stuy." He had returned to the hassock and he was leaning back, his hands clasped around his knees for balance. "Middle-class house, lawn to mow and leaves to rake and a driveway to shovel. I can slip in and out of the ghetto talk, but it's mostly a shuck. We weren't rich but we lived decent. And there was enough money to send me to Hofstra."

"What did you study?"

"Majored in art history. And didn't learn shit about African art there, incidentally. Just that dudes like Braque and Picasso got a lot of inspiration from African masks, same as the Impressionists got turned on by Japanese prints. But I never took a look at an African carving until I got back from Nam."

"When were you over there?"

"After my third year of college. My father died, see. I could have finished all the same but, I don't know, I was crazy enough to drop out of school and enlist." His head was back and his eyes were closed. "Did a ton of drugs over there. We had everything. Reefer, hash, acid. What I liked, I liked heroin. They did it different there. You used to get it in cigarettes, used to smoke it."

"I never heard of that."

"Well, it's wasteful," he said. "But it was so cheap over there. They grew the opium in those countries and it was cheap. You get a real muzzy high that way, smoking skag in a cigarette. I was stoned that way when I got the news that my mother died. Her pressure was always high, you know, and she had a stroke and died. I wasn't nodding or anything but I was high from a skag joint and I got the news and I didn't feel anything, you know? And when it wore off and I was straight again I still didn't feel anything. First time I felt it was this afternoon, sitting there listening to some hired preacher reading Ralph Waldo Emerson over a dead whore." He straightened up and looked at me. "I sat there and wanted to cry for my mama," he said, "but I didn't. I don't guess I'll ever cry for her."

He broke the mood by getting us both more coffee. When he came back he said, "I don't know why I pick you to tell things to. Like with a shrink, I suppose. You took my money and now you have to listen."

"All part of the service. How did you decide to be a pimp?"

"How did a nice boy like me get into a business like this?" He chuckled, then stopped and thought for a moment. "I had this friend," he said. "A white boy from Oak Park, Illinois. That's outside of Chicago."

"I've heard of it."

"I had this act for him, that I was from the ghetto, that I'd done it all, you know? Then he got killed. It was stupid, we weren't near the line, he got drunk and a jeep ran over him. But he was dead and I wasn't telling those stories anymore, and my mama was dead and I knew when I got home I wasn't going back to college."

He walked over to the window. "And I had this girl over there," he said, his back to me. "Little bit of a thing, and I'd go over to her place and smoke skag and lay around. I'd give her money, and, you know, I found out she was taking my money and giving it to her boyfriend, and here I was having fantasies of marrying this woman, bringing her back Stateside. I wouldn't have done it, but I was thinking about it, and then I found out she wasn't but a whore. I don't know why I ever thought she was anything else, but a man'll do that, you know.

"I thought about killing her, but shit, I didn't want to do that. I wasn't even that angry. What I did, I stopped smoking, I stopped drinking, I stopped all kinds of getting high."

"Just like that?"

"Just like that. And I asked myself, Okay, what do you want to be? And the picture filled in, you know, a few lines here and a few lines there. I was a good little soldier for the rest of my hitch. Then I came back and went into business."

"You just taught yourself?"

"Shit, I *invented* myself. Gave myself the name Chance. I

started out in life with a first name and a middle name and a last name, and wasn't any of them Chance. I gave myself a name and created a style and the rest just fell into place. Pimping's easy to learn. The whole thing is power. You just act like you already got it and the women come and give it to you. That's all it really is."

"Don't you have to have a purple hat?"

"It's probably easiest if you look and dress the part. But if you go and play against the stereotype they think you're something special."

"Were you?"

"I was always fair with them. Never knocked them around, never threatened them. Kim wanted to quit me and what did I do? Told her to go ahead and God bless."

"The pimp with the heart of gold."

"You think you're joking. But I cared for them. And I had a heavenly dream for a life, man. I really did."

"You still do."

He shook his head. "No," he said. "It's slipping away. Whole thing's slipping away and I can't hold onto it."

Chapter 31

We left the converted firehouse with me in the back seat and Chance wearing a chauffeur's cap. A few blocks away he pulled over and returned the cap to the glove compartment while I joined him in front. The commuter traffic had pretty much thinned out by then and we made the trip into Manhattan quickly and in relative silence. We were a little aloof with each other, as if we'd already shared more than either of us had anticipated.

No messages at the desk. I went upstairs, changed my clothes, paused on the way out the door and got the .32 from my dresser drawer. Was there any point in carrying a gun I seemed unable to fire? I couldn't see any, but I put it in my pocket anyway.

I went downstairs and bought a paper, and without thinking too much about it I walked around the corner and took a table in Armstrong's. My usual corner table. Trina came over, said it had been a long time, and took my order for a cheeseburger and a small salad and coffee.

After she headed for the kitchen I got a sudden flash of a martini, straight up and bone dry and ice cold in a stemmed glass. I could see it, I could smell the odor of juniper and the tang of a lemon twist. I could feel the bite as it hit bottom.

Jesus, I thought.

The urge for a drink passed as suddenly as it had come on me. I decided it was a reflex, a reaction to the atmosphere of Armstrong's. I'd done so much drinking here for so long, I'd been eighty-sixed here after my last bender, and I hadn't crossed the threshold since. It was only natural that I'd think of a drink. It didn't mean I had to have one.

I ate my meal, drank a second cup of coffee afterward. I read my newspaper, paid my check, left a tip. Then it was time to go over to St. Paul's.

THE qualification was an alcoholic version of the American Dream. The speaker was a poor boy from Worcester, Mass. who worked his way through college, rose to a vice-presidency at one of the television networks, then lost it all drinking. He went all the way down, wound up in Los Angeles drinking Sterno in Pershing Square, then found AA and got it all back.

It would have been inspiring if I could have kept my mind on it. But my attention kept straying. I thought about Sunny's funeral, I thought about what Chance had told me, and I found my thoughts wandering all over the whole case, trying to make sense out of it.

Damnit, it was all there. I just wasn't looking at it right.

I left during the discussion, before it was my turn to speak. I didn't even feel like saying my name tonight. I walked back to my hotel, fighting the urge to stop in at Armstrong's for a minute or two.

I called Durkin. He was out. I hung up without leaving a message and called Jan.

No answer. Well, she was probably still at her meeting. And she'd go out for coffee afterward, probably wouldn't get home until after eleven.

I could have stayed at my own meeting until it ended, then gone to coffee with some of the others. I could join them now, as far as that went. The Cobb's Corner where they hung out wasn't all that far away.

I thought about it. And decided I didn't really want to go there.

I picked up a book but couldn't make sense out of it. I tossed it down, got undressed, went into the bathroom and ran the shower. But I didn't need a shower, for Christ's sake, I just had a shower that morning, and the most strenuous activity I'd had all day was watching Chance working out with weights. What the hell did I need with a shower?

I turned the water off and got dressed again.

Jesus, I felt like a caged lion. I picked up the phone. I might have called Chance but you couldn't just call the son of a bitch, you had to call his service and wait for him to call back, and I didn't feel like doing that. I called Jan, who was still out, and I called Durkin. He wasn't there either, and once again I decided against leaving a message.

Maybe he was at that place on Tenth Avenue, unwinding with a couple of belts. I thought about going over there and looking for him, and it struck me that it wasn't Durkin I'd be looking for, that all I wanted was an excuse to walk through the door of that bucket of blood and put my foot upon the brass rail.

Did they even have a brass rail? I closed my eyes and tried to picture the place, and in an instant I was recalling everything about it, the smells of spilled booze and stale beer and urine, that dank tavern smell that welcomes you home.

I thought, You've got nine days and you went to two meetings today, a noon meeting and an evening meeting, and you've never been closer to a drink. What the hell's the matter with you?

If I went to Durkin's boozer I'd drink. If I went to Farrell's or Polly's or Armstrong's I would drink. If I stayed in my room I'd go crazy, and when I went crazy enough I'd get away from those four walls and what would I do? I'd go out, to one bar or another, and I'd drink.

I made myself stay there. I'd gotten through the eighth day and there was no reason why I couldn't get through the ninth. I sat there and every now and then I looked at my watch and sometimes a whole minute went by between looks. Finally it got to be eleven o'clock and I went downstairs and hailed a taxi.

THERE'S a midnight meeting seven nights a week at the Moravian Church on the corner of Thirtieth and Lexington. The doors open about an hour before meeting time. I got there and took a seat, and when the coffee was ready I got myself a cup.

I didn't pay attention to the qualification or the discussion. I just sat there and let myself feel safe. There were a lot of newly sober people in the room, a lot of people who were having a hard time. Why else would they be there at that hour?

There were some people who hadn't stopped drinking yet, too. They had to put one of them out, but the others didn't make any trouble. Just a roomful of people getting through one more hour.

When the hour was up I helped fold the chairs and empty the ashtrays. Another chair folder introduced himself as Kevin and asked me how long I'd been sober. I told him it was my ninth day.

"That's great," he said. "Keep coming back."

They always say that.

I went outside and signaled a passing cab, but when he cut over and started to brake I changed my mind and waved him off. He gunned his engine as he drove away.

I didn't want to go back to the room.

So instead I walked seven blocks north to Kim's building,

bluffed my way past her doorman, let myself into her apartment. I knew there was a closetful of booze there but it didn't bother me. I didn't even feel the need to pour it down the sink, as I'd done with the bottle of Wild Turkey earlier.

In her bedroom, I went through her jewelry. I wasn't really looking for the green ring. I picked up the ivory bracelet, unfastened the clasp, tried it for size on my own wrist. It was too small. I got some paper towels from the kitchen and wrapped the bracelet carefully, put it in my pocket.

Maybe Jan would like it. I'd pictured it on her wrist a few times—at her loft, during the funeral service.

If she didn't like it she didn't have to wear it.

I went over, picked up the phone. The service hadn't been disconnected yet. I supposed it would be sooner or later, just as sooner or later the apartment would be cleaned and Kim's things removed from it. But for now it was still as if she'd just stepped out for a moment.

I hung up the phone without calling anyone. Somewhere around three o'clock I got undressed and went to sleep in her bed. I didn't change the linen, and it seemed to me that her scent, still faintly discernible, constituted a presence in the room.

If so, it didn't keep me awake. I went right off to sleep.

I woke up bathed in perspiration, convinced that I'd solved the case in a dream and then forgot the solution. I showered and dressed and got out of there.

There were several messages at my hotel, all of them from Mary Lou Barcker. She'd called just after I left the night before and a couple of times that morning.

When I called her she said, "I've been trying to reach you. I would have called you at your girlfriend's but I couldn't remember her last name."

"Her number's unlisted." And I wasn't there, I thought, but left it unsaid.

"I'm trying to reach Chance," she went on. "I thought you might have talked to him."

"Not since around seven last night. Why?"

"I can't get hold of him. The only way I know is to call his service—"

"That's the only way I know."

"Oh. I thought you might have a special number."

"Only the service."

"I've called there. He always returns his calls. I've left, God, I don't know how many messages and he hasn't called me back."

"Has that ever happened before?"

"Not for this length of time. I started trying him late yesterday afternoon. What time is it, eleven o'clock? That's over seventeen hours. He wouldn't go that long without checking with his service."

I thought back to our conversation at his house. Had he checked with his service in all the time we were together? I didn't think he had.

Other times we'd been together he called in every half hour or so.

"And it's not just me," she was saying. "He hasn't called Fran, either. I checked with her and she called him and he never returned her calls."

"What about Donna?"

"She's here with me. Neither of us wanted to be alone. And Ruby, I don't know where Ruby is. Her number doesn't answer."

"She's in San Francisco."

"She's where?"

I gave her a brief explanation, then listened as she relayed the information to Donna. "Donna's quoting Yeats," she told me. " 'Things fall apart, the center cannot hold.' Even I can recognize that. Apt, though. Things are falling apart all over the place."

"I'm going to try to get hold of Chance."

"Call me when you do?"

"I will."

"Meanwhile Donna's staying here and we're not booking any tricks or answering the door. I already told the doorman not to let anybody come up."

"Good."

"I invited Fran to come over here but she said she didn't want to. She sounded very stoned. I'm going to call her again and instead of inviting her to come over I'm going to *tell* her to come over."

"Good idea."

"Donna says the three little pigs will all be hiding in the brick house. Waiting for the wolf to come down the chimney. I wish she'd stick to Yeats."

I couldn't get anywhere with his answering service. They were happy to take my message but wouldn't disclose whether Chance had called in recently. "I expect to hear from him shortly," a woman told me, "and I will see that he receives your message."

I called Brooklyn information and got the number for the house in Greenpoint. I dialed it and let it ring for a dozen times. I'd remembered what he'd told me about removing the clappers from the bells of his telephones, but I thought it was worth a check.

I called Parke Bernet. The sale of African and Oceanic art and artifacts was scheduled for two o'clock.

I had a shower and a shave, had a roll and a cup of coffee and read the paper. The *Post* managed to keep the Motel Ripper on the front page, but it took some stretching to do it. A man in the Bedford Park section of the Bronx had stabbed his wife three times with a kitchen knife, then called the police to tell them what he'd done. This normally would have rated two paragraphs on the back page at the most, but the

Post put it on the front page and topped it with a teaser headline that wondered, DID THE MOTEL RIPPER INSPIRE HIM?

I went to a meeting at twelve-thirty and got to Parke Bernet a few minutes after two. The auction was being held in a different room from the one where the sale lots had been displayed. You had to have a sale catalog to get a seat, and the catalogs cost five dollars. I explained I was just looking for someone and scanned the room. Chance wasn't there.

The attendant didn't want me to hang around unless I bought a catalog, and it was easier to do that than argue with him. I gave him the five dollars and wound up registering and getting a bidder's number while I was at it. I didn't want to register, I didn't want a bidder's number, I didn't want the goddamned catalog.

I sat there for almost two hours while one lot after another went under the hammer. By two-thirty I was fairly certain he wasn't going to show but I stayed in my seat because I couldn't think of anything better to do. I paid minimal attention to the auction and looked around every couple of minutes for Chance. At twenty to four the Benin bronze was offered for bids and sold for $65,000, which was just a little higher than the estimate. It was the star of the sale and quite a few bidders left once it had been sold. I hung on a few minutes longer, knowing he wasn't coming, just trying to grapple with the same thing I'd been grappling with for days.

It seemed to me that I already had all the pieces. It was just a question of fitting them together.

Kim. Kim's ring and Kim's mink jacket. *Cojones. Maricón.* The towels. The warning. Calderón. Cookie Blue.

I got up and left. I was crossing the lobby when a table full of catalogs of past sales caught my eye. I picked up a catalog of a jewelry auction held that spring and leafed through it. It didn't tell me anything. I put it back and asked the lobby attendant if the gallery had a resident expert on gems and jewelry. "You want Mr. Hillquist," he said, and told me what room to go to and pointed me in the right direction.

Mr. Hillquist sat at an uncluttered desk as if he'd been waiting all day for me to consult him. I gave him my name and told him I wanted some vague approximation of the value of an emerald. He asked if he could see the stone, and I explained that I didn't have it with me.

"You would have to bring it in," he explained. "The value of a gem depends upon so many variables. Size, cut, color, brilliance—"

I put my hand in my pocket, touched the .32, felt around for the bit of green glass. "It's about this size," I said, and he fitted a jeweler's loupe into one eye and took the piece of glass from me. He looked at it, went absolutely rigid for an instant, then fixed his other eye warily upon me.

"This is not an emerald," he said carefully. He might have been talking to a small child, or to a lunatic.

"I know that. It's a piece of glass."

"Yes."

"It's the approximate size of the stone I'm talking about. I'm a detective, I'm trying to get some idea of the value of a ring that has disappeared since I saw it, I—"

"Oh," he said, and sighed. "For a moment I thought—"

"I know what you thought."

He took the loupe from his eye, set it on the desk in front of him. "When you sit here," he said, "you are at the absolute mercy of the public. You wouldn't believe the people who come here, the things they show me, the questions they ask."

"I can imagine."

"No, you can't." He picked up the bit of green glass and shook his head at it. "I still can't tell you the value. Size is only one of several considerations. There's also color, there's clarity, there's brilliance. Do you even know that the stone is an emerald? Did you test it for hardness?"

"No."

"So it could even be colored glass. Like the, uh, treasure you've given me here."

"For all I know it is glass. But I want to know what it could be worth if it did happen to be an emerald."

"I think I see what you mean." He frowned at the piece of glass. "You have to understand that my every inclination is to avoid naming any sort of a figure. You see, even assuming the stone is a genuine emerald, its range in value could be considerable. It could be extremely valuable or very nearly worthless. It could be seriously flawed, for example. Or it could simply be a very low-grade stone. There are mail order firms that actually offer emeralds by the carat for some ridiculous sum, forty or fifty dollars the carat, and what they're selling is no bargain, either. Yet they are genuine emeralds, however worthless they may be as gemstones."

"I see."

"Even a gem-quality emerald could vary enormously in value. You could buy a stone this size—" he weighed the chunk of glass in his hand "—for a couple thousand dollars. And that would be a good stone, not industrial-grade corundum from western North Carolina. On the other hand, a stone of the highest quality, the best color, perfect brilliance, unflawed, not even Peruvian but the very best Colombian emerald, might bring forty or fifty or sixty thousand dollars. And even that's approximate and imprecise."

He had more to say but I wasn't paying attention. He hadn't really told me anything, hadn't added a fresh piece to the puzzle, but he'd given the box a good shake. Now I could see where everything went.

I took the cube of green glass with me when I left.

Chapter 32

Around ten-thirty that night I walked in and out of Poogan's Pub on West Seventy-second Street. A light rain had begun falling an hour or so earlier. Most of the people on the street were carrying umbrellas. I wasn't, but I had a hat, and I paused on the sidewalk to straighten it and adjust its brim.

Across the street I saw a Mercury sedan with its motor riding.

I turned to my left and walked to the Top Knot. I spotted Danny Boy at a table in back but went to the bar anyway and asked for him. I must have spoken loudly because people looked at me. The bartender motioned toward the rear and I went back there and joined him.

He already had company. He was sharing his table with a slender fox-faced girl whose hair was as white as his own, but in her case nature couldn't take the credit. Her eyebrows were severely plucked and her forehead had a shine to it. Danny Boy introduced her as Bryna. "Rhymes with angina," he said, "among other things." She smiled, showing sharp little canine teeth.

I pulled a chair out and sat down heavily. I said, "Danny Boy, you can pass the word. I know all about Kim Dakkinen's boyfriend. I know who killed her and I know why she was killed."

"Matt, are you all right?"

"I'm fine," I said. "You know why I had so much trouble getting a line on Kim's boyfriend? Because he wasn't an action guy, that's why. Didn't go to clubs, didn't gamble, didn't hang out. Wasn't connected."

"You been drinking, Matt?"

"What are you, the Spanish Inquisition? What do you care if I've been drinking or not?"

"I just wondered. You're talking loud, that's all."

"Well, I'm trying to tell you about Kim," I said. "About her boyfriend. See, he was in the jewelry business. He didn't get rich, he didn't starve. He made a living."

"Bryna," he said, "suppose you powder your nose for a few minutes."

"Oh, let her stay," I told him. "Her nose doesn't look shiny to me."

"Matt—"

"What I'm telling you's no secret, Danny Boy."

"Suit yourself."

"This jeweler," I went on. "The way it looks, he started seeing Kim as a john. But something happened. One way or another, he fell for her."

"These things happen."

"They do indeed. Anyway, he fell in love. Meanwhile, some people got in touch with him. They had some precious stones that never went through Customs and that they had no bill of sale for. Emeralds. Colombian emeralds. Real quality stuff."

"Matt, would you please tell me why in the hell you're telling me all this?"

"It makes an interesting story."

"You're not just telling me, you're telling the whole room. Do you know what you're doing?"

I looked at him.

"Okay," he said, after a moment. "Bryna, pay attention, darling. The crazy man wants to talk about emeralds."

"Kim's boyfriend was going to be the middleman, handling the sale of the emeralds for the men who'd brought them into the country. He did this sort of thing before, made a few dollars for himself. But now he was in love with an expensive lady and he had a reason to want some real money. So he tried a cross."

"How?"

"I don't know. Maybe he switched some stones. Maybe he held out. Maybe he decided to grab the whole bundle and run with it. He must have told Kim something because on the strength of it she told Chance she wanted out. She wasn't going to be turning tricks anymore. If I were going to guess, I'd say he did a switch and went out of the country to unload the good stuff. Kim got herself free of Chance while he was gone, and when he got back it was going to be Happily Ever After time. But he never came back."

"If he never came back, who killed her?"

"The people he crossed. They decoyed her to that room at the Galaxy Downtowner. She probably thought she was going to be meeting him there. She wasn't hooking anymore, she wouldn't have gone to a hotel room to meet a john. In fact she'd never been much on hotel tricks. But suppose she gets a call from somebody who says he's a friend and the boyfriend's afraid to come to her place because he thinks he's being followed, so would she please meet him at the hotel?"

"And she went."

"Sure she went. She got all dressed up, she wore the presents he gave her, the mink jacket and the emerald ring. The jacket wasn't worth a fortune because the guy wasn't rich, he didn't have money to burn, but he could give her a terrific emerald because the emeralds didn't cost him anything. He was in the business, he could take one of those smuggled stones and have it set in a ring for her."

"So she went over and got killed."

"Right."

Danny Boy drank some vodka. "Why? You figure they killed her to get the ring back?"

"No. They killed her to kill her."

"Why?"

"Because they were Colombians," I said, "and that's how they do it. When they have a reason to hit somebody they go for the whole family."

"Jesus."

"Maybe they figure it's a deterrent," I said. "I could see where it might be. The cases make the papers pretty regularly, especially in Miami. A whole family gets waxed because somebody burned somebody else in a coke deal. Colombia's a rich little country. They've got the best coffee, the best marijuana, the best cocaine."

"And the best emeralds?"

"That's right. Kim's jeweler wasn't a married guy. I figured he was, that's why he was so hard to get a line on, but he never married. Maybe he never fell in love until he fell in love with Kim, and maybe that's why he was ready to kick his life over. Anyway, he was a bachelor. No wife, no kids, no living parents. You want to rub out his family, what do you do? You kill his girlfriend."

Bryna's face was as white as her hair now. She didn't like stories where they killed the girlfriend.

"The killing was pretty professional," I went on, "in that the killer was careful about evidence. He covered his tracks pretty well. But something made him do a butcher job instead of a couple of quick bullets from a silenced handgun.

Maybe he had a thing about prostitutes, or maybe it was women in general. One way or another, he went and did a number on Kim.

"Then he cleaned up, packed the dirty towels along with the machete, and got out of there. He left the fur jacket and he left the money in the purse but he took her ring."

"Because it was worth so much money?"

"Possibly. There's no hard evidence on the ring, and for all I know it was cut glass and she bought it for herself. But it might have been an emerald, and even if it wasn't the killer might have thought it was. It's one thing to leave a few hundred dollars on a dead body to show you don't rob the dead. It's something else to leave an emerald that might be worth fifty thousand dollars, especially if it's your emerald in the first place."

"I follow you."

"The room clerk at the Galaxy Downtowner was a Colombian, a young kid named Octavio Calderón. Maybe that was a coincidence. There are a lot of Colombians in town these days. Maybe the killer picked the Galaxy because he knew somebody who worked there. It doesn't matter. Calderón probably recognized the killer, or at least knew enough about him to keep his mouth shut. When a cop came back to have another talk with him, Calderón disappeared. Either the killer's friends told him to disappear or Calderón decided he'd be safer somewhere else. Back home in Cartagena, say, or another rooming house in another part of Queens."

Or maybe he got killed, I thought. That was possible, too. But I didn't think so. When these people killed, they liked to leave the corpses in plain sight.

"There was another whore that got killed."

"Sunny Hendryx," I said. "That was a suicide. Maybe Kim's death triggered that, so maybe the man who killed

Kim has some moral responsibility for Sunny's death. But she killed herself."

"I'm talking about the street hustler. The TV."

"Cookie Blue."

"That's the one. Why did she get killed? To throw you off the track? Except you weren't on the track to begin with."

"No."

"Then why? You think the first killing turned the killer nuts? Triggered something in him that made him want to do it again?"

"I think that's part of it," I said. "Nobody would do a second butcher job like that unless he enjoyed the first one. I don't know if he had sex with either of his victims, but the kick he got out of the killings had to be sexual."

"So he just picked up Cookie for the hell of it?"

Bryna blanched again. It was bad enough hearing about someone who got killed for being the wrong person's girlfriend. It was even worse hearing about a girl getting killed at random.

"No," I said, "Cookie was killed for a specific reason. The killer went looking for her and passed up a batch of other streetwalkers until he found her. Cookie was family."

"Family? Whose family?"

"The boyfriend's."

"He had two sweeties, this jeweler? A call girl and a transvestite hustler?"

"Cookie wasn't his sweetie. Cookie was his brother."

"Cookie—"

"Cookie Blue started life as Mark Blaustein. Mark had an older brother named Adrian who went into the jewelry business. Adrian Blaustein had a girlfriend named Kim and some business associates from Colombia."

"So Cookie and Kim were connected."

"They had to be connected. I'm sure they never met each

other. I don't think Mark and Adrian had any contact in recent years. That may explain why it took the killer so long to find Cookie. But I knew there had to be some kind of link. I told someone earlier that they were sisters under the skin. That wasn't far off. They were almost sisters-in-law."

He thought about this, then told Bryna to give us a few moments alone. This time I didn't interfere. She left the table and Danny Boy motioned to the waitress. He ordered vodka for himself and asked me what I wanted.

"Nothing right now," I said.

When she brought back the vodka he took a careful little sip and set the glass down. "You've been to the cops," he said.

"No cops."

"Why not?"

"Just didn't get around to it yet."

"You had to come here instead."

"That's right."

"I can keep my mouth shut, Matt, but Bryna the Vagina wouldn't know how. She thinks unexpressed thoughts build up inside your head and explode your skull, and she's not taking any chances. Anyway, you were talking loud enough for half the room to pick up on what you were saying."

"I know that."

"I figured you did. What do you want?"

"I want the killer to know what I know."

"That shouldn't take long."

"I want you to pass it on, Danny Boy. I'm leaving here, I'm walking back to my neighborhood. I'll probably spend a couple of hours in Armstrong's. Then I'll walk around the corner to my room."

"You're gonna get killed, Matt."

"This fucker only kills girls," I said.

"Cookie was only half a girl. Maybe he's working his way up to men."

"Maybe."

"You want him to make a move on you."

"Looks that way, doesn't it?"

"Looks to me as though you're crazy, Matt. I tried to head you off the minute you came over here. Tried to cool you down some."

"I know."

"It's probably too late now. Whether I pass it on or not."

"It was too late before then. I was uptown before I came down here. You know a man named Royal Waldron?"

"Sure, I know Royal."

"He and I talked some. Royal's been known to do a little business with some fellows from Colombia."

"He would," Danny Boy said. "The business he's in."

"So they probably already know. But you could pass it on anyway, just for insurance."

"Insurance," he said. "What's the opposite of life insurance?"

"I don't know."

"Death insurance. They may be waiting outside for you right now, Matt."

"It's possible."

"Why don't you go pick up the phone and call the cops? They could send a car and you go somewhere and make a statement. Let the bastards earn their money."

"I want the killer," I said. "I want him one-on-one."

"You're not Latin. Where'd you get this *macho* hangup?"

"Just pass the word, Danny Boy."

"Sit down a minute." He leaned forward, dropped his voice. "You don't want to walk out of here without a piece. Just sit here a minute and I'll get you something."

"I don't need a gun."

"No, of course not. Who needs one? You can take his machete away from him and make him eat it. Then break both his legs and leave him in an alley."

"Something like that."

"Will you let me get you a gun?" His eyes searched mine. "You've already got one," he said. "On you, right now. Haven't you?"

"I don't need a gun," I said.

AND I didn't. On the way out of the Top Knot I put my hand in my pocket and felt the butt and barrel of the little .32. Who needed it? A little gun like that doesn't have a whole lot of stopping power anyway.

Especially when you can't make yourself squeeze the trigger.

I went outside. It was still raining but no harder than before. I tugged the brim of my hat and took a good look around.

The Mercury sedan was parked on the other side of the street. I recognized it by its crimped fenders. While I was standing there the driver started the engine.

I walked over to Columbus Avenue. While I waited for the light to change I saw that the Mercury had come around in a U-turn and was approaching. The light changed and I walked across the street.

I had the gun in my hand and my hand in my pocket. My index finger was on the trigger. I remembered how the trigger had trembled beneath my finger not too long ago.

I'd been on this same street then.

I walked on downtown. A couple of times I looked over my shoulder. The Mercury stayed a little less than a block behind me all the way.

I never relaxed, but I was especially tense when I got to the block where I'd drawn the gun once before. I couldn't help looking back, expecting to see a car careening toward me. I spun around involuntarily once at the sound of brakes screeching, then realized the sound was a good two blocks away.

Nerves.

I passed the spot where I'd dropped to the pavement and rolled. I checked the place where the bottle had broken. There was still some broken glass there, though I couldn't be sure it was the same broken glass. A lot of bottles get broken every day.

I kept walking all the way to Armstrong's. When I got there I went in and ordered a piece of pecan pie and a cup of coffee. I kept my right hand in my pocket while my eyes scanned the room, checking everybody out. After I was done with the pie I put my hand back in my pocket and drank my coffee left-handed.

After awhile I ordered more coffee.

The telephone rang. Trina answered it, walked over to the bar. There was a heavyset fellow there with dark blonde hair. She said something to him and he went to the phone. He talked for a few minutes, looked around the room, came over to my table. Both of his hands were where I could see them.

He said, "Scudder? My name's George Lightner, I don't think we met." He pulled a chair out and sat in it. "That was Joe just now," he said. "There's no activity out there, nothing at all. They're laying doggo in the Mercury plus he's got two sharpshooters in second-floor windows across the street."

"Good."

"I'm in here, and there's the two fellows at the front table. I figured you made us when you walked in."

"I made them," I said. "I figured you were either a cop or the killer."

"Jesus, what a thought. This is a nice place. You more or less hang out here, huh?"

"Not as much as I used to."

"It's pleasant here. I'd like to come back sometime when I can drink something instead of coffee. They're selling a lot of coffee tonight, what with you and me and the two guys down front."

"It's pretty good coffee."

"Yeah, it's not bad. Better than the shit in the station house." He lit a cigarette with a Zippo lighter. "Joe said there's no activity elsewhere either. There's two men staked out downtown with your girlfriend. There's a couple others with the three hookers on the East Side." He grinned. "That's the detail I shoulda drawn. Can't win 'em all, huh?"

"I guess not."

"How long you want to stay here? Joe's guess is that the guy's either set up by now or he's not gonna move tonight. We can cover you every step from here back to the hotel. Of course we can't insure against the possibility of a sniper firing from a rooftop or a high window. We did a rooftop check earlier but there's no guarantee."

"I don't think he'll do it from a distance."

"Then we're in pretty good shape. And you're wearing the bulletproof vest."

"Yes."

"That's a help. Of course it's mesh, it doesn't always stop a blade, but nobody's about to let him get that close to you. We figure if he's out there he'll make a move between here and the doorway of your hotel."

"That's what I figure, too."

"When do you want to run the gauntlet?"

"A few minutes," I said. "I might as well finish this coffee."

"Listen," he said, rising, "what the hell. Enjoy it."

He returned to his spot at the bar. I finished my coffee, got up, went to the lavatory. There I checked my .32 and made sure I had a round under the hammer and three more rounds to back it up. I could have asked Durkin for a couple more cartridges to fill the empty chambers. For that matter, he'd have given me a larger gun with more of a punch to it. But he didn't even know I was carrying the .32 and I hadn't wanted to tell him. The way things were set up, I wasn't going to have to shoot anybody. The killer was supposed to walk right into our arms.

Except it wasn't going to happen that way.

I paid the check, left a tip. It wasn't going to work. I could feel it. The son of a bitch wasn't out there.

I walked out the door. The rain had let up some. I looked at the Mercury and glanced at the buildings across the street, wondering where the police sharpshooters were planted. It didn't matter. They weren't going to have any work to do tonight. Our quarry wasn't taking the bait.

I walked down to Fifty-seventh Street, staying close to the curb just in case he'd managed to find a spot in a dark doorway. I walked slowly and hoped I was right and he wouldn't try to do it from a distance, because a bulletproof vest doesn't always stop a bullet and it doesn't do anything to protect you from a head shot.

But it didn't matter. He wasn't there. Damnit, I knew he wasn't there.

Still, I breathed easier when I walked into my hotel. I may have been disappointed but I was also relieved.

There were three plainclothesmen in the lobby. They identified themselves right away. I stood around with them for a few minutes, and then Durkin came in alone. He went into a huddle with one of them, then came over to me.

"We struck out," he said.

"Looks that way."

"Shit," he said. "We didn't leave many loopholes. Maybe he smelled something but I don't see how. Or maybe he flew home to fucking Bogotá yesterday and we're setting a trap for somebody who's on another continent."

"It's possible."

"You can go get some sleep, anyway. If you're not too wired to unwind. Have a couple of drinks, knock yourself out for eight hours."

"Good idea."

"The guys have had the lobby staked out all night. There've been no visitors, no check-ins. I'm gonna keep a guard down here all night."

"You think it's necessary?"

"I think it can't hurt."

"Whatever you say."

"We gave it our best shot, Matt. It's worth it if we can smoke the fucker out because God knows how we could get anyplace combing the city for emerald smugglers. Sometimes you get lucky and sometimes you don't."

"I know."

"We'll catch the cocksucker sooner or later. You know that."

"Sure."

"Well," he said, and shifted his weight awkwardly. "Well, listen. Get some sleep, huh?"

"Sure."

I rode up on the elevator. He wasn't in South America, I thought. I knew damned well he wasn't in South America. He was here in New York and he was going to kill again because he liked it.

Maybe he'd done it before. Maybe Kim was the first time he found out it felt good to him. But he'd liked it enough to do it again the same way, and the next time he wouldn't need an excuse. Just a victim and a hotel room and his trusty machete.

Have a couple of drinks, Durkin had suggested.

I didn't even feel like a drink.

Ten days, I thought. Just go to bed sober and you've got ten days.

I took the gun out of my pocket and put it on the dresser. I was still carrying the ivory bracelet in another pocket and I took it out and set it down next to the gun, still wrapped in paper towels from Kim's kitchen. I got out of my slacks and jacket, hung them in the closet, and took off my shirt. The bulletproof vest was a tricky thing to get out of and a cumbersome thing to wear, and most of the cops I knew hated wearing them. On the other hand, nobody likes getting shot.

I took the thing off and draped it over the dresser next to the gun and bracelet. Bulletproof vests aren't just bulky, they're also warm, and I'd perspired inside this one and my undershirt had dark circles under the arms. I took off the undershirt and my shorts and my socks, and something clicked, some little alarm went off, and I was turning toward the bathroom door when it flew open.

He sailed through it, a big man, olive skinned, wild-eyed. He was as naked as I was and there was a machete in his hand with a gleaming foot-long blade.

I threw the mesh at him. He swung the machete and knocked it aside. I grabbed the gun off the dresser and dove out of his way. The blade arced down, missing me, and his arm rose again and I shot him four times in the chest.

Chapter 33

The LL train starts at Eighth Avenue, crosses Manhattan along Fourteenth Street, and winds up way the hell out in Canarsie. Its first stop across the river in Brooklyn is at Bedford Avenue and North Seventh Street. I left it there and walked around until I found his house. It took me a while and I took a couple of wrong turns, but it was a good day for walking, the sun out, the sky clear, and a little warmth in the air for a change.

There was a heavy windowless door to the right of the garage. I poked the doorbell but got no response, and I couldn't hear the bell sounding within. Hadn't he said something about disconnecting the bell? I jabbed it again, heard nothing.

There was a brass knocker mounted on the door and I used it. Nothing happened. I cupped my hands and shouted, "Chance, open up! It's Scudder." Then I pounded on the door some more, with the knocker and with my hands.

The door looked and felt awfully solid. I gave it a tentative nudge with my shoulder and decided it was unlikely I could kick it in. I could break a window and get in that way, but in Greenpoint some neighbor would call the cops, or pick up a gun and come over himself.

I banged on the door some more. A motor worked, and a winch began lifting the electrically operated garage door.

"This way," he said. "Before you knock my damn door down."

I went in through the garage and he pushed a button to lower the door again. "My front door doesn't open," he said. "Didn't I show you that before? It's all sealed shut with bars and shit."

"That's great if you have a fire."

"Then I go out a window. But when'd you ever hear of the firehouse burning down?"

He was dressed as I'd last seen him, in light blue denim pants and a navy blue pullover. "You forgot your coffee," he said. "Or I forgot to give it to you. Day before yesterday, remember? You were gonna take a couple pounds home with you."

"You're right, I forgot."

"For your girlfriend. Fine-looking woman. I got some coffee made. You'll have a cup, won't you?"

"Thanks."

I went into the kitchen with him. I said, "You're a hard man to get hold of."

"Well, I sort of stopped checking with my service."

"I know. Have you heard a newscast lately? Or read a paper?"

"Not lately. You drink it black, right?"

"Right. It's all over, Chance." He looked at me. "We got the guy."

"The guy. The killer."

"That's right. I thought I'd come out and tell you about it."

"Well," he said. "I guess I'd like to hear it."

* * *

I went through the whole thing in a fair amount of detail. I was used to it by now. It was the middle of the afternoon and I'd been telling the story to one person or another ever since I'd put four bullets into Pedro Antonio Marquez a little after two in the morning.

"So you killed him," Chance said. "How do you feel about that?"

"It's too early to tell."

I knew how Durkin felt about it. He couldn't have been happier. "When they're dead," he had said, "you know they're not going to be back on the street in three years, doing it again. And this one was a fucking animal. He had that taste of blood and he liked it."

"It's the same guy?" Chance wanted to know. "There's no question?"

"No question. They got confirmation from the manager of the Powhattan Motel. They also matched a couple of latent prints, one from the Powhattan and one from the Galaxy, so that ties him to both killings. And the machete's the weapon used in both killings. They even found minute traces of blood where the hilt meets the handle, and the type matches either Kim or Cookie, I forget which one."

"How'd he get into your hotel?"

"He walked right through the lobby and rode up in the elevator."

"I thought they had the place staked out."

"They did. He walked right past them, picked up his key at the desk and went to his room."

"How could he do that?"

"Easiest thing in the world," I said. "He checked in the day before, just in case. He was setting things up. When he got the word that I was looking for him, he went back to my hotel, went up to his room, then went to my room and let himself in. The locks in my hotel aren't much of a challenge.

He took off his clothes and sharpened his machete and waited for me to come home."

"And it almost worked."

"It should have worked. He could have waited behind the door and killed me before I knew what was happening. Or he could have stayed in the bathroom a few more minutes and given me time to get into bed. But he got too much of a kick out of killing and that's what screwed him up. He wanted us both naked when he took me out, so he waited in the bathroom, and he couldn't wait for me to get into bed because he was too keyed up, too excited. Of course if I hadn't had the gun handy he'd have killed me anyway."

"He couldn't have been all alone."

"He was alone as far as the killings were concerned. He probably had partners in the emerald operation. The cops may get somewhere looking for them and they may not. Even if they do, there's no real way to make a case against anybody."

He nodded. "What happened to the brother? Kim's boyfriend, the one who started everything."

"He hasn't turned up. He's probably dead. Or he's still running, and he'll live until his Colombian friends catch up with him."

"Will they do that?"

"Probably. They're supposed to be relentless."

"And that room clerk? What's his name, Calderón?"

"That's right. Well, if he's holed up somewhere in Queens, he can read about it in the paper and ask for his old job back."

He started to say something, then changed his mind and took both our cups back to the kitchen to refill them. He came back with them and gave me mine.

"You were up late," he said.

"All night."

"You been to sleep at all?"

"Not yet."

"Myself, I doze off in a chair now and then. But when I get in bed I can't sleep, I can't even lie there. I go work out and take a sauna and a shower and drink some more coffee and sit around some more. Over and over."

"You stopped calling your service."

"I stopped calling my service. I stopped leaving the house. I guess I been eating. I take something from the refrigerator and eat it without paying attention. Kim's dead and Sunny's dead and this Cookie's dead, and maybe the brother's dead, the boyfriend, and what's-his-name is dead. The one you shot, I disremember his name."

"Marquez."

"Marquez is dead, and Calderón disappeared, and Ruby's in San Francisco. And the question is where's Chance, and the answer is I don't know. Where I think I am is out of business."

"The girls are all right."

"So you said."

"Mary Lou isn't going to be turning tricks anymore. She's glad she did it, she learned a lot from it, but she's ready for a new stage in her life."

"Yeah, well, I called that one. Didn't I tell you after the funeral?"

I nodded. "And Donna thinks she can get a foundation grant, and she can earn money through readings and workshops. She says she's reached a point where selling herself is starting to undermine her poetry."

"She's pretty talented, Donna. Be good if she could make it on her poetry. You say she's getting a grant?"

"She thinks she's got a shot at it."

He grinned. "Aren't you gonna tell me the rest of it? Little Fran just got a Hollywood contract and she's gonna be the next Goldie Hawn."

"Maybe tomorrow," I said. "For now she just wants to live in the Village and stay stoned and entertain nice men from Wall Street."

"So I still got Fran."

"That's right."

He'd been pacing the floor. Now he dropped onto the hassock again. "Be a cinch to get five, six more of them," he said. "You don't know how easy it is. Easiest thing in the world."

"You told me that once before."

"It's the truth, man. So many women just waiting to be told what to do with their damn lives. I could walk out of here and have me a full string in no more than a week's time." He shook his head ruefully. "Except for one thing."

"What's that?"

"I don't think I can do that anymore." He stood up again. "Damn, I been a good pimp! And I liked it. I tailored a life for myself and it fit me like my own skin. And you know what I went and did?"

"What?"

"I outgrew it."

"It happens."

"Some spic goes crazy with a blade and I'm out of business. You know something? It would have happened anyway, wouldn't it?"

"Sooner or later." Just as I'd have left the police force even if a bullet of mine hadn't killed Estrellita Rivera. "Lives change," I said. "It doesn't seem to do much good to fight it."

"What am I gonna do?"

"Whatever you want."

"Like what?"

"You could go back to school."

He laughed. "And study art history? Shit, I don't want to do that. Sit in classrooms again? It was bullshit then, I went into the fuckin' army to get away from it. You know what I thought about the other night?"

"What?"

"I was gonna build a fire. Pile all the masks in the middle of the floor, spill a little gas on 'em, put a match to 'em. Go out like one of those Vikings and take all my treasures with me. I can't say I thought about it for long. What I could do, I could sell all this shit. The house, the art, the car. I guess the money'd last me a time."

"Probably."

"But then what'd I do?"

"Suppose you set up as a dealer?"

"Are you crazy, man? Me deal drugs? I can't even pimp no more, and pimping's cleaner'n dealing."

"Not drugs."

"What, then?"

"The African stuff. You seem to own a lot of it and I gather the quality's high."

"I don't own any garbage."

"So you told me. Could you use that as your stock to get you started? And do you know enough about the field to go into the business?"

He frowned, thinking. "I was thinking about this earlier," he said.

"And?"

"There's a lot I don't know. But there's a lot I do know, plus I got a feel for it and that's something you can't get in a classroom or out of a book. But shit, you need more'n that to be a dealer. You need a whole manner, a personality to go with it."

"You invented Chance, didn't you?"

"So? Oh, I dig. I could invent some nigger art dealer same way I invented myself as a pimp."

"Couldn't you?"

"'Course I could." He thought once more. "It might work," he said. "I'll have to study it."

"You got time."

"Plenty of time." He looked intently at me, the gold flecks glinting in his brown eyes. "I don't know what made me hire you," he said. "I swear to God I don't. If I wanted to look good or what, the superpimp avenging his dead whore. If I knew where it was going to lead—"

"It probably saved a few lives," I said. "If that's any consolation."

"Didn't save Kim or Sunny or Cookie."

"Kim was already dead. And Sunny killed herself and that was her choice, and Cookie was going to be killed as soon as Marquez tracked her down. But he'd have gone on killing if I hadn't stopped him. The cops would have landed on him sooner or later but there'd have been more dead women by then. He never would have stopped. It was too much of a turn-on for him. When he came out of the bathroom with the machete, he had an erection."

"You serious?"

"Absolutely."

"He came at you with a hard-on?"

"Well, I was more afraid of the machete."

"Well, yeah," he said. "I could see where you would be."

HE wanted to give me a bonus. I told him it wasn't necessary, that I'd been adequately paid for my time, but he insisted, and when people insist on giving me money I don't generally argue. I told him I'd taken the ivory bracelet from Kim's apartment. He laughed and said he'd forgotten all about it, that I was welcome to it and he hoped my lady would like it. It would be part of my bonus, he said, along with the cash and two pounds of his specially blended coffee.

"And if you like the coffee," he said, "I can tell you where to get more of it."

He drove me back into the city. I'd have taken the subway but he insisted he had to go to Manhattan anyway to talk to Mary Lou and Donna and Fran and get things smoothed out. "Might as well enjoy the Seville while I can," he said. "Might wind up selling it to raise cash for operating expenses. Might sell the house, too." He shook his head. "I swear it suits me, though. Living here."

"Get the business started with a government loan."

"You jiving?"

"You're a minority group member. There's agencies just waiting to lend you money."

"What a notion," he said.

In front of my hotel he said, "That Colombian asshole, I still can't remember his name."

"Pedro Marquez."

"That's him. When he registered at your hotel, is that the name he used?"

"No, it was on his ID."

"That's what I thought. Like he was C. O. Jones and M. A. Ricone, and I wondered what dirty word he used for you."

"He was Mr. Starudo," I said. "Thomas Edward Starudo."

"T. E. Starudo? *Testarudo?* That a curse in Spanish?"

"Not a curse. But it's a word."

"What's it mean?"

"Stubborn," I said. "Stubborn or pig-headed."

"Well," he said, laughing. "Well, hell, you can't blame him for that one, can you?"

Chapter 34

In my room I put the two pounds of coffee on the dresser, then went and made sure nobody was in the bathroom. I felt silly, like an old maid looking under the bed, but I figured it would be a while before I got over it. And I wasn't carrying a gun anymore. The .32 had been impounded, of course, and the official story was that Durkin had issued it to me for my protection. He hadn't even asked how I'd really come by it. I don't suppose he cared.

I sat in my chair and looked at the place on the floor where Marquez had fallen. Some of his bloodstains remained in the rug, along with traces of the chalk marks they place around dead bodies.

I wondered if I'd be able to sleep in the room. I could always get them to change it, but I'd been here a few years now and I'd grown accustomed to it. Chance had said it suited me, and I suppose it did.

How did I feel about having killed him?

I thought it over and decided I felt fine. I didn't really know anything about the son of a bitch. To understand all is to forgive all, they say, and maybe if I knew his whole story

I'd understand where the blood lust came from. But I didn't have to forgive him. That was God's job not mine.

And I'd been able to squeeze the trigger. And there'd been no ricochets, no bad bounces, no bullets that went wide. Four shots, all in the chest. Good detective work, good decoy work, and good shooting at the end.

Not bad.

I went downstairs and around the corner. I walked to Armstrong's, glanced in the window, but went on walking to Fifty-eighth and around the corner and halfway down the block. I went into Joey Farrell's and stood at the bar.

Not much of a crowd. Music on the jukebox, some baritone crooner backed up with a lot of strings.

"Double Early Times," I said. "With water back."

I stood there, not really thinking of anything, while the bearded barman poured the drink and drew the chaser and set them both before me. I had placed a ten dollar bill on the counter. He cracked it, brought my change.

I looked at the drink. Light danced in the rich amber fluid. I reached for it, and a soft inner voice murmured *Welcome home*.

I withdrew my hand. I left the drink on the bar and took a dime from my pile of change. I went to the phone and dropped the dime and dialed Jan's number.

No answer.

Fine, I thought. I'd kept my promise. Of course I might have misdialed, or the phone company might have fucked up. Such things have been known to happen.

I put the dime back in the slot and dialed again. I let it ring a dozen times.

No answer.

Fair enough. I got my dime back and returned to the bar. My change was as I'd left it, and so were the two glasses in front of me, the bourbon and the water.

I thought, *Why?*

The case was finished, solved, wrapped up. The killer would never kill anyone again. I had done a whole lot of things right and felt very good about my role in the proceedings. I wasn't nervous, I wasn't anxious, I wasn't depressed. I was fine, for Christ's sake.

And there was a double shot of bourbon on the bar in front of me. I hadn't wanted a drink, I hadn't even thought of a drink, and here I was with a drink in front of me and I was going to swallow it.

Why? What the hell was the matter with me?

If I drank the fucking drink I would end up dead or in the hospital. It might take a day or a week or a month but that was how it would play. I knew that. And I didn't want to be dead and I didn't want to go to the hospital, but here I was in a gin joint with a drink in front of me.

Because—

Because what?

Because—

I left the drink on the bar. I left my change on the bar. I got out of there.

AT half past eight I walked down the flight of basement stairs and into the meeting room at St. Paul's. I got a cup of coffee and some cookies and took a seat.

I thought, You almost drank. You're eleven days sober and you went into a bar you had no reason to be in and ordered a drink for no reason at all. You almost picked up the drink, you were that close to it, you almost blew eleven days after the way you sweated to get them. What the hell is the matter with you?

The chairman read the preamble and introduced the speaker. I sat there and tried to listen to his story and I couldn't. My mind kept returning to the flat reality of that glass of bourbon. I hadn't wanted it, I hadn't even thought about it, and yet I'd been drawn to it like iron filings to a magnet.

I thought, My name is Matt and I think I'm going crazy.

The speaker finished what he was saying. I joined in the applause. I went to the bathroom during the break, less out of need than to avoid having to talk to anybody. I came back to the room and got yet another cup of coffee that I neither needed nor wanted. I thought about leaving the coffee and going back to my hotel. The hell, I'd been up two days and a night without a break. Some sleep would do me more good than a meeting I couldn't pay attention to in the first place.

I kept my coffee cup and took it to my seat and sat down.

I sat there during the discussion. The words people spoke rolled over me like waves. I just sat there, unable to hear a thing.

Then it was my turn.

"My name is Matt," I said, and paused, and started over. "My name is Matt," I said, "and I'm an alcoholic."

And the goddamnedest thing happened. I started to cry.

Enter the World
of Lawrence Block's
Matthew Scudder

Lawrence Block is widely acknowledged by both fans and reviewers to be one of the best mystery writers working today. He is also one of the most prolific, and his varied series—from the lighthearted romps of Bernie the Burglar to the cool musings of Keller the Hit Man—have impressed readers with their versatility. He is a Mystery Writers of America Grand Master and a multiple winner of the Edgar, Shamus, and Maltese Falcon awards.

Block's most intriguing hero may be the deeply flawed and deeply moral ex-policeman, recovering alcoholic, and unlicensed private investigator Matthew Scudder. Scudder has walked New York's mean streets for almost thirty years and in that time a lot of change has come both to this dark hero and to the city he calls home. But he's still the complex detective who caused The Wall Street Journal to say, "Block has done something new and remarkable with the private-eye novel" and Jonathan Kellerman to exclaim, "The Matthew Scudder novels are among the finest detective books penned in this century."

Read on, and enter Scudder's world . . .

The Sins of the Fathers

The hooker was young, pretty . . . and dead, butchered in a Greenwich Village apartment. The murderer, a minister's son, has already been caught and become a jailhouse suicide. The case is closed as far as the NYPD is concerned. But the victim's father wants it reopened—he wants to understand how his bright little girl went wrong and what led to her gruesome death. That's where Matthew Scudder comes in. He's not really a detective, not licensed, but he'll look into problems as a favor to a friend, and sometimes the friends compensate him. A hard drinker and a melancholy man, the former cop believes in doing an in-depth investigation when he's paid for it, but he doesn't see any hope here—the case is closed, and he's not going to learn anything about the victim that won't break her father's heart.

But the open-and-shut case turns out to be more complicated than anyone bargained for. The assignment carries an unmistakable stench of sleaze and perversion, and it lures Scudder into a sordid world of phony religion and murderous lust, where children must die for their parents' most secret, unspeakable sins.

Time to Murder and Create

Small-time stoolie Jake "The Spinner" Jablon made a lot of new enemies when he switched careers from informer to blackmailer. And the more "clients," he figured, the more money—and the more people eager to see him dead. So he's greedy but scared, and he turns to his old acquaintance Matthew Scudder, who used to pay him for information back in Scudder's days as a cop. Scudder's his insurance policy—if anything happens to "The Spinner," Scudder can check up on the people who wanted him dead.

No one is too surprised when the pigeon is found floating in the East River with his skull bashed in. Blackmail's a dangerous business. What's worse, no one cares—except Matthew Scudder. The unofficial private eye is no conscientious avenging angel. But he's willing to risk his own life and limb to confront Spinner's most murderously aggressive marks. A job's a job, after all, and Scudder's been paid to find a killer—by the victim . . . in advance.

In the Midst of Death

Jerry Broadfield thinks he's a good cop. But now he's been charged with extortion—and his former buddies in the NYPD would like to see him laid out on a morgue slab for squealing to a committee on police corruption. Suddenly, he's got a lot of enemies, and when a dead call girl turns up in his apartment his troubles get even bigger.

Broadfield screams "setup," but nobody believes him—except ex-policeman now unlicensed p.i. Matthew Scudder. Because Broadfield turned traitor no cop is going to give Scudder any help with this investigation, so Scudder's on his own. But finding a killer among the stoolie cop's sleazebag connections is going to be as difficult as pouring a cold beer in hell—where some of Broadfield's enemies would like to see Scudder if he gets himself in too deep.

A Stab in the Dark

Nine long years have passed since the killer last struck—nine years since eight helpless young women were brutally slaughtered by an icepick-wielding maniac. The trail grew cold and the book was unofficially closed on a serial killer who stopped killing. But now "The Icepick Prowler" has confessed—but only to seven of the killings. Not only does he deny the eighth, he has an airtight alibi.

Barbara Ettinger's family had almost come to accept that the young woman was the victim of a random killing. Now they must grapple with the shocking revelation that not only was her death disguised to look like the serial killer's work, but her murderer may have been someone she knew and trusted. Matthew Scudder has been hired to finally bring her slayer to justice, setting the relentless detective on the trail of a death almost a decade cold, searching for a vicious murderer who's either long gone, long dead . . . or patiently waiting to kill again.

Eight Million Ways to Die

Nobody knows better than Matthew Scudder how far down a person can sink in the dirty city of New York. A young prostitute named Kim knew it also—and she wanted out. Maybe Kim didn't deserve the life fate had dealt her. She surely didn't deserve her death.

The alcoholic ex-cop turned p.i. was supposed to protect her, but someone slashed her to ribbons on a crumbling waterfront pier. Now finding Kim's killer will be Scudder's penance. But there are lethal secrets hiding in the slain hooker's past that are far dirtier than her trade. And there are many ways of dying in this cruel and dangerous town—some quick and brutal . . . and some agonizingly slow.

When the Sacred Ginmill Closes

The 1970s were dark days for Matthew Scudder. An ex-New York cop, he had drowned his career in booze. Now he was drinking away his life in a succession of seedy establishments that opened early and closed late, reduced to doing paid "favors" for the cronies who gathered to drink with him.

However, in a lonely place like so many others, opportunity comes knocking: a chance to both help the ginmill's owner recover his stolen, doctored financial records and exonerate a drinking buddy accused of murdering his wife. But when cases flow together in dangerous and disturbing ways—like the nightmare images of a drunkard's delirium—it's time for Scudder to change his priorities to staying sober . . . and staying alive.

Out On the Cutting Edge

Paula Hoeldtke was a nice girl from Indiana who came to New York to be an actress and disappeared. Her father wanted Scudder to find her. Eddie Dunphy was a small-time hood trying to give up drinking who wanted Scudder to sponsor him in AA. Ex-cop, ex-drunk, ex-innocent Matthew Scudder is trying to stay sober in a city gone mad, but he'll try to give Paula's father and Eddie what they need.

But Eddie turns up dead, apparently in an ugly accident. And Paula may be dead, too—her cold trail leads Scudder to the blistering heat of a dark part of the city called Hell's Kitchen. All Scudder wants to do is find a straight path out of trouble, but on the road he's following all he can find easily is death.

A Ticket to the Boneyard

Matthew Scudder knew James Leo Motley was the most dangerous kind of man: one who hurts people for pleasure. So twelve years ago Scudder, then a cop, lied to a jury to put Motley behind bars.

But now the brilliant psychopath is free—and Scudder must pay. Friends and former lovers, even strangers unfortunate enough to share Scudder's name are turning up dead because a vengeful maniac won't rest until he's driven his nemesis back to the bottle . . . and then to the grave.

A Dance at the Slaughterhouse

In Matt Scudder's mind money, power, and position elevate nobody above morality and the law. Now, in this Edgar Award-winning novel, the ex-cop and unlicensed p.i. has been hired to prove that socialite Richard Thurman orchestrated the murder of his beautiful, pregnant wife.

During Scudder's hard-drinking years, he left a piece of his soul on every seedy corner of the Big Apple. But this case is more depraved and more potentially devastating than anything he experienced while floundering in the urban depths. Because this investigation is leading Scudder on a frightening grand tour of New York's sex-for-sale underworld, where an innocent young life is simply a commodity to be bought and perverted . . . and then destroyed.

A Walk Among the Tombstones

A new breed of entrepreneurial monster has set up shop in the big city. Ruthless, ingenious murderers, they prey on the loved ones of those who live outside the law, knowing that criminals will never run to the police, no matter how brutal the threat. So other avenues for justice must be explored, which is where ex-cop turned p.i. Matthew Scudder comes in.

Scudder has no love for the drug dealers and poison peddlers who now need his help. Nevertheless, he is determined to do whatever it takes to put an elusive pair of thrill-kill extortionists out of business—for they are using the innocent to fuel their terrible enterprise.

The Devil Knows You're Dead

In this city, there is little sense and no rules. Those who fly the highest often come crashing down the hardest—like successful young Glenn Holtzmann, randomly blown away by a deranged derelict at a corner phone booth on Eleventh Avenue. Unlicensed p.i. Matt Scudder thinks Holtzmann was simply in the wrong place at the wrong time. Others think differently—like Thomas Sadecki, brother of the crazed Vietnam vet accused of the murder, who wants Scudder to prove his brother innocent.

But no one is truly innocent in this unmerciful metropolis, including Matthew Scudder, whose curiosity and dedication are leading him to dark, unexplored places in his own heart . . . and to passions and revelations that could destroy everything he loves.

A Long Line of Dead Men

An ancient brotherhood meets annually in the back room of a swank Manhattan restaurant, a fraternity created in secret to celebrate life by celebrating its dead. But the past three decades have not been kind to the Club of 31. Matthew Scudder—ex-cop, ex-boozer—has known death in all its guises, which is why he has been asked to investigate a baffling, thirty-year run of suicides and suspiciously random accidents that has thinned the ranks of this very select group of gentlemen.

But Scudder has mortality problems of his own, for this is a city that feeds mercilessly on the unsuspecting—and even the powerful and those who serve them are easy prey. There are too many secrets here, and too many places for a maddeningly patient serial killer to hide . . . and wait . . . and strike.

A *New York Times* Notable Book

Even the Wicked

Matthew Scudder knows that justice is an elusive commodity in the big city, where a harmless man can be shot dead in a public place while criminals fly free through holes in a tattered legal system. But now a vigilante is roaming among the millions, executing those he feels deserve to die. He calls himself "The Will of the People," an ingenious serial killer who announces his specific murderous intentions to the media before carrying through on his threats. A child molester, a Mafia don, a violent anti-abortionist, even the protected and untouchable are being ruthlessly erased by New York's latest celebrity avenger.

Scudder knows that no one is innocent—but who among us has the right to play God? It is a question that will haunt the newly licensed p.i. on his journey through the bleak city grays as he searches for the sanity in urban madness . . . and for a frighteningly efficient killer who can do the impossible.

Everybody Dies

════════

Matt Scudder is finally leading a comfortable life. The crime rate's down and the stock market's up. Gentrification's prettying up the old neighborhood. The New York streets don't look so mean anymore.

Then all hell breaks loose.

Scudder quickly discovers the spruced-up sidewalks are as mean as ever—dark and gritty and stained with blood. He's living in a world where the past is a minefield, the present is a war zone, and the future's an open question. It's a world where nothing is certain and nobody's safe, a random universe where no one's survival can be taken for granted—not even his own. A world where everybody dies.

**A *New York Times* and *Publishers Weekly*
Notable Book**

Available in hardcover
from William Morrow

HOPE TO DIE

A Matthew Scudder Crime Novel

When a prominent Manhattan couple is killed in a brutal home invasion, the whole city catches its breath. A few days later, their killers turn up dead behind a locked door in Brooklyn. One has killed his partner, then himself.

The city sighs with relief. The cops close the case.

Private investigator Matt Scudder and his wife were in the same room with the couple just hours before their death, and in spite of himself, Scudder is drawn to the case. The closer he looks, the more he senses the presence of a third man, a puppet master who manipulated his two accomplices, then cut their strings when he was done with them.

The villain who looms in the shadows is cold and diabolical, murdering for pleasure and profit. Nobody but Scudder even suspects he exists—and he's not done killing.

He's just getting started . . .